D0098820

BY JOHN DIXON

Phoenix Island

Devil's Pocket

The Point

THE POINT

THE POINT

JOHN DIXON

DEL REY | NEW YORK

Published in the United States by Del Rey, an imprint of Random House, a division of Penguin Random House LLC, New York.

DEL REY and the HOUSE colophon are registered trademarks of Penguin Random House LLC.

Hardback ISBN 978-1-101-96756-0
Ebook ISBN 978-1-101-96754-6

Printed in the United States of America on acid-free paper

randomhousebooks.com

1 2 3 4 5 6 7 8 9

First Edition

Title-page and chapter-opener art: iStockphoto/Adelevin
Book design by Susan Turner

For Allison Skiff,
the best sister-in-law in the world

THE POINT

ONE

"YOU CAME HERE AS CHILDREN," KEYNOTE SPEAKER Senator Wesley Ditko said, "but you leave here as men and women."

Mid-May was typically beautiful in the Philadelphia suburbs, but today the sun beat down mercilessly on the 411 graduating seniors seated before the stage. Their suffering families sagged along open bleachers.

Master Sergeant Charles Winter, U.S. Army, retired, gray-haired and bespectacled, sat ramrod straight on the top bleacher, watching the proceedings with a stony face that betrayed neither pride nor impatience.

Mrs. Winter, resplendent in a bright yellow dress, moved incessantly, fanning herself with the graduation program. She shifted in her seat and whispered to her son.

Sergeant Daniel Winter, U.S. Marine Corps, sat as straight as his father but failed to replicate the man's stoicism. He beamed, proud and relieved. His kid sister actually was going to graduate after all.

"A plane in its hangar is safe," Senator Ditko said, and smiled down at the fidgeting seniors, pausing to make eye contact with the valedictorian: his daughter. "But planes aren't meant to sit in hangars.

Ladies and gentlemen, you are clear for takeoff. Spread your wings and fly!"

Principal Santana returned to the microphone, her face shining with perspiration, and began calling students onstage. Douglas Abbey stumbled coming up the stairs but caught himself and gave the crowd a big grin before shaking the principal's hand and accepting his diploma.

One by one, students crossed the stage. Whatever each had been—athlete or scholar, geek or dullard, stud or square—it was over now. He or she had run the gauntlet, surviving the thirteen years of institutionalized insanity that constitute the American public school experience.

Mrs. Winter fanned her face, which grew redder with each passing minute.

Principal Santana called, "Demarcus Winslow."

Mrs. Winter tucked the makeshift fan into her purse and grabbed the hands of her husband and son. "Here we go."

This was it.

After all these years, all these worries—troubles at school and problems with police and endless emergency room visits in which nurses cooed over her pretty daughter, the girl with a wild streak, a daredevil who seemed to have broken every bone in her body—her baby finally was graduating.

Wild but sweet, her Scarlett. Always sweet and loving, full of kindness.

Mrs. Winter loved her husband and son, but they were cold and self-reliant, as her own father had been. Not Scarlett. Scarlett was her heart, her only warmth in the Winter household.

The long suffering was finally over. At last, a new beginning.

Principal Santana called, "Scarlett Winter."

Mrs. Winter laughed and leaned forward, her vision blurry with tears of joy.

There was a brief pause.

From the student seating, choppy bursts of laughter rattled like sporadic gunfire.

"Scarlett Winter?" Principal Santana repeated.

No one stood. No one climbed the stairs. No one crossed the stage.

More laughter rippled through the crowd, and for a frantic second Mrs. Winter feared she might join in with a peal of hysterical laughter.

Principal Santana cleared her throat. "Jeffrey Wood."

A blond-haired boy whooped loudly, charged up the stairs, and Frisbeed his mortarboard into the applauding crowd.

Mrs. Winter dropped her face into her hands and sobbed.

Master Sergeant Winter, his mouth a grim slash across his sunburned face, stood and nodded to his son. Together they took Mrs. Winter's arms and helped her to her feet. If not overtly sympathetic, the men were inarguably gentle and protective. Fiercely so, even.

As the family made its slow descent, people turned to watch with sympathy, amusement, or horror. Master Sergeant Winter stared straight ahead, betraying nothing.

The eyes of the broad-shouldered Marine, however, burned with rage. Marching stiffly toward the parking lot, he growled, "Where the hell is Scarlett?"

TWO

STRETCHED OUT HIGH ATOP THE STONE QUARRY cliff, loving the bright sunshine baking her bare skin, Scarlett grinned, naked save for bright blue knee socks, aviator shades, and perhaps too many scars for a girl of eighteen.

Nick, the cute, inked-up vegan she'd been hanging with lately, lay beside her. His blond dreads spilled over his tanned shoulders as he sat up and took a deep pull off the pipe.

Scarlett liked the way that sunlight twinkled on his nose ring and glistened along the light sheen of perspiration covering his lean body. They'd broken a sweat climbing the cliff and had kept it rolling with a spirited celebration at the top. Life was good.

Her phone vibrated, rattling on the rocky ground between their towels.

"Uh oh," Nick said, smiling slyly.

Scarlett's stomach lurched. Picturing her mother's face, she felt a pang of guilt. She started to reach for the phone, but then she pictured her father's face and . . .

Nick capped the bowl with the red Bic. "You going to answer it?"

She just stared, her hand hovering there. The phone stopped vibrating.

"Guess not," Nick said, and handed her the pipe.

She sucked in a deep hit of Super Lemon Haze. It was good weed. A little tart, a little sweet, like smoking Lemonhead candy. "It's my life, not theirs," she said, holding the citrusy smoke. "I'm the one who has to live with my choices."

Mom wanted her to go to college, which right now held about as much appeal as chugging a gallon of spoiled milk. She was tired of rules and homework and sitting around, listening to people talk.

Her father wanted her to go into the Army.

Screw that . . .

Scarlett had plans. She and Ginny were going to backpack in Europe. Sleep in youth hostels, drink good beer, see the sights—Paris, Madrid, Rome—and meet up with Ginny's dad in Amsterdam. They'd sail to the Caribbean and check out the yacht culture, rich people partying 24/7 and swapping business cards.

She just had to break it to her parents.

She handed Nick the pipe. Then she picked up a rock and pitched it over the cliff and watched it tumble down, down, down and smack into the quarry pond a hundred feet below. Impact rings pulsed across the surface.

Nick took another hit and held the pipe out to her again.

She waved him off and leaned back. "I'm good." High above, an airplane glinted in the sky. She imagined the people sitting up there, doing crosswords and playing solitaire at several hundred miles an hour.

She stood and pulled on her shorts and bikini top. She had to shake this mood. Here she was, free at last, but she felt like she was being smothered.

"Don't let it get you down," Nick said. "We're celebrating, right?" He unzipped the backpack and pulled out a pair of Yuenglings beaded with condensation. Smiling over his shoulder—the one tattooed *carpe diem*—he said, "Wanna do it again?"

"No," she said, stuffing her phone and sandals into her backpack.

"I have to do something," she said. "I have to shake things up."

"But we were—"

Scarlett didn't stick around to hear the rest of it. She took three running steps and leaped into the void.

THREE

CLOSER, CLOSER, CLOSER . . .

Jagger opened his eyes. He lay in the gloom beneath a highway overpass. He heard the whoosh of cars driving overhead and smelled smoke and the savory aroma of campfire cooking.

He didn't know where he was or how he had gotten here. He'd blacked out again.

He sat up, squinted.

Beyond the gloom, daylight illuminated a weedy slope clumped with sumac and strewn with highway litter. Nearer, half in light, half in shade, loomed a hulking bum holding a two-by-four, one end of which bristled with rusty nails, like one of the *masus* that the Hutus had favored during the Rwandan genocide.

Not that Jagger had been in Rwanda. That had been before his time. His time was now—and of course, his time was yet to come.

Closer, closer . . .

Fragmented memories returned to him, blurry and out of sequence: walking the highway, whistling, alone; the bright green quad of a college campus, two dozen crisp young hipsters gathered around, eyes gleaming; the hulking vagrant down on his knees, crying, begging forgiveness. Trying to make sense of these piecemeal flashes was like trying to reassemble a stained-glass window smashed into muddy ground.

Jagger rolled with it. He understood everything that he needed to understand for now, such as the fact that the gigantic hobo had stood watch over him all night.

Downslope, near the dirt road at the bottom of the gully, dozens of bums and madmen gathered around campfires, waiting. He saw others arriving, looking this way, craning their necks, and receiving pamphlets. He remembered preaching beneath a full moon and understood that his congregation had doubled, possibly tripled, during his slumber.

The dreams had been strong. Sadie's voice echoed in his ears. The sense of her driving this way on the open road lingered like a taste.

Yes.

Despite his recent blackouts and Penny's meltdown and the colossal mess in Atlanta, everything finally was coming together.

The big bum turned, six and a half feet of flat-out crazy, dressed—despite the sweltering heat—in a badly soiled Army cold-weather field jacket. The man's grizzled beard was streaked in grease and dark matter, blood or tobacco juice. With his bushy hair pulled back in a warrior's ponytail and bound by a filthy red-white-and-blue Budweiser headband, he looked like a backwoods hobo-demon long on the road but now returning, the worst nightmare of the Wall Street 1 percent coming at last for his share of the American dream.

But he isn't their worst nightmare, Jagger thought. *I am.*

Seeing Jagger smile, the giant bum smiled, too. His wolfish teeth were yellow and spotted with rot. His eyes gleamed.

Jagger could feel adoration and loyalty coming off the man in waves.

"He is risen!" the man called downhill, his voice husky with emotion.

Jagger rose and dusted himself off. He slipped into his well-worn combat boots and lifted his rucksack from the ground.

More memories arrived, increasing in clarity.

Before coming here to this hobo jungle, he'd spent the evening twenty miles away at Rutherford University, spreading the good word to moneyed young scholars there.

A very different good word than he'd spread here, of course.

And a much different good word than he'd be spreading tomorrow evening.

Everything drawing together. The dawn of a new world. Not so much a birthing as a manifestation.

Bums hobbled timidly up the trail, murmuring quietly, gentle as sheep.

He wondered what their eager eyes saw. Each would see someone different, of course, but how different? How significantly did their fears and desperation shape his vision?

He approached the hulking man and asked, "What is your name, my son?"

"Ezzard," the man whispered.

"Excellent," Jagger said. He placed a hand on the giant's shoulder and turned him gently to face the crowd. "This is my high priest, Ezzard. You will listen to him until my return."

He set the rucksack on the ground and undid the clasps and opened it and pulled out the remaining stacks of bundled hundred-dollar bills. These he offered to Ezzard, who laid his weapon on the ground and accepted the teetering pile of cash with his massive filthy hands.

"Feed these people," Jagger said. "Heal these people."

Ezzard nodded his shaggy head. One glistening tear rolled down his creased and weather-beaten face and disappeared into the forest of his graying beard. "I will."

Jagger stared into the man's eyes. "I know you will, Ezzard," he said. "You understand what to do with the rest, yes?"

Ezzard nodded enthusiastically.

Jagger patted his shoulder gently. "I will speak to you in dreams, my son, and you will prophesy to my people, the People of the Road, the People of the Underpass, the Shadow People, whom society has exiled . . . until we return on the Day of Reckoning."

He raised his voice, addressing the zealots. "You are my people."

"Yes!" a bald man with a scabbed forehead shouted, and the others nodded enthusiastically. A crooked old woman in a ragged dress offered a surreal curtsy.

"You are no longer alone, no longer forsaken. Every day, our numbers grow. You will go forth on roads and rails and spread my word to those you recognize as our people."

"Yes!"

"Yes, we will!"

Jagger nodded back at them. "Dark days are coming, my children."

"Signs and wonders!"

"Yes," Jagger said. "You will know me by these signs and wonders, but until our time arrives, you will endure great tribulation. Do not lose faith. These sufferings will cleanse you, preparing you for my return, and this is my promise to you. Every persecution you suffer in my name will multiply your reward upon my return." He raised a fist overhead and extended his four fingers, leaving only the thumb tucked.

The transients mimicked him.

"The Crown of Glory bathes you in its blessed light," he told them.

"Yes, Lord!"

Downhill, the green sedan appeared, bumping toward them over the rutted access road.

Perfect.

Gesturing to the bundled money, he said, "I am the god who sacrifices *to* his people. My blessings unto you, children. May these gifts and my promise sustain you until we are rejoined."

As he descended the weedy hillside, vials and syringes crunched beneath his boots. The faithful cleared a path, bowing and kneeling. Some shied away, terrified in their awe.

As they should, he thought.

The sedan stopped. Beautiful Sadie, twenty-five years old and already gray, beamed at him and slid into the passenger seat.

Jagger gave Sadie just the hint of a smile.

She beamed up at him. "You're filthy," she said, but her tone was all joy and lust.

"I've been on the road for a long time."

"Too long," she said, and the pink tip of her tongue peeked from between her white teeth.

He turned back to the gathering of transients staring down at him.

"Signs and wonders," he said to them, and raised his hand overhead, once again making the sign of the Crown of Glory.

The motley congregation aped him.

Then he extended his thumb and did something they could never, ever replicate.

They cried out in terror and adulation as the rucksack he'd left behind rose into the air, drifted over their heads, and lowered slowly into his hand.

He shouldered the bag, walked around the car, and slid into the driver's seat.

Sadie grinned like the cat who'd tortured the canary to death before eating it. "You're getting stronger."

He nodded. His power swelled every day. Yet he'd lost time again, hadn't he? There were times when it felt—

But no. He couldn't consider those things now. Not with everything coming together.

"I am pleased with you," he said, putting the car into gear and bumping away over the rough road. "Give me the sitrep."

"Operation Softball Glove is good to go," Sadie said. "They'll deliver your message tonight—with a *bang*."

FOUR

THE HOUSE WAS DIM AND SILENT AND COLD. GOOSE-flesh rose along Scarlett's exposed skin. Ever since Afghanistan, her father had kept their home at morgue temperature.

"Mom?"

Silence save for the faint ticking of a clock.

She felt a twinge of hope. Maybe they'd bumped into friends at the ceremony. If so, she could leave a note and bolt. Spend the night at a friend's. Let the whole thing blow over.

Jumping off the quarry cliff had jarred her out of the funk, but now she felt the blues flooding back in.

"Mom?"

Coming down the hall, she smelled food, and her stomach growled, reminding her that she hadn't eaten since ... when, precisely? Last night? She stepped into the kitchen but stopped dead in the doorway.

What is this?

She saw chips and pretzels, crackers and cheese, fruit and vegetables, lunch meat and sandwich rolls; glass dispensers filled with tea and lemonade and Mom's cucumber water; stacks of red plastic cups alongside tubs of melting ice packed with wine and beer and soda; two dozen liquor bottles sitting beside mixers and wedges of freshly cut lime.

A cake covered half the kitchen table. Across white icing, blue lettering shouted, CONGRATULATIONS, SCARLETT! WE KNEW YOU COULD DO IT! LOVE MOM, DAD, AND DAN.

They'd planned a huge surprise party for her, but . . .

I ruined it.

No one had even bothered to cover the food. In the reckoning silence, she could hear flies buzzing back and forth from feast to feast.

A shotgun blast of emotion filled her with conflicting impulses. She felt like shooing the flies and covering the food . . . or speeding away on her Yamaha to go somewhere and get blackout drunk.

Instead, she picked up a handful of salami and stood there eating, caught in an unfocused stare. Hearing a sound, she blinked. Her father stood in the doorway, staring at her with disgust.

"Use a plate," he said, and offered a bitter smile. "There are plenty left."

Scarlett grabbed a plate from the counter, but her hunger was gone. She set the meat on the plate and placed the plate on the counter and grabbed a napkin and wiped the grease from her fingers. Crumpling the napkin, she noticed the custom printing: CONGRATULATIONS, SCARLETT!

Her father stared, saying nothing. Flies buzzed.

"Where's Mom?" she finally asked.

"She's resting."

Resting. That meant she was up there crying, waiting for the Xanax to kick in.

Her father uncapped a bottle of Jack and poured himself a double.

She couldn't believe it. He'd been on the wagon for years. "You're drinking?"

He lifted the tumbler, gulped down half the whiskey, and turned to her with dead eyes. "Want to make this about me? After what you did?"

"Hey, I—"

"Your mother did all of this for you," he said, gesturing toward the ruined feast, "and you just blew off graduation. Didn't even call her."

"I texted her."

"Bull." He sipped his whiskey. "You know she never checks her phone."

"I—"

"You bailed and didn't have the guts to tell us. Now you're blaming your mother?" He shook his head and swallowed the rest of the whiskey. "You're a real peach, kid."

Scarlett said nothing. Out in the world, nothing scared her—not cliff diving, popping wheelies on the freeway, or running from the cops—but her father always made her feel weak.

He poured another double. "I spoke with Sergeant Mitchell this afternoon."

It took her a second. "The recruiter?"

Her father sipped his whiskey. "You meet with him Monday morning, 6:30 a.m."

She shook her head. "I'm not joining the Army. I have plans."

He rolled his eyes. "You missed the application deadline. Besides, you wouldn't last a semester. Forget flunking. You'd self-destruct."

"No I wouldn't," she said, but her words came out in a whisper.

"The Army will teach you the things your mother wouldn't let me teach you. Responsibility, discipline, character."

"Is that what you were doing when you hit Dan? Building character?" The man had never hit Scarlett, only Dan. He'd just ignored her and scowled at her with contempt.

He spread his hands. "Look at your brother now . . . and look at you. For all of your mother's mollycoddling, are you happier than Dan? No. He's proud, part of something *real*, working hard toward a goal that's bigger than himself."

She looked at her feet.

Her father said, "You're a beautiful, athletic, intelligent girl, but you're soft. You dominated every sport you tried . . . and quit every one. You coasted through school. You don't even keep a steady boyfriend. There's more to life than just scooping ice cream and chasing boys. It's time to grow up, quit sampling flavors, and commit to something real."

She looked up. "Nice vanilla life, huh? Be happy, like you and Mom?"

"You're selfish," he said. "That's the point. You have the potential to make the world a better place, but you just sit on the sidelines and twiddle your thumbs."

"I don't owe the world anything."

"You owe the world everything," he said, "and the world demands far more of women than it does of girls."

"In two weeks, I'm going to Europe with Ginny," she said, wanting to be done with this. "We're going backpacking and—"

He gave a condescending snort, tossed back the rest of the whiskey, and reached again for the bottle.

"You can't stop me," she said, hating the weakness of her own voice.

He laughed. "My daughter, Peter-frigging-Pan in female form."

"I have money saved."

"You'd burn through it in a week, partying. Sure, Ginny would loan you more, because she's a spoiled brat, but sooner or later you'd piss her off, and she'd leave you in the lurch. And who would have to bail you out? Me, that's who. Because your mother would divorce me if I let her baby learn a real lesson."

Scarlett felt sapped. "No, it won't be—"

"What about a passport?" he asked with a grin. "Were you planning on picking one up at Wawa on your way to the airport?"

Something crumbled inside her. *The passport . . .*

"The party's over, Scarlett. Time to quit scooping tutti-frutti and become an adult."

Everything was crashing down. She'd printed the passport application months ago, but . . .

Something in her father's eyes softened. "Hell, kid. I know you've got it in you. You've proved that. What you did that night last summer . . ." He shook his head.

A tickling sensation crawled over her scars, and she could all but hear the woman and her child screaming as the car burned around them. "You would've done it, too."

Her father shook his head and stared into the empty tumbler. "No, I couldn't have."

"In the heat of the moment, anyone can be a hero."

He stared into her eyes. "You did something miraculous that night."

She could only shrug. The tickling along her scars turned to an itch.

"There's a special strength inside you," he said, "waiting for you to call upon it."

Scarlett remembered the woman smiling as her hair burned. "I hope I never have to call on it again."

"Sometimes we must suffer to find happiness. It's the nature of mankind. At leisure, we stagnate. But under the worst conditions, we evolve."

They stood there, neither of them capable of anything like a de-escalating embrace. In the silence, Scarlett again heard the flies—and music now, faintly, classic rock, playing in the backyard. She looked out the window and saw the old Jeep parked beside the garage, speakers and a beer sitting on its hood.

"Dan's home?" she asked, shocked.

"He came to see you graduate."

She felt a surge of excitement. She hadn't seen Dan since Christmas.

Her father swirled his whiskey and smirked. "Careful. He isn't very happy with you."

Scarlett walked past him and pushed out the door, leaving the tomblike home and stepping into the heat and noise of the backyard.

"Don't say I didn't warn you," her father's voice said, and the door shut between them.

FIVE

OUT IN THE WARMTH OF THE SUNNY BACKYARD, with classic rock blasting and the world sprawling away in all directions, Scarlett instantly felt lighter and more energetic.

Dan's legs jutted from beneath the Jeep, a new tattoo shining on one muscular calf. Zeppelin replaced the Stones.

Scarlett grinned. Such a Dan scene.

A thick arm covered in tats shot out from beneath the Jeep and patted around the grass. The hand closed on a wrench and dragged it back into darkness.

"Dan," Scarlett called. "Hey, Dan!"

Nothing.

Scarlett stopped the music. "Hey, bro."

A grunt. The wrench shot from beneath the Jeep. Next came a thick arm streaked in motor oil.

Scarlett flinched. When they were kids, Dan had been terrifying, but he'd changed after joining the Corps and escaping the beatings. He'd never apologized, but he went out of his way to be nice to her now. She knew that he was sorry for how he'd treated her growing up and knew that she had been catching secondhand beatings from an older brother driven half out of his mind by steady abuse. Dan hadn't hurt her in years, but hearing the grunt and seeing that thick arm—did oil always look that much like blood?—she stiffened with apprehension.

"Why didn't you tell me you were coming?" she asked, trying to sound natural.

Dan's face emerged, looking weathered and hard. "Where were you?"

"At the quarry," she said, "celebrating with a friend."

Dan stood, looking pissed. He'd put on even more muscle since she'd last seen him. "You blew off graduation for some guy?"

"He's smoking hot," she said, trying to keep it light. "Hey, I'm sorry. If I had known you were coming, I would've been there." She spread her arms. "Give me a hug."

Dan stuck out his palm like a traffic cop. "You made Mom cry."

She took a step back. "I texted her."

He advanced, jabbing the air between them with his stubby finger. "Don't try to talk your way out of this."

"Hold on," she said. "I'm sorry that—"

"Sometimes sorry isn't enough," he said. "Your actions have consequences." He drove his finger into her shoulder, hard.

"Hey," she said. The poke must have hit a nerve. Even as the pain faded, force radiated in little waves from her shoulder into her chest.

"Dad's drunk," Dan said, and shoved her. "Because of *you*."

"Hey," she said, suddenly angry but also afraid of her brother in a way she had never expected to feel again. The force of the shove pulsed into her, lingering like an echo. Weird. "Don't pin that on me. Dad's an alcoholic. The guy's wired to drink."

"Spare me, Scarlett. Your whole life you've tried to sweet-talk your way out of everything."

He stiff-armed her high on the chest—half shove, half strike—and she stumbled backward, shocked. The force of the thumping blow radiated through her . . . but not *out* of her. It bounced around inside her chest, joining the echo of his earlier attacks. Her whole body was thrumming now with fear, anger, and whatever was happening inside her. "Quit pushing, Dan. We're not kids anymore."

"Exactly. You're eighteen now. Time to grow up."

Another push. This time both hands thudded into her chest. She almost fell but caught herself, feeling strangely steady and *strong,* as if her body was absorbing the force and feeding her muscles, supercharging them. Pent-up pressure filled her, demanding release. Through gritted teeth, she said, "Stop. Pushing. Dan."

He pointed toward the hedge and the folding tables draped in white linen. "They called off the party. You humiliated the family."

"Nobody told me about the stupid party," she said, "and I sure didn't ask for one." The pressure inside her shook and hissed like an angry rattlesnake. It hurt like the world's worst heartburn. Was she having a panic attack? A heart attack? Whatever the case, the whole scene was hurtling toward disaster. "I'm out of here."

"Don't turn your back on me," he said.

She came back around, meaning to tell her brother to shut up, and—*smack*!

Her head jerked sideways. She was stunned not by the blow, which wasn't that hard, but by the sheer fact that Dan had slapped her in the face for the first time in years. She had thought that all of that was behind them, that things had changed, that *he* had changed. She felt shocked and angry but also distracted and bewildered because rather than lingering as hot pain on her face, the force of the slap plunged straight into her, stoking the inferno in her chest.

"I won't let you ruin your life," Dan said, marching straight at her. "You're joining the military."

"I'd rather die," she said, and something in her, perhaps spurred by the firestorm at her center, ratcheted into place like a cocked revolver, spinning her away from fear and shock and locking her into anger.

Dan bulled forward, dipped low, and drove his shoulder into her gut.

Her back slammed into the Jeep, and the volcano within her erupted.

She lashed out with both hands, shoving. Her palms hammered into his burly chest, and her arms snapped to full extension. Dan flew away, tumbling through the air, and thudded to the ground *several feet away*.

Scarlett blinked in disbelief. She breathed hard, shaking. The pressure was gone, its energy released. What had she just done?

Dan sat up slowly, holding his chest and grimacing with rage and something Scarlett had never seen on her brother's face before: fear. He picked up a wrench. "Don't know how you did that, but I'm going to—"

"Stop!" a voice screamed from behind them.

Her mother leaned from an upstairs window. The fancy hairdo she'd been so proud of now hung in crazy disarray, framing a face twisted with anguish. "I can't take it anymore! You're killing me. Is that what you two want? Are you trying to kill me?"

The shame was too much to bear. "I'm sorry," Scarlett said, her voice a faint whisper.

Her father came out the back door, shouting.

She sprinted around the house, shouldered through the fence gate, and jumped onto her Yamaha. Her muscles throbbed. Explosions of pain popped like fireworks in her skull.

She kicked the motorcycle to life just as her father rounded the house.

"Scarlett, you come back here!"

"I'm sorry," she said. She popped the clutch and zoomed out of the driveway. A horn blared. She jerked hard to the right, narrowly avoiding a head-on collision. Then she leaned over the gas tank, twisted the throttle, and shot away from the mess she'd made.

SIX

WHY ARE YOUR FRIENDS NEVER AROUND WHEN YOU need them?

Nobody at the park but that old creeper Biscoe, the guy somewhere between thirty and fifty, used to buy Scarlett and her friends booze for an extra buck or two. In those days, Scarlett would search the park, desperate to find Biscoe and score a cheap six-pack or a fifth of rotgut. Now, with seemingly limitless access to any drink or drug on God's green earth, she saw Biscoe not as a bastion of hope but as what he really was: a sad troll with rotting teeth and a bad liver, the guy's brain so pickled from sleeping outside and drinking cheap piss that he couldn't even hold a conversation anymore. You'd slit your wrists out of boredom before he got to the frigging point.

Now he was waving some crazy pamphlet, ranting about the "Day of Reckoning."

Scarlett split and rode out to the mall.

Younger kids roamed in packs, showing off, making the same old jokes. One pack catcalled her from a distance, then laughed and dashed. Worse were the older guys, losers a year or two out of high school, trying to act cool, like it wasn't lame, hanging with high school kids.

One of them, this guy Willie Fay, leaned outside the arcade, puffing an e-cigarette and holding court over half a dozen boys in black T-shirts and a girl with purple streaks in her hair. His shirt read, *I hate being bipolar. It's awesome!*

"Hey, Scarlett," Fay called. "How's it going?"

The kids turned to appraise her. The eagerness in their eyes—all of them waiting around for someone to idolize—made her feel like she was covered in ticks.

She kept walking. To hell with Fay, his e-cig, stupid T-shirt, and ten-cent groupies.

Dad thinks I'm going to become the female Fay. No way. I'll show him.

But even that declaration lacked power now. She was at low tide.

She paused near the fountain. People walked past, talking about nothing, swinging bags of stuff they didn't need.

Maybe I should just call it quits. Head home, apologize, make Mom feel better.

She liked the idea. Lure Mom out of her room. Give her a big hug, work on her until she started smiling again. Spend a quiet night in, watch one of Mom's favorites, like *The Sound of Music* or *The Breakfast Club*. Patch things up. Do it right, pick up a card and flowers.

But Dad was drinking again, and Dan would be sitting there, cracking his knuckles.

So home wouldn't work. Not yet. Not tonight. What, then?

Ginny was at her mom's in Tahoe. She didn't know where Nick was and didn't care. She didn't feel like getting high or getting laid, and that was all he was good for, honestly. Everybody else was at Savannah's big graduation party, and Scarlett definitely wasn't welcome there, not since the trouble in the Poconos, after which Sav's father, *Senator* Ditko, had declared their friendship officially dead.

She stared into the dirty water of the gurgling fountain. The pennies on the bottom stared back up at her like coins covering the eyes of dead dreams.

Scarlett Winter, she thought, *the world's lamest poet.*

She felt weird. Listless yet restless, too.

She pictured Dan, all pissed off, coming at her, hitting her. She felt sad and angry and completely disillusioned. So much of her life was up in the air. Now she couldn't even trust her brother, couldn't even trust her vision of the past. She'd thought that that was all long behind them, that he'd only ever lashed out at her because Dad had hurt him so much. But now she knew that wasn't true. Where did that leave them?

She remembered Dan tumbling through the air as if he'd been hit by a truck. It made no sense, but truth be told, it wasn't the first time something like that had happened, was it?

An invisible feather tickled over her scars.

One night last summer, when she and Savannah were still friends, they'd almost gotten themselves killed, snooping around a field of pot plants they'd discovered not far from Sav's cabin in the Poconos. A dog started barking. Then people were shouting, coming for them. Scarlett hopped on the Yamaha, Sav rode pillion, and they screamed away down the dirt road through the darkness. A truck roared after them. Scarlett heard the flat crack of a rifle and hunched low and buried the throttle. The Yamaha pulled away. Farther downhill, she fishtailed to a stop. She could still hear the truck roaring toward them. She went down an embankment into a field and killed the lights. They plowed through weeds and bumped over ruts, squinting against the grit and pollen and night bugs until at last they picked up another dirt road and headed downhill through a tunnel of pines. They paused on a darkened logging trail, giving the truck time to disappear, and Scarlett shook off her fear with a bark of nervous laughter. Sav was still in a panic, of course. If her father, the senator, knew about this . . .

They started downhill again. When they came out of the woods, the road leveled out. They rounded a corner, and suddenly it was daylight—or so it seemed.

The car burned so brightly.

Nearby, the horn of the overturned vehicle blared steadily. Dead men lay in the grass. Bits of shattered windshield caught the firelight and sparkled like rhinestones on their bloody faces.

My baby! The woman had cried from the burning wreckage of the sedan. *Save my baby!*

Scarlett remembered the woman's pleading eyes and Sav trying to stop her, telling her, *No, the fire is too hot*, and the tremendous heat and pain she'd felt, plunging into the flames.

That night, her surge of strength had come out of nowhere. Tonight, with Dan, had been different.

Her head throbbed. Occasional spasms twitched through her aching muscles like the aftershocks of an earthquake.

This afternoon had kicked her mojo square in the teeth, made her start second-guessing herself, made her think about heading home with her tail tucked.

Whole legions of people—teachers, cops, parents—were always waiting for you to mess up so they could offer a way out, a *second chance*. All you had to do was confess, cry, and sign on the dotted line. You'd been a fool. They'd been right all along. You were so sorry. Yes, it was over. *Now, sir or ma'am, could you please point me in the right direction? I need you to tell me how to live my life.*

Not Scarlett. She wouldn't let fear turn her into a perfect little penitent.

She would fight back twice as hard.

Scarlett straightened, surging with enthusiasm. To generate real mojo, though, she needed help. As they said in physics class, you can't create or destroy energy, only transform it.

She needed to hook into something fun, get her engines running again. She needed people, action. Needed to shake stuff up, do something crazy.

Sav's party.

No one would expect Scarlett. Their astonishment would fill her like rocket fuel.

Besides, she wanted to congratulate Sav on making valedictorian.

Sav had worked hard and had struggled to keep it together after her sister had disappeared.

If Scarlett got caught crashing the party, the senator would have her arrested, but that risk only spurred her on.

She went into Hallmark and bought a blank card with horses on the front—Savannah loved horses—and asked to borrow a pen and wrote a nice note inside.

The party was black-tie formal. To fit in, she would need a gown, heels, and, most of all, a shower.

She laughed. She'd buy a cute top and show up in cut-offs and sandals, smelling of sweat and smoke and sex.

Ten minutes later, she pulled out of the mall, wearing a fabulous new shirt over her bikini top and feeling better. Way better. She twisted the throttle and weaved the Enduro in and out of cars on the highway, her long hair whipping in the wind, and shouted laughter at the beeping horns of the angry drivers she blew past.

SEVEN

SCARLETT PARKED ON A SLEEPY SIDE STREET LINED with luxury cars and started walking toward what sounded like live elevator music. A stone wall surrounded the sprawling estate, most of which was shrouded in darkness.

Near the Ditko mansion, the grounds glowed in candle flame and canopy lighting. Around the shimmering blue rectangle of the pool, hundreds of well-dressed attendees burbled politely. An army of tuxedoed caterers weaved from group to group with trays of hors d'oeuvres and tall skinny glasses that meant champagne for the senator and his well-scrubbed supporters and spritzers for the newly minted grads, most of whom would already be high, half in the bag, or deeply messed up on pills anyway. Everyone knew that wealthy suburban kids got loaded but looked the other way as long as they kept up appearances. Great training for the adulthoods awaiting them in the land of milk and cubicles.

A black suit was checking invitations at the gate, so Scarlett backtracked to the end of the block and hopped the fence. She would cross the parklike main lawn and sneak into the party. Easy as—

She ducked behind a towering sycamore, curses rattling like machine-gun fire in her mind. A pair of patrolling security guards . . .

Had they seen her? She didn't dare to peek around the trunk.

Her legs wanted to bolt, but her gut told her to stay put, so she held her breath, digging her fingers into the stiff bark of the sycamore, and sighed when the guards passed, murmuring softly, and disappeared into the shadows.

She grinned. That had been close.

Then she strolled toward the lights, taking her time, loving the feel of the cool night air, and leaned her head back, digging the bright sliver of moon overhead and the sprinkling of stars twinkling against the hard darkness between rags of silver cloud. A beautiful night to—

Oh, great. She'd forgotten to stash her weed. A trespassing charge would suck. But possession charges, with her record, now that she was eighteen, would mean jail time.

She had to hide the bag. But where? Then, glancing across the yard, she smiled.

The guest house was dark save for the twinkling of electric window candles. She'd stash her weed in the basement, where she had first given in to Sav's persistent curiosity and shared a bowl with the future valedictorian.

Above the guest house door hung a familiar flag: yellow lightning bolts crossed over a field of blue, with the motto of the 2nd Infantry Battalion—*Ride the Lightning*—in white letters. Her father had one just like it in the den. During the first Gulf War, Master Sergeant Charles Winter, then *Corporal* Charles Winter, had served under Sav's father not only in the same battalion but the same *platoon*. What a lighthearted outfit that must've been.

The door was ajar. She listened, heard nothing, and slipped inside the kitchen. She crossed the creaking floorboards, opened the basement door, started down the steps, and closed the door behind her in case the security guards came by. Halfway down the stairs, the good smell of apples struck her, ushering in memories. Good times, getting lit, Sav finally chilling out, laughing.

Scarlett tucked the bag between two apple bins and drew her lungs full of the sweet aroma. She remembered this one time when they'd gotten baked and Sav had made up this hilarious song about—

Eeee . . .

The floorboards creaked overhead. Scarlett heard scuffling feet and muffled voices. A loud thump rattled the cellar door. Dust shook down from the floor joists over her head.

The guards? Or some couple pulling at each other's clothes?

She tiptoed up the cellar stairs. Her heart hammered with adrenaline, but she had to smile. She loved the edge.

Then a woman's voice said, "Set it for a minute forty-five."

Caterers? Was someone using the microwave?

"Cutting it a little close," a man's voice said.

"Want someone to see us, come in here, and cut the wires, deactivate it?"

Deactivate?

A third voice, male, chuckled. "You just want a front row seat when this thing blows up."

Blows up?

The tremor started in Scarlett's feet, rolled up through her legs, rumbled through her core, and rattled out her shoulders. She clacked her teeth shut to trap the scream inside. She hunched in panic and dug her fingers into the wooden handrail. Leaning forward, she peered through the keyhole and went cold.

Like the security guards, this trio wore black. Not suits but jumpsuits. Ski masks covered their faces. One man crouched before the keyhole, fiddling with something.

A bomb, Scarlett thought. *That's what he's fiddling with.* Right there, inches away.

The woman held a stubby machine gun. "No front row seat," the woman said. "Even from here the blast could knock over the van."

The man standing beside her gripped a blocky pistol. In his other hand, he held—and this was so strange that Scarlett did a double take—a tiny baseball glove.

"All set," the crouching man said. His pupils were huge. "Tell me when to punch it."

The woman's smile was very bright against the black ski mask. "No gods . . ."

"No masters," the men replied in unison.

Something beeped, and the three of them hurried from the room.

Scarlett gripped the doorknob but forced herself to wait. If she sprinted out now, they would gun her down. She could barely breathe. Her fingers felt like ice on the doorknob.

Finally, unable to wait another second, she twisted the handle, pushed the door, and rushed forward. Then she was falling, tumbling backward down the stairs.

She lashed out, grabbed a rail post, and jarred to a stop before hitting the cellar floor.

The knob had turned, but the door hadn't opened, so she'd bounced off it—*Stupid-stupid-stupid!*—and fallen down the stairs.

She raced back upstairs, twisted the handle hard, and pushed again.

"No!" The door was jammed.

The terrorists—her mind cringed at the word, but what else could you call them?—had worried about making it to their van and driving to safety in a minute and forty-five seconds. How much time was left now? A minute? Less?

She pushed again, and the door barely budged. It was the bomb. The bomb was against the door, blocking her escape.

Wild with fear, she ran downstairs—and instantly realized her mistake. Even if she survived the blast down here, the house would collapse on her. She ran back up, screaming.

She slammed against the door. It gave the tiniest bit. In a mad panic, she threw her weight against the door, cursing, knowing it was too late, knowing that in mere seconds the bomb would explode. Each attempt filled her with desperate strength and pushed the door open a bit farther. With a burst of strength, she drove the door forward and squeezed through the gap.

The device, a large cube within a skeletal frame, looked very much like the generator her father had wired into their electric box to power the fridge and computers whenever they lost power, but of course a generator didn't display red numbers counting down.

19, 18, 17 . . .

No time to run.

She had to stop it, needed to—what had they said? *Cut the wires and deactivate it*—but she saw no wires and had no wire cutters and . . .

She launched herself at the bomb. She jabbed buttons, but the countdown continued—*15, 14, 13 . . .*—and she almost leaped away in panic but forced herself instead to reach inside the skeletal framework, patting madly, searching for wires.

11, 10, 9 . . .

Her fingers closed on a wire, but she couldn't get a grip, couldn't pull it loose.

6, 5 . . .

Then she did panic, leaping away—*No-no-no!*—and immediately jerked around again, understanding her mistake—*The wires are your only chance!*—but the counter slid from 2 to 1 to—

Standing five feet away, Scarlett screamed as the bomb exploded.

EIGHT

WITH HIS GRAY HAIR AND MARATHONER'S BUILD, team leader Brady Webster might not have looked like a bona fide supertrooper, especially next to the heavily muscled members of his security detail, but he'd done a dozen combat tours before switching over to private security, first with Blackwater, then in South America, and finally here, guarding Senator Ditko and his family.

He was searching the orchard when something flashed brightly inside the guest house. With it came the all-too-familiar *whump* of high explosives—or rather a *whu,* because the sound cut off abruptly.

Like someone jumped on a grenade, he thought.

He called to Taylor and Fuchs, and together they ran toward the guest house, which was dark and silent again.

"Fan out," he told the men. They took up flanking positions, pistols drawn.

Faint light flickered indistinctly within the guest house, but he saw no flames or smoke, no sign that the place was afire. Had someone detonated a dud in there?

Whatever the case, something weird was going down, so he reminded himself to go slow and keep his guys in check. *Weird* got people killed.

The guest house door swung open, and a girl stumbled outside. Instantaneously, his brain registered the facts: a Caucasian female, late teens or early twenties, approximately five feet, six inches tall, perhaps 120 pounds with a dancer's build, no discernible weapon, barefoot, dressed in raggedy shorts, a pink bikini top, and the charred and smoking remains of what had been a blouse. She staggered, obviously disoriented, into the yard.

She certainly didn't look dangerous, but then Webster remembered the rumors about what had happened down in Atlanta—talk about not looking dangerous—and shouted, "On the ground!" Taylor and Fuchs closed, echoing his command, weapons held out before them, ready to fire.

The kid turned toward them, a look of bewilderment on her pretty face.

"On the ground, miss," Webster repeated. Then to Taylor, "All call."

Taylor nodded and lifted his lapel mic.

"Fuchs," Webster said, "keep a sharp eye. The house, the orchard, everywhere."

But Fuchs only continued to stare at the girl.

"Get away!" the girl shouted.

Then Webster saw it. The girl was glowing, radiating a faint, flickering light. She shuddered like a dog coming out of a river, only that wasn't water coming off her.

Webster stood firm despite every fiber of his being wanting to retreat. "Drop and roll," he said. "You're on fire."

The girl looked down at herself in terror. Flames were coming off her bare skin in small bursts, arching and huffing like geysers on the surface of the sun. Then she looked up again, locking eyes with Webster. "Run," she pleaded. "I can't hold it much longer."

Time for talking was over, Webster knew. The girl was out of her mind and in big, big trouble. Webster holstered his pistol and pulled his Taser. "On the ground, miss. Last chance."

The girl's eyes went wide. "No," she said, backing up, afraid of the Taser in some way that she hadn't feared the pistol. "Don't—"

There was no time to repeat the warning. She was huffing flame, burning alive, whether she knew it or not. Webster fired the Taser—

And flew backward, knocked unconscious by a wave of heat and light and force.

He came to a moment later, coughing and confused, ears ringing, the bright flash of the explosion still lingering in his eyes. He sat up, felt the heat, and shied away, shielding his eyes.

Where the girl had stood, a massive column of flame pillared brightly skyward. The ground shook beneath Webster for several seconds until the flames weakened and fell away, revealing what looked like the aftermath of a rocket strike. The girl was gone. The place where she had stood was now a smoldering crater.

REACHING THE EDGE of the lawn, Scarlett struggled up the wall, tumbled over the edge, and hit the ground hard, jarring the wind from her lungs. Behind her, car alarms wailed, triggered by . . . whatever had happened back there.

She had to hurry, had to get out of here.

She crawled into the street. Too slow, she knew. Crawling was too slow. But what else could she do when she felt weak as a baby?

Get up, she told herself. *Get up or you are going to be in such huge trouble.*

She fought through the pain and weakness and forced herself to stand. She wanted to run, but painful spasms wracked her muscles, and she stumbled toward her motorcycle in a lurching hobble. Her ears rang, and her head pounded. Her spine was a column of fire, and her entire body sizzled head to toe as if she'd plugged her nervous system into a light socket.

She climbed onto the Yamaha, head swirling. Her bare feet—she'd somehow lost her sandals—felt weird on the pegs. Her shorts were charred and tattered. The new blouse was a tattered mess of smoking rags.

She finally glanced back in the direction from which she'd staggered. What she saw shocked her so much, she almost fell off the bike. Where she'd been standing, smoke poured from a gaping crater. In the weird, flickering light of the flames, she saw the smoldering battalion flag and the guest house windows broken open like screaming mouths.

You caused this . . .

Around the crater, dark shapes staggered to their feet. Thank God they'd survived.

What had happened back there? The bomb had exploded right in front of her, its light and heat and noise blasting outward, filling the room in a microsecond, hitting her like a hurricane gust, rushing past—but just as quickly, the explosion had collapsed, *pulling back into her.* All that bright fire and roaring force had whooshed into her body, filling her, and she'd staggered outside, dazed and desperate, struggling to hold in the tremendous ball of flame swelling inside her, like a human volcano about to erupt. She'd tried to warn the men, but they wouldn't listen . . .

In the distance, sirens howled, drawing nearer, rousing her from her shocked state. With this new clarity, she realized that she could hear nearer sounds, too: doors opening, footsteps and voices, people coming from various directions.

Get out of here!

She mustered all the strength remaining in her, started the bike, and pulled away. The world pulsed in and out of focus with every heartbeat of the migraine hammering in her skull. She didn't trust her twitching muscles or blurry vision, but with the sirens closing fast, she was out of options. She gritted her teeth, twisted the throttle, and sped away through the night.

NINE

A BLACK SUBURBAN WITH TINTED WINDOWS TURNED into the crowded driveway of the Ditko guest house and pulled up behind the bomb squad van.

Seconds later, a pug-faced policeman swaggered over and rapped officiously on the darkened driver's-side window.

The window hummed down, revealing the driver, a short-haired black man with no expression on his face. His hands remained on the wheel, a heavy golden ring glowing on one finger.

"You can't park here, sir," the policeman said. "Emergency services only."

"We *are* emergency services," the driver said.

The passenger door opened, and out stepped a broad-shouldered man in a dark beret and Army dress blues resplendent with citations and badges. Beneath his silver eagle insignia, a nameplate read *Rhoads*. He glanced at the smoldering crater, shook his head, and gave an impressed whistle. Then he came around the vehicle and handed the policeman his credentials.

The policeman straightened a little. "With all due respect, Colonel, we have an active investigation under way here, and I haven't received word of military involvement."

"I am the word," Rhoads said. His smile managed both warmth and warning. "A clarion call, you might say. Now, be a good man and fetch me Senator Ditko."

Police officers have a sixth sense for danger, one that detects not only thugs and muggers but also more subtle threats, such as political pitfalls, that could prove as deadly as a bullet to one's career. The pug-faced officer hesitated only a fraction of a second before trotting off.

Rhoads stood at parade rest and surveyed a familiar scene of aftermath and fresh destruction with an interested smile. Groups of people scouring fresh destruction, talking in hushed tones, each team's windbreakers with a different three-letter acronym on the back.

A moment later, Senator Ditko came across the yard, hailing Rhoads. "That was fast, Oscar, even for you."

"In light of recent events, they've assigned me a jet," Rhoads said. The men shook hands. "Sure beats driving over the George Washington Bridge. How's Margie holding up?"

Ditko nodded. "You know Margie. She's tough. Thanks for coming."

Rhoads nodded. "And Savannah? How's she handling this?"

"She's upset," Ditko said. "Not exactly what she had planned for her graduation party." Ditko glanced back toward the house. "I'm just so damned glad that they're okay."

Rhoads laid a hand on his shoulder. "Me, too, Wes. Me, too." The men had worked together for a long time even as their lives had diverged, and Rhoads could see how badly the night's events had rattled his old friend. "I'm sorry, Wes. This is a terrible thing, and I know you're shaken up, but she's okay. Truly. Now, why don't you tell me what you know?"

Ditko nodded. "CSI found a detonated bomb in the guest house. A big one. Semtex."

Rhoads glanced at the guest house then back to Ditko. A detonated bomb packed with Semtex—even a small one—should have leveled the house. "Looks like someone misplaced the crater. Second device?"

"No," Ditko said. "Not exactly. Come inside."

The bomb squad was finishing up and didn't offer much resistance after seeing Rhoads's credentials. He asked them to leave the kitchen and promised not to touch anything. Once they were gone, he crouched down next to the bomb and started poking at the debris.

Strange smells in there. Charred air. Ozone. Something sharp, like ammonia. And beneath it all, like the ghost of autumn, the faint aroma of apples.

The device carriage was blown wide open, just what you'd expect from that sort of explosion, but the kitchen had sustained almost no damage. A flash burn on the floor, shattered windows, a few gouges in the walls, but the shrapnel lay in a tight circle around the detonated bomb, as if it had all blasted away for a fraction of a second . . . and then just dropped.

"Something hinky happened here," Rhoads said.

"Something very hinky," Ditko agreed. "Like the bomb started to explode but stopped."

"It exploded," Rhoads said, "but then, somehow, it stopped exploding."

"Security saw the flash, heard the noise, and came running," Ditko said. "A girl staggered out of here and shouted for them to get away. Then *boom* . . . You probably noticed the crater."

"Suicide vest?" Rhoads said.

Ditko shook his head. "She was half naked. Shorts and a bikini."

"Underwear bomber?"

"You couldn't fit enough ordnance in your pants to make a crater that size."

Rhoads thought for a moment, then nodded. "So . . . a human torch, then?"

Ditko nodded. "That's what they're saying."

"Where are your men? I'd like to ask them some questions."

"They're with the sketch artist now."

Rhoads looked pensive for several seconds, then glanced in all directions. They were alone. "You think it's him, his people?"

Ditko hesitated. "I don't know."

"But you called me."

"I thought you should know."

"Well, I appreciate it."

The pug-faced officer interrupted, excusing himself and handing Ditko a sketch. "Artist just finished up."

Rhoads looked over the senator's shoulder to see the sketch artist's rendering of a pretty girl with a halo of wild hair and scar tissue on her neck and chest and shoulders.

The cop asked, "Recognize her, Senator?"

"No," Rhoads said, and took the sketch from Ditko's hands, "he doesn't."

The cop scowled but said nothing, those good instincts kicking in again.

Rhoads dismissed him, and they were alone once more. "You know her, don't you?"

Ditko nodded. "You?"

"I do," Rhoads admitted. "But she's not one of theirs, right?"

"No," Ditko said, looking troubled. "Not as far as I know. But why . . . ?"

The door opened, and the policeman returned, looking sheepish. "Senator, we found this near the blast zone." He crossed the room, handing Ditko a softball glove. "Looks like it has your daughter's name in it."

Ditko's eyes went wide. He mumbled thanks. As the officer once again fled the room, Ditko studied the mitt with his mouth hanging open.

"What is it, Wes?" Rhoads asked.

"Evidence," Ditko said. He clutched the baseball glove to his chest like a toddler hugging a security blanket. "Evidence that my daughter, despite making valedictorian, still can't seem to put her things away properly." He paused, obviously battling emotion. "It's Savannah's. I guess I reacted, seeing it. I just . . . it's too easy to imagine how this could have gone wrong."

Rhoads patted his back. "She's okay, and I have every confidence that we'll get to the bottom of this, Wes," he said. "Every confidence."

They talked for a time, then went back outside and shook hands and said their good-byes. Wesley Ditko watched the man who twenty-some years ago had been his most trustworthy lieutenant head toward the emergency services coffee klatch just beyond the cordoned-off area, where Rhoads no doubt would be asking some pointed questions. Ditko wondered if Rhoads even knew that he'd just echoed the exact same assurance—*I have every confidence that we'll get to the bottom of this, Wes. Every confidence*—that he'd offered last spring when Ditko's younger daughter had been kidnapped as she'd been walking home from softball practice.

He looked down at the glove about which he'd just lied.

It wasn't Savannah's name scrawled across the thumb. It was her sister's. His eyes misted just to see her familiar handwriting and the signature heart she'd always used to complete the tail of the *y*.

The handwriting beneath her name was not hers, however. Blocky caps read, *if found, call* . . . and listed an unfamiliar number.

He had no idea what Scarlett Winter had to do with this but would happily skin her alive to find out. Unfortunately, Rhoads had jurisdiction. She was his. For now, at least for now.

Senator Ditko groaned his daughter's name and departed the scene, heading off to find privacy to make the call. He would do anything to get her back.

TEN

"WELL, LOOK WHO DECIDED TO WAKE UP AND JOIN the world," Scarlett's mother chimed.

"Hey," Scarlett said, leaning in the doorway. The kitchen was spotless. No sign of the decomposing food or the wasted graduation cake. No sign of her father or brother, either. Bright sunshine flooded the room. All was well in the world, the kitchen proclaimed, and her mother's chirpy greeting agreed. "Where's Dan?"

"Oh, he had to head back to base," Mom said, wiping down the counter. "So nice of him to surprise you like that, though, wasn't it?"

"Yeah," she said. If Mom was going to be nice enough to let her off the hook for last night's debacle, Scarlett could make her happy by playing along.

She shuffled to the refrigerator. Her head wouldn't stop pounding, and she was sore from head to toe, but most of all she was hungry and thirsty, so incredibly thirsty, thirstier than she'd ever been in her entire life.

"Sit down, honey," her mother said. "Let me make you something nice."

Scarlett grabbed a two-liter of cola from the fridge and chugged straight from the bottle. The cold bubbles felt great on her parched throat. She let her eyes close and drank and drank and drank.

"Oh, my goodness," her mother said. "Did you just drink that whole thing?"

She nodded, wanting more, and released a tremendous belch that made both of them laugh.

Mom scolded her halfheartedly, then told her how proud she was. "You did it, Scarlett," she said, crossing the room. "You graduated high school." She threw her arms around Scarlett, cooing, then stepped back with a look of revulsion on her face. "You smell *horrible.*"

She faked a smile. "Gee, Mom . . . thanks."

Her mother waved a hand in front of her face. "I'm serious, Scarlett Marie. Phew! You smell like someone set fire to a pile of sweaty gym socks. What did you get into last night?"

You'd need to waterboard that out of me, Mom, she thought, but she just shrugged and said, "Not much."

Her mother stepped closer, frowning. "Is your hair singed?" She touched the side of Scarlett's head. "Sweetie, how did you burn your hair?"

"Oh, that?" She forced a chuckle. "Bonfire party in West Chester last night. Guess I got too close."

"Well, I don't like that one bit," her mother said, fussing with her hair. "I hate to say it—I know how you are about cutting your hair—but you're going to need a haircut to fix this." She stepped back again, wincing. "Oh, the stench."

Scarlett roared another soda burp.

Mom grimaced and made a shooing motion with her dish towel. "You're a monster."

Despite her pounding head, Scarlett had to laugh. Few things in life are funnier than grossing out your mom.

Cooking eggs and sausage, Mom said, "Well, I sure am glad that you aren't hanging around with that Ditko girl anymore."

Scarlett feigned ignorance and listened as her mom described the explosion. "It's all over the news," she said, scraping eggs onto Scarlett's plate. "Praise God no one was killed."

"Thanks," she said, and started shaking hot sauce onto her eggs. "What caused the explosion?"

The iron skillet clattered in the sink, and the faucet gushed to life. "Gas main explosion," her mother said. "Can you believe it?"

Actually, no, she thought, and let her shoulders relax.

The doorbell rang.

"I got it," Scarlett said, hopping up.

Two soldiers stood outside, smiling. One white, one black, the white guy in dress blues with a whole bunch of colorful ribbons on his chest, the black guy looking very fit in a black jumpsuit with a Spartan helmet and sword logo.

"Hey," Scarlett said. She tensed at the sight of them—thinking, *Recruiters?*—but then she noticed the white guy's insignia and relaxed. Wooing third-rate prospects was below a colonel's pay grade. She hollered over her shoulder, "Dad, someone here to see you."

"Actually," the colonel said, "we're here to see you, Scarlett. My name is Colonel Oscar Rhoads." He stuck out his hand.

Scarlett shook it but hung back. "What for?"

"Let's say I wanted to see what the daughter of a hero looked like," Rhoads said.

Hero? Dad? Yeah, right . . .

"If you'll invite us inside," Rhoads said, "we can talk all about it."

Then her father's voice spoke up in the hall behind him. "Major Rhoads?"

"Well, it's *Colonel* Rhoads now, but yes," Rhoads said, beaming.

"Sorry, sir," Scarlett's father said, and saluted. "I hadn't heard."

"At ease, soldier," Rhoads said, and strode forward to gather Scarlett's father into an embrace. "How the heck are you, Charlie?"

Charlie? Scarlett watched in disbelief, confused by her father's huge smile, the man suddenly looking less like one of those stone heads on Easter Island and more like a living, breathing human capable of admiration and friendship and maybe even humor.

The other soldier stepped forward, smiling warmly. "Hey, Scarlett. I'm Captain Fuller."

In the kitchen, Scarlett's mom gave Rhoads a big hug. "Sit down to lunch with us."

Scarlett expected a jab from her father—*we have plenty of leftovers*—but no, her father beamed as he insisted, "Yes, please, come and eat with us."

After some polite hemming and hawing, the men agreed.

"Don't set a place for me, Mom," Scarlett said. She gave the soldiers a wave. "Hey—nice meeting you guys."

"I was hoping you'd join us, Scarlett," Rhoads said.

Scarlett put a hand to her stomach. "Sorry, just ate. I'm stuffed."

"Do an old friend of your father's a favor and sit with us, anyway," Rhoads said.

"Thanks, but—"

"Scarlett," her father said, drilling her with death eyes. "Help your mother set the table, please. And set a place for yourself."

BY THE TIME they had filled their plates with burgers, coleslaw, and salad, Scarlett's stomach was growling again, and she understood that her father had served under Rhoads a million years ago, in the first Gulf War. Rhoads had relied heavily on Scarlett's father, whom he continued to call *Charlie* and to whom he again referred as a hero. Scarlett's father looked happier than Scarlett had ever seen him, and her mother looked almost tearfully proud.

"Scarlett," Rhoads said, "I'd like to talk to you about the Harvard of the military: West Point."

Scarlett nodded, chewing a big mouthful of burger and slaw.

"Have you ever heard of Operation Signal Boost?" Rhoads asked.

Scarlett shook her head.

"Each year," Rhoads said, "West Point receives fifteen thousand applications from highly qualified individuals. Valedictorians, star athletes, legacy kids whose brothers, fathers, and grandfathers were all members of the Long Gray Line . . . every last one of them with a personal recommendation from a senator or congressman. Yet we ultimately accept only 9 percent of these applicants."

"Wow," Scarlett said, not bothering to put much into it. "Hey, Mom, could I have another burger, please?"

"I run Operation Signal Boost," Rhoads said. "We keep an eye on top military families around the country, watching for young people of high potential who, for one reason or another, would not officially qualify for West Point yet could, we believe, succeed there given proper structure and support."

Her mom turned with wide eyes and looked at Scarlett's father, who stared at Rhoads.

Rhoads smiled broadly. "Scarlett, how would you like to attend West Point?"

"Me?"

"Yes, you," Rhoads said, and laughed. "No application or congressional recommendation necessary."

"But I—"

Rhoads waved her off. "We know you've been in trouble. We know your grades have been . . . erratic. But we know other things, too: your IQ score, your athletic ability, the service your family has paid this nation. Operation Signal Boost is all about channeling raw potential."

Scarlett leaned back, grinning nervously. This was insane. West Point? Her? "I really appreciate it, but no." She stood. "I'd make a terrible soldier."

"Scarlett," her father said. He sat very straight, and his eyes were wide and intense like those of a choking man. "Sit down right now."

Scarlett lowered herself into the seat but didn't bother to push back to the table. Rhoads was a lunatic if he thought she was going to go to West Point and ruin her life.

"Honey, at least hear him out," Mom pleaded, reaching for Scarlett's hand.

She pulled it away. "No. Look, Colonel, like I said, I really appreciate it, but—"

"Colonel Rhoads made you an amazing offer," her father said. "Show some respect."

Scarlett stood again, suddenly angry. "I told you yesterday," she said, finally finding the strength to glare back at her father. "I'm not joining the Army. Period. I don't care if it's West Point. It's still the Army, and I'm done taking orders!"

Her father rose to his feet. "Don't raise your voice in this house, young lady. Now sit down and—"

"Scarlett," Rhoads said. Somehow his voice, though quiet, cut through the shouting. "Would you do me a favor, please? Give me five minutes. Outside. I'd hate for you to turn us down without understanding what you're saying no to and why I'm so confident that you'd make a great cadet."

Scarlett was shaking with anger but not at Rhoads. "All right," she said. "Just the two of us, though."

Rhoads smiled. "I wouldn't have it any other way."

ELEVEN

BE NICE TO THE GUY, SCARLETT THOUGHT, LEADing Rhoads out to the backyard, *but give it to him straight and be done with it: You're wasting your time. I'm no soldier.*

But no sooner had they stepped into the midday sun than Rhoads knocked her off balance, saying, "Tell me about Senator Ditko's party." His smile was gone. He stared, waiting.

"I don't know what you're talking about."

Rhoads frowned. "Come on, Scarlett. Do you really want to play this game?" He reached inside his jacket, withdrew a square of paper, and handed it to her. "Unfold it."

She hesitated. Her fingers felt ice cold. Then, slowly, she opened the paper, and the iciness from her fingers spread up her arms and filled her body. She managed to shrug her shoulders, though inside, she was howling. "So what? Is this supposed to be me?"

"It *is* you, Scarlett. A police sketch artist's rendition, anyway. You were seen."

Scarlett shook her head. "I don't know what you're talking about."

"Senator Ditko already identified you," Rhoads said, "to me, anyway. He's agreed not to share that information with the police, FBI, or Homeland unless I give him the green light . . . which all depends on the conversation we're having right now."

"What do you mean?"

Rhoads spread his hands. "Commit to the program. Four years plus four more active duty."

"Eight years?" she said. "You must be crazy."

"Those eight years will pass one way or the other," Rhoads said. "It's your choice: the program . . . or whatever happens. The bomb squad is cooperating for now, backing our gas main story, but the truth will come out sooner or later if I step away."

Scarlett felt frozen in place. "So if I don't join, you'll have them haul me off to jail?"

Rhoads shrugged. "These are volatile times, Scarlett. You've seen the news. The paranormal terror attacks have people jumpy. We did a pretty good job muting Springfield, Round Rock, Mobile, and a dozen small-town tragedies . . . but then Atlanta happened."

He didn't have to clarify. The web had been buzzing over the attacks for months, crying government cover-ups, but Atlanta had been a full-on horror show with gruesome footage playing night and day on the major news networks. All those people, more than a hundred of them, bursting spontaneously into flames as if someone had soaked them in napalm and struck a match.

"America is clamoring for answers," Rhoads said. "One more Atlanta and we'll see the Salem Witch Trials reborn coast to coast. Crazed with fear, this country will eat itself alive. That's something the U.S. government will not allow. If you refuse my offer, I can't support you. Your capture will take pressure off the agencies, and the public will finally have its scapegoat. Paranormal terrorism will finally have a face—yours."

"Mine?" She couldn't believe this. "I'm no terrorist."

"I know that," Rhoads said, and offered a wistful smile, "but this would be the story of the century. Do you think the network news will give you fair treatment? Or do you think they'll sensationalize the story for all it's worth?"

"I don't believe it," Scarlett said. "I don't believe you." But Rhoads didn't look like he was lying. She just didn't want to believe him.

"Senator Ditko will be all too happy to prove me right. All I have to do is walk away. He'll have you in handcuffs before you can say *Guantanamo Bay*."

Over the years, she had been chewed out by principals, grilled by cops, and chastised by judges. Through it all, she'd kept her cool even when the judge had sentenced her to lockdown, but this was trouble on a whole different level. No way out. No coming back. Nothing.

She had the urge to spill everything and be done with it but slammed on the brakes at the last second. "I want to talk to my lawyer."

"Makes sense," Rhoads said, "but can you really trust Mr. Tiliakos?"

That knocked her off balance again. Rhoads knew about Tiliakos, the cut-rate lawyer she'd used to get out of an underage drinking rap and two more serious charges. Well, he'd gotten her out of one of the more serious charges, anyway. The second time, Tiliakos had fumbled the ball, and Scarlett had caught two months in lockdown.

"You really trust Tiliakos with your life? We're not talking underage drinking this time."

Scarlett pictured Tiliakos, the guy quick with a smile and a joke, but . . .

Her mind leaped to the time when she'd been sitting in a small room, waiting for the cops. Just Tiliakos and her in there, Scarlett half drunk, wondering how bad it was going to be this time, Tiliakos sitting there, scrolling through his phone. Then she'd smelled the fart. Just the two of them in there, and she hadn't cut it, but Tiliakos hadn't said word one. No *excuse me*, no grin, not even a lawyer joke, and Tiliakos had a million of those. He just sat there in the stink, scrolling through his phone, silent as a hanged man.

"No," Scarlett told Rhoads, sure of it. "I won't trust him with my life."

"Great," Rhoads said. "Frankly, there isn't a lawyer on earth who could save you this time." His smile beamed. "Only I can do that."

The walls of the world were pressing in on her, crushing everything she'd ever hoped or dreamed or believed.

"Look, Scarlett," Rhoads said. "I know you didn't intend to hurt anyone. Sometimes collateral damage is impossible to avoid. I'm offering you a way out. This has to be your choice and yours alone. I won't lie and tell you that West Point will be easy, but I will make this trouble disappear, and I'll help you control that power of yours so that you never hurt an innocent person again." Rhoads laid a hand on her shoulder. "Well, what do you say?"

TWELVE

R-Day
United States Military Academy, West Point, New York

A SUCCESSION OF OFFICERS WELCOMED THE 1,300 new cadets and their families seated in Eisenhower Hall Auditorium. The Winters sat in the middle, adrift in a sea of eager candidates and proud families.

At different points over the weeks since Colonel Rhoads's visit, Scarlett had experienced a puzzling range of emotions: fear, incredulity, remorse, even excitement. This morning, she felt wary but determined.

The officers talked about the past and the future, about the Long Gray Line, their name for the unbroken succession of West Point graduates stretching now over 200 years, including great generals, even presidents, soldiers like Grant, Lee, Patton, MacArthur, and Eisenhower, all of them dedicated to the three-word West Point code that seemed to Scarlett an American Bushido: *Duty, honor, country*.

Scarlett had never been much of a team player. Motivational

speeches had never motivated her. Patriotism, embodied in her father, was a mixed bag: admirable, sure, but from her experience kind of like a drug, providing a necessary high to its cabal of dedicated users, who would sing its praises in a shared argot that set them apart from mainstream society as they went about their bloody way, killing and dying for a country that everybody loved and nobody much liked anymore. So yeah, a mixed bag.

But this place, West Point, this granite fortress atop a high plateau, with its epic topography, the green slopes plunging as sharply as Scandinavian fjords to the Hudson far below, all beneath the bluest sky Scarlett had ever seen, rattled her irreverence. She could *feel* the academy's proud history coming off the gray stones of its buildings, which reminded her of castles, the realm of American knights. There was an undeniable gravity all around her, and an electric optimism emanated from both the institution and its people, this place somehow inextricable from the Long Gray Line it had produced. Together, they had offered great sacrifice in the name of duty, honor, and country. Those three words united the living and the dead, the past, the present, and the future, untethering the Long Gray Line from time and lashing it to an eternal promise to the academy, the Army, and the nation.

She was surprised to feel a tentative glimmer of pride sparking to life within her just to be associated with the Long Gray Line. That was absurd, of course. She didn't belong. She hadn't earned her way here. But she was here nonetheless, part of something much greater than she'd ever expected. It was a surprise, feeling this way. She'd expected to retain her characteristic cynicism. But here, in this place, surrounded by these people and all this history, cynicism seemed suddenly weak and childish, like a crutch. These people had dispensed with irony and sarcasm, rolled up their collective sleeves, and gotten down to the business of creating the best Army officers they could make, and they'd been doing this for 200 years. One serious tradition, the Long Gray Line. She felt a little rocked, truth be told, and as she sat there, her burgeoning optimism played tag with self-doubt. How could she measure up? How could she possibly keep up with these fiercely attentive recruits, this gathering of valedictorians, sports stars, school presidents, and Eagle Scouts?

The ceremony ended, and the officer announced, "You have ninety seconds to say your good-byes."

She hugged her mother, who cried and told Scarlett that she loved her. Scarlett and her father shook hands awkwardly. Her mother reminded her to call home when she could, Scarlett said that she would, and then she joined the flood of cadets leaving the auditorium, grinning with unexpected excitement. Maybe she could do this . . .

TWENTY MINUTES LATER, she stood in a tightly packed line of new cadets, thinking, *What have I done?*

The stone-faced junior glaring at them was just as crisp as her uniform. *The stone-faced cow,* Scarlett reminded herself, recalling the West Point word for a third-year cadet. She was already sick of the lingo, the cuteness of it, everybody here playing a game, but serious, too, shouting at the new recruits, burying them with information, telling them to *hurry, move, go*.

Now the stone-faced cow had them at attention. "New Cadets, from this second forward and for the next four years, you will move with a purpose. You will clench your fists, lock your arms straight, and swing them at your sides. You will keep your head straight and your eyes forward. When you pass upperclassmen, you will greet them with the regimental motto, and when you are in formation, you will stand at the position of attention. Do you understand?"

"Yes, ma'am!" Scarlett chorused with the others, but the optimism she'd felt in the auditorium was long gone, replaced by a burgeoning sense of dread. Everybody here was so serious. Standing at attention, marching everywhere, everyone wearing the same uniform, echoing code phrases like a bunch of militant parrots. How did they do it?

Up and down the hall, upperclassmen were reading the same riot act to squads of new cadets. Most of the new recruits were twitchy with nerves. Nobody smiling, nobody cracking jokes, nobody rolling eyes, nobody even talking. They were to speak only when spoken to by a superior. Even then, they had only four responses: *Yes, sir or ma'am; No, sir or ma'am; I don't know, sir or ma'am;* and *No excuse, sir or ma'am.*

Insanity.

How could she possibly deal with this for four years?

How didn't matter. She had to. Rhoads had made that clear. If Scarlett washed out of West Point, she'd go straight to lockdown, awaiting the results of a reopened investigation, and ultimately would spend a long, long time in prison.

The day rushed forward, line to line, station to station, everything *go-go-go, stand here, do this, say that,* the upperclassmen a bunch of high-strung nitpickers, messing with the new cadets every step of the way.

Scarlett traded in her street clothes and personal effects for black shorts, a black T-shirt, and dog tags. Each new cadet received a big blue bag into which went the clothing and equipment issued at each station. The bags grew heavier and bulkier and more awkward with every acquisition. People dropped them, spilled stuff, got chewed out. For Scarlett, the physical stuff wasn't so bad, but her head was spinning, and she had a lot of trouble remembering to say stuff the right way. The upperclassmen rode her hard, rode everybody hard. She knew that they were following a script designed to shake up the new cadets, but it still rattled her cage. She felt jumpy, off balance, uncertain.

There were no breaks. The tension never let up. They remained with a squad, supervised at all times, every second planned and observed.

Scarlett's squad marched into Lee Barracks and entered a buzzing space where twenty barbers stood upon a calico carpet of shorn locks. The barbers were civilians. Some talked. Some didn't. They moved with the quick efficiency of sheep shearers. A middle-aged woman with baggy eyes and a blue apron called Scarlett to the chair and ran her fingers through her hair, saying how nice it was. Scarlett thanked her, remembering to call her "ma'am," and ninety seconds later, most of her hair was gone. "Well," the woman said, her fingers moving along Scarlett's scalp, "you sure are hiding a lot of scars under that pretty hair."

Scarlett looked in the mirror. Her hair had hung to the small of her back. Somehow, the sight of her new pixie cut made this situation real in a way that nothing else had to this point. She was in the Army. No more street clothes, no more long hair, no more nothing. From here on out, life would consist of shouting four responses, standing at attention, and marching with her fists swinging at her sides.

The new cadets each received a *knowledge book* and the stellar news that they would have to memorize all of it, as in every word, verbatim. Grim news for a girl who'd never quite managed to memorize the two dozen ice cream flavors she'd spent two summers scooping. At a flip, Scarlett saw songs, West Point trivia, quotes from famous officers, a glossary of cadet slang, and a long Q&A section on West Point lore and tradition that reminded her of the catechism book one of her old boyfriends, a Catholic, had shown her. Some of the answers were a full paragraph, and they needed to know every last word by heart. Whenever they were waiting, whether to fill out a form, eat, or take a leak, they should be reading their *knowledge book.*

Grand.

Upperclassmen marched them into Central Area, a paved courtyard surrounded by high gray buildings that looked now to Scarlett less like castles and more like prison walls. The sun beat down as the cadre explained how to stand, how to speak, how to listen, delivering these instructions in a breathless cadence, sounding like impatient hard-bitten auctioneers.

Roll with it, she told himself. *You have the haircut, uniform, and dog tags. Play their game, do your time, and get on with your life.*

They formed lines facing away from a row of upperclassmen wearing red sashes on their white uniforms. Scarlett understood what she was supposed to do. When called, she would execute an about-face, march to the line, drop her bag, salute, and report to the Cadet in the Red Sash, saying, *Sir, New Cadet Winter reports to the Cadet in the Red Sash for the first time as ordered.* Then listen to the guy, salute, and say, *No retreat, sir.*

Simple.

They called her forward, and she found herself face-to-face with the human manifestation of a Jack Russell terrier, a muscular little guy whose close-set eyes drilled into Scarlett, giving her the kind of hard look thugs had tried back in juvie. Big deal.

"New Cadet," the guy said, eyeballing Scarlett, "step up to the line not on the line not over the line not behind the line. New Cadet, step up to my line."

Scarlett stepped up, dropped her bag, and—

"New Cadet, do not stand on my line. Step up to the line not on the—New Cadet! Do not look down. Step back, New Cadet. Pick up your bag and get to the back of the line."

Scarlett went back and waited, annoyed, until it was her turn again. She stepped up to the line, dropped her bag, saluted, and said, "Sir, New Cadet Winter reporting to the Cadet in the Red Sash for the first time as ordered."

"New Cadet," the Jack Russell said, and Scarlett tensed, waiting for it. "Was this the first time you reported to me?"

"No, sir."

"New Cadet, can't you count to two?"

"Yes, sir."

"Yes, you can't, New Cadet? You're telling me that you can't count to two?"

"No, sir."

"Back of the line, New Cadet. Try again."

She marched back down the steps, went to the back of the line, and turned away, fuming.

The Cadet in the Red Sash called her again. She marched back up the steps, listened to him bark, toed the line, dropped the bag, and—

"New Cadet, get your bag off my line."

Scarlett bent and reached, but the bag wasn't on the line. "Sir, it isn't on—"

"New Cadet," the guy said, "you do not speak unless spoken to by a superior. Did I speak to you, New Cadet?"

"No, sir, but—"

"New Cadet, what are your four responses?"

Scarlett rattled them off.

"Do any of those responses contain the word 'but,' New Cadet?"

"No, sir."

"You said 'but,' New Cadet. Are you calling me a butt, New Cadet?"

"No, sir."

"New Cadet, why haven't you saluted me?"

Scarlett felt like a piñata. "Sir, I—"

"You'd better hope you're not in my squad, New Cadet. Back in line."

Again and again Scarlett approached the Cadet in the Red Sash, and again and again the little hammerhead found some reason to trash her. Where she stood, how she saluted, where her eyes looked, how she reported. The guy was on a power trip. Scarlett grew more frustrated and angry with each failed attempt.

He called her forward once more. She marched to the line, dropped her bag, saluted, and started to report again.

The Cadet in the Red Sash cut her off. "New Cadet, you seem upset. Do you have an attitude problem, New Cadet?"

"No, sir."

"You look like you want to cry, New Cadet. Is that what you want to do, New Cadet? Do you want to cry?"

"No, sir," Scarlett said, and glared down at him. "I want to smash your ugly face."

THIRTEEN

SCARLETT EXPERIENCED AN INSTANT OF INTENSE satisfaction, watching the cocky guy's face contort with shock. Then screaming upperclassmen surrounded her, bellowing orders, demanding answers, talking over one another, an absolute feeding frenzy . . .

"Cadets!" a deep voice thundered, and Scarlett's tormentors snapped to attention.

Scarlett smiled with relief. It was Rhoads's right-hand man, Fuller, dressed now in an officer's uniform with captain's bars.

"Hey, Captain Fuller," Scarlett said.

Fuller scowled. "New Cadet, pick up your gear and follow me—now."

"Yes, sir," Scarlett said. She grabbed her bag and followed Fuller, who marched rapidly across the courtyard. She hurried after him, feeling ridiculous as she struggled with the ungainly blue bag. New cadets watched with wide eyes.

Scarlett caught up to Fuller just as the man entered the cool dimness of the sally port beneath one of the tall dormitories. "Sir? I'm sorry about that, but—"

"Lock it up, Winter," Fuller said. "You do not speak unless spoken to."

"Yes, sir," she said, thinking, *What a jerk.* He'd been all smiles back at the house, saying how nice it was to meet her and yucking it up at lunch. Now, he was suddenly all business, a gung-ho ramrod just like her father and all the rest of these guys, only worse, because he'd actually pretended to be friendly.

They turned down a street and marched on without speaking. Fuller went up the steps of a dormitory. Scarlett followed him inside.

"Sir, I . . . permission to speak, sir?"

"Denied," Fuller said.

They couldn't just kick her out for one argument, could they?

Yes, they can, her own mind answered. This wasn't high school, wasn't even college . . . not real college. This was the military. West Point. *The Harvard of the Military,* Rhoads's voice echoed in her mind, which added, *no place for someone like you.*

Fuller led her down into a basement. The low ceiling was busy with fluorescent lighting, exposed wiring, pipes, and conduits. They passed a locker room with wooden benches and walls tiled beige and walked past storage rooms enclosed by wire fencing. Fuller went up three steps and stopped in front of a tan door that read I-2 TRUNK ROOM. He unlocked the door and turned on the lights, and Scarlett followed him into a room filled, aptly enough, with storage trunks.

Fuller closed the door.

Scarlett tensed. Why had he closed the door?

Fuller moved past her and pushed aside a cart stacked with trunks, revealing a scuffed section of wallboard marked with the imprint of a boot sole where some beleaguered plebe had apparently blown off steam by kicking the wall. Fuller reached out and pressed his thumb into the heel of the boot print.

The wall whooshed aside, revealing the space behind: what appeared to be the top landing of a circular stairwell that spiraled down into the darkness beneath West Point.

"This way," Fuller said, and Scarlett followed him into the stairwell. Lights clicked automatically to life overhead. The air here was cool and stale. Fuller gestured to a button on the wall. "Hit that."

She slapped the button. The wall slid shut behind them.

They descended, twisting around and around the stone steps for what felt like several flights until the staircase ended at a wall of burnished steel. Fuller reached out and pressed a thumb into the steel, which whipped aside, revealing a large concrete corridor with a high ceiling. Against the opposite wall, a line of around twenty new cadets turned their heads to stare at them.

"Eyes forward," a wiry cadet in the white uniform of an upperclassman told them.

Some obeyed. Others kept looking.

These recruits were different from the squads in the courtyard. Up there, maybe one in five were girls. Here, the split was fifty-fifty. This crew was more racially diverse, too, and better looking. The girls were pretty, and the guys were handsome, though three guys and one girl were freakishly huge, bigger than bodybuilders. This group was apparently less disciplined, too. Watching over them were additional upperclassmen and MP types in camouflage BDUs with Tasers on their belts and nightsticks in their hands.

"Back of the line, New Cadet Winter," Fuller said.

"Yes, sir," she said. She went to the back of the line and stood behind a girl who'd pulled her bright red hair into a tight ponytail, revealing the blue tattoo on the back of her neck: a Z intersected by an infinity symbol.

"Winter's the last," Fuller told the cadre. "Made it to the Red Sash, then failed epically."

The wiry upperclassman—his name tag read *Hopkins*—gave Scarlett a tough-guy glare that harkened back to the Cadet in the Red Sash, only Hopkins looked more like a Doberman than a Jack Russell, long, lean, and angular, with just enough muscle to generate damage and no excess mass to slow him. Hopkins said, "We'll fix her attitude, sir."

Scarlett ignored the guy, trying to understand the implications of what Fuller had said. She'd made it the farthest? These others had all been pulled *before* the Red Sash?

Oh, man. She'd joined some kind of reject brigade.

Fuller led them down the cavernous corridor to a massive door twenty feet high, twice as wide, and built seemingly of concrete and steel, like the blast door to a nuclear bunker. The door ground heavily aside to reveal a large concrete box of a room. They marched into the box, and the door behind them groaned shut. The majority of each wall was another blast door. Scarlett looked up and saw cameras high above in each corner.

The door in front of them slid open. They marched into a well-lit, brightly tiled corridor past a glassed-in space that reminded her of a police station reception counter except that the half dozen people she saw inside all wore camouflage BDUs. Fuller checked in at a sliding window, then a door opened at the end of the hall, and the new cadets marched into a two-story lobby. To the right was another glassed-in room, this one looking more like the main office of a school than a police station. To the left were what looked like classrooms, the small windows in their doors dark. Above, situated along the rail of a metal walkway, a pair of guards stared down, holding, she was startled to see, M4 machine guns.

Fuller marched them toward a pair of double doors over which a sign read *Welcome to The Point* and beneath that *Training Tomorrow's Leaders Today*. Between those lines was a logo much like West Point's: the same black and gold design, same Spartan helmet, same star beneath, only instead of a sword, this logo had a lightning bolt.

They entered an auditorium with a gleaming wooden stage and tiered seating for perhaps 300. Hopkins and the other upperclassmen joined uniformed cadets lining the far wall. Scarlett and the other misfits sat in the first row, as directed—and shot to their feet again as Rhoads strolled onto the stage, wearing his dress blues but no beret. His gaze swept over them. "At ease, New Cadets. You may be seated."

They sat.

"My name is Colonel Rhoads," he said, standing behind the podium. "Welcome. I know that some of you—" He paused and smiled. "—heck, *all* of you, had a rough morning, right?"

The new cadets responded in an affirmative jumble blending *Yeah* with *Yes* with *Yes, sir,* and the freakishly muscular girl piped up, "You got that right, sir!"

Fuller cut through the babble, saying, "You will all respond 'Yes, sir!' "

They chorused, "Yes, sir!"

"Motivated!" Rhoads said. "Way to sound off, New Cadets. You might be wondering what in God's name you're doing down here, eighty feet below the annual R-Day dog-and-pony show. Well, I'm here to tell you. What you just experienced was the shock-and-awe rite of passage through which all West Point cadets enter Beast Barracks and their plebe year. Unlike those above us, every last one of you failed."

Here we go, Scarlett thought, shifting in her seat. *He's kicking us out.*

"In all fairness, your failure was expected," Rhoads said. "Presently, you don't have what it takes to make it here at West Point."

Fuller shushed the grumbling.

"I speak only the truth," Rhoads said, "but let's be fair. How many of you actually *applied* to West Point?"

Scarlett glanced down the row. Not a single hand rose.

Rhoads said, "We recruited you. Yes, you need remedial assistance, but we will get you up to West Point standards. You will become professionals of the highest order, part of the Long Gray Line, men and women defined by three words." As he spoke each of these three words, he knocked his ring against the wooden podium. "Duty. Honor. Country. Do you understand?"

"Yes, sir!" she chorused along with the others. She was confused yet relieved. Rhoads wasn't giving them the boot. No jail, then—at least not yet.

"You will live and train in this facility, with me, my cadre, and the upperclassmen who preceded you. Eventually, you will interact with the regular plebes and cadets, dining with them, taking classes alongside them, training with them, and, of course, attending football games beside them."

"Beat Navy!" Fuller shouted.

"Beat Navy!" the cadre and upperclassmen echoed.

"Cadet Amer," Rhoads said.

"Right here," a female voice responded. Scarlett swiveled in her seat. Cadet Amer, a striking brunette with dark eyes and a heart-shaped face, leaned against the wall, smirking. Of all the cadets, she was the only one leaning, the only one smirking, the only one with her arms crossed.

"How many days until Army beats Navy?"

"One hundred and sixty-two days," Amer said.

"Outstanding," Rhoads said.

Whoa, Scarlett thought. Amer must be some kind of savant, one of those people, you tell her your birthplace and date, and before you can say *Rain Man*, she says you were born on a snowy Tuesday and recites your hometown phone book from memory.

Rhoads straightened, gripping the podium like a steering wheel, and smiled down at the new cadets. "You're no doubt wondering *why* we brought you here. Brace yourselves."

Here we go, she thought, and pressed her palms into her thighs.

Rhoads said, "Ten years ago, the government was alerted to the existence of 'posthumans,' an emerging breed of men and women with incredible abilities that manifest around the age of eighteen."

The new cadets murmured among themselves. Fuller squashed the chatter.

Rhoads said, "The first of these posthumans were detained, studied, and in many instances trained by the U.S. Army—with varying degrees of success. Since that time, armed with a better understanding of the strengths and liabilities of posthumans, West Point has taken on the mantle of instruction. Posthumans are genetically superior to the general population in numerous ways, including their special powers, but we have learned that they often face challenges as well. Difficult home lives, frequent discipline issues, social problems, struggles against authority." Rhoads knocked his ring once more against the podium. "I suspect that each of you is a posthuman."

Posthuman? Scarlett thought. *I couldn't be*—but an invisible feather tickled over her scars. She remembered the burning car, her brother flying through the air, the incredible explosion outside the guest house.

She glanced at her classmates and saw confusion, amusement, and wariness but no absolute shock, no outright denial.

Rhoads said, "Each of you brings incredible talent . . . and formidable challenges. How many of you came here straight from some sort of detention center?"

A third of the hands went up.

Rhoads nodded. "And which of you came here to avoid incarceration?"

Scarlett raised her hand. Others joined her. Half the group either in jail or on the way . . .

"Society is not ready for you," Rhoads said. "The oldest, fiercest fear is ignorance. Sooner or later—and probably sooner, given the strange nature of recent terror attacks—the general population would burn you at the metaphorical stake."

Rhoads paused, letting the message resonate. The cadre didn't need to hush anyone. The new cadets were utterly silent, trained with absolute attention on the man behind the podium.

Rhoads said, "Here, you will train alongside other posthumans. With our instruction, you will learn to control and maximize your powers and to use them for the greater good. You will discover camaraderie and purpose. You will become a part of something bigger than yourselves: the Long Gray Line." A faint smile lifted the corners of his mouth. His eyes, however, remained intense, almost sad. "Ladies and gentlemen, welcome to The Point, ground zero for the development of tomorrow's supersoldiers, the future leaders of the coming Posthuman Age."

FOURTEEN

RHOADS STOPPED THEM OUTSIDE THE ENTRANCE to a gymnasium. Standing at the front of the line, Scarlett heard shouting and clapping, the pounding of running feet, and sneakers squeaking on the wooden floor. Over Rhoads's shoulder, she saw a shining basketball court, bleachers, and above the seating an elevated running track on which stood a guard in camouflage.

"At ease, New Cadets," Rhoads said. "Once I release you, you'll be free to wander the gymnasium and observe the activities. At all times, you will maintain a safe distance."

At last, she thought. *A little freedom*. This would be the first liberty she'd had since leaving her parents at Eisenhower Hall Auditorium.

Rhoads stepped aside and gestured for Scarlett to lead them inside.

She entered the gym and lurched to a halt.

Something—or, rather, several somethings—blurred past. She staggered backward, bumping into another new cadet.

"Whoa," someone said.

Whoa, indeed . . .

Half a dozen sprinters in shorts and T-shirts tagged the far wall, spun, and sprinted back this way. They flashed past, running faster than Olympic sprinters. Way faster. The female cadet in front crossed the pylon finish line with a whoop and kept hurtling straight at the wall.

Scarlett tensed, expecting her to smash into the cinder blocks, but the sprinter ran straight up the wall to the elevated track twenty feet above, sprang away, executed a graceful flip, and stuck the landing like a champion gymnast.

How in the world?

Shouting drew her attention across the court to the weight room, where a circle of gigantic cadets hollered encouragement while a kid built like a professional wrestler did standing shoulder presses with a massive metal I beam atop which sat a pair of grinning cadets.

Posthumans . . .

The new cadets fanned out, murmuring with amazement.

The sprinters blurred past again.

Scarlett approached another corner, then stopped and stared.

A pair of cadets played Ping-Pong. Only their eyes moved. The ball smashed back and forth as if being pounded by invisible paddles.

Amazing . . .

Behind them, a petite cadet shuffled like a boxer around a leather heavy bag suspended from a metal frame. Though her hands remained close to her face in a peekaboo defense, the bag jerked and hopped, the chains overhead jangling crazily, as if a young Mike Tyson were pounding out combinations.

Scarlett spoke to the nearest new cadet, the redhead with the weird tattoo on her neck. "This is crazy."

The redhead nodded, looking afraid, and pointed to a table where a pair of cadets, one male, one female, were playing chess.

Scarlett drifted in that direction. The player of the black pieces, a tall, skinny girl wearing spectacles, leaned forward, staring at the complex position. Drawing closer, Scarlett analyzed the board—a nice, calming exercise for her brain. Material was equal. The player of the white pieces was safe behind stonewalled pawns with one curious structural aberration. He'd pushed the pawn in front of his castled king, weakening his defense. He moved the pawn recklessly forward again, threatening black's knight.

Coming around the side of the board, Scarlett saw the player of the white pieces for the first time. He was *gorgeous*. An athletic-looking Asian guy with a strong jaw, freckles, and luminous blue eyes, he stared like a predator at his opponent's threatened piece.

The player of the black pieces leaned back and crossed her arms. The threatened knight lifted from the board as if it had been picked up by an invisible hand, retreated through the air, and settled gently onto black's back rank.

Amazing . . .

"Ha," the guy said, obviously unimpressed by his opponent's use of telekinesis, and used his hand to push his bishop across the board, snatching black's H pawn. "Check, DeCraig."

Scarlett shifted her focus. She hadn't even considered the move, and with good reason. The bishop had no protection. He'd just traded a bishop for a pawn.

Guess his special power isn't chess.

DeCraig shrugged, half laughing. "Okay," she said, and took the bishop with her king.

The guy grabbed his queen.

"No," said one of the observing white-clad firsties, an intense-looking girl whose name tag read UBA. "Use your mind, not your hand, Kyeong."

Kyeong gave Uba a hard look but released his queen and stared at the piece.

Hopkins, the officious Doberman from the corridor, slid up beside Uba, chuckling. "Ten bucks says he can't do it."

Kyeong glared at him. "Shut up, Hopkins."

Hopkins leaned in, eyes flashing. "That's 'Shut up, sir' to you, yearling. Let's go, Kyeong. It's simple. That piece is only a few ounces. Push it."

Kyeong stared venomously for a second longer, then returned his attention to the piece.

Now Scarlett saw his intended move. It was pretty awesome. Kyeong had sacrificed the bishop to open the king's defenses. His queen would move out on its diagonal to the H file and throw check, forcing the king back behind its damaged pawn shield. Meanwhile, his own defense, though wonky at a glance, was actually rock solid. After throwing check, he could lift his rook, line up a battery with his queen, and probably force mate in a few moves. Scarlett wasn't good enough to guarantee it, let alone count it out, but she could see that Kyeong's seeming recklessness had actually been carefully calculated.

DeCraig, Uba, Hopkins . . . none of them seemed to see it. Scarlett grinned. Smart and ballsy stuff, aggressive and sly. She liked Kyeong's style.

Kyeong stared at the queen with narrowed eyes, the tip of his tongue poking from one corner of his mouth.

The piece wobbled in place.

Come on, Scarlett thought. *You can do it.*

"Whoa, Kyeong," Hopkins said. "Easy does it. Don't mess up."

A couple of Hopkins's buddies sidled up. "Kyeong the Cannon," one of them jeered.

Don't listen to them, Scarlett thought. *You can do this.*

Kyeong's face twisted with concentration. The queen jerked out its diagonal. One square, two . . .

Scarlett smiled. *That's it, Kyeong.*

The queen shot off the board and *tink-tink-tink*-ed across the floor.

Hopkins and his buddies burst into laughter.

"Hey!" Kyeong said. "Who did that?"

"It's okay," DeCraig said. "I'll get it." She frowned at the laughing upperclassmen and twisted in her seat. The piece lifted into the air and started to drift back in their direction.

Uba turned on the laughing cadets, unamused. "Hopkins, did you—"

"Assholes!" Kyeong shouted, and the board and pieces flew from the table and clattered loudly off the floor.

"Kyeong the Cannon blew up the board!" Hopkins shouted. His friends roared with laughter.

Kyeong shot to his feet.

Hopkins's laughter died, and he fell back, ready to fight. "Come on, Kyeong. Do us all a favor. Try to blast me like you did Harrison. The faster you buy The Farm, the better."

"Enough," Uba said, stepping between them.

Scarlett grunted as a pair of soldiers knocked her aside, hurried past, and grabbed Kyeong by the arms.

"Hey," Scarlett said. "He didn't do anything."

Kyeong turned in her direction. They made eye contact, and then he was shouting curses as the guards dragged him from the gym.

Hopkins and his buddies exchanged high fives.

DeCraig and Uba frowned.

Scarlett bent to pick up a piece at her feet, but a hand fell on her shoulder.

"Don't bother, Scarlett," Rhoads said. "We have work to do."

Fuller called the new cadets to formation near the door.

Scarlett lingered beside the colonel. "But sir," she said, "Kyeong didn't do anything."

Rhoads looked at her but said nothing, then turned and marched away.

Scarlett started after him.

Hopkins stepped in her way. "New Cadet, why aren't you in formation?"

"I—"

"New Cadet, get into formation . . . now," Hopkins said, and she didn't need any special power to read the challenge in the firstie's eyes. Hopkins wanted her to disobey so that he could . . . what? Far above, on the campus of West Point, he might shout or tell her to do push-ups. Here, anything was possible.

"Yes, sir," she said, and marched across the gym floor, fists swinging at her side.

FIFTEEN

AT THE END OF A VERY LONG DAY, THEY MARCHED into a long cinder block corridor lined with metal doors. They paired off, one chaperone per cadet. Scarlett ended up with Fuller.

Unlocking one of the metal doors and gesturing her inside, Fuller said, "Home sweet home, Winter. Your dorm."

Oh, no . . .

The place reminded her of juvie: same concrete floor and block walls, same metal door set with a square of impact glass, same stainless steel toilet, even the same faint smell of Pine-Sol. All this room lacked was a bunk bed and an acne-scarred roomie spouting hopped-up stories about stuff they both knew she'd never done. Only one bed here and no roommate, apparently. Solitary confinement, then.

"This isn't a dorm," she said. "It's a prison cell."

"Do not speak unless spoken to, New Cadet," Fuller said. He opened a freestanding metal cabinet, revealing drawers, a space for hanging clothes, and a small shelf. Pointing to each section, he explained—rapidly, in great detail—what went where and how everything needed to be positioned: the order of the hats on the shelf, the order and direction in which each uniform piece was to hang, the correct methods for rolling and storing socks. Scarlett would never remember it all. No one could. Except maybe that Amer girl . . .

"Square away this room, New Cadet," Fuller said. "All equipment stored properly and secured at all times." Then he stepped back into the corridor. "Study your knowledge book. Taps at 2200, breakfast formation at 0630." Then he swung the door shut with a heavy clang. The lock clacked into place.

What a day . . .

She was exhausted. The cadre had kept them busy every second, nearly drowning them with a pounding waterfall of procedural information. She wanted to pass out but had to unpack her stuff while she still remembered some of Fuller's instructions. She dumped the contents of the blue bag and got to work folding, hanging, and positioning everything, all the while trying to process everything.

I'm surrounded by people who can lift trucks and run up walls and move stuff with their minds. Comic book stuff, but real.

Once she'd put her stuff away and locked the cabinet, she sat on her cot. The mattress was as thin and hard as a wrestling mat, but it was nice to just sit and breathe, no one telling her what to do, what to remember. She panned her gaze across the block wall, industrial yellow in color, across the metal sink and toilet, the locked metal door.

She went to the square of thick glass and looked out onto a hallway of metal doors. Blurry faces stared from some windows, the thick glass making their features as indistinct as those of half-formed people.

She wanted to sleep but needed to study this stupid knowledge book, which was apparently specific to The Point. Guaranteed they'd quiz everybody in the morning, and she was determined to follow her father's advice: *Just do your job correctly and never volunteer for anything.* That, her father insisted, was the key to survival in the Army.

So she opened the knowledge book.

THE POINT HONOR CODE

"A cadet will not lie, cheat, steal, or tolerate those who do."

LYING: A cadet will not deceive another cadet through an untruth or an omission of truth. A cadet will not withhold their abilities or work to withhold the uncommon abilities of those around them. A cadet will use their uncommon ability to its utmost when they are called upon to do so; to do otherwise is lying.

CHEATING: A cadet will not fraudulently act out of self-interest to gain an advantage. A cadet will not use their uncommon ability to deceive anyone about their strengths or weaknesses or blame an uncommon event on circumstance. A cadet will not use their uncommon ability outside of the Point compound.

STEALING: A cadet will not wrongfully take, obtain, or withhold the money, property, belongings, or service of another cadet, the faculty, or The Point itself. This includes refusing to use one's uncommon ability when it is requested of them or required to continue business as usual at the academy, or using one's uncommon ability to unfairly take power, thought, or ability from another cadet.

TOLERATION: A cadet must report to a superior if they are witness to or learn of any violation of the Honor Code. A cadet is required to use their uncommon ability to its strongest to learn of an Honor Code violation if they suspect such a violation to have occurred.

The Three Rules of Thumb:

• Does this action attempt to deceive anyone or allow anyone to be deceived about what I truly am?

• Does this action gain or allow the gain of privilege or advantage to which I, someone else, or a common human being would not be otherwise entitled?

• If I were on the receiving end of this action, would I desire to use my uncommon ability to change the outcome?

Always Remember:

You are not a common human being. You possess an uncommon ability which you cannot control. You require our aid to help you hone your uncommon ability and be the best American you can be. In return, it is your duty to use that ability for the good of the United States of America and the Academy.

Scarlett frowned. She'd never been a thief, rarely cared enough to cheat, and had gotten into way more trouble over the years for telling the truth than she had for lying, but the *toleration* thing bothered her. She was no tattletale. Getting in trouble for *not* ratting on somebody sounded more like Cold War Hungary than West Point.

But this wasn't West Point. This was The Point. Different population, different policies.

She turned the page.

PUNISHMENT:

Given their state of constant observation and their awareness of it, it is incredibly rare that a cadet violates the Honor Code. However, if such an infraction occurs, levels of punishment have been considered. Punishment numbers are reset every semester unless mitigating circumstances come into play.

Basic offense: Committing through ignorance, hubris, or deviousness a violation of the honor code; discovery of an intention to commit an act that violates the honor code.

Major offense: An offense that threatens the confidentiality of The Point; any attempt to remove Point technology or medication from the compound; unsolicited aggression toward a staff member.

First Basic Offense: Two hours observation with one extra duty, no lunch.

First Major Offense: Physical reprimand, two hours in the Chamber.

Second Basic Offense: One day observation with three extra duties, no breakfast or lunch.

Second Major Offense: Physical reprimand, one day in the Chamber, no rations.
Third Basic Offense: One week observation with three extra duties, two hours in the Chamber.
Third Major Offense: Physical reprimand, three days in the Chamber, no rations.
Fourth Basic Offense: Inhibition, expulsion, transfer to The Farm.
Fourth Major Offense: Physical reprimand, one week in the Chamber, no rations, transfer to The Farm, chemical processing, stasis.

She sat up straighter and reread the punishments. Okay, so this explained—cryptically, at least—the tension simmering between the guards and the cadets, but what did it all mean?

What constituted a *physical reprimand*?

She was surprised by the withholding of food—was that even legal?

What was the *Chamber*?

The final block, punishments for fourth offenses, bothered her most of all. What was *The Farm? Chemical processing? Stasis?*

The hallway outside the door filled with music.

She rose from her cot and went to the door and looked out the small window but saw nothing. Just the empty corridor and a few indistinct faces looking out from their cell windows.

She recognized the sad, tinny bugle music from funerals she'd attended with her parents. It was taps.

The second the music ended, darkness fell. Scarlett huffed with surprise. The hall, her room, everything had gone pitch black.

She crossed the darkness carefully but still stubbed her toe getting into bed. Exhaustion pressed her into the thin mattress. At least she'd glanced at the knowledge book. If the cadre quizzed them in the morning, she was bound to know more than *someone*. That would be the key here. Don't be the worst or the best. Hide in the middle.

She drifted off but woke a short time later to someone whispering her name.

"Winter," a male voice said. "Hey, Winter."

Scarlett sat up in the darkness, confused. The voice sounded like it was coming from outside the door. She called, "Hello? Who's—hey!"

She jolted back against the wall. Someone had poked her in the side. Someone was in the dark with her. "Who's there?"

She heard laughter in the hall. More than one voice.

Then the whisperer said her name again, drawing it out. "Wiiiiinterrrrr . . ."

Scarlett didn't like the taunting tone or the laughter. It sounded like a few people out in the hall. But someone had poked her. How had anyone gotten inside without waking her?

Someone had jabbed her in the thigh.

"Hey," she said, startled. She pushed out defensively but hit nothing.

The people in the hall thought this was hilarious.

"What's the matter, Winter?"

In the corridor, a flashlight clicked to life. Hopkins held it beneath his chin. His leering face, illuminated in a Halloween show of light and shadow, pressed against the window. Vague countenances pushed in to either side of his, toothy moons with staring eyes.

"You afraid of the dark?" Hopkins asked. He turned his light and pressed it to the glass.

"Leave me alone," she said, shielding her eyes, but even half blind, she knew the unnerving truth: poking or no poking, she *was* alone in the room. They'd jabbed her from out there. She was locked in this cell and completely at the mercy of their telekinetic whims.

"No speaking out of turn, New Cadet," Hopkins said. "I asked you a direct question. Answer promptly and efficiently and end your response with 'sir.' Now . . . are you afraid of the dark?"

"No, sir," she said, doing her best to block the bright light.

"Well," Hopkins said, "we'll change that."

The first strike knocked the wind out of her. The next blow

shoved her from the cot. She hit the hard ground, cursing, and they were on her. Their attacks thumped into her like pillows soaked in half-hardened cement.

There was no way to fight back. She tried to stand and was knocked down again. She tried to push and kick, but that only exposed her to the blows. Ultimately, she curled into a ball and covered her face, thinking, *Don't cry out, no matter what. Don't give them the satisfaction.*

And then it was over.

She lay there, hurting—but not from the blows, she realized. A ball of fire pulsed at her center. She didn't dare to move. She couldn't risk blowing something up and getting in trouble.

"Welcome to The Point," Hopkins said. "Square yourself away, show us respect, and stay away from Kyeong. He is tore up from the floor up, a bona fide broke-dick washout."

"Bona fide," another cadet's voice echoed in the hall.

Hopkins said, "You cop an attitude, you'll pay. You're not safe here. You're not safe anywhere. You aren't even safe locked behind a metal door. Do you understand, New Cadet?"

"Yes, sir," she said.

The flashlight clicked off. Her tormentors moved down the hall. She heard them laughing and calling at another door.

Scarlett lay there, moaning. The burning energy within her throbbed, demanding release. Her muscles twitched and screamed. She gritted her teeth, fighting the fire filling her body. *What in the world have I gotten myself into?*

SIXTEEN

"YOU DON'T BELONG HERE," THE HULKING, HEAVILY scarred drill sergeant said. He was the most muscular person Scarlett had ever seen, like a prize bull, with muscles on top of muscles, all swelling and striated bulges taut against bronze skin. His head seemed small atop the broad shoulders and thick neck, and his face was skull-like, an emaciated mask of scar tissue. An unlit cigar stub jutted from the corner of his mouth. His nameplate read Lopez.

Scarlett stood halfway back in the row of new cadets. They were lined up single file in the corridor outside the gymnasium. The air was thick with perspiration. Before Lopez's arrival, the upperclassmen had smoked them with push-ups, jumping jacks, and sit-ups for the better part of an hour. Even the smallest mistakes justified punishment here.

"Compared to the *real* West Point cadets, you are abominations," Drill Sergeant Lopez said, pacing back and forth, his voice deep and garbled, as if born of flexed muscle. "They *earned* their way here. You, on the other hand, are nothing more than genetic freaks. You did not earn this placement."

True enough, Scarlett thought. She hadn't earned it . . . or asked for it.

Lopez squared himself with them. "Keep that in mind when Colonel Rhoads throws around words like *special* and *powers*." He exhaled sharply through his nose. The sound was loud and shockingly abrupt, like a big rig's air brakes or the bloodcurdling screech of a diving hawk. Scarlett's muscles, still sore and weak from the hazing aftermath, leaped involuntarily.

"You see my *unnatural* physique," Lopez said, "you might think I'm one of you, that I'm going to wrap up with some feel-good story, how I remember being in your shoes and went through the same stuff and hung in there and how it changed my life, made me all *hooah,* and how I believe in you and all that happy horseshit you're hoping to hear. Well, you can shoot that little notion right between the eyes."

Upperclassmen chuckled. A few new cadets faked laughter. Scarlett knew she should, too—*don't stand out; hide in the middle*—but she couldn't even fake a smile. After getting hazed and listening to this guy, she was suffering from a severe case of *screw-this-place-itis*.

Lopez reviewed again the rules of dining, which sounded like an enormous pain in the ass. Every table would hold eight people, two from each class. New cadets served the upperclassmen, and there was a highly specific way to do everything, from announcing the beverage of the day to cutting the dessert. If seven people wanted cake, the new cadets had to figure out how to cut a rectangle into seven *equal* parts. Inwardly, Scarlett groaned. She was not cut out for any organization that placed this much value on pointless attention-to-detail nonsense.

On R-Day, they'd eaten C-rations in the gym. From this morning forward, however, Lopez explained, they would take their meals in the West Point mess hall alongside *real* cadets. "You will be polite and respectful, New Cadets," he said. "Over time, you will learn professional bearing from your surface-dwelling superiors. And if any of you uses your powers—even to pass the fucking salt—you will take a trip to the Chamber."

When it was time to eat, Lopez and the guards stayed behind. Fuller escorted the cadets. They left The Point, passing back out through the blast doors, and took an elevator that deposited them above ground, ten at a time, in the lobby of what appeared to be a barracks.

Once all sixty-some cadets had assembled, they left the dormitory. From the outside, it looked like a narrow row house squashed between two much larger barracks, one old, one new.

Scarlett drew her lungs full of fresh air. It had rained in the night, and the air was cool and damp. A light mist cloaked the river. The rising sun crowned the Hudson Highlands in red. She wished she could break ranks and hang out for a while, soak in the dawn. She'd been underground for less than twenty-four hours, but it felt like a week.

They marched across campus, passing between buildings of gray stone. Other formations appeared from all sides. They passed the library and joined hundreds of cadets forming up on the apron outside the mess hall. She noticed the neat ranks and perfect postures of the real cadets. Lopez's strange voice echoed in her mind: *They earned their way.*

The doors opened. The cadets entered the mess hall in an orderly yet purposeful fashion.

It's the Great Hall from Harry Potter, Scarlett thought, taking in the high-vaulted and coffered ceilings, massive stone pillars, and medieval archways. Hundreds of tables in neat rows filled multiple wings of dining space. Colorful flags and banners hung everywhere, and a huge mural covered one wall.

The cadets reported to their assigned seats, eight to a table, and Scarlett groaned inwardly. Hopkins sat at the opposite end of her table.

AFTER EATING, UPPERCLASSMEN marched them back to the strange dorm between dorms.

As bad as the whole serving-the-upperclassmen setup had sounded, the reality ended up being far worse. Announcing and distributing the cold beverages, Scarlett messed up countless times—in all fairness, how could anyone remember everything they were supposed to say and do?—and the upperclassmen took great delight in insulting her and forcing her to do things over. Making matters worse, she'd shared serving duties with Bentley, this nervous kid who messed up even more than she did. Before they'd even finished feeding the upperclassmen, the thirty minutes was up, so she and Bentley went without breakfast.

Scarlett was in the final group to take the elevator. Her chaperone was DeCraig, the tall bespectacled cadet who'd played Kyeong in chess.

Waiting for the elevator, DeCraig told the new cadets about the strange barracks. It served as a secret portal but was also a real dormitory. Firsties from The Point roomed in the upper floors. "There's a little motivation for you, New Cadets," DeCraig said with a grin lighting her face. "Senior year, you room above ground like civilized folk."

On the ride down, DeCraig told them to relax. "It's a short walk back to The Point, but it's the best part of your day, so I expect to see slouching and smiling."

Scarlett grinned and slowed her pace. DeCraig was cool, and even this small freedom felt great. As they strolled along, it was possible to hope that things here might chill out a little.

Up on campus, the upperclassmen had moved stiffly and seemed almost nervous. Down here, they once again swaggered with bravado. Their conversations grew louder. She heard laughter up ahead from Hopkins and his friends.

Ahead of them, Kyeong walked alone.

Hopkins called to Kyeong. Scarlett couldn't hear much, just Hopkins's mocking tone. Without looking back, Kyeong lifted a fist and extended his middle finger.

Scarlett grinned.

Then, out of the blue, Kyeong stumbled and sprawled to the ground.

Hopkins and his pals cackled. They had tripped him with their minds.

"Hey," Scarlett said. She started forward, pissed—and jerked to a stop. Someone had grabbed her shoulder.

She whirled and found herself face-to-face with DeCraig, "Leave it, Winter."

"They tripped him," Scarlett said, shaking free.

DeCraig shook her head. "You go barking up that tree, Hopkins will make your life a living hell. Guaran-friggin-teed."

"You think I care?"

DeCraig raised her brows. "Pace yourself. Okay? And trust me, if there's one person here who can take care of himself, it's Seamus Kyeong."

SEVENTEEN

SCARLETT STRUGGLED THROUGH ONE MORE REP and racked the barbell. Her spotter was Dunne, the yearling who'd shoulder pressed an I beam and two cadets during orientation. He had the face of a country boy and a Southern drawl to match. The outside world might assume he'd grown huge by tossing hay bales and drinking raw milk.

"One thirty-five for eight," Dunne called to another meathead, who scratched on a clipboard.

Scarlett couldn't help but smile. Eight reps with 135 pounds. Not bad, considering she hadn't lifted weights in about a million years.

But Dunne chimed a singsong "Not wor-thy," and the other meatheads echoed him. "Not wor-thy!" They roared with laughter and slapped high fives with their calloused, chalky palms, just as they had with the cadets who'd come before Scarlett.

Another test, another unremarkable result. Great.

Earlier in the week, she'd cranked out a mile in five and a half minutes, knocked out fifty push-ups, eighty-three sit-ups, and seventeen chin-ups, and thrown a basketball nearly ninety feet from a seated position, but none of these scores was good enough to impress the cadre here at The Point. The mental tests had been difficult but not overwhelming. A lot of the stuff she just didn't know. Higher-level math and grammatical minutiae were tough when you'd spent high school baked out of your gourd. Not knowing stuff didn't mean you were stupid. It just meant you weren't prepared.

Most of her classmates seemed smart, fast, and strong, but each test identified genuine outliers, such as the guy who'd run the mile in under four minutes and the girl who'd benched 500 pounds, earning hoots and high fives from the meatheads.

One by one, the new cadets were finding their places. Not Scarlett, though. Maybe she'd no-score her way out the door . . . and straight into a prison cell.

Dunne handed Scarlett her paper. "Head over to Room 20, weakling."

"I'm strong for my size," she said.

Dunne laughed, gave her a light shove that sent her halfway across the floor, and called "Next weakling" to the lean kid who was next in line. *Jakes*, Scarlett thought, remembering the kid's name from when she'd seen his nameplate during a meal. Jakes didn't look concerned as he approached the bench and didn't seem to mind being called a weakling. No surprise there. After all, Jakes had won his hundred-meter heat by about thirty meters.

Heading toward Room 20, Scarlett jerked to a stop. Someone was screaming in Room 17.

"Keep moving," the guard posted outside Room 17 said.

Arriving at Room 20, she signed in at the door and entered a classroom with desks and a white board and a few new cadets waiting silently to be tested.

She sat next to Perich, the pale redhead with the blue tattoo. Perich was wearing a nervous half smile.

Scarlett smiled back. "Hey."

Across the room, a scowling guard pointed his nightstick at them.

A pretty brunette cadet whose name tag read CRAMER sat across the teacher's desk from Vernon, one of the hulking new cadets. Thin wires ran from a black box between them to what looked like a pair of acupuncture needles half buried in Vernon's thick forearm.

Cramer twisted a dial. Vernon tensed and grunted.

"Sorry," Cramer said, turning back the dial. "The juice always burns you meatheads."

Vernon shook his head. "I don't juice, ma'am."

Cramer looked confused for a second, then grinned. "Oh, my," she said. "You thought I meant steroids. It's okay, New Cadet; you just sit there quietly, and we'll get you back to your heavy things real soon, mmm-kay?" She removed the needles and called out numbers to the upperclassman recording results. Turning back to Vernon with a friendly smile, she said, "Typical meathead numbers."

Vernon shrugged his huge shoulders. "I yam what I yam and that's all that I yam, ma'am."

"Only speak when spoken to, New Cadet," Cramer told him, but she said it with a grin, not the hard-bitten delivery favored by so many of the upperclassmen.

"Yes, ma'am," Vernon said.

"Haul your thick self over to Room 11, where you will no doubt fail like a champ."

"Yes, ma'am," Vernon said, grinning. He'd pumped out ten reps with 455 pounds and was already receiving good-natured ribbing of the "not bad for a girl" variety from the other meatheads. He'd found his tribe.

Next up was Perich. As always, she looked nervous.

Cramer smiled and told her to sit down, and Perich gave her sheet to the upperclassman with the clipboard. "A little pinch," Cramer said, and inserted the thin needles into Perich's arm. "Juice on," Cramer said, and twisted a dial.

Scarlett waited for Perich to stiffen, but she giggled as if someone had tickled her.

Reading the meter, Cramer smiled and raised her brows. "Let me guess," she said. "It started with an animal?"

Perich tilted her head. "Ma'am?"

"A pet got hit in the road, or maybe a bird flew into the bay window, and you helped it."

Perich shook her head.

Cramer pulled the needles free and looked at the redhead with waiting eyes.

"My grandmother," Perich said. "She fell on the ice last winter."

"Broke her hip?"

Perich shook her head. "Her wrist."

Cramer nodded. "You can tell me the rest of the story later. I have a feeling we'll be working pretty closely." She returned her paperwork and smiled brightly. "Your electrical impedance numbers are fantastic."

Perich beamed. "Thank you, ma'am."

"All right. Head on over to Room 11. Don't let the TKs bother you."

"Yes, ma'am."

Perich left with a satisfied smile, her characteristic anxiety nowhere in sight.

"Next," the tester said.

Scarlett sat down, handed Cramer her paper, and smiled.

Cramer gave the sheet to a cadet with a clipboard. "Okay, Winter," she said, all business now. "Little pinches." Her touch was soft, and the needles slid home with very little discomfort. "All right," Cramer said, inspecting the needles and wires. "You might feel a little burn."

Scarlett braced herself as Cramer twisted the dial, partly in anticipation of the burn, partly in hopes that this test finally would reveal her calling.

A subtle trickle of warmth dribbled into the muscle near the needles.

Cramer gave a confused *"huh"* and told Scarlett that she had to adjust the needles. "Killing the juice," she told the clipboard cadet.

"Numbers?"

"None for now," Cramer said, and pulled the needles. She touched

Scarlett's arm for a second, pressing two fingers into the muscle close to her elbow. Scarlett felt a little patch of warmth where Cramer pressed. "Right here," Cramer said to herself, then, robotically, "little pinch," as she reinserted the needles. This time it did pinch a bit.

"Let's try this again," Cramer said. A few seconds later, she stopped the test, removed the needles, and gave Scarlett an annoyed look. "What are you made of, rubber?"

"No, ma'am," she said, confused.

"Zero," Cramer called over her shoulder to the cadet with the clipboard.

"Zero?"

"Zero," she said. Turning back to Scarlett, she said, "If you broke my machine, New Cadet, I'll have your head. Room 11."

Scarlett left, more confused than ever. Whatever test she'd just taken, she'd failed yet again. Out in the hall, passing excited new cadets, she felt like a kid waiting to get picked last in a game of kickball.

Inside Room 11, Hopkins took her paper and pointed to a clipboard. "Sign in, Winter."

"Yes, sir," she said, and wrote her name.

"Wow," Hopkins said, looking up from Scarlett's sheet. "You take mediocrity to a whole new level. You're not strong *or* smart." His eyes scanned the sheet. "Normal . . . normal . . . normal. I've never seen a less remarkable recruit. You sure you even belong here, Winter?"

"No, sir," she said.

Hopkins handed her the sheet. "Ten bucks says you blow this test, too."

She didn't have to wait long. Perich drifted past, unperturbed as a spring breeze.

"The Winter of my discontent," DeCraig said from behind the desk where she sat, and gestured to the chair across from her. A strange assortment of items covered the desktop: a deck of cards, a pen, a canteen, and two pieces of green yarn.

When Scarlett handed her sheet to the results taker, her heart gave a flutter.

Kyeong slipped the sheet into a clipboard, not even sparing her a glance.

Don't read it, Scarlett thought, suddenly embarrassed.

DeCraig picked up the cards and started shuffling them with the nonchalant precision of a Vegas blackjack dealer. "You qualify yet, Winter?"

"No, ma'am."

"Well, maybe this is your lucky station."

"I hope so, ma'am," Scarlett said. In truth, she wasn't so sure. On the one hand, DeCraig was the coolest person she'd met here, and qualifying as a telekinetic would mean training around Kyeong, getting to know him. On the other hand, Hopkins and his crew were also TKs.

"All right," DeCraig said, "bear with me. I'm going to ask you to try a few things that might sound kind of crazy. Just give it a shot, okay?"

"Yes, ma'am," Scarlett said. Behind her, Hopkins was giving some new arrival a hard time.

DeCraig pulled a single card from the deck and laid it facedown on the desk between them. Above her spectacles, her brows lifted. "What card is that?"

"I don't know, ma'am."

"Try," DeCraig said. "Think for a second. Pretend that you can see the face."

Scarlett stared at the blue-and-white paisley. She saw no numbers, no suits, nothing. "I don't know, ma'am."

"Guess, then."

"Ace of spades."

DeCraig picked up the card and sighed. "Your answer is as incorrect as it is unoriginal, I'm afraid." She turned it toward Scarlett. The four of hearts.

"No worries, Winter," DeCraig said, tucking the card back into the deck. "My whole time here, we've only had one remote viewer, and he ended up buying The Farm by Thanksgiving."

Scarlett still wasn't sure what The Farm was. Punishment or exile. Maybe both.

Next, DeCraig asked her to move the pen with her mind.

Scarlett asked how she was supposed to do that, and DeCraig told her to stare at the pen and picture it moving. "Hope for a pushing feeling in your forehead, force going out."

Scarlett tried and failed. Utterly.

"She's negative," DeCraig told Kyeong, who looked neither surprised nor disappointed. "Oh, well, Winter. I was rooting for you, but . . ." DeCraig shrugged. "Seamus, where do we send her now?"

"Um," Kyeong said, and hesitated. "Room 17."

DeCraig looked surprised. "Seventeen?"

"That's what her paperwork says."

DeCraig nodded, looking puzzled . . . and troubled. Then she recomposed her face, half smiling. "Room 17, then, Winter—and good luck."

"Yes, ma'am," Scarlett said, standing. "Thank you, ma'am."

Hopkins chuckled as she left. "So long, goat. Have fun in 17."

EIGHTEEN

SCARLETT REPORTED TO ROOM 17, BUT THERE WAS no one there. There wasn't even a sign-in sheet. She looked at herself in the big mirror that covered the upper half of one wall. It was undoubtedly two-way glass like they had in police stations. A metal desk was shoved up against the pale cinder blocks of the opposite wall, presumably to make space for the odd chair dominating the center of the claustrophobic room. The thing looked like some kind of S&M wheelchair, with straps hanging from several points.

She stepped closer, realizing she'd seen a chair like this before, back in juvie, when that kid from Downingtown had flipped out and attacked a guard and they'd strapped him into—

The door banged open behind her.

She spun around, startled.

A wave of camouflage pounded into her, knocked her from her feet, and drove her to the ground. The air rushed from her lungs. Several soldiers pinned her down, ignoring her protests and talking to one another calmly, calling out which arm they had, which leg, as mechanically as robots.

She shouted and struggled and cursed. They ignored her.

They lifted her, carried her to the center of the room, set her in the chair, and started fastening the straps. A deep, garbled voice said, "Don't bother to fight, Winter."

Lopez swaggered into the room and stood at parade rest, watching with cold eyes as the guards restrained Scarlett's arms and legs and cinched belts around her waist and chest.

"Make them tight," Lopez said.

"Drill Sergeant," she said as the soldiers torqued the restraints, "I didn't do anything."

"No talking out of turn," Lopez said. Then, to the guards, "Get her head."

They pulled Scarlett's head back, yanked another strap over her forehead, and cranked it tight. Claustrophobia filled her with squeaking rats scratching madly for escape.

"Leave us," Lopez told the guards.

Scarlett watched them go with a sense of panic. Heat throbbed at her center. Her muscles twitched beneath the restraints. "Drill Sergeant, I—"

"Lock it up, Winter." Lopez swept Scarlett's testing results from the ground and stood beside the chair, reading. A dirty boot print covered the back of the paper.

Lopez shook his head and gave that sharp animal snort again.

Her aching muscles tensed involuntarily. That noise hit her right in the bone marrow.

Lopez crumpled the paper and dropped it to the floor. "You're holding back."

"No, Drill Sergeant, I—"

"What are you hiding, Winter?"

"Nothing, Drill Sergeant."

"What's this, then?" He stomped on the crumpled paper. "Zeros across the board? You're not strong or fast or smart, and you can't do any cute little magic tricks . . . or at least that's what you want us to think." Lopez leaned close. Scars crosshatched his emaciated face. Scarlett could smell the unlit cigar stub and coffee and Lopez himself, an animal smell like yet unlike sweat, with something sharper underneath, a scent that belonged in a barn or a zoo, the man not fully human any longer. "You're going to tell me the truth."

"I am telling you the truth, Drill Sergeant. Honest."

"Lock it up!"

Scarlett's eyes slammed shut against the force of the drill sergeant's bellow.

Lopez continued in a calm voice. "I was in an outfit called the High Rollers. My team leader taught me all about truth. You've heard of black ops?"

"Yes, Drill Sergeant."

"Well, High Roller ops were dark-side-of-the-moon black. Deep undercover, no rules of engagement. We fixed problems that the country couldn't admit to fixing. You follow?"

"Yes, Drill Sergeant."

"You sure are agreeable, Winter. I like that."

She forced a smile. Her muscles throbbed with the force they'd absorbed. She had to get out of here.

Lopez scowled. "Maybe charm's your hoodoo. You gonna sweet-talk your way out of that chair?"

"No, Drill Sergeant," she said. Her memory dredged up Dan's voice. *Your whole life you've tried to sweet-talk your way out of everything.* "Drill Sergeant, ask Colonel Rhoads. He recruited me. He can tell you why I'm here."

Lopez ignored her, saying, "The High Rollers get this target, a driver for the bad guys. He's heard stuff. Stuff that can save lives. So we grab him and take him someplace where nobody can hear him scream and tie him to a chair and ask him where the bad guys are hiding. This driver, he's a squirrelly little guy, about your size, twitchy. He doesn't look tough. But this isn't America, you know? He's hard as a lifer in the state pen. Says he doesn't know anything. My Team Leader looks at him and says yes, he does. So we keep asking. We even make him a little uncomfortable." Lopez reached out and squeezed Scarlett's shoulder, his thick fingers digging into the throbbing muscle. "You know what I mean, Winter?"

"I think so, Drill Sergeant." She had to get away from this crazy son of a bitch.

Lopez nodded. "We worked on him a little, knocked out a tooth or two. The TL had a way of whipping us into a fury. But this driver, he was tough, the type of guy if he wasn't such a scumbag, you could almost respect him. The TL asks him a question, this guy spits blood and shakes his head. So Gerber, this real twisted bastard who'd been in law school before he got recruited into the High Rollers, he pulls a blade, lays it across the guy's cheek."

Lopez pressed a finger so close to Scarlett's eye that her eyelid snapped reflexively shut.

"Gerber tells the guy that blind people have great memories on account of they're not distracted by visual input. Tells him he'd better start remembering or we were going to improve his memory. But the driver still wouldn't tell us anything. Kind of like you."

"I'm telling the truth, Drill Sergeant." Wild with fear and pain, she squirmed within her restraints. "Let me talk to Colonel Rhoads."

"Don't interrupt, Winter. I'm just getting to the good part. The TL says, 'The truth is elemental.' Says with a stubborn bastard like this driver, we have to 'use the elemental to extract the elemental.' And he walks out of the room . . ."

Lopez swaggered from the room as if acting out the scene. From the hallway, his garbled voice said, "And he comes back with his element of choice." Lopez reentered the room holding a blue cylinder with an angled brass stem on top and a small dial at the juncture. "Fire."

The guy had a blowtorch. "I want to talk to Rhoads," she said again.

Lopez said, "The TL opens the valve and sets the torch on the ground." He twisted the dial and set the thing on the floor between them. She heard the hiss of gas. "Lets the guy hear it."

"This is crazy," she said. "I'm not lying, okay? I'm just not like these other people. I'm not special."

"The TL pulls out a match," Lopez said, talking over her. He reached in his pocket, came out with a wooden match, and held it close to her face. "By now the guy's eyes are bulging, and he's jabbering away, but he just keeps telling us the same lies."

"Maybe he didn't know anything," she said. "Did that ever cross your mind?"

Lopez didn't appear to hear her. "The TL lights the match." Lopez held out a palm and scratched the match across his thick calluses. The match popped to life, shining brightly.

The smell of sulfur made Scarlett feel like screaming.

"The TL picks up the torch—" Lopez bent, doing the same thing. "—and lights it."

With a huff, the blowtorch came to life, burning blue.

"I have some weird power, but I don't understand it," she said. "Okay? Like this bomb blew up and should've killed me but didn't, and like right now, my muscles hurt, because—"

"The driver sees the flame," Lopez said, "remembers everything. Tells our interpreter the bad guys are holed up across town. But the TL shakes his head, says, 'No, they're not,' and we believe him, because nobody could read people like the TL. He says, 'Fire will reveal the truth.'"

Lopez held the blue flame inches from Scarlett's face. Its sound swelled to a roar. Feeling the heat, she tried to cringe away, but she was locked in place, paralyzed by the restraints.

"And you know what?" Lopez bared his teeth, clamping the stubby cigar in a hideous grin. "The TL was right. Fire brought truth."

"You're crazy," she said. "Keep that thing away from me."

Lopez shook his head. "An hour later, the bad guys were dead. Our problems in that sector disappeared overnight, abra-bye-bye-cadabra."

"Rhoads is going to hear about this."

Lopez chuckled derisively. "You poor stupid girl. Colonel Rhoads sent me in here." He turned up the torch and lowered the flame toward her restrained forearm.

"No!" she shouted, struggling wildly. "Help!"

Lopez pushed the brass nozzle closer.

She screamed in horror as the blue flame touched her forearm—and plunged *inward*.

She felt a rush of warmth but no pain, as if Lopez were holding a hair dryer rather than a blowtorch. Heat rushed up her arm through the meat and bone, filling the aching bicep and shoulder, and whooshed into her chest, where it joined the burning vortex.

Lopez pressed the nozzle closer, filling her with flame.

"Get the hell off of me!" she shouted, and she pushed out at Lopez reflexively and instinctively, not with her restrained body but with her will, her intention, her mind.

Lopez bellowed with surprise, shielding his face from the wave of heat that had burst from Scarlett. The blowtorch fell to the tiled floor with a loud *clank* and lay there, huffing flame.

Lopez lowered his arms, pulled the cigar from his mouth, and smiled at the smoldering stub. "Thanks for the light, Winter," he said, all the menace gone out of him. He picked up the torch, killed the flame, and gave the mirror a thumbs-up. "And for future reference, that's 'Get the hell off of me, *Drill Sergeant*.'"

NINETEEN

AFTER LOPEZ LEFT, SCARLETT RAGED IN IMPOTENT solitude until a worried-looking DeCraig appeared, coming through the door as tentatively as a visitor at a wake.

"Hey, Winter," she said. "You all right?"

Scarlett snapped, telling her everything in an angry torrent.

DeCraig nodded thoughtfully and explained it the way she saw it. Scarlett had to be patient, had to put this behind her. They couldn't know what Lopez was up to, let alone Rhoads, but hey—*no harm, no foul, right?*

"No harm?" Scarlett said. "Did you miss the part about the blow-torch?"

"Lopez must have assumed that the flame wouldn't hurt you," DeCraig said.

"So this is what, the world's most twisted practical joke?"

DeCraig shrugged. "Maybe they needed you to *think* it was dangerous. Maybe your ability hinges on adrenaline or something. Maybe—"

"If you say it was for my own good," Scarlett said, "I will hurt you . . . ma'am."

DeCraig grinned. "I administered your TK test, Winter, so I'm not worried about you hurting me while you're tied up."

Scarlett surprised herself by chuckling. She was still pissed at Lopez and Rhoads, but DeCraig was cool.

"You good, bro-tato chip?" DeCraig asked.

"Did you just bro-joke me?"

"Why not?" DeCraig said, undoing the restraints. "Why should guys get all the good nicknames? A girl can only call her friend Sistine Chapel so many times."

Since they were too late for the mess hall, they ate MREs together in the gym. DeCraig's first name was Lucy. She was a few years older than Scarlett, a college dropout from New Jersey. She liked books, horror movies, and cats and had a serious boyfriend who currently was serving on a submarine. That brief meal, with its easy flow of conversation, was the first Scarlett had enjoyed here.

Then, as if nothing had happened, it was back to business as usual. Days passed, and no one mentioned the blowtorch incident. Lopez acted like nothing had happened.

Captain Fuller, who turned out to be the official liaison to West Point, disappeared. Rhoads appeared only at first formation each morning, where he provided a sunny pep talk before abandoning them to Lopez, his menacing guards, and the malicious upperclassmen.

Scarlett envied the other new cadets, among whom a fledgling camaraderie was forming. When a guard knocked the wind from one sprinter, Jakes helped the breathless cadet to her feet. After Lopez belittled Vernon for singing "The Star Spangled Banner" too loudly, another meathead surreptitiously patted the burly new cadet's back.

She missed home, her friends, her mom, her motorcycle, weed. She missed laughing and getting laid and catching a buzz. She missed *freedom*.

She trudged on alone and bore up as best she could. There was no time to make friends, not for her. The cadets couldn't talk in formation, at meals, or during class. As a group, they had no downtime, and the new cadets all lived in solitary confinement. The only place for mingling was ability-based training . . . and she was alone.

Meanwhile, guards lurked, punishing anyone who showed up late to formation, whispered in line, or nodded off in class, a thing they all fought against. The schedule lied: lights out at 2200, first formation at 0500 . . . seven hours of rack time, right? In reality, they trained after lights out and then cleaned and studied by flashlight. They woke at 0400 to prepare for the day. Add frequent midnight hazing and rotating charge of quarters and fire guard duties, and sleep became a lost dream. They were punchy with sleep deprivation.

Lopez and the upperclassmen rode them hard, nitpicking constantly and stressing professionalism and pride at every turn.

Every morning, the cadre presented leadership and ethics classes. Scarlett winced at their hypocrisy, especially when Hopkins led a class on the core values: *duty, honor, country*. Just the night before, Hopkins and his thugs had again battered her through the door, leaving her unable to sleep because of the painful force throbbing in her muscles. She glowered as Hopkins reminded the class of the most important rule here at The Point: cadets could use their special powers only as directed. Breaking this rule would result in immediate and severe punishment. Repetition would result in the Chamber or even transfer to The Farm.

The Chamber was either solitary confinement or some type of torture device. The Farm was almost certainly a prison or insane asylum. Her fear of both grew daily.

They ate lunch in the main mess hall alongside real cadets. More stress, more nitpicking, all for nothing. Just a bunch of high-strung overachievers playing the stupidest game in the world.

Then the dreaded afternoons.

They received their daily medications. Then, as her visibly excited classmates split into ability-based training groups, guards led Scarlett away. Her classmates watched her go, eyeing her with suspicion and contempt and pity. She hated it.

She hated Room 17 even more. Here, day after day, they subjected her to what they called *testing* and she called *torture*.

One day, the guards in rubber suits restrained her, attached electrodes, and shocked her repeatedly, filling her with rage and desperation and a crackling yellow static that burned her head to toe until she released it in a blast of miniature lightning bolts.

Another day, half a dozen meatheads in padded suits slammed into her and thumped her with punches and kicks. The strikes didn't hurt. Their force sank into her, filling her muscles with sizzling force, and *that* hurt. Then the pressure exploded, and she tossed them away like so many scarecrows stuffed with straw.

After each session, Lopez gave the big mirror a thumbs-up and left without so much as a "nice torturing you, Winter."

Then Lucy DeCraig. Always Lucy entering the room, asking, "You okay, sis?"

Mail call was bittersweet. Scarlett loved receiving letters from home, but the guards kept confiscating stuff. When Mom sent cookies, Scarlett got only the accompanying letter. When Ginny sent a flattened joint inside three pages of Bukowski poems, Scarlett received "hours," which amounted to marching back and forth in the gym alongside other petty offenders. One night, three female guards pulled Scarlett into their office and held up a picture of Nick lying naked on a shag carpet. A leering guard pocketed the photo and said, "No pornographic material allowed." Scarlett earned more hours for telling the guard where she could stick the photograph.

Scarlett didn't have time to answer most letters, but she did write to Dan. She wanted an apology but instead demanded an explanation. She considered saying that she was sorry for her role in the fight but decided that he needed to apologize first.

Dan didn't write back.

This was her life for weeks. Suffering, solitude, and constant pressure.

Then came the afternoon that changed everything.

Restrained in Room 17, waiting for Lopez, was like waiting for a dentist who refused to use numbing agents.

Lopez entered, wearing ear protection and pushing a cart that held a boxy machine with what looked like a silver megaphone on top. Shouting, Lopez told her that in his experience all new cadets had impaired hearing. "A natural side effect of having their heads so far up their asses." He gritted his cigar stub in a sneering smile and started the machine.

An invisible muscle car with a bad muffler roared to life in the small room. Scarlett scrunched back in her chair. Lopez turned a knob, increasing the volume. Pulsing waves of sound buffeted her like gusts of wind. She shut her eyes and wished she could plug her ears, but her arms were strapped at her sides. Vibration rattled her teeth and bones.

Lopez cranked the noise louder.

This force built within her more slowly than had other forms of energy, but eventually her vibrating bones felt like they would burst from her skin, ripping her to pieces.

"Quiet!" she screamed.

Or at least that was what she'd *intended* to scream. What came out was a wallop of force, a loud boom punctuated by a sharp rifle crack sound.

The mirror exploded inward, revealing a hidden room.

Inside, a smiling Colonel Rhoads gave Scarlett a thumbs-up.

TWENTY

THIS TIME, RHOADS, NOT LUCY DECRAIG, LED SCARlett away.

"I apologize about the testing," Rhoads said. "I know that it's been difficult."

He ushered her into the noisy gymnasium. Sprinters dashed in blurry packs along the elevated track; gymnasts tumbled across mats, the picture of power and grace; meatheads clapped and roared to the clanking music of pumping weights.

"These cadets are Level I posthumans," Rhoads said, leading her across the gym. "Their powers are physical in nature. No one's better at breaching doors and kicking butt."

The gymnasts had stopped training. They stood in a huddle and eyed Scarlett, whispering among themselves.

Rhoads led her away from the gym and down the hall. They paused at the doorway of a classroom. Inside, telekinetic upperclassmen were coaching new cadets.

"These TKs, along with healers, trackers, tech jammers, and antihealers," Rhoads said, "are Level II posthumans. Their power comes from their minds."

New cadets watched as Uba, standing at parade rest, rapidly folded a sheet of paper into an origami swan. Seamus stood against the far wall, looking hot as always. His blue eyes stared intensely at the origami demonstration. He was lean and compact but muscular, with the physique of a gymnast.

Then, as she stared, he turned his head and stared straight at her. He looked from her to Rhoads, looked back to her, and scowled.

Great, she thought, and looked away.

Rhoads led her away from the classroom.

"Sir," she said, "Cadet Winter requests permission to speak."

Rhoads chuckled. "When we're talking, Scarlett, have at it. Forgo the formalities."

"Thank you, sir," she said. "So, am I Level II?"

"No," Rhoads said. He pushed through a fire door. They ascended a flight of stairs, their footsteps echoing in the stairwell. On the next level, they entered a bright corridor. The hall's many doors, drop ceiling, and busy corkboards reminded Scarlett of her mother's office at West Chester University.

"Every now and then," Rhoads said, "we recruit a cadet whose powers are neither Level I nor Level II. These rare individuals are Level III posthumans, and their powers are unique."

"So I . . ."

Rhoads nodded. "You are Level III."

She didn't know what to say. *Thanks? Wow? What in the world are you talking about?*

"Your power is fascinating," Rhoads said, turning a corner and walking down a short hallway that ended in a set of double doors. "Your body absorbs and rereleases energy."

Scarlett had figured that much. "How?"

"We don't know yet, but we're excited. You have incredible potential."

She could have groaned. She'd heard about her "incredible potential" all her life and knew that it led only to incredible disappointment.

"And now," Rhoads said, pushing through the double doors, "I want you to meet The Point's only other Level III cadet."

They entered a bright, spacious room walled with floor-to-ceiling mirrors. A dark-haired girl in yoga pants and a pink tank top sat with her legs crossed at the center of the hardwood floor, arms lying on her thighs, palms up. Soft music played in the background. The air smelled faintly of fruit or flowers or both.

The girl opened her eyes and smiled without standing or saluting. "Hey, Colonel. What's up?"

"Dalia Amer," Rhoads said, "meet Scarlett Winter. Scarlett, Dalia."

Dalia stood, and Scarlett recognized her as the cadet who had impressed her so much the first day, when Rhoads had asked how many days were left until the Army–Navy football game. Now, of course, Scarlett could give the answer just as quickly. The number of days until "Army beats Navy" was one of the countless stupid facts that they needed to be able to report at an instant's notice.

Dalia shook her hand and said it was nice to meet her.

Scarlett said, "Thank you, ma'am."

"Oh," Dalia said, and reached out to pinch Scarlett's cheek. "So cute. Straight from the cabbage patch."

What the hell?

Rhoads said, "Scarlett is our new Level III, Dalia. I want you to take her under your wing."

Dalia crossed her arms, cocked a hip, and studied Scarlett with seeming amusement.

"She can do amazing things with energy," Rhoads said, "but—"

"She's still a newb."

Rhoads nodded. "I'd like you to teach her yoga and meditation. Hopefully, it will help her control her power."

Dalia rolled her eyes, and a smile crept onto her face. "I suppose," she said. "Can I send her to the Chamber if she doesn't follow directions?"

Rhoads smiled uncomfortably. "She'll comply. Won't you, Scarlett?" Before Scarlett could respond, Rhoads clapped her on the shoulder and said, "We really must be going."

They left to the sound of Dalia's echoing laughter.

Rhoads led her back downstairs via a new stairwell. "I expect great things from you, Scarlett. Great things."

She thanked him. Nothing seemed quite real. For weeks, she'd suffered isolation, confusion, and pain. Now . . .

They entered a residential wing that looked like the world's cleanest college dormitory. Rhoads ushered her into a spotless room twice the size of her cell. It looked like a hotel room. A *nice* hotel room.

"Welcome to your new quarters," Rhoads said.

"New quarters?"

"Correct," Rhoads said. "Your gear has already been secured in that footlocker."

Too good to be true, her bones whispered. *Good things always come with a price.*

"Quite an upgrade, yes?" Rhoads said. "Your own desk, a larger footlocker, a semiprivate bathroom."

And bunk beds, Scarlett thought. *So I have a—*

"Ah," Rhoads said, turning toward the door, "your roommate."

Lucy DeCraig entered the room, grinning like a madwoman, and shook Scarlett's hand. "Cheers, Scarlett Bro-hansson. You don't snore, do you?"

TWENTY-ONE

THE NEXT AFTERNOON, INSTEAD OF REPORTING TO Room 17, Scarlett went to the yoga studio.

"Namaste, newbie," Dalia said, and gave her a smirk.

"Hey," she said.

They started stretching. Dalia asked some questions but didn't seem particularly interested in Scarlett's responses. Dalia was from Pennsylvania, too, but upstate. Wyalusing, a little town on the Susquehanna.

"You miss it?" Scarlett asked.

Dalia looked at Scarlett like she was crazy. "Miss it? I wish I could burn it to the ground." Her voice was as bitter as a winter wind. Then she smiled. "It's better here. Being Level III kicks butt. We get nice rooms, skip most of the bad stuff, and don't have to walk and talk like robots. And we *can* walk around. Pretty much anywhere, anytime. The other cadets whine about it, but so what? Why should we suffer just because they're having a hard time?"

"Cool," Scarlett said. She felt uneasy about receiving preferential treatment, but hanging out in this bright music-filled room sure beat getting tortured and hazed.

"You have to work hard," Dalia said. "Rhoads expects *results*."

"Like what?"

Dalia shrugged. "Whatever he tells you to do. With you, it's this energy thing. Hence meditation and yoga. They're all about mindfulness and energy flow. Rhoads thinks it will help you understand and control your ability."

"I hope so," Scarlett said, and followed Dalia's lead, twisting sideways. So far, yoga just felt like stretching. "And what's your power?"

"I'm a somnopath," Dalia said.

Scarlett thought for a second and came up empty. "What's that mean?"

Dalia looked her in the eye. "It means don't mess with me."

She raised her palms. "Hey, I didn't—"

Dalia laughed. "Just kidding, plebe-o. You're cute. So jumpy."

Jumpy, she thought. *There's something no one's ever called me before.*

She remembered Lucy's advice during the previous night's chess match: *Tread lightly with Dalia, sis. You don't want her as an enemy.* Treading lightly would be tough if Dalia kept treating her like a little kid.

"I don't fully understand it myself," Dalia said. "Basically, I tap into people's subconscious, make them remember their dreams, stuff like that." She crossed the room and turned off the music. "I'm all yoga-ed out for today. Let's take a walk instead."

"But Rhoads said—"

"Scarlett, Scarlett, Scarlett," she said, giving her a pitying look. "What am I going to do with you? Forget Rhoads. I want to take a walk . . . and I always get what I want."

Scarlett spread her hands. "Whatever you say."

"I like your attitude, newbster," Dalia said. "Go change into your uniform and meet me outside Room 7 in fifteen minutes."

SCARLETT SHIFTED FROM foot to foot in the hallway outside Room 7.

Dalia was late.

She pressed her back to the wall, hoping the instructor inside wouldn't wander over and glance into the hall because she recognized the instructor's voice.

Hopkins said, "The team with the slowest time goes without dinner, hooah?"

Come on, Dalia.

Hopkins's voice crossed the room. "Meatheads, you breach the door and get out of the way. Speedsters, you enter next. Engage and disrupt. TKs, follow at an angle. Precision work, TKs. Eliminate all threats."

Dalia came around the corner in her uniform and gave Scarlett a little wave. She grabbed her arm—and dragged her straight into Room 7. Cadets of all disciplines packed the chairs and lined the walls. They turned as one to stare.

Scarlett's stomach cleared the top of the roller coaster and plunged downhill at 200 miles an hour.

Hopkins stopped in midsentence. "May I help you, Cadet Amer?"

Dalia ignored Hopkins and pointed to Dunne. "Clayton, come with us. Tour time."

Hopkins's predatory eyes narrowed. "Dunne is training."

"You want him to prove he can kick in a door?" Dalia said. "Give me a break. Come on, Clayton."

The class's nervous laughter died under Hopkins's glare.

Dunne gathered his things, avoiding eye contact with Hopkins, and crossed the room.

Dalia squeezed Scarlett's arm and whispered, "Dunne is crazy about me. Kind of sad, really. Follows me around like a big puppy dog. But he's sweet."

"Hmm," Scarlett said, aware of everyone—particularly Hopkins—staring at her.

"Clayton, darling," Dalia said with an affected voice. She gave the hulking cadet a hug, kissed him on both cheeks, and pulled him into the hall.

Scarlett hurried after them, eager to get out of there, but someone tapped her shoulder, and she turned back around.

There was no one there.

Across the room, Hopkins's lips curled into a smile that didn't reach his glaring eyes.

Oh, great . . .

An invisible hand propelled her out the door. She hurried after Dalia and Dunne.

"That son of a bitch is meaner than hot sauce on hemorrhoids," Clayton said. "You hear him in there? 'Breach the door and get out of the way.' Like we're just battering rams or something."

Dalia laughed. "Clayton, meet my new sex slave, Scarlett. Try not to be too jealous."

Clayton snorted.

Dalia slipped her arm into his. "Nobody knows West Point better than Clayton."

Clayton looked suddenly worried. "We going outside again? Rhoads said—"

"Let me worry about Rhoads," Dalia said, and beckoned impatiently for Scarlett to walk on her other side. Scarlett caught up, and Dalia slid her free arm through hers. "Let's get some fresh air."

"All right," Scarlett said, but she wasn't so sure. She'd spent her life breaking rules. You had to be smart or you ended up smashed like a bug on a windshield. "They're going to let us out?"

"Aw, how cute. Is little Scarlett afraid?"

"I didn't say I was afraid," she said. "I just asked if—"

"Don't you worry," Dalia said. "I take care of my babies."

Scarlett wasn't buying her cool. Dalia was cocky and condescending, but she was insecure, too, the type of person who needed to surprise and impress. In that instant, Scarlett understood that Dalia would endanger her and Clayton just to highlight how untouchable she was here.

Dalia led them past the infirmary and the kitchen and out into a hall that ended in a door marked *Do Not Enter*. She paused, grinned theatrically, and pushed through the door.

Great, Scarlett thought. *Here we go.* And just when things had started looking up.

They descended a flight of stairs and pushed through another door.

"Whoa," Scarlett said.

It was like stepping into the New York subway system, only this place was much cleaner and empty of people, and the train itself looked older.

"Surprised, plebe-o?" Dalia said. "Stick with me and you'll see a lot more than this."

Clayton gestured at the train. "Without that thing, The Point wouldn't exist. The train's top secret. Runs all the way to Grand Central. Ever hear of Track 61?"

Scarlett shook her head.

"M42?" Clayton asked.

"No," she said.

"The Point started as a bunker back in the thirties, a bug-out zone for bigwigs."

"Nerd alert," Dalia said. "Don't bore the poor girl to death."

"Actually, it's pretty interesting," Scarlett said.

"Oh, boy," Dalia said. "I'm surrounded by geeks. Let's go." She hopped down onto the tracks, led them across, and climbed up the other side.

They walked along that ledge until they came to a rusted door in the tile wall. "This way," Dalia said, and opened the door. The rusted metal sounded like metal nails on a metal chalkboard.

Beyond the door was a dark shaft. Dalia clicked a flashlight to life, and Scarlett saw a metal ladder bolted to the block wall. Its rungs disappeared up into darkness.

"Hope you're not afraid of heights, plebe-o," Dalia said.

Scarlett, who jumped off cliffs for fun, laughed. "Not quite."

After a long climb—something like 100 feet, Scarlett guessed—they emerged through a camouflaged door in the stony hillside overlooking the Hudson, just below the West Point train tracks. They climbed what looked like a deer path to the edge of campus.

It was a beautiful day, sunny and warm, the grass very green beneath the hard blue sky, a faint breeze sighing off the Hudson. Scarlett filled her lungs and grinned at the warmth of the sunshine. She was not built for subterranean living.

Above ground, Dalia and Clayton acted like actual cadets, walking with a purpose, cupped hands, the whole nine.

Clayton pointed out landmarks to Scarlett. Dalia hadn't been kidding. Despite his drawl and irreverence, Clayton made an excellent tour guide. Every building, every monument, every piece of open ground triggered a history lesson.

"During the first War of Independence," he said, pointing at a sharp bend in the river, "they worried the Brits might come sneaking down the Hudson, attack New York."

"The *first* War of Independence?" Scarlett said. "There was more than one?"

Clayton shook his head. "Spoken like a true Yank." Then he went on to explain how the forces at West Point had stretched a heavy chain across the river to slow British boats. He turned and pointed across campus to the hills. "We had artillery up there. Would've pounded the Brits to pieces if they'd gotten caught in the chain, like spearing catfish in a bathtub, but the redcoats never tried it. We'll see some of the chain links over there, at Trophy Point."

Clayton pointed out Thayer Hall, the Superintendent's House, and Flirtation Walk—"Flirtie," Dalia chimed in—a riverside path off limits to the cadre.

"This is General Sedgwick's monument," Clayton said, leading them around the back of the statue, which stood atop a stone pediment, putting the general's boots at eye level. Clayton pointed to the statue's heels. "Behold General Sedgwick's spurs."

"Note the color," Dalia said.

"West Point cadets are superstitious as Southern grandmothers," Clayton said. "Everything here is tradition and superstition and do-this-don't-do-that hoodoo juju. Cadets get behind, need some luck, they come out here and spin ol' Sedgwick's spurs."

Scarlett grinned. The statue was made of dark metal—bronze, she thought—but the spurs were lighter, as if many hands had spun them over the years.

Clayton laughed. "There's a whole bunch of rules. You gotta be desperate. I'm talking stone broke in the hope department. And you gotta spin it at midnight on the dot."

"Which means they have to be *really* desperate," Dalia said, "since they're not allowed out of their rooms at that hour." Up here Dalia was way cooler.

Or maybe I'm less uptight, Scarlett thought. Either way, she'd judged Dalia too harshly down in The Point.

"Well," Scarlett said, "I hope I'm never that desperate."

Coming back, as they passed the Combating Terrorism Center, they saluted a ruggedly handsome colonel, who smiled and wished them a good afternoon.

"That guy's one of the baseball coaches," Clayton said.

Incredible, Scarlett thought. West Point had some sincerely high-speed individuals. This colonel could teach classes, combat terrorism, and still find time to coach a sport?

The thought made her feel small. She knew that she'd been born with natural advantages even without this crazy energy thing, but her whole life was a series of blown opportunities, limping failures, and pitiful implosions. She had a lot of quit in her. What was she doing here among all these incredible people?

Clayton was laughing at Dalia's joke as he pushed through the *do-not-enter* door and back into The Point, but his laughter disappeared as shouting filled the hall.

"Cadet Dunne! What do you think you're doing?"

Scarlett recognized the guard by his chipped tooth and unibrow. He was one of the meanest. He leveled a Taser at Clayton.

"Wait," Clayton said. "Don't—" Then he howled with pain, his big muscles going stiff as the Taser *crack-crack-crack*-ed.

Dalia pushed past Scarlett and into the hall.

The Taser stopped, and Clayton stumbled backward. Scarlett lowered her shoulder and bent her knees and managed to keep Clayton from tumbling backward down the stairs.

"Cadet Amer," the guard said, "I didn't see you there. I never meant—"

And then he was skittering backward, brushing frantically at the front of his uniform. The Taser fell to the ground. A high-pitched *eeeee* whistled from his throat like helium escaping a pinched balloon.

Scarlett gasped.

A shadow appeared, shifting over the guard's body . . . then came clearer, and she saw that the shadow was made of smaller shadows, tiny pockets of darkness scampering up the guard's chest and arms and neck.

The guard slammed into the wall, eyes wide, brushing furiously. "Get off me!"

The shadow grew clearer still, and Scarlett felt like brushing her own uniform. The guard was covered in spiders. Hundreds of spiders. Thousands. Crawling over him with jerky spider speed, pouring into his collar and up his sleeves and into his ear canals.

Scarlett twitched with revulsion.

A ghastly grin twisted Dalia's face into a mask of cruelty. Her eyes gleamed, merciless and insane. The guard collapsed to the ground.

"Stop," Scarlett said.

Dalia panted, enraptured. She didn't seem to hear Scarlett, didn't seem even to be aware of her or anything but the shuddering, blubbering guard she was torturing.

He flailed on the floor, making horrible animal sounds, his form indistinct now beneath a mound of scurrying spiders. His bowels let go, filling the corridor with stink.

She was killing him.

"Dalia, stop," Scarlett said.

But Dalia was growling now, growling and panting and laughing all at once, her fingers arched like claws.

Scarlett reached out and touched her shoulder, saying, "Please, Dalia, stop—you're killing him," and Dalia's fiery eyes turned in her direction.

Scarlett shouted and stepped away, suddenly covered with spiders, millions of tiny spider legs tickling across every inch of her body. They packed her ears and nostrils and filled her mouth, choking her, and—

Then they were gone.

Gone from Scarlett, gone from the guard. Gone.

Dalia loomed over the weeping man, hands on hips, and spoke in a cold whisper. "Do *not* mess with the Queen Bitch."

TWENTY-TWO

"YOUR REAL GOAL," RHOADS SAID, SETTING A BLACK case on the floor at Scarlett's feet, "is holding on to energy, letting it build."

Room 17 again. Day after day after day . . .

Scarlett sat in a wooden chair, unrestrained. Strange gloves—hard black plastic on the outside, soft rubber on the inside—covered her hands. The rubber insulation ended at her fingertips, which pressed against something cold and smooth. Probably metal. The gloves ran nearly to her elbows, and a black cable ran from each wrist to the boxy machine atop the cart that Rhoads had pushed into the room, one of its wheels squeaking like a lab rat.

"I already hold on to energy, sir," she said.

"To a degree," Rhoads said, "but mostly you're *channeling* energy. There's a brief pause while force builds inside you, but you're basically acting like a conduit. Force flows in, force flows out. We need to hold the energy longer, let it build."

She shook her head. The force dictated its own release. Once it built to a certain point, the energy just exploded. If anything, she should release it sooner. Holding on hurt. "Impossible."

"*Impossible* is a word I hear more frequently from new cadets than from upperclassmen," Rhoads said, unsnapping the latches of the black case. "The Point's motto is '*Training tomorrow's leaders today*,' but I've always favored '*Never say never*.' Not very original, perhaps, but true. And truth trumps both originality and any notions of what is or isn't possible. Certainly you've seen enough here to understand that."

Remembering the frantic fraction of a second when she'd been covered in ghostly spiders, she nodded. That had been terrifying but somehow not as scary as the casual way Dalia had joked afterward. *Geez*, she'd said, never even addressing the fact that she'd nailed Scarlett with what amounted to somnopathic friendly fire, *that guy really hates spiders*, and then, squeezing Clayton's bulging biceps, *Nobody messes with my teddy bear.*

In the weeks since that night, Scarlett had continued to meet with Dalia for meditation and yoga. Not that they actually meditated or did yoga. They just stretched and talked. Well, Dalia talked. And talked and talked and talked . . .

Scarlett had never met someone so stuck on herself. Everything was about her.

Rhoads made things worse by doting on Dalia. The guards feared her. The cadets didn't really interact with her. Dalia felt nothing but contempt for her classmates, including Clayton, who clearly had a thing for her. Sometimes she pulled Clayton from class, but only when she wanted an audience, Scarlett figured.

Dalia talked about Scarlett like a pet project, some poor little lost kid she'd been kind enough to take under her wing. All that head patting drove Scarlett nuts, but she didn't feel like getting covered in spiders, so she kept her mouth shut.

The best days were the ones when Dalia left The Point to work with active-duty teams, though she was even cockier after returning from those sessions, glowing with her own importance and dropping constant and cryptic hints at what she'd been doing, clearly wanting Scarlett to pry.

Those days, Scarlett just chilled in the yoga room or used the time to catch up on studying, cleaning, or writing letters. Every few days, she wrote Dan another letter. No reply yet from her brother. She shouldn't be surprised, she knew—Dan was probably still pissed and never had been much of a letter writer, anyway—but she honestly missed her big brother and wanted to bury the hatchet. That was clear now.

Another thing she'd learned since coming here: she *needed* freedom.

Evenings, she and Lucy talked and played chess. That freedom—hanging out and losing herself in a game—felt great, like getting back to her true self.

Lucy was cool and smart. Decisive and realistic. Perpetually upbeat but tough, too. A confident, hardworking professional. At twenty-three, she was the oldest third-year cadet. In posthuman terms, she'd been a late bloomer, and then she'd hidden her talent, which had scared her badly. As she'd become more comfortable with the fact that she could move things with her mind, she'd used it to scam free beers at college bars. At Rutgers, before The Point found her, she'd been studying electrical engineering, with a minor in German. Sometimes, when she and Scarlett played chess, she spoke with an overdone German accent. When she was feeling particularly upbeat, she even sang with the exaggerated accent. It was horrible and hilarious.

Lucy had another side, too, a strength born of genuine morality and impulsive boldness. One night, when Scarlett was complaining about Hopkins, Lucy shrugged matter-of-factly. "He's a big shot now, but he'll never hack it in the real Army."

Scarlett grinned. She'd never heard Lucy bad-mouth anybody. Normally, she was Miss Upbeat, a very positive individual who didn't seem bothered by anything.

Even now, Lucy smiled happily as she said, "Hopkins is more suited to rising through the political ranks than he is to leading troops. Think he has some magic switch that he can flip at will, turn him into a strong, compassionate leader? No way. Out in the field, he's done. Honestly, his best bet would be to get out and go corporate. But he would never do that. He wouldn't have the confidence."

Scarlett leaned back, warming to the idea of Karma going upside Hopkins's angular head. "You really think so?"

"Absolutely. He'd better avoid combat arms. He'd draw friendly fire like honey draws flies. He should get into supply, something like that, create a petty empire. King of the Fobbits."

Scarlett laughed. "He would never go supply. His ego wouldn't let him."

Lucy's grin stretched wider. "Exactly, Bro-fessor. Don't sweat Hopkins. He's doomed."

Unfortunately, Lucy wasn't impulsive enough to join Scarlett on her nighttime excursions. After lights out, Scarlett used Dalia's secret subway exit and escaped from The Point. She loved to drink the night air and stroll the darkened campus alone, with great stone buildings rising all around her like sleeping giants. Whenever a vehicle approached, she hid. Twice, she'd run from MPs, which had been fun and strangely nostalgic. She'd been dodging cops since middle school.

Luckily, she'd always been a fast runner. Since coming to The Point, she'd gotten much faster. Stronger, too. Swapping out partying for PT had no doubt helped, but she figured the gains had more to do with the pills and injections they forced on her daily.

Medicine to enhance your genetic advantages, Rhoads told the cadets.

Steroids, Scarlett guessed, among other things.

Just fucking take them was Lopez's answer when Scarlett asked about the pills.

Scarlett shrugged, popped the pills, and spit them into the latrine down the hall.

Unfortunately, she couldn't escape injections. Maybe they were causing her crazy dreams, which had been incredibly vivid, like reliving the past. Her fight with Dan, troubles she'd gotten into, guys she'd gotten with—and boring stuff, too: brilliant dreams of her room at home, perusing her books and music and posters. Weird.

She was tempted to ask Dalia about them, but what would be the point? Instead of helping, Dalia would call her "poor baby" and go off about how she had no troubles with dreams and how she simply wouldn't accept such a reality.

Dalia wanted her to be in awe of her powers, the fear she engendered, the way she had Rhoads wrapped around her finger, her wit, and her unpredictability.

Scarlett didn't have her power, Lucy's focus, or the work ethic of the USMA cadets. She just hoped to ride whatever talent she did have. Daily, she vowed to work hard, but in her heart, she feared that eventually she would let everyone down.

"Okay, Scarlett," Rhoads said, and opened the case. Inside, what looked like a car battery with dials and meters sprouted a tangle of red and yellow wires. "Let's begin."

Your turn, Scarlett felt like saying, but she nodded and said "Yes, sir" instead. As a Level III, she had escaped her cell, her solitude, and hazing, not to mention the unrelenting pressure of a nonstop day with no breaks, no freedom, and no friendship. She couldn't go back. She had to keep Rhoads happy.

"Relax," Rhoads said. He unstrung a thin red wire with a round sticker at the end. "No big blast today."

"What, then?"

Rhoads stuck leads onto Scarlett's arms, neck, and forehead. "We'll go slowly. Just a trickle of current."

Scarlett smiled bitterly. "Low and slow, huh? Like a chicken."

Rhoads looked confused for a second, then grinned. "Ah, barbecue humor. Yes, like a chicken. We know that you can absorb a tremendous amount of energy in a blast, but we're hoping that you can absorb even more this way. With faster methods, I'm afraid that you might absorb too much energy too quickly. We can't have you blowing out your circuit board." He turned a dial on the battery. "Can you feel that?"

Scarlett couldn't.

Rhoads adjusted the dial. "Now?"

Scarlett started to say no, but then she felt a slight warmth at the contact points on her neck. "A little."

"Good," Rhoads said. "I want you to try to hold on to this energy as long as you can, okay?"

Scarlett nodded. She could feel warmth in her temples and arms and back.

So pointless. She had no control. You couldn't ask a quart jar to hold a gallon of juice.

Rhoads indicated the control box. "This will register how much energy you can build prior to release. Congratulations. You're now storing as much energy as a nine-volt battery."

"Gee, thanks, sir."

"Now a whole pack of batteries."

Scarlett raised an eyebrow.

Rhoads nodded, looking serious. "You're approaching the capacity of a car battery."

Scarlett concentrated on her breathing. Earlier, they'd tried hooking her directly to batteries but to no avail. She had no way of drawing upon potential energy.

"Creeping up now," Rhoads said.

After several minutes, she felt the all too familiar burn at the center of her chest. Her muscles tensed. She wanted to release the energy and tell Rhoads, *Sorry, I just can't do it,* but the colonel wouldn't believe her, not with all those meters at his disposal.

"It hurts, sir," Scarlett said.

Rhoads nodded without looking up from the readouts. "Training is often painful, Scarlett. Better to suffer here than die in battle."

Force built. Each point of contact burned now. Each stream of energy moved in a line of fire toward her center. The leads at her temples burned like twin suns and sent fiery spiderwebs around the back of her skull to join the river of electricity coursing into her neck. The force at her center pulsed white hot and urgent.

“I have to let it out,” she said. She was sweating now.

Rhoads shook his head. “Hold on, Scarlett. Keep trying. This is very important.”

Scarlett gritted her teeth. Her eyes twitched uncontrollably. Her muscles hummed, hard as rocks, aching. Inside the gloves, her fingers pulsed, tingling against the metal tips. Everything hurt, and it was all so stupid, so utterly pointless.

And *whoosh* . . . the force blasted out of her fingers, into the cables, and away. She fell back in her chair, shaking. Her head pounded, her muscles twitched, and her chest ached as if Clayton Dunne had nailed her with a haymaker.

A red light atop the meter stared coldly up at her.

Rhoads frowned and gave the slightest shake of his head.

Scarlett started ripping wires away, a clumsy affair in the bulky gloves. “Can’t just . . . hold it,” she said, struggling to catch her breath. “Like chugging spoiled milk . . . and trying not to puke.”

“That’s enough for today,” Rhoads said. “Soon, however, I’m going to need *results*.”

She tore away the last of the leads and glared at Rhoads.

“You obviously have some kind of internal capacitor,” Rhoads said, “or current would just flow through you. No build, no blast.”

If only, she thought.

“Find that capacitor within yourself,” Rhoads said. “Learn to control it, like concentrating your mind or flexing a muscle.”

“What if it isn’t like a muscle?” she said. “What if it’s like a bone, just a thing inside me, something I have no control over?”

“Even bones bend,” Rhoads said.

LATER, IN THE yoga room, Dalia rolled her eyes. “You’re a Level III, Scarlett. Tell Rhoads to chill out.”

“Yeah,” Scarlett said, shifting to stretch her other leg. “I don’t know if that would really work.”

They sat opposite each other, soft music playing in the background.

Dalia leaned back. "Don't be such a wimp. People will walk all over you if you let them. That's why I'm the Queen Bitch." She showed her cocky smile, ready to ditch Scarlett's concerns and go off again about how she was so awesome.

"He's losing patience," Scarlett said, hurrying so that Dalia wouldn't interrupt. "Can we step up the yoga and try meditation? They might help me break through."

"What are you talking about? We're here every day."

"Yeah, but—"

Someone knocked at the door.

"Be a dear and answer that, would you?" Dalia said.

Anger rose in Scarlett—she was so sick of Dalia's condescending attitude—but she stood and crossed the room and opened the door.

Clayton filled the doorway, looking anxious. "Hey, Scarlett," Clayton said, looking past her, "Dalia here?"

"She's the one over there," she said, "the one you're looking at."

She stepped aside, but Dalia said, "Not now, Clayton. We're busy."

Clayton looked at her with hurt eyes.

"Come on, Scarlett," Dalia said without even looking at Clayton, then turned and stretched her arms overhead, lifting onto her tiptoes, giving Clayton a good look at her yoga pants. "Let's go."

Clayton stood there, transfixed. "But in the dreams," he whispered so softly that Scarlett barely even heard him, "you said . . ." His hands twitched at his sides as if they were looking for something they could lift.

"Get him out of here, Scarlett," Dalia said, and touched her toes.

Clayton let out a soft groan. What had happened to him?

"Sorry," Scarlett said, and patted one big shoulder. "Got work to do."

Clayton stared at Dalia. The fire of desperation in his eyes dimmed to hopelessness. He stalked off down the hall without even saying good-bye.

Scarlett closed the door and returned to her mat.

Dalia rolled her eyes again. "God, why can't he just leave me alone?"

"I thought you were friends."

"Guys can never leave it at that," she said, and her smile glowed with cruel delight.

THAT WEEKEND, FULLER reappeared and marched the new cadets above ground to witness the *real* cadets march past the superintendent's house. They'd spent the summer in Beast Barracks, learning to soldier. This march signified their switch from new cadets to plebes.

They had arrived at West Point this summer a bunch of wide-eyed high school kids. Now they looked like soldiers. Leaner and tougher. Serious and proud. They had suffered, sacrificed, and survived. Camaraderie thrummed off them.

Scarlett wondered what that would feel like.

"Congratulations," Fuller announced unceremoniously once the real West Pointers disappeared. "You're plebes now." Then he marched them back underground, far from sunlight, fresh air, and class camaraderie.

At least she had a friend in Lucy. That night, they played chess in their room.

"You know, you can just move the pieces with your hand," Scarlett said, pushing her pawn, strengthening her center, and nullifying Lucy's threat, "especially if you're going to make moves like that."

"Talk is cheap, sis," Lucy said, "on the chessboard and in life. The more I do with my mind, the better my control. I can't generate crazy force out of thin air like Seamus or move heavy stuff like Hopkins. All I can do is practice, practice, practice. I might not be the flashiest or most powerful TK, but I'm the most reliable, and Rhoads knows it."

Scarlett pushed another pawn. "You work too hard. Why don't you shake things up, sneak out tonight, take a walk?"

Lucy shook her head. "Not me. I don't share your self-destructive tendencies, Marilyn Mon-bro. I play it safe. Besides, summer's over. You need your sleep. Once classes start on Monday, you'll forget what sleep is."

Seamus appeared at the door, holding a plastic bin. "Mail call," he said, and tossed Lucy an envelope. "Another love letter from your sailor boyfriend."

"He's a submariner, not a sailor, and he's not my boyfriend. He's my *man*friend." Lucy's eyebrows bounced up and down.

"Spare me the details," Seamus said.

"You're on mail duty now?" Lucy asked, opening the letter. "What did you do this time?" Seamus had only recently finished weeks of laundry duty.

Lucy had explained to Scarlett that Seamus was always in trouble for something, usually for speaking his mind.

"Maybe I volunteered," Seamus said with a cockeyed grin.

He turned and started for the door without so much as glancing at Scarlett, which was normal. Whenever she smiled at him or said anything, he either ignored her or got snarky. He still had a chip on his shoulder about her Level III privileges.

"Wait," Scarlett called to him. Mail was pure gold, the best thing, even better than food or sleep, and she'd been waiting for mail call in hopes that she might hear from her brother. Dan had to respond someday. "Any mail for me?"

"Oh, Winter . . . yeah, sorry," he said. "You got letters from friends."

Scarlett rose from her seat, grinning. "Really?"

"Yeah," Seamus said. "You got a letter from every . . . last . . . one of them." He turned the bin upside down. Nothing dropped to the ground. No letters, no packages, nothing. He burst into laughter, executed a crisp about-face, and flipped her the bird as he left the room.

TWENTY-THREE

Hey, Dan. What's up?

You heading home for Thanksgiving next week? I can't. Maybe I'll see you for Christmas. I can't come home then, either, but family can visit.

Write back, okay?

Later,
Scarlett

SHE FOLDED THE LETTER AND PUT IT IN AN ENVElope and addressed it and set it aside to mail. Not much of a note, but so be it. She'd sent her brother seven or eight letters, but Dan still hadn't responded. She was losing patience. Maybe she'd blasted him through the air, but he'd started it, and he'd crossed a line that they'd both understood that he was never supposed to cross again.

She was too busy to dwell on his silence.

Fall semester had been brutal. Every day was packed. Mornings were given over to math, American history, and physics. They were hard. Really hard.

Afternoon training sucked. Rhoads expected her to hold on to more energy. It was impossible. Trying harder just hurt worse and made it harder to deal with Dalia.

Yoga and meditation was a joke. All she did was sit around and listen to Dalia talk. If they were in high school, it wouldn't have been so bad, but here she was under constant stress and never with enough time to stay on top of stuff.

The Point killed its lights at 2200, which meant staying up for hours to study, yet she somehow never managed to study everything she needed to study, and she was always scrambling to keep up with the mile-long list of stuff they expected her to do, from polishing her boots to memorizing the knowledge book.

Lucy suggested that she quit taking nighttime walks, but if she didn't get out of The Point from time to time, she'd go crazy, and not *bounce-your-leg-in-class* crazy. She'd go full on *Jack-Torrance-in-*The-Shining crazy. All work and no midnight walks made Scarlett a dull girl, after all.

One evening, when Seamus dropped in to collect laundry—this time he'd talked back to a classroom instructor—he agreed to play Scarlett in chess. She knew he was good, but she didn't expect him to beat her. That was what he did, though, attacking aggressively out of the same weird Stonewall position he'd used against Lucy on Scarlett's first day at The Point.

Seamus was good-looking and smart and interesting but unfortunately still had a chip on his shoulder about her Level III status. She wished she'd known him back in high school. He probably would have been way cooler after smoking a bowl or two. Even now, she'd love to take him for a ride on her Yamaha, stay up all night, and split a six-pack while watching the sun rise.

Instead, she was stuck here. The one advantage to being so busy was that fall semester flew. Everyone was scrambling, trying to find enough time to read and study. They were under constant pressure to think, act, and speak like leaders. Various milestones loomed, cranking their stress levels: midterms, PT and obstacle course tests, ability-specific threshold deadlines, and countless events—Ring Weekend, Branch Night, Sandhurst—that cluttered the calendar and demanded constant preparation. At any moment, cadre or upperclassmen could stop a plebe and quiz him or her on the knowledge book, demanding that the plebe sing "Benny Havens, Oh!"; explain the composition, deployment, and destructive power of an M18A1 claymore mine; or correctly identify the number of days until Army beat Navy. Whenever someone asked Scarlett—usually it was Hopkins, who remained pissed at Scarlett for escaping from her cell and midnight hazing—how many days it was until Army would beat Navy, she felt like saying, *Well, sir, based on their record against Navy, I wouldn't hold my breath.*

Here at West Point, people lost their minds over football. After the constant pressure and right-dress-right nitpicking, football games gave cadets a chance to hang out and holler, and football, like most things at West Point, was layered with tradition and ritual. For members of The Point, football was even nicer. During home games, they were able to join the regular cadets above ground and just have fun. It was pretty exciting, and with each game, Scarlett, who'd never been a football fan, felt some of her prior cynicism falling away.

Thanksgiving came and went. The cadets had a big meal at The Point. The food was pretty good, though Clayton ruined the cranberry sauce, saying it looked like it had "come out the ass end of a gut-shot hog." After the meal, the cadre had even given them a few hours of liberty, but for Scarlett, that just meant more studying. Her mom sent a card shaped like a turkey and said that "they" were looking forward to seeing Scarlett over Christmas break. No word, however, whether *they* included Dan, and Dan himself certainly hadn't given any clues. Her brother still hadn't responded.

By the time December rolled around, she was pumped for the Army–Navy game. Army had beaten Navy only once since 2002, but the Black Knights were having a good season and might have a shot. Making matters even more exciting, the game was being held at Lincoln Financial Field in Philly, close to where she had grown up. She wouldn't be allowed to see family or friends, but it was cool to be back in Philly, and for the first time she felt unified with the cadets of The Point and West Point.

Bundled in their dark woolen long coats, Scarlett and her classmates cheered like maniacs. It was the second Saturday in December, a bitterly cold yet beautiful day, the sky impossibly blue and the wind blowing so hard and cold that Scarlett grinned at the chill, her eyes leaking tears. Lucy shouted German insults whenever Navy celebrated a play. Everyone was excited. Even Lopez cheered. Two rows down, Seamus smiled, his cheeks pink from the cold, his eyes glistening. For once, he looked happy.

Dalia had refused to attend. Football was beneath her. Scarlett was glad. Dalia would have complained the whole time.

Navy had jumped out to an early lead. Going into the half, they were up by two touchdowns and a field goal. The enthusiasm of the West Point cadets never wavered, however. The Black Knights must have had a pretty good pep talk in the locker room, because when they came out for the second half, they looked like a whole new team. They scored quickly, shut down Navy's first drive, and marched straight back up the field. Scarlett and her classmates cheered like crazy. Army failed to score a second touchdown that drive, but their kicker nailed a 40-yard field goal, making the score 17–10. They held Navy again on the next drive and ended the third quarter with another touchdown. Scarlett's section of the stadium erupted in a volcano of celebration. Army had tied the game! Or so it had seemed . . .

Unfortunately, a gust of wind roared across the field at the absolute worst moment, and Army's kicker missed the extra point, leaving Navy with a one-point advantage, 17–16.

During the fourth quarter, both defenses dominated, and when Army got the ball back with just under a minute left in the game, they were still down by a single point. They didn't need a touchdown. With so little time on the clock, all they had to do was charge up the field one more time and get close enough for their kicker to score a field goal. Navy wouldn't have time to fire back with a drive of their own.

Scarlett was screaming at the top of her lungs. Army completed a pass for a first down, taking it out to their own 35-yard line. Lucy raged in German, eyes gleaming like an absolute madwoman. Seamus pumped a fist in the air, hollering encouragement.

They had to get the ball up the field. Scarlett was on the edge of her seat. The whole stadium was going insane. She'd never felt anything like this in her entire life. The next pass was incomplete. And the next. And the next. The collective groan was thunderous. Suddenly it was fourth and 10, with ten seconds left on the clock and 65 yards of turf between Army and their big win.

"*Deine Mutter masturbiert im stehen!*" Lucy shouted.

Army snapped the ball. Navy attacked. The quarterback dropped back, pumping his arm, looking for a receiver downfield, scrambled, broke a tackle, and hurled the football. Just past midfield, a Black Knight made the catch and stepped out of bounds, making the first down and stopping the clock at two seconds.

They had time for one more play, one chance at winning glory for West Point. The kicking team trotted onto the field. It would be a 50-yard attempt, and a frigid crosswind was hammering across the field.

Both teams got into position. The stadium went insane. Army kicked, Navy tried to block, and the ball sailed, tumbling end over end, toward the goalposts.

Scarlett tensed—this was it!—and Lucy grabbed her arm, screaming German filth.

But then the crosswind strengthened, and Scarlett joined the collective groan as the ball veered left, going wide . . .

At the last second, however, the ball wobbled, jerked back to the right, clipped the post, and scored for the win.

As the USMA cadets roared with excited bewilderment, Scarlett noticed Seamus turn from the field, doing his best to cover a secret smile. Seeing his suppressed excitement and satisfaction, she understood.

He'd done it. He'd nudged the ball with his mind, winning the game for West Point.

At that moment, Seamus looked up and saw her. At first his eyes widened—he knew that she knew—but then they exchanged a smile, and he raised a finger to his lips.

Shhh.

She smiled and nodded, then frowned as Lopez grabbed Seamus by the shoulder and dragged him away.

TWENTY-FOUR

SCARLETT RAN, THE JEERS OF HOPKINS'S CREW echoing after her like sounds from a nightmare. If only this were a dream. She'd certainly been having a lot of them, most of which dragged her kicking and screaming back into the past, back to the explosion at Sav's guest house, back to the fight with Dan, back to the night of the burning car.

But here, now, the catcalls and laughter closing in—this was no dream. She couldn't let them catch her. Because then . . .

"We're coming for you, Wiiiiinnterrrr . . ."

She'd slipped out earlier and strolled the West Point campus just to clear her head. The TK bullies had spotted her and given chase after she'd returned to The Point. If they caught her, she was going to be in huge trouble. Ever since Scarlett had escaped from the cells, Hopkins had been eye mauling her like a muzzled Doberman.

At the end of the hallway, she came to a door marked RESTRICTED: CADRE ONLY.

She hesitated, laying her fingertips against the cool metal of the door. If she ran, they almost certainly would catch her. If she hid behind the restricted door, she might be able to wait them out and slip away.

She heard them drawing closer.

"She went this way."

"Finally got her."

"Come on. Hurry."

She pushed through the door, hating the clack the latch made closing behind her, and braced herself against the door, listening, her heart pounding.

The TKs' laughter swelled now, coming into the hallway, filling it. If they pushed through this door, trapping her here, her worst nightmare would come true.

She looked over her shoulder, hoping to see a way out. But she was disappointed. There was no escape. She'd trapped herself in a short hallway that was dark save for a weird flickering blue light coming from a room at its dead end.

The jeering cadets ran past, calling for her.

Scarlett froze there, paralyzed with indecision. Hopkins would double back eventually. Should she run in the opposite direction and risk being seen or hide here and hope they didn't check this corridor?

Wrestling with this dilemma, she became increasingly aware of a low mechanical groan coming from down the hall and, beneath it, a quieter, more troubling sound: not the squeaking of machinery but a soft and terrible whimpering. The sound drew her toward the light, which flashed through a little square window set in a metal door.

Down this off-limits hall, within the room pulsing eerie blue light, someone was suffering.

Overtop the door, a plaque read THE CHAMBER.

She leaned into the window and squinted against the flashing blue light. The machine ground on—*ruh, ruh, ruh*—as her eyes adjusted to the horrible scene beyond the door.

At the center of the room, Seamus writhed atop a table. He

struggled against his restraints, which held him at the center of what looked like a gleaming rib cage, curved metal bars rising from both sides of the table and arching overhead. Sizzling blue light arced in the slight gap between the metal ribs. A robotic arm moved up and down, back and forth, inches from his skull. At the end of the robotic arm spun a silver disk from which beams of blue light pulsed into Seamus's temples and forehead. His eyes were squeezed shut. His chin jutted forward. He whimpered and thrashed, lost to pain and terror.

The sight sickened her.

All because of the stupid football game. What was the big deal? They'd all been cheering their heads off, hoping Army would win.

Nobody deserves to suffer like this.

Seamus strained against his bonds. The veins in his neck stood out in the pulsing light.

Scarlett opened the door. "Seamus, are you all right?"

He didn't reply. How could he? He was lost to pain and terror.

The robotic arm shifted. The spinning disk jackhammered his temples with pulses of blue light.

Seamus's eyes flew wide open. His mouth yawned as if to scream, but only a faint moan, long and soft and terrible, escaped, and she understood that in his private world of pain, Seamus was screaming louder than he—or anyone else—had ever screamed before.

Something was wrong with the machine. It was killing him.

She crouched beside the machine, found a switch, and flicked it.

The groaning stopped, the blue lights died, and Seamus let out a bloodcurdling scream. He thrashed even harder against his restraints. She talked to him, but he didn't seem to hear her.

"It's okay," she told him. "The machine was broken." She reached through the metal bars to touch his shoulder. "I stopped it. You're going to—"

Seamus turned his head to glare at her. "What have you done?"

She nearly stumbled backward from the force of his anger. "It was killing you."

"You're so stupid! You've ruined everything!"

"But it wasn't—" Scarlett stammered.

Laughter sounded from behind her. She jumped at the sound of it, then turned with a sinking feeling in her chest.

Hopkins and his TK crew filled the doorway.

"Winter," Hopkins said, drawing it out like a growling attack dog. "You are in sincerely deep doo-doo."

"She stopped the machine," one of the others said, and laughed incredulously.

Seamus wept, mumbling curses.

Scarlett let her eyes close and pinched the bridge of her nose. Everything was wrong, wrong, wrong. She'd tried so hard to stay out of trouble, tried so hard to do the right thing, to help him, but now . . .

"Step out into the hall, Winter," Hopkins said. "Kaiser, start the machine over again . . . *from the beginning*. Winter bought Seamus an extra—" He whistled. "—six hours of suffering."

Scarlett opened her eyes and put herself between Kaiser and the machine.

Kaiser grinned and glanced toward Hopkins.

"Don't," Scarlett said. "There's something wrong with the machine. It was killing him."

"There's nothing wrong with the Chamber," Hopkins said. "That's the way it works. Why do you think Kyeong is so crazy?"

"Just do it," Seamus said, his voice thick with tears. "Just get it over with."

Kaiser started around Scarlett, but she sidestepped, blocking him. "Don't. This is my fault, not his. Write me up and leave him be."

Hopkins laughed. "Write you up? We're going to teach you a lesson. Remind you that you're still a plebe even if you have a fancy room. Running around at night, interfering with punishment? Those are heavy offenses, Winter." He grinned wolfishly. "You remember how we used to visit your cell at night?"

Invisible hands shoved Scarlett. She staggered back. "Yeah, I remember," she said, and a resigned weariness settled over her. "I'd been worried you'd catch me some night."

"You were right to be scared," Hopkins said, and looked to his friends. "Beat her down."

Blows rained down. These weren't the heavy pillow thuds they'd given her in the cell. These were crunching blasts, prizefighter hooks slamming into her ribs and gut and the side of her face. They pummeled her from all angles, smashing into her head and thumping into her body again and again, hundreds of hammer blows pounding, pounding, pounding . . .

When a furious strike smashed into her ribs, she realized that it was an actual boot, not telekinetic force. She opened her eyes to see Hopkins grinning down.

"Thought you could run from us," Hopkins said. "How'd that work out for you, Winter?"

Scarlett looked at him with no expression on her face. "I wasn't running because I was afraid of you," she said. "I was afraid of myself."

And then, with the force of their attacks raging like a tornado of fire within her, Scarlett finally let them have it.

TWENTY-FIVE

DALIA LEANED BACK IN THE CHAIR ACROSS FROM Rhoads, watching the man straighten the papers atop his desk, knowing what that compulsive tidying meant.

He was going to ask her again.

Before he'd asked the first three times, he'd unnecessarily straightened his work space.

"I hope you're right, Dalia," he said, not looking her in the eye. "For now, I'll take your advice and be lenient with Scarlett." He straightened the framed photo of his deceased parents.

She stood, knowing that Rhoads wasn't finished, and told him that that sounded great. She'd give Scarlett a talking to, straighten her out.

Scarlett had really done a number on Hopkins and his toadies. Broken noses, cracked ribs, deeply bruised egos. So stupid of her to snap like that—and beyond stupid, helping Seamus—but hilarious, too, because it all backfired, earning Pretty Boy several extra hours in the Chamber.

Rhoads frowned. His anxiety was delicious.

"A moment longer, please," he said, gesturing toward her chair.

"Sure," she said, and sat down again.

"I hate to ask," Rhoads said, forcing himself to meet her eyes now, "but I want you to do another recon mission."

She feigned concern. "But you said—"

"I know," Rhoads said, "and I remain worried. I still have nightmares about Appleton . . ."

I know you do. In those nightmares, Appleton stumbled through dense fog, blood and pulp draining from the ruined mess within his eye sockets, crying out for Rhoads to help him.

"You want me to spy on Scarlett?" she asked.

Rhoads cleared his throat, visibly uncomfortable, and nodded. "Given this recent incident," he said, and trailed off. He straightened the picture again. "I never saw it coming. I made a similar error once before, and I'll regret it for the rest of my life. I can't afford to let something similar happen again. I'm hoping you can take a look. I need to know if I can trust her."

"I'll try," she said.

His relief was obvious and pitiful. "Thank you."

"But if I end up at The Farm . . ."

Rhoads laughed nervously, shaking his head. "Don't even joke like that."

She raised one brow. "I wasn't joking. I'm willing to help, but this is a risky mission. If something . . . goes wrong . . . I hope that you'll . . . give me a second chance. You wouldn't—"

He waved her off. "Dalia, you know that I will protect you."

Like you protected Appleton? From time to time, she visited the dreams of Appleton, who had been one of only two other somnopaths ever to attend The Point. Observing his dreams now was like walking on the dark side of the moon, everything dark and dusty, airless and lifeless, a bleak and cratered wasteland. She'd burrowed beneath that stark moonscape, drilling for the hidden subconscious, but all she'd found was a dry riverbed devoid even of fossilized memories. Appleton was *gone.*

"If you're not certain—" Rhoads said.

"I'll do it," she interrupted. She stood once more and offered what she intended would look like a forced smile. A *brave* smile. "But you owe me one."

"Anything," he said, "and please do be careful."

She paused at the door, showing him the brave smile again. "I'll try to have something for you soon."

In reality, she'd been watching Scarlett's dreams for weeks, since Rhoads first had introduced them. Of course, she could never let Rhoads know that. He thought that she had a difficult time doing dream recon and worried that she would snap, as Appleton had, and end up drooling in a padded cell at The Farm.

A ridiculous concern. Truth be told, Appleton was weak.

She was strong.

Far, far stronger than Rhoads would ever guess.

Let him toss and turn tonight, worried that he'd asked too much of her.

In truth, she had moved *way* beyond simply peeping into people's dreams.

Tomorrow, she would skip her shower and set her hairpins loosely and report back to him that it had been difficult, but yes, she'd managed to open a window onto Scarlett's dreams. Then she'd give him something, a piece of the truth, probably, just enough to satisfy him yet certainly not enough to make him suspect the true power of her abilities. But yes, she would have to give him *something*. Despite Rhoads's genuine concern for her well-being, he remained a results-oriented, goal-driven man. He would, she knew, offer her up without the slightest hesitation as a living sacrifice if that would guarantee the safety of The Point.

What to tell him, though? Shadows and whispers, blurry impressions, enough to make him mull. She could guide his interpretations easily enough.

Returning to her room, she closed and locked the door, sat on the bed, and folded her legs in a lotus position. She laid her forearms atop her thighs and let her palms open toward the ceiling. Then she concentrated on her breathing and sank into her mind.

Inside, she strolled the cool stone hallway she'd created there, what she thought of as a pyramid passageway, although she knew that it had more in common with the European castles over which she had obsessed as a little girl than with the ancient architectural wonders of her father's Egyptian bloodline. Whatever. It didn't matter. She'd never seen either structure in real life. Besides, this was her place and her place alone, and she liked it like this, historical accuracy be damned.

She drifted—*drifted* was more accurate than *walked* in this internal world where she felt only half corporeal—beneath the great stone archway and into the dusty dream archives, which she'd modeled after the cozy old stacks of her hometown library, where she'd spent so much of her youth, hiding from the cruelty of other children, who could see only her dark skin and strange last name, and escaping into the much happier worlds offered by books. Here she stored the fragments of dreams she visited each night. These dream snippets lacked the length and orderly narration of the library books of her childhood, but what they lacked in completeness and clarity they more than made up for in brilliance and emotion and the draw of the puzzle that even the simplest of them offered. These were intimate glimpses of her classmates and cadre, archived alongside the fears and hopes and confessions of those she'd left behind in her hometown, Wyalusing. Also stored here were scenes clipped from the dreams of people she'd met only in passing and, increasingly, people she'd never met at all. Over the last several months, she'd taken to ranging out into the world. She'd learned to drift through the dream ether until, like a hawk spying movement in the grass, she detected a vibrant dream. Then she would swoop straight into the heart of it.

Here in the archives, she could revisit dreams. Unlike living dreams, dream snippets were as static as film clips, though you couldn't enter film clips, couldn't stand there and feel the grass of someone's dream beneath your feet, couldn't pause to study the sparkling glass in the hair of the dead men or smell the smoke or hear the crackling of the fire and the screaming of the woman and her child and Scarlett's friend Savannah or know that Scarlett and Savannah were no longer close or that Scarlett worried over this sometimes, though nowhere nearly as frequently or fiercely as she worried over her brother, Dan.

Scarlett fascinated her. Night after night, Dalia went to her dreams. Some nights, she observed. Other nights, she waited for a lull between dream sequences, dipped into the river of Scarlett's subconscious, dredged out something iconic—the burning car; her brother jabbing her; the smell of apples, which for some reason meant friendship and laughter and hope—and used the flashbacks to cast Scarlett into dreams woven principally of memory.

In this way, she had come to know Scarlett. She had watched scenes from her difficult childhood. She'd seen her ignored by her father, beaten yet loved by her brother, and smothered by her loving but pitiful mother. She'd seen the boys—so many of them—and her friends, and all the partying, and she'd known that if she and Scarlett had attended the same school, they wouldn't have been friends, though Scarlett wouldn't have teased her. Scarlett was wild and irresponsible, but she wasn't mean.

Dalia saw so much in her. So much potential but anxiety, too, and laziness and fear of failure. In Scarlett, confidence and shame were conjoined twins, sharing a single heart, and she experienced and delivered equal parts bitterness and sweetness. Sloth and ambition. Scarlett was struggling with who she had been, who she was, and who she would become. She missed her friends and her mother, partying and her motorcycle, climbing cliffs and diving off bridges and laughing. She worried that the good times were over for good. She didn't belong here and couldn't square herself with that reality. She didn't trust the power she was developing. More than anything, she wanted to heal her relationship with her brother.

Dalia could give Rhoads that much. The fight with Dan. Scarlett's desire to bury the hatchet. Dalia would mention the blowtorch, too, so Rhoads would know that she wasn't making stuff up. She was certain that Rhoads already knew about the blowtorch. After all, she'd seen it in his dreams before it had appeared in Scarlett's.

That would be enough for tomorrow. That and her general impression. *You don't have to worry about her,* she'd say, and that much was true. Scarlett posed no danger to The Point.

For now, she had unfinished business back in Wyalusing.

She vanished from the archives, casting her consciousness out and away. She left The Point and returned to her hometown, zeroing in on the dreams of Brad Turpin. She smiled, recognizing at once the blurry edges and general murkiness. He was still on sleeping pills, then. Still trying to fight her visits, still scared out of his mind.

She laughed. Well, he should have considered that a long time ago. It was too late now.

She found him stumbling numbly through some stupid dream about the factory where he now worked, having gotten the job through his father, a longtime foreman, Brad two years out of high school and already wearing a white hat. No college, no real experience, just good looks and Daddy's influence and a surprising penchant for kissing butt. It shamed her to know that she'd fallen for the tricks of such a simpering suck-up. The shame made her hate her former self even more than she already had.

Cold purpose frosted over her as she stared at Brad in his khaki pants and shirt and tie and white hat. He was getting a gut, shifting into middle age at twenty. How could she ever have given herself to him?

Because you thought he was sweet, she told herself. *And handsome. And he was nice to you, the first boy in the whole town to be nice to you.*

Feeling ashamed and furious, she changed the dream.

The factory disappeared. Gone were its steel and cement maze and caution tape and the constant droning of machinery.

Brad huffed with fear as his new environment coalesced. He recognized it, of course. He knew its smell of hay and horse manure, the creak of old wooden floorboards beneath his feet and the soft sunlight sparkling with spinning dust motes, the cooing of doves high above in the rafters, the heat of the barn. He would never, ever forget this place no matter how much he drank or what kinds of pills he took, because she would drag his dreaming mind back every night to this place, the barn where he had taken her virginity exactly one day before he'd made her the laughingstock of their high school.

No, he would never forget it. Because she would never forget it. Never forget, never forgive.

"Brad," she said, entering the dream behind him.

He jumped—and even that was a clumsy affair, given his drugged state—and turned, his handsome face white with terror. She noticed that his face was getting fat now, too. In five years, people no longer would think of him as handsome. In ten, he'd have a full set of jowls, and his hair would recede like a swamp in drought. By forty, he'd be fat and bald and unloved, and through it all she'd be here, bringing him back to this place.

"I'm sorry," Brad said, blubbering like a frightened toddler. "Dalia, I'm so, so sorry."

She was naked now. Naked and beautiful. She made herself extra beautiful. She wanted each nightly visit to be what Brad had said that he'd wanted her first time to be: *special.*

Of course, at that time, she had no idea that *special* meant recorded on a GoPro, shared with friends, and uploaded to Pornhub with the caption *Amateur Egyptian First Time Slut.*

"Look at me, Brad."

"No," he said, crying and shaking his head. "I don't want to."

She was disgusted to see the dark circle spreading across his pants. She hoped he'd wet the bed at home in Wyalusing, too.

"I'm sor-r-r-y," he sobbed, falling to his knees. "Don't . . . please . . . I can't take—"

"Too late, Brad," she said. "A friend is here to see you."

Brad fell to all fours, squeezed his eyes shut, and shook his head back and forth, crying, "No, no, no!"

She cued the laugh track—a chorus of raucous howls that she knew Brad recognized all too well. "Your friends are laughing at you, Brad. They're all watching and all laughing at you. Your father is laughing at you." And she added the laughter of his father, looping the big belly laugh Brad's father had used when Brad was six and wet his pants on the roller coaster.

"Please stop!" Brad cried.

"If you're expecting mercy from me, you're even stupider than I thought. You're going to pay for what you did every night for the rest of your life."

Heavy footsteps approached from the shadows behind him. *Boom* . . . dust popped from the rattling floorboards . . . *boom* . . .

Brad shut his eyes, muttering prayers.

Boom . . .

Behind Brad, the monster stepped into view. She was proud of her creation. She had based him on the neighbor's giant bull, which had terrified Brad as a young boy. This version of the bull, however, walked upright on its muscular hind legs, had hands instead of front hooves, and had a humanoid face, the features of which she had borrowed from Dale Groover, the hulking and sadistic dimwit who had terrorized Brad in his freshman year. Groover used to wait outside the showers for Brad, then snap his wet, naked body with a towel twisted up into a whip. The towel would crack; Brad would shriek, hating the sound of his own voice; and long welts would raise along his back and butt and belly.

"Look, Brad," she said.

He shook his head, whimpering.

"Look!"

Brad turned and saw. She made his screams high and girlish and filled him with the old locker room self-loathing and all the fear of the bull and the bully and drowned out his cries with the laughter of his friends and father.

Brad's clothes disappeared. He yelped and did his best to cover himself. She added beads of highly chlorinated water to his body and the soft sound of showers running not far away. He whimpered.

The bull-thing snorted, advancing slowly.

Brad's screams knifed the steamy air, but his legs wouldn't move. He was locked in place.

"You never should have messed with me, Brad," she said.

Brad tried to apologize again, but his weakness disgusted her so much that she rushed the narrative, and a gruesome towel, twisted and knotted and clotted with blood, manifested in the knobby hand of the bull-thing. The towel slashed the air, cracked like a bullwhip, and sliced Brad's hip to the bone. The bull-thing drew back its muscular arm for another swing. Brad blubbered, begging for mercy. When the whip cracked again, splitting his butt cheek and painting his naked leg in blood, Brad screamed in terror and pain and desperation, but the sound was lost beneath the crazed laughter of his buddies and the father whose love he'd always chased and never earned.

Much later, when it was all over and the boy who had wronged her was reduced to a quivering mess of meat and fat hanging ragged on bloody bones, Dalia whisked Brad away from the pain and terror and deposited him, as she did every night after his punishment, in a comfortable chair in the bright kitchen of his grandmother. From watching his dreams and dredging his subconscious, she knew how much he missed his grandmother and the meals she had made him, the sprawling Sunday dinners and her cookies—sugar and molasses, freshly baked and waiting for him in the green glass cookie jar on the counter whenever he visited, which was frequently, especially when things were hard at home, when his dad was drinking and running around on his mom and Brad couldn't concentrate on his schoolwork or focus at football practice. Whatever was wrong, Grandma was always there for him, always with a warm hug, the woman as soft and comforting as a pillow. Dalia was always careful to replicate the smell of the old woman's cheap perfume, a scent as sweetly cloying as her grandmotherly voice, telling him to sit down and have a cookie . . . *freshly baked sugar today* and *here, Bradley, have a cold glass of milk.*

Food is comfort, Dalia whispered in his grandmother's voice each night as Brad fluttered down, shredded, from the heights of terror. With every bite that Brad took, Dalia reduced his pain and horror. *Food will make you feel better*, she cooed in the old woman's voice. *I love you, I love you, I love you . . .*

TWENTY-SIX

"YOU REALLY DODGED A BULLET, HAN BRO-LO," Lucy said when Scarlett explained Rhoads's ruling. "Stay out of trouble for a while, okay? No more midnight walks. You so much as sneeze in class, they'll crucify you."

Scarlett nodded. All things considered, she felt pretty lucky.

Not that she would enjoy missing lunch or spending two hours of marching back and forth in the gym, but she'd expected far worse punishment. Rereading the discipline code, she was surprised that they hadn't charged her with a major offense—or even two major offenses, splitting the assault and interference charges—and sent her to the Chamber.

The next day, Dalia gave her a knowing smile. "I told you not to worry. Didn't I say I'd take care of you?"

Scarlett thanked her. Had Dalia really gone to Rhoads on her behalf? She didn't know and wasn't about to ask. After skipping lunch and spending two long and incredibly boring hours marching back and forth, Scarlett wasn't in the mood for games. Nor was she in the mood for the lecture that Dalia and Dunne gave her about Seamus.

"Keep your distance," Dalia said. "Bad things happen to people who hang around Seamus."

A grin spread across Dunne's broad face. "I reckon Scarlett probably might've figured that out."

Well, Scarlett thought, *it'll be easy enough to avoid Seamus.* He probably hated her now.

NO, SCARLETT THOUGHT. *No, no, no . . .*

She was dreaming again, but it was all so real, so accurate, like traveling back in time.

She didn't want to be here, just as she hadn't wanted to be here last May, with Dan swaggering toward her, red-faced.

No. Not this again.

Though she understood that she was dreaming, she remained powerless, doomed to relive the past. It was like being a passenger in a car accident, hearing the squeal of tires, seeing the onrushing truck, everything slowing as impact approached . . . yet having no chance to do anything to change the outcome.

Dan jabbed a finger into her shoulder.

It's a dream, she told herself, but this detached narration did little to quell the burgeoning terror within her because she could feel the pressure building all over again, just as it had built that horrible day in the backyard.

Her own mouth spoke without her consent, saying, "Stop. Pushing. Dan."

But he kept pushing, and the dream dragged her back through that horrible afternoon, everything escalating until the force inside her exploded, and she pushed back, and Dan flew through the air and crashed into the ground, and the window rattled up behind them—Scarlett's brain screaming, *No-no-no-no!*—and Mom cried, "Are you trying to kill me?"

She sprinted away, pounded through the side gate, hopped onto the Yamaha, and sped into the street, where a horn blared, and she narrowly dodged an onrushing car and wound through a pine-dark bend in the dirt road, Sav's arms tight around her. Scarlett's terror ramped up as she downshifted the motorcycle and the forest whipped away behind them, and the world was suddenly noonday bright. She lifted an arm to shield her eyes and pulled into the field where the car burned and dead men with sparkling hair lay near an overturned pickup with the horn jammed, blaring . . . yet she could still hear the woman's voice crying out, "Save my baby!"

Again and again, all the way through the flames and the woman's hideous smile as she burned alive, smiling to see her child pulled to safety, Scarlett having somehow managed to wrench the door from the smashed car, to pull the metal free, snapping its hinges, and toss it like an empty cardboard box across the field and into the darkness.

She carried the child away from the flames and out the guest house door, where its cries became insistent commands—"On the ground!" and she tried to tell them to back away, and the explosion was in her, swelling again, and she knew it was a dream, yet there was nothing she could do about it, and for the fiftieth or hundredth or thousandth time—it was impossible to say, her nights being so fraught with these repetitive nightmares—the explosion boomed out of her . . .

And then, suddenly, it was over, and she felt good—scratch that, *great*—the sun warm on her bare skin as she moved against Nick, who was naked and delicious beneath her. His big hands encircled her waist as she rode him, the two of them moving in perfect harmony, not too fast, not too slow, not too hard, not too soft, a rhythmic pleasure machine made of flesh, both of them a little high and incredibly happy, and in another flash of detached semilucidity she realized that this was it, the apex of life, the definition of true happiness, both of them digging it, digging each other, and she was free, free, free—

A gasp behind her ruined everything. She covered herself and turned. "Dalia?"

Dalia stood there, staring not at Scarlett or Nick but off in the other direction, toward the tree line.

And then Scarlett's consciousness whipped away.

She woke to darkness, in her room at The Point, fighting for breath, heat throbbing in her.

What the hell?

TWENTY-SEVEN

DALIA WAS HAVING THE SAME THOUGHT.

Still in the dream, she shielded her eyes to better see the Watcher at the edge of the forest. It was a young woman with long hair as dark and shining as obsidian. From that distance, Dalia couldn't make out the features on the woman's pale, heart-shaped face, but the sense of beauty sighed over her like a warm breeze.

The woman raised a hand, beckoning, and began to fade back into the trees.

Dalia stood, took one step in that direction, and froze, the intuitive wind shifting, chilling her with a concern as faceless as the distant woman, who looked now like a fading ghost as her pale skin receded into the forest.

What's going on here?

Scarlett hadn't dreamed this—*and I'm certainly not dreaming.*

Scarlett was gone, yet Dalia lingered here, as if touring an archived dream . . . only this place, these events, they were still active. She remained in control of her own actions, but this other woman, the Watcher, was still here, too, even if she'd vanished into the trees.

What to do?

Common sense told her to fly back to The Point. This was strange, perhaps dangerous—*so get out*—yet she hesitated, because this was by far the most interesting thing that had happened to her since she'd learned to dream walk. Who was this woman? What did she want? How had she found Dalia? And where were they now, if not in Scarlett's dream?

Too many questions.

Yet she wanted to know. *Needed* to know.

Of course, she would never admit this to Rhoads, but she got lonely at times. Very lonely. And it hit her there in that strange dream space that she had always been lonely. Back in Wyalusing, she'd skulked at the edges of society like a scapegoat wolf. At The Point, she was the alpha female, but even if she now ate first, at the head of the pack, she still ate alone.

Could this woman be another dream walker, a kindred spirit . . . a friend?

Realizing she'd been walking toward the tree line, she stopped.

A friend? she thought, disgusted by her own neediness. *You're still pining for friends?*

No. She rejected this weakness wholesale. It was the same attitude that had led her to such intense misery back in her hometown.

She was powerful now. She wouldn't whimper for friends like some abandoned puppy.

Besides, none of this made sense. The woman, the continuation of the dream, the steps she'd taken without quite knowing it.

Another cold breeze passed over her.

Was she in danger? Was Scarlett in danger? Had Dalia somehow opened a gate onto Scarlett's dream space and allowed someone else to enter? By staying here, was she further endangering Scarlett?

With that thought, she pulled back. The sunny summer scene whipped away, and she returned to the shadowy confines of her dimly lit room.

So strange. So very strange.

She sat up, remembering the woman. Here, in the world of flesh and bone, Dalia felt more alert and more aware. Something tickled up her spine like a spider, making her shudder.

Fear. That was what had whispered up her back, a thing she'd thought she'd done away with . . . fear.

She shook her head.

Nothing to fear, she told herself. *You're in control. Only you.*

With that thought, she glanced to her nightstand and the item she'd printed from *The Daily Review* before going to sleep. The service would be Saturday morning at the Bolan Funeral Home in Towanda, followed by a noontime internment at Oak Hill Cemetery.

The funeral notice didn't say if the Turpin family would have an open casket for Brad. She supposed it depended on how he'd done it.

But of course, a newspaper wouldn't spell out suicide, let alone the method.

She'd gone off to play with Brad this evening and had come up empty, not even tapping into the static subconscious of a wakeful mind. There was nothing. After pulling back, she'd hopped online. Something was wrong . . .

What a shame. She'd expected to punish him for years, and she'd been really interested to see if she could make Brad eat himself to death. He'd cheated her of that pleasure.

A part of her wanted to go back in now to range the dream lands, looking for the Watcher, but she decided against it. It was time for sleep now. Real sleep, deep and dreamless.

She fed the funeral notice slowly into the paper shredder and stretched out on her thousand-count Egyptian cotton sheets.

Even the Queen Bitch needed her beauty rest.

TWENTY-EIGHT

"WE'RE SO PROUD OF YOU, SWEETIE," SCARLETT'S mother said, her eyes shining like the Christmas lights adorning this wing of the West Point dining hall. "Aren't we, Charles?"

Scarlett's father grunted, chewing, and wiped his mouth with a napkin. "This food isn't half bad for mess hall grub," he said. "Lot better than the slop they fed us in basic." He turned and shared the same opinion with Perich's father, who sat at the other end of the table. "White Christmas" crooned from the mess hall speakers.

It had been a surprise when the Operation Signal Boost parents arrived at the big holiday dinner laughing and hugging like old friends, which in many cases appeared to be the case. Every cadet in Operation Signal Boost had a parent who'd served alongside Scarlett's father in Operation Desert Storm. An excruciatingly awkward moment ensued when her father had recognized his "old buddy" and dragged her over, both sets of parents rejoicing and grilling their kids with questions. Did they know each other? Why—*wink, wink, nudge, nudge*—were they blushing? The two of them weren't . . . dating . . . were they?

"No," the cadets had answered in unison.

Awkward, indeed, but she had to give it to Hopkins. The way he acted, no one would guess how much he hated her or that she'd wiped the Chamber floor with him and his buddies. Since returning from the infirmary, Hopkins had ridden her twice as hard at meal-times and with every stupid regulation in the book, but he hadn't laid a finger—made of either flesh or telekinetic force—on her since she'd fought back.

Luckily, the Hopkins family had been on the other side of the cafeteria when Colonel Rhoads had invited everyone to sit down.

The rest of the campus was empty, the cadets on exodus for Christmas and the holidays. Today, the grand dining hall belonged solely to The Point.

Scarlett's mother reached across the table and squeezed her fore-arm. "Cadets need quality nutrition."

Scarlett put her hand on top of her mother's. She missed her.

Her father seemed smaller somehow. Diminished. Maybe he'd lost weight. Or maybe it was context, the man not looming quite so large in this vast dining hall.

Or maybe this is his real size and you couldn't see that until you'd escaped from his house.

Whatever the case, she was glad to see them. Mom looked happy and well rested. She'd earned a promotion at the university, and she'd been taking yoga classes three nights a week.

She considered telling her that she'd been taking yoga, too, but decided against it, wanting to avoid questions. *My instructor? Oh, she's great. Unless you make her angry. Then she'll wrap you in a living blanket of spiders.*

Scarlett couldn't see Dalia from where she sat, but she could certainly *hear* her. Dalia was talking loudly to her parents—an older, timid-looking couple—and shouting laughter that had everyone in the hall casting glances. Rhoads, who'd been going from table to table and glad-handing like a politician, smiled uncomfortably after one particularly loud squawk.

Dalia had been acting really weird lately, sometimes showing up for yoga, sometimes not. She looked uncharacteristically disheveled and had dark circles under her eyes. She'd shifted into a kind of manic state, talking even more than usual and so erratically that she was often hard to follow. Of course, Scarlett's boredom and distraction probably hadn't helped. It was hard to sit through the same half dozen story types again and again: how Dalia had shocked Rhoads that day, how she'd humiliated some guard, how so-and-so was expecting her to do one thing but—here she'd pause and give Scarlett the sideways grin—he or she was in for a "little surprise."

Dalia been moody, too, and anything less than total attention annoyed her. Scarlett didn't mean to piss her off, but honestly, it was getting harder to care. She was stressed out, battered by life, and worn out by sleep deprivation and her crazy dreams, which amounted to so many nightmare recollections, dragging her through the worst of her memories. She was a captive participant. She went through the motions, saying and doing and experiencing things as if her body had been enslaved while her semilucid thoughts remained, taking it all in and trying to analyze things with absolutely no power to change what was happening. If she couldn't escape the crazy dreams, she wished she could at least be dreaming about Seamus.

She could see him over her father's shoulder, toward the back of the room. Seamus ate alone, no friends, no family. As she watched, he leaned back from his food, interlaced his fingers behind his head, and stared up at the gigantic mural that covered the back wall.

If Seamus's family didn't show, maybe Scarlett could talk with him so that he wouldn't have to be alone. The Point wouldn't let the cadets go home for the holidays, but they would have an unusual amount of free time for the next week and a half. She could ask him to play chess or walk around campus, show him some of the cool stuff she'd discovered while roaming at night.

Yeah, right . . . after what you did? He hates you, girl.

"I wish Dan could have made it," Mom said. "Wouldn't that have been nice? The whole family together for Christmas dinner?"

"No soldier can count on Christmas dinner, let alone with his family," her father said.

"How is Dan?" Scarlett asked, trying and failing to sound natural. He still hadn't replied to her letters.

Mom smiled wistfully. "He's his father's son. Always coming and going, taking on this and that. I hope he isn't taking on too much."

"Working his way up the ranks," her father said. "He has no say in the matter."

"My," Mom said, leaning forward, "that girl sure laughs loudly."

Scarlett half turned. Dalia flapped her arms up and down like a bird and let out another squawk of loud laughter. What was going on with her?

Dalia's parents smiled awkwardly, looking like they might bolt for the door.

"Of course, Dan will be even busier now with the wedding."

Scarlett tilted her head. "What wedding?"

Mom looked confused. "You didn't know? Your brother is engaged."

"Engaged? Dan? Are you serious?"

She nodded, her smile fading a little. "He didn't tell you?"

"No," Scarlett said. "He didn't." What should have been happy news hit her like a punch in the gut. All those letters she'd written, and Dan couldn't even bother to tell her that he was getting married? "I didn't even know he had a girlfriend."

"Well, he does. A fiancée," Mom said. "Daisy. She's very nice. I mean, we were surprised that they decided to get married so quickly, but she's really very nice. Isn't she, Charles?"

"Men aren't like women," her father said, mopping up the last of his gravy with half a roll. "We don't need to tell each other everything. Dan will get around to it when he gets around to it. You going to eat that cranberry sauce or what?"

A beaming Rhoads appeared and launched into a long spiel about how hard Scarlett was working and how she'd impressed everyone here at The Point. He didn't mention the trouble that she'd been in or the poor grades she'd earned in math and physics. To hear Rhoads, you'd think Scarlett was the finest cadet at West Point, a modern-day Douglas MacArthur.

As Fuller assembled the families for a group tour of the grounds, Rhoads offered the Winters a personal tour. Scarlett squirmed, hoping her classmates wouldn't notice, and squirmed again when she saw Seamus watching with icy eyes as Rhoads led them away.

Light snow fell from slate skies, padding the mantle of white covering the campus. As they walked, Rhoads identified dark granite buildings and spouted West Point trivia. Through it all, he continued to praise Scarlett, whose mother's eyes were shining an hour later, when Rhoads led them to their car and bade them good-bye, embracing Scarlett's parents and thanking them again for the daughter they'd sent him.

Mom opened the car door and pulled a box from the backseat and handed it to Scarlett. "It's a care package," she said. "Stuff you like. Cookies, things like that."

Scarlett hefted the box. Good smells wafted out. "Thanks, Mom."

"You'd better eat them before someone confiscates them," she said.

"Eat them before your battle buddies scarf them down is more like it," her father said with a rare smile. He'd grown quiet during the walk but didn't seem angry. "I don't think I ate more than three cookies during basic, and my mother sent a fresh batch weekly." He laughed, shaking his head, his eyes a thousand miles away.

Scarlett didn't have the heart to tell him that she didn't train with a platoon and barely knew her fellow plebes. It was just her. And Dalia, sort of.

"Well," her father said, reaching into the car and coming out with a small box wrapped in red paper. "They can't eat this, anyway." He handed it to Scarlett. "Merry Christmas."

She turned the gift in her hands, taking in the terrible wrap job.

Too much paper, too much tape. Mom would never wrap something so sloppily. She blinked. Her father had wrapped it. For the first time in her life, her father was giving her a present.

She looked up, and there was something wrong with her father's face. His mouth was slightly ajar, and his eyes looked almost nervous. He reached awkwardly toward her, but his hand paused in the gap between them, as if he couldn't decide whether to pat Scarlett's arm or maybe snatch the present out of her hands.

She glanced at her mother for a clue. Mom was crying and smiling, looking back and forth between them, her gaze lingering on her father with something like pride.

"Well," Mom said, wiping at her eyes, "open it, Scarlett."

What's going on here? Suddenly her face felt hot.

Her father ended the moment. "She can open it back in the barracks," he said. "It's nothing big. Just a little something I thought you might like. If not, you can toss it." He looked at Scarlett strangely again, offered a wriggling smile, and started to walk around the car.

Mom started to protest, clearly disappointed, and Scarlett said it was fine, she'd open it now, but her father shook his head and said they had to get on the road before the storm got any worse. "Merry Christmas, Scarlett," he said. "Keep your powder dry."

"Merry Christmas, Dad," Scarlett said, but her voice came out funny, having a hard time working its way around the lump in her throat. *Keep your powder dry*. Dad always said that to Dan, never to Scarlett.

Her father slipped in behind the wheel and slammed the door. Mom took the care package from Scarlett and set it on the car so she could give her a hug. Mom kissed her cheek and wished her a Merry Christmas and told her that she loved her, and Scarlett said the same things to her and stood at the curb with the cookies and the mysterious, poorly wrapped gift and watched her parents pull away, heading toward the gate and home. And then they were gone.

She stood there for a moment, alone, the world suddenly silent beneath its muffling layer of snow, quiet enough that she could hear the tiny flakes *tap-tap-tap*-ing against the wrapping paper of the little red present. She turned it in her hand. Part of her wanted to open it now, hoping to shed light on her father's strange behavior, but she felt a little odd, reverent or afraid or maybe a little of both, so she tucked the mysterious present into her coat pocket and shifted the care package under one arm and started for the barracks, hoping Mom had packed brownies and banana bread, too. Maybe she could catch Lucy before formation. Lucy would love the cookies. Maybe they'd even throw a little meat on her skinny frame.

These were her happy thoughts as she looped back past Trophy Point, but she and her thoughts lurched to an abrupt halt when she spotted a familiar figure striding away through the strengthening snow, heading toward the edge of campus and Flirtation Walk.

Though he was a fair distance away and dressed like any cadet, she recognized the solitary figure instantly by his trim, muscular build and fast-paced gait.

Seamus.

TWENTY-NINE

HIS WERE THE ONLY TRACKS IN THE NEWLY FALLEN snow. They were spread far apart, Seamus walking at his characteristic clip, fast with long strides.

She hurried after him.

He had disappeared onto Flirtie, the rocky footpath overlooking the Hudson, where cadets came to escape from prying eyes and honor code violations.

She followed the tracks around one corner, then another, heart pounding. What would she even say if she caught up with him?

Hey, I know I caused you hours of pain and terror, but . . .

She wound around another corner, and an invisible truck slammed into her. She stumbled backward, more from surprise than from the invisible force, some of which entered her and spun at her center. The wall pushed slowly forward, inching her off the trail, and pinned her back against raw stone.

Seamus stepped from the bushes, his face twisted with anger. "Why are you following me, Winter?"

"I—" she stammered, her brain freezing. "I wanted to talk to you."

"Why would a big shot like you want to talk to someone like me?"

"I'm not a big shot."

He made a face. "Yeah, right. I see you, strolling with Rhoads. You guys are all buddy-buddy, like him and the Queen Bitch."

He meant Dalia, she knew. That was what the cadets called her behind her back. Dalia knew it, liked the name, and perpetuated it.

"Well?" Seamus asked. "What did you want to talk about?"

She'd planned to apologize, but suddenly she didn't want to mention the Chamber at all. Her mind scrambled. "I saw you in the dining hall."

"So?"

"You were all alone."

"And?"

"It's Christmas."

He rolled his eyes. "Spare me."

"But your family."

"They're dead," he said. "No one told you? Seamus the orphan, Seamus the unloved."

"No," she said. "I'm sorry."

"Being a rock star isn't enough? You have to be the rock star with a heart? Well, save it. I don't want your pity."

"It wasn't like that. I've been trying to talk to you since forever."

He looked at her for a second without saying anything. "I'm not interested. Okay? Just because you're a rock star doesn't mean everybody wants to be your groupie."

"Drop the rock star crap, okay?" she said. "You don't even know me. If people back home could see me now . . ."

"Let me guess," he said. "You were the prom queen bound for Harvard, right?"

She laughed. "I was in juvie during prom. I barely graduated."

Back on campus, the clock chimed. Thirty minutes until formation at The Point.

"Too cool for school, huh?" The invisible wall evaporated. He started to walk away.

"I just never got my act together," she said, falling in beside him.

"That's why I laughed. I mean, *nobody* thought of me as a rock star. Well, my mom, maybe."

"And your dad?"

She laughed again, not bothering to hide the bitterness. "I was an embarrassment to him. He's all Army, all the time. Said I had to enlist. I said no way . . . then Rhoads showed up."

He slowed his pace. "What's in the box?"

She looked down. One corner was dented from the wall of force. "Cookies."

"What kind?"

"I don't know yet," she said, and stopped walking. "Let's find out."

He watched her open the box. The sweet smell of baked goods wafted out. Her face went hot, seeing the sheet of paper sitting on top:

> *Merry Christmas, Scarlett! Here are some sweets for the sweetest young lady I know! I love you! XXXOOOXXXOOO, Mom.*

Laughing awkwardly, she snatched away the paper and stuffed it into a pocket.

Seamus laughed. "Mama's girl, huh?"

She shrugged, perusing the treasure. "Chocolate chip. Snickerdoodles. Molasses."

"Yuck."

She grinned up at him. "Don't knock 'em till you try 'em. And—oh, yes . . . *brownies*." She opened the bag, breathed in the good smell, and offered them to Seamus. "Want one?"

He looked thoughtful. "I'd rather have a chocolate chip."

She shook the bag. "Try these first."

He bit into a chocolaty square and closed his eyes. "Mmm . . ."

She bit into one, too, and they stood there, groaning with appreciation, until a cold wind blew off the Hudson, forcing them both to pin their hats to their heads with their hands.

"Why don't you use telekinesis to hold your hat?"

Seamus had a great smile. "Sometimes it's easier to do it the old-fashioned way. Besides, my brain's busy right now, grooving on these cookies."

They strolled along, sampling the chocolate chip cookies next.

He liked them even better than the brownies. "My mom used to make cookies."

"You miss her?" she asked. "Sorry—dumb question."

"Let me have another chocolate chip and I'll pretend you didn't ask."

She opened the flap. His hand slipped inside. "I do," he said. "I miss her a lot."

"And your dad?"

He shrugged. "Not so much." He looked out at the river.

They rounded the corner, and there was the end of the path and campus beyond. "I hate it here," he said. "Deeply."

"Yeah," she said. "It sucks."

He snorted in disdain. "You have it made, Miss Level III. I'm trapped. I never would have come, but it was this or prison."

She nodded. "Me, too. By the time I got out, I would've been ancient. Like thirty or thirty-five."

"They *never* would have let me out," he said, looking across the campus, toward Constitution Island, which was nearly obscured now by falling snow. "Not ever."

The clock tower chimed again, and the color drained from his face. "Oh, no . . . we're late."

THIRTY

THEY BUZZED THROUGH THE BLAST DOORS, OUT OF breath from their mad sprint back to The Point. They cleared the first checkpoint, stepped into the lobby, and for a second Scarlett thought that they'd made it.

Then the guards blocked their way, smirking.

There were three of them, including the guard with the chipped tooth and unibrow. The man had been almost timid since Dalia had tortured him with dream spiders, but punishment never cures bullies. Sooner or later, the mean boils up in them again. And Unibrow led the charge, grabbing Seamus by the arm and snarling, "Late again, Kyeong, and this time, you're all out of warnings."

"Get off me," Seamus said, trying to shake his arm free, but another guard grabbed him from behind and twisted his arm behind his back.

Seamus shouted in pain and went to his tiptoes. "All right, all right."

The third guard stepped toward Scarlett, seemed to recognize her, and hesitated.

Unibrow leered, grinning much as Dalia had the day she'd tortured him. "Chamber time, Kyeong."

Being tortured hadn't taught this guy empathy or even sympathy, she realized. It had only made him want to torture somebody else. You couldn't reason or plead with a savage like this. He understood only one language: brutality.

She stepped past the hesitant guard.

Unibrow narrowed his eyes, and in that moment she *saw* him recognize her. He tensed, licking his lips, but didn't release Seamus. "This doesn't concern you," he told her.

"Let him go," she said.

"Scarlett, don't," Seamus said. "You'll just get into trouble, too."

She ignored him and drilled Unibrow with death eyes. She was shaking with anger now. "Let him go now or I'll make you suffer so bad, you'll *wish* you were covered in spiders."

Unibrow cleared his throat and let go of Seamus and stepped away. He mumbled to the other guard, who did the same.

She glared at the three guards, one after the other, until each had dropped his eyes. Then she stomped her boots on the tile floor, knocking loose snow and ice. "Clean that up," she said. Then she took Seamus by the arm and led him away, shaking with adrenaline and feeling half sick at how easily she'd gone Queen Bitch on the guy.

Then she looked ahead, and—speak of the Devil—saw none other than Dalia watching from the entrance to the main corridor.

Before Scarlett could so much as wave, Dalia turned and disappeared.

"Geez," Seamus said, "remind me not to piss you off, okay? What happened back there?"

"Nothing," she said, suddenly filled with dread. Not at the guards—they were nothing more than stinging insects—but at the look she'd seen on Dalia's face.

The flashing eyes and snarl meant that Scarlett had somehow just fucked with the Queen Bitch.

LATER, ALONE IN her room, Scarlett pulled her father's mysterious gift from her pocket. She'd forgotten all about it, swept along by her day, bumping into Seamus, clashing with the guards, worrying over Dalia's strange anger, and then joining formation late. She'd explained to Colonel Rhoads that they'd been held up by the guards, and he'd miraculously let them off without punishment, though he did look back and forth from Scarlett to Seamus and raised a brow, looking thoughtful . . . and displeased.

It sucked, having to spend Christmas break at The Point, but at least she and the other cadets of Operation Signal Boost would have a ton of free time. For the next week and a half, things would loosen up. They'd be allowed to goof around, play games, walk around campus, and sleep in a little. Accompanied by a firstie, they could even go off base as long as they signed out, stuck together, and adhered to all the rules and regulations.

She sat on her bunk, leaned back against the wall, and turned the awkwardly wrapped little present in her hands. Black marker read *To Scarlett . . . Dad.* There was another word before "Dad," but melting snow and time in her pocket had smeared the ink. She couldn't tell whether the missing word said "love" or "from."

The box was heavy for its size. She gave it a shake. Something knocked around in there.

Hmm. She had no idea.

Hearing voices in the hall, she tore away the paper, revealing a tan box with a picture of a portable cell phone charger on the front. Go figure. The first gift he ever gives her is a charger to a phone she won't be allowed to use for the next six months.

She lifted the lid.

On top was a shred of yellow paper that read, For luck. Dad.

The box held a gold-plated watch. A man's watch, used and sort of old-timey, with one of those elasticized metallic bands that made gaps between the metal segments when you stretched them, like the one her father used to wear.

And then she understood. This didn't just *look* like her father's old watch. It *was* his old watch.

Why would he . . . ?

She lifted the watch from the box and examined it. She hadn't seen the thing for a long time. Her father had worn the watch for only a few years, back when things were at their worst, and he was like a bear that sometimes shouted and sometimes brooded and sometimes went upside her brother's head with a meaty palm, often without even the slightest provocation. She remembered sitting at the dinner table, afraid to meet his eyes and staring at the watch instead, distracted by the way his dark arm hair sprouted here and there between the band's golden segments.

An inscription on the back of the watch read, WITH THANKS TO CORPORAL CHARLES WINTER, WHO DESERVES A HELL OF A LOT MORE THAN A WATCH.

Huh?

Then the door banged open, and Lucy's voice chimed, "Honey, I'm home."

Scarlett stuffed the strange gift back into its box, shoved the box into her pocket, and scooped her mom's care package from the cot. Standing, she said, "Who's the best roomie in the world?"

Lucy grinned, and the eyes behind the spectacles brightened with that crazy light. "That depends. What's in the box?"

Scarlett lifted the lid.

"*Gott in Himmel!*" Lucy said. Her jaw dropped . . . and a snickerdoodle lifted from the box and floated to her open mouth.

Later, as they were resetting the chess board, both of them half sick on sugar, Lucy snapped her fingers and smiled. "Your mom's cookies hijacked my brain, so I forgot to tell you, sis. Cramer said we can tag along."

Scarlett didn't know what Lucy was talking about but liked the way she was smiling. "Tag along where?"

"Say *vaya con di-bros* to The Point," Lucy said. "We're heading off base for a little R&R!"

THIRTY-ONE

SCARLETT GRINNED AS LUCY APPROACHED THE TABLE. Carrying two large pitchers of beer in one hand and five frosted mugs in the other, Lucy looked like the world's skinniest Oktoberfest girl, only instead of a low-cut top, she wore a heavy wool sweater. Scarlett wore a black West Point hoodie, jeans, and work boots. Being off base and wearing civvies, no one eyeballing them or telling them what to do, was *awesome*.

Cramer, a firstie healer, had driven. Her car was small. Vernon, a meathead plebe, had looked utterly ridiculous crammed into the front passenger seat. Scarlett had squeezed into the backseat, sandwiched between Lucy and Seamus, who seemed just as surprised to see her as she was to see him.

The roads were snowy but passable. Instead of heading to Highland Falls, with all its bars and restaurants, they had driven to Fort Montgomery, happily sacrificing dining options for an increased likelihood of privacy. Nothing would ruin a night out more quickly than Hopkins showing up and spouting regulations.

The lot of Barnburners BBQ had been almost empty, but a neon pig had glowed orange in the steamy window, a good omen if ever there was one, and now they had the place practically to themselves.

Lucy's submariner boyfriend, Malcolm, who'd driven all the way from Connecticut, stood and asked if Lucy was sure that she didn't need a hand.

"No thanks, Jacques Coust-bro," Lucy said, and set the pitchers and mugs on the green-and-white checkered tablecloth without spilling a single drop.

Telekinesis, Scarlett realized with a grin.

Technically, they weren't supposed to use their special powers outside The Point. Scarlett was happy to see her generally rule-abiding roomie loosening up a little bit. Lucy slid in next to Malcolm, who put his arm around her waist. The two of them seemed very happy together, very natural.

"That's what I'm talking about," Seamus said, smiling at the beer.

"Oh, no, you don't," Cramer said with a smile. Scarlett didn't really know her, but she seemed cool. "Underage drinking is a serious honor code violation."

Seamus laughed. "Speaking of honor code violations, *ma'am*," he said, pointing to where Vernon's big arm was draped over Cramer's shoulders, "what are your feelings about The Point's zero-tolerance policy on upperclassmen dating plebes?"

"We're not dating," Cramer said. "I'm just healing his arm. It gets so tired lifting all those heavy things."

Vernon, who'd been smiling like a 300-pound infant with a new rattle, turned toward Cramer, confusion dawning on his face. "My arms don't get tired."

Cramer pinched his cheek. "Cute and dumb, just how I like 'em."

Vernon beamed. "She said I'm cute."

Scarlett laughed. Playing dumb was a thing with the meatheads. *Not a bad plan*, she thought. *Do your job, play stupid, and keep expectations low. Not a bad plan at all.*

"Here you go, Eleanor Bro-sevelt," Lucy said, sliding a mug toward Scarlett.

"Thanks," Scarlett said. The cold mug felt good in her hand despite the cold night outside, and the smell of beer filled her with crackling anticipation. She hadn't had a sip of alcohol in months.

"A toast," Lucy said, raising her mug.

They all lifted their beers.

"*Zu Freundschaft und Bier*," she said.

"I'll drink to that," Malcolm said.

"I'll drink to anything," Scarlett said, and gulped down half her beer in a pull. It was pale and cheap, cold and bitter . . . the best thing she'd ever tasted.

"Go easy," Cramer said, "and beware the freed plebe curse."

Scarlett grinned across the table and took another drink. If there was one thing she could do, it was party.

"After all this clean living, you won't handle alcohol the way you did in high school," Cramer explained.

"Thanks for the warning," Scarlett said, and finished the mug.

They drank and talked and laughed. Vernon turned out to be a funny storyteller. When he told the story of crashing a golf cart, even Seamus laughed so hard that tears rolled from his bright blue eyes. They ordered cheese fries, a colossal nacho plate with meat and cheese and guac piled on top, two dozen "nuclear" chicken wings, and another round of pitchers. Vernon also ordered a cheesesteak and a loaded pizza, explaining that he was "a little hungry."

At one point, Lucy leaned across Malcolm and nudged Scarlett. "It's good to see you smiling, sis."

Scarlett realized that she'd been grinning nonstop since sitting down. It was awesome to be off base, hanging out like real people, laughing and telling stories and busting on one another. "Thanks for inviting me."

"Right on," Lucy said, and clinked her mug against Scarlett's.

The group's optimism surprised her. She'd known that Lucy was an optimist, but Cramer and Vernon felt lucky and thankful and hopeful, too. Cramer couldn't wait to graduate this spring. "I'm looking forward to doing something real," she said, holding up her hands. "This gift, I want to do something with it, you know? I want to save lives."

"Must be nice," Seamus said, examining his own hands. "I wish I was a healer."

Lucy poked him. "No complaining, bro," she said. "The rest of us TKs would kill to have your natural talent."

"That's exactly what I don't want," Seamus said, suddenly serious, "to *kill*."

"Very few soldiers *want* to kill," Malcolm said, "but we accept that we might have to kill."

"I won't be Rhoads's weapon," Seamus said.

"Why attend The Point at all, then?" Malcolm asked.

"I got into some trouble," Seamus said. "The Point made it go away. Now I'm just trying to get an education."

Cramer and Lucy busted on Seamus then. Apparently, he was all business in the classroom, the hyperfocused Dr. Jekyll to the rebellious Mr. Hyde that Scarlett had witnessed.

Seamus shrugged. "I'm not going to cut off my nose to spite my face. Laugh all you want. I was a good student in high school. But I wouldn't even be able to attend community college on my own. We walk out of here with basically an Ivy League education."

"How about you, Scarlett?" Cramer asked. "How do you like The Point?"

Scarlett had finished another beer. She was just beginning to feel the alcohol, a slight buzz coming back to her like an old friend who'd been gone for far too long. She reached for the pitcher. "Things have been better lately, but I hated it for a long time. Everybody else was pairing off in ability groups, but I was alone. Training sucked."

Vernon laughed. "You think it sucked for you?" He told everyone about the time he and half a dozen meatheads had geared up in padded suits and reported to Room 17. He made the story funny, all these big guys waddling down the hall and everybody confused at the order to pummel this skinny little girl, and then how she'd tossed them across the room like so many bowling pins.

Lucy shared some of the strange aftermaths she'd witnessed. Limping meatheads. A charred Lopez champing his smoldering cigar stub. The shattered two-way mirror.

Cramer said she'd healed a lot of people who had participated in Scarlett's training.

Seamus nudged Scarlett playfully. "You should've seen her intimidate the guards today."

Scarlett smiled uncomfortably and took another drink.

Malcolm looked impressed if not surprised. "Lucy said you can absorb energy."

Then they were all asking questions. *Did it hurt? What were her limits? What were Rhoads's plans for her?*

Scarlett leaned back against the wall, surprised by their interest in her powers. She answered their questions, holding nothing back. It all came tumbling out of her. Someone filled her beer again. At one point, she stopped, realizing that she'd been monopolizing the conversation, and apologized for talking too much, but they urged her on, clearly fascinated.

They ordered more pitchers. The food came. Vernon tried a nuclear wing. His eyes went comically wide. He dropped the wing. "Those are really hot," he said, and fanned his tongue.

"Maybe that's why they call them nuclear," Cramer said.

Vernon gulped beer and winced. "They're really hot," he said, and pressed his tongue into the mug.

Seamus handled the wings, but his face turned red, and Scarlett saw beads of sweat forming on his forehead and his freckled nose. He kept eating them, though.

"What are you, a masochist?" she asked him, and gave his arm a squeeze. The muscle was compact but rock hard.

"You want hot," Seamus said, "try my grandmother's kimchi. She buries it for months. You open up a jar, set it on the counter, and stand back." He leaned into her, away from the invisible kimchi. "Your eyes start burning, and your nose starts running. Stuff's like tear gas—but it tastes great."

"Guys," Vernon said, addressing everyone. "Those wings are really hot."

"Let's see," Cramer said, and leaned to kiss the big plebe.

After a while, Scarlett and Seamus left the couples and went into the other room to play a game of pool. When she stood up, Scarlett realized that she had a good buzz on. A *very* good buzz. After months of forced sobriety, blurring the edges of reality was absolutely delicious.

"No TK tricks," she said, chalking her stick.

Seamus laughed and said that she could trust him, and that was when she noticed that he was looking at her differently.

That was okay. She was taking a closer look at him, too. His square face was chiseled and angular, with a strong jaw and high cheekbones. She liked his glossy black hair and the spray of light freckles across his nose and cheeks. He had a great smile and full lips that softened his otherwise rugged face to a degree.

They played and drank and talked, everything suffused with the energy of two young people drawing closer for the first time.

Seamus asked about her life. Not her powers, not The Point. Her life before.

She told him about home, her friends and parents and brother, about school and her Yamaha, about partying and some of the trouble she'd gotten into over the years.

He nodded and winced and asked more questions, taking it all in stride.

She liked that. Usually, you met a guy who'd been locked up, he was more trouble than he was worth no matter how good he looked or how cool he acted. Most of them were angry, crazy, or just plain stupid. But Seamus had brains and didn't seem to be out to impress anybody or manipulate the world. It was nice talking to somebody smart who'd also experienced his share of trouble, someone who understood the things she'd experienced, someone who wouldn't judge her when she told the truth. It felt almost conspiratorial.

Seamus's life had been up and down—pretty much in that order. Like most army brats, he'd moved around a lot, growing up. He'd lived all over the world and met some pretty cool people, and he'd been happy as a kid, but his father had changed over the years, becoming increasingly abusive. That was rough. Still, Seamus had managed to carve out a life for himself wherever they went. "Until I came home one day," he said, avoiding her eyes then, pretending to line up a shot, "and found my family dead. Murdered."

"Oh, Seamus, that's terrible," she said, and touched his arm. She'd known that his parents were dead, but this was shocking. "I can't imagine. I'm so sorry."

He nodded, took his shot, and sank a ball. "That's enough about that, though," he said, and straightened, showing her a forced smile. "Did you really have a job scooping ice cream?"

"Ah," Lucy said, leading the others to the pool table, "it's Bromeo and Juliet."

The others crowded around, offering refills and cracking jokes, Vernon asking with mock seriousness if Scarlett knew that her roommate was a complete derelict.

Scarlett laughed, but she felt preoccupied by the sense of time having passed, of things having changed. She felt closer to Seamus. As the others laughed and drank and talked smack, filling the space with noise and movement, Scarlett felt disappointment. For as much as she enjoyed everyone, she wished that she could have spent more one-on-one time with Seamus.

Oh, well, she thought, and remembered one of her brother's favorite sayings: "Wish in one hand, shit in the other . . . and see which one fills up first."

Dan was engaged—and hadn't even bothered to tell her.

But no . . . she wouldn't let Dan ruin her night.

She leaned against the wall and drank and sneaked glances at Seamus.

A couple of ugly pool games later, Cramer asked Scarlett what she could do other than absorb and rerelease energy. What could she initiate on her own?

Scarlett just shrugged. "Nothing?"

"Whoa," Vernon said, and she could tell by his grin and tone that he was busting on her. "So you're just like . . . a lightning rod?"

"Pretty much," she said.

Vernon looked back and forth between the others with *can-you-believe-this* mock amazement. "Wow, Scarlett . . . that's superboring. Guys, I don't know if we should let her hang out with us anymore." He shrugged his big shoulders. "I mean, we have standards, don't we?"

Scarlett laughed and rolled her eyes. "Let's see you do this, Bronan the Barbarian."

"Nice one!" Lucy said.

Scarlett crossed the room to the bar and climbed onto a stool.

"Hey," the bartender said, looking up from his phone. "That's enough."

Scarlett leaned forward and popped into a handstand. Her sweatshirt dropped to her armpits, and she could feel cool air on her stomach and ribs.

The bartender stopped complaining.

She walked on her hands, traveling the whole length of the bar before springing off and landing on her feet.

The cadets applauded. The bartender grinned.

"A perfect ten, Nadia Bro-maneci," Lucy said, patting Scarlett on the back.

Then the bartender was saying, "All right, that's enough," and Scarlett looked down the bar, where Seamus had climbed onto a stool.

People talked over one another, telling him to come down.

Seamus clapped his hands and cartwheeled into an impressive

handstand. His shirt fell, too, revealing a narrow waist and six-pack abs.

Scarlett felt a grin spread across her face.

"Piece of cake," Seamus said. He reached out a hand . . . and came crashing down. His head knocked into the bar, and he tumbled to the floor, knocking over a row of bar stools and cursing the whole way down.

They helped him to his feet. Seamus laughed woozily and dabbed at his split eyebrow, wiping away blood. His eye was ballooning rapidly.

Scarlett cupped his jaw and turned his head, examining the wound. "You okay?"

"I'm good," Seamus said, and winced. "Ouch."

"Dude," Vernon said. He looked around, smiling incredulously. "Dude . . . that was *awesome*!"

"Come on," Cramer said, pulling Seamus away from the bar. "I think I have a Band-Aid in the car."

Lucy raised a finger, catching the bartender's attention. "Check, *bitte*."

OUTSIDE, THE NIGHT had grown even colder, and a fine snow was falling. Scarlett shifted her weight back and forth and hugged herself, shivering, her breath coming out in pale clouds like bong hits.

Behind her, she heard the restaurant door lock. The orange pig went dim for the night.

Cramer looked around the empty lot as if scanning for witnesses. "In the car."

"I'm fine," Seamus protested as Vernon pushed him into the backseat.

Lucy stood ten feet away, kissing Malcolm.

Good for them, Scarlett thought. Then she piled into the backseat beside Seamus.

Cramer twisted around in her seat and told Seamus to lean forward. Diaphanous sheets of green and purple light wavered between her palms and Seamus's injured eye, reminding Scarlett of an aurora borealis. Light pooled over the wound, congealing like coagulating blood. A few minutes later, Cramer sucked the light back into her hands, and Seamus was as good as new.

The door opened, letting in a blast of cold air, and Lucy slid in beside Scarlett. Lucy rolled down her window and called to Malcolm in German as they pulled away.

Scarlett elbowed Seamus in the ribs. "That was pretty dumb back there."

"I couldn't let you show me up," he said.

"How'd that work out for you?"

"I'm good as new," he said. "Are your teeth chattering?"

"It's cold as balls," she said.

"Here," he said. She felt his arm go over her shoulders. Then he pulled her tight against him. "Get warm."

Then they were kissing. Passionately, desperately.

What did it mean?

She didn't care. She was buzzed and happy, and this was the first real fun she'd had since coming here.

They made out all the way back to the base.

THIRTY-TWO

DALIA'S EYES BURNED.

Rhoads droned on and on as Captain Fuller drove them down the long driveway through the tunnel of pines.

Shut up!

She wanted to scream it—he'd given the same lecture a thousand times—but instead she fought to keep her burning eyes open and to nod in all the right places. To Rhoads, this recon mattered more than anything.

She was exhausted. Night after night, she'd sacrificed real sleep to go looking for the Watcher. Most nights, she caught fleeting glimpses of the woman, always at a distance. The Watcher was almost ethereal, felt as much as seen. Dalia had called out to her, but the Watcher never answered, never even lingered. Whenever Dalia shouted to her or started in her direction, the Watcher faded away into whatever wilderness edged that particular dream, leaving Dalia aching with curiosity and more: a need to see this woman, to speak with her, to know if what she was beginning to suspect actually could be true.

Was she obsessed?

Yes, she supposed that she was. At least that was what others would say, but so be it. Who could judge her? No one, that's who. Not Rhoads, not Appleton, and certainly not Valerie Schmidt.

Only Dalia could judge Dalia. So what if she'd grown a little obsessed with the Watcher? That was natural enough, considering that she was surrounded day in and day out by a legion of laughable weaklings.

She also had continued to observe Scarlett's dreams—and Kyeong's. She'd known that Scarlett liked him—she'd seen it in her eyes and dreams—but she'd never expected him to reciprocate. He was an island, a jungle island filled with nightmares.

Scarlett should have spent her break with Dalia. They could have relaxed and had fun, become good friends. But no. Despite all Dalia had done for Scarlett, taking her under her wing, keeping her safe, teaching her, Scarlett had abandoned her for the biggest loser at The Point. Well, that was Scarlett's loss, not hers, Scarlett's mistake.

Still, she couldn't let Scarlett destroy herself, especially not when she had vouched for her. She had to keep an eye on Scarlett's dreams, had to be ready in case she needed an intervention.

"We're running out of time," Rhoads said. "We have to find them before they strike again."

She nodded, knowing from Rhoads's dreams that he was frightened of more than another act of terrorism. Things were getting personal.

They drove out of the woods and entered the snowy expanse of The Farm. Fields and orchards spread away from the fenced compound encompassing a large barn, several outbuildings, and a huge old farmhouse complete with a wraparound porch, a weather vane, and Christmas lights twinkling along the eaves.

"We need names," Rhoads said. "Times, dates. Any clues to where he might be now."

A few residents in orange jumpsuits and matching jackets stumbled along shoveled paths between the buildings, doing the Thorazine shuffle.

Back at The Point, everyone feared The Farm, but it wasn't that bad. Not really.

During warmer months, the trees blossomed and bore fruit and the pastures turned a beautiful emerald green. Most residents moved more or less freely about the main compound. They had volleyball and badminton, tetherball and a sandbox. They even tended the orchards and gardens themselves, all to the music of wind chimes and birdsong.

Fuller parked beside the barn. Some of the residents looked up, saw the black Suburban, and looked away.

"Ready?" Rhoads asked.

"Ready," she said.

Fuller stayed with the Suburban. She and Rhoads went inside and signed in at the front desk. The officer behind the glass buzzed them through the door.

Residents in orange jumpsuits occupied the enormous recreation area. A dozen stared dully at a big-screen TV, watching a cooking show. Another dozen sat in the separate lounge area, reading or writing or talking quietly or rocking back and forth. A meathead gone to fat stood alone at the Ping-Pong table. He knocked the little white ball across to the other side, then shuffled after it, no doubt to knock it back the other way and start his shuffle again.

Hours of fun . . .

She recognized a few of the residents as cadets who'd washed out during her time at The Point. One, a TK named Sharonda, had snapped at dinner one evening, given a bloodcurdling scream, and overturned a table in the West Point dining hall. Previously, the girl had been nice, quiet, and utterly pitiful. The meltdown in the dining hall—which had been a *very big deal*—was the first and last interesting thing Sharonda had done at The Point.

Sharonda sat in the lounge area, knees drawn up, hugging her shins, her med-slackened face watching a slow game of checkers. Looking up and seeing Dalia, she smiled and started to wave. Then she spotted Rhoads, dropped her hand, and stared once more at the board.

Good, Dalia thought. She hated seeing Sharonda. Waving back felt like hugging a leper.

Still, this place isn't as bad as everyone at The Point thinks.

They crossed the main floor and came to the elevators.

No, they shouldn't fear The Farm.

The elevator doors slid open. She stepped inside and shuddered.

They should fear The Mushroom Farm.

They descended in silence. Rhoads crunched TUMS and checked his watch. Dalia waited, feeling the creep of revulsion and anxiety as they sank deep into the earth.

The elevator stopped. The doors slid open. They passed through another checkpoint, buzzed through a heavy door coated in flame-resistant rubber, and entered the underground facility she'd come to think of as The Mushroom Farm.

She followed Rhoads down the narrow corridor, hating the nursing-home smell of the place, a stale and fleshy odor underscored with ammonia and poorly masked with cleaning products, like old hamburger marinating in cat piss and Pine-Sol.

The tinkling Muzac down here did little to muffle the disconcerting sounds coming from behind the cell doors: screams, laughter, and the endless murmur of people talking to themselves. When Dalia first had started coming here, she'd made the mistake of glancing through the thick window slits of this maximum-security wing. Rubber walls, padded walls, scorched walls. People in straitjackets, rocking back and forth, moaning, wailing, weeping; people pacing their cells, mumbling and gesticulating wildly; and several people too dangerous even for consciousness—including Appleton, she was disturbed to see—strapped atop gurneys like corpses in a morgue, hooked by tubes and wires to machines that sustained them, carried off waste, and monitored all manner of things that she didn't want to consider.

They arrived at 113. The door slid open. Rhoads led her inside. The door slid shut behind them with a dull thump. Within the cell, the odor grew chokingly pungent.

Valerie Schmidt, an ashen woman who looked much older than her twenty-eight years, lay as dry and stiff as driftwood atop her cot. Valerie was a High Roller, a member of the posthuman black ops unit trained at Fort Bragg before Rhoads started The Point. The High Rollers had gone rogue. Captured after the Atlanta tragedy, Valerie split her rare waking hours among mocking laughter, scalding tirades, and prophecies of doom.

A wooden chair waited for Dalia beside the cot. Rhoads would stand behind her, as always, his hands on the seat back, as if he were propelling her in a wheelchair, pushing her into the dream recon.

Of course, Rhoads had no idea that she could strafe Valerie's dreams just as effectively back at The Point. The less he knew, the better.

She sat.

Rhoads moved in behind her, gripping the chair. "We're counting on you."

Valerie's respirator sucked and hissed, sucked and hissed.

Dalia closed her eyes. The smells and sounds of the subterranean cell disappeared, replaced by the smells of cinnamon and vanilla and the ticking of an old clock down the hall. The cottage again. Valerie's memory dream. The place was warm and happy and, yes, a memory. Dalia could feel that veracity, its nostalgia.

This was the same dream Valerie had every time Dalia checked, a short but vivid scene repeated on an unvarying loop, as if broadcast from some magical dream tower.

As usual, Valerie lay on a comfortable-looking old sofa, smiling drowsily.

"We haven't forgotten you," the unseen man said from outside the dream frame. His voice was deep and soothing. The room brightened and warmed at the sound of it. "Have faith."

"All my faith is in you," Valerie purred.

"We will come for you," his voice, low and seductive, told her.

Valerie shifted languorously. "Come for me."

Dalia felt a twinge of absurd jealously at the obvious sexual undertones. Valerie didn't deserve this man . . .

The dream ended and started over. Dalia remained. If she pulled out now, Rhoads would just send her back in again.

Valerie sighed.

The deep voice returned. *We haven't forgotten you . . .*

And then a door opened to her left.

Dalia could have screamed. In all the hundreds of times she had observed Valerie's dreams, they had never deviated. How had the door opened?

She moved forward, the main script still playing behind her, Valerie's voice murmuring, *Come for me.*

Dalia stepped through the open door and into a sweet-smelling summer scene of rustic perfection. Birdsong filled the air. A warm breeze passed, bending the hay and tall grasses between her and the wooded hillside.

The Watcher is here . . .

Dalia could feel the Watcher's warmth in the dream breeze, could hear her soft heartbeat stitched into the birdsong, could smell her floral scent mixed with the sweet aroma of the dream meadow. Sensing her, Dalia quavered with loss and longing and a twist of dread. Then she saw the Watcher, beckoning from the tree line.

Dalia started across the field, her eyes locked on the Watcher, from whom a sense of familiarity now emanated like heat blurring the air over hot macadam.

The Watcher beckoned, fading back into the trees.

Dalia pumped her arms and legs, running, pulled forward by familiarity, urged on by bone-deep desperation that she almost but didn't quite understand.

Entering the forest, she slowed. Beneath the trees, the world was cool and dim yet no less sweet than the meadow. She stumbled forward, desperate to find the Watcher.

There!

Glimpsing the Watcher through the trees, Dalia moved downhill into a ravine.

She heard the creek first, then smelled it—a good, green smell that reminded her of childhood, the happy years before everything had gone bad—and then she was clattering across the stones of the narrow brook, jumping from mossy rock to mossy rock, and she reached the opposite bank and stumbled into the embrace of the Watcher.

For a long time, Dalia held on tight, crying and laughing.

"Dalia," the Watcher said, stroking her hair gently.

"Mom," Dalia said. "I've missed you so much. I . . . life has—"

"Shh," her mother said, pulling her once more into an embrace. She looked . . . normal. "Everything's all right now. I never forgot you, Dalia."

"But you're gone," Dalia said. "You killed yourself. You left me all alone." She stepped back again, half expecting a nightmare twist, some awful transformation in the thing pretending to be her mother, but Mom still stood there, smiling sadly, telling her how sorry she was for leaving her alone, explaining that Dalia had reunited them through her dream walking. Mom had been trying to reach her for months. Now, finally, they were together again, reunited.

"I'm so happy," Dalia said. "I'm so tired, and I'm so happy."

Her mother brushed away Dalia's tears with the soft touch she'd missed so much. "There's someone I want you to meet."

"Who?"

"Someone wonderful," her mother said. Had so much gray always streaked her hair? "He's waiting for you." She took Dalia's hand and led her alongside the creek, moving downhill through the forest. Dalia had no idea who was waiting for her, but at that point, feeling her mother's familiar hand, she would have followed her straight through the gates of hell.

The stream flowed over a tumble of mossy stones, cascaded several shimmering feet, and spilled into a glimmering pool beside which stood a beautiful man, dark-haired with bronze skin and dark eyes, dressed all in white. His full lips spread, revealing a dazzling smile.

"Dalia," he said, his voice deep and soothing. It was *the* voice. "Dalia, at long last. Come. Come to me."

She went to him and fell into his embrace, which was somehow even more comforting than that of her mother. He held her and smoothed her hair and said her name, the low bass of his voice another embrace. He understood her, how she'd worked and suffered, how she'd hidden her pain, overcome it, how people had betrayed her again and again. But that was over now, his deep voice assured her, all over now.

She was so relieved.

Then, holding her and rubbing her back, the man began to ask questions about her life, about The Point, about dream walking, and especially about the girl she knew, Scarlett.

And Dalia, no longer lonely, told him everything.

THIRTY-THREE

CONSIDERING THERE WAS NO BOOZE, THE POINT'S New Year's Eve party was a lot of fun. They had food and soda and games, and big speakers ringed the gymnasium, blasting music by a surprisingly good live DJ: Scarlett's mythology professor, Major Petrie, who apparently had a thing for EDM and hip-hop. Who could have guessed?

The cadets danced and ate junk food and shouted and laughed and generally acted like the excited fools the cadre was allowing them to be, if for one night only.

Scarlett hung with Seamus, Lucy, Cramer, and Vernon but also talked to dozens of cadets who drifted in and out of conversations, everyone living it up, high on this temporary freedom.

She was incredibly happy. She was starting to feel that she actually belonged here, and she could finally understand, if not yet wholly echo, the optimism of people like Lucy, Cramer, and Vernon. The last few days had been incredible.

She'd had fun with Lucy, swapping bro-jokes and girl talk, and each night they'd ridden along with friends, hitting the bars and restaurants of Highland Falls and Fort Montgomery. Best of all, however, was the time she spent with Seamus.

She and Seamus played chess, cards, and Ping-Pong but spent most of their break above ground, walking the campus. She especially loved their late-night excursions. After everyone came back from town and hit the rack, she and Seamus would sneak out through the subway ladder. These walks were the best. Seamus liked to climb, too, and they made a pact to tackle the stone face of Thayer Hall after the snow and ice melted.

Wherever they went, whatever they did, they talked, getting to know each other. Seamus was smart and tough and sometimes funny, though she liked that he didn't *need* to be funny. Most guys, if they made you laugh a couple of times, soon ruined everything, trying way too hard to be witty or ironic.

Half Korean, half Irish, Seamus got his largely Asian appearance and love of spicy foods from his father's side and his blue eyes, freckles, and fiery temper from his mother's people. For most of his life, he'd been relatively happy. Until sophomore year, he'd liked school, actually had enjoyed studying and learning, and had been a pretty good athlete, excelling in a few sports despite moving a lot. His favorite sport was gymnastics.

After his dad had gotten mean, Seamus started avoiding home and running the streets with other kids. Overseas bases, he explained, never have a shortage of wild army brats. While running the streets, he used his gymnastics skills to hang with a group of kids who were into parkour. Scarlett loved it when he talked about those times. He lit up, his eyes distant but gleaming, telling her how those kids would run and jump and climb all across the base, driving the MPs crazy. She wished she could have run with them.

She didn't say so, but she also wished she could have been around to help him through those dark times. He didn't bring up his murdered family again, but she sensed it often in things unsaid, like a rumbling storm cloud behind anecdotes. He did mention—choking up a little as they walked the campus one night—how much he missed his two little brothers, twins named Sean and Liam.

Over the course of those days, Scarlett and Seamus drew together in the curiously expedient manner exclusive to young people living in close quarters, away from home, and under heavy institutional pressure. In this manner, unlikely friendships form quickly and fiercely among boot camp battle buddies, college freshmen, prison inmates, and teens trapped in rehab.

But this was more than friendship. Scarlett had wondered, the morning after their trip to Barnburners BBQ, if their make-out session had been nothing more than two drunk kids having ten minutes of steamy fun in a backseat. The next day, however, she'd known the instant she'd seen Seamus at lunch—both by the way she felt and by the way he looked at her—that their story had more chapters, and later that afternoon, returning to Flirtie, they'd kissed again.

Because she was a plebe and he was a yearling, they couldn't let on that they were anything other than friends, but that went out the window when they were off base, surrounded only by friends, and during their campus strolls, especially after they discovered the famous drafting room, a dusty, abandoned space that West Point cadets used to find true privacy. Sometimes it was nice to take a break from talking and thinking and just lose themselves in each other.

Tonight, of course, they couldn't even hold hands, but that was all right. Just being with Seamus and her new friends made things a million times better and made this the best New Year's Eve of her life.

Around eleven-thirty, Major Petrie cut the music, and Rhoads took the microphone.

"Play 'Free Bird,'" someone called out.

"All right, Cadets," Rhoads said, flashing a grin. "It's great to see all of you having a nice time tonight. I'm very proud of the things you've achieved over the course of the past twelve months here at The Point, and we look forward to incredible things in the coming year. Now let's move this party down the hall to the auditorium so we can watch the ball drop."

The cadets gave a loud "Hooah!" and made their way toward the auditorium.

"Last New Year's Eve," Scarlett told Seamus, keeping her voice low, "I got so high that my friend Ginny convinced me that we'd gone *back* a year."

They filed into the auditorium. Much to Scarlett's relief, they were allowed to spread out and move around rather than having to sit for the ball drop. The big screen at the back of the stage cut among network commentators, celebrity performers, and parties around the country, focusing, as tradition would have it, on the jubilant masses crowding Times Square.

As the minutes slipped away, Scarlett couldn't help but marvel over the many ways this year had changed her life and wonder what changes the rapidly approaching year ahead would reveal.

"What's your New Year's resolution?" she asked Seamus.

"Find cooler friends," he said, grinning.

She elbowed him, wishing they were someplace else, someplace away from the rules of The Point, someplace that didn't frown on public displays of affection.

They should at least be allowed to kiss at the stroke of midnight.

And in that instant, as the final minute of the year arrived, she decided that she *would* kiss Seamus, rules be damned, right at midnight. If anybody gave her a hard time, she'd play stupid. *Hey, it's New Year's Eve.*

The thrill of excitement fluttered in her chest. She couldn't wait to see the expression on Seamus's face.

"Here we go," he said, pointing at the screen. The descending ball flashed and shimmered.

The final ten seconds arrived. Scarlett stole a quick glance at Seamus's face as he joined the other cadets, who all shouted along with the countdown.

"10, 9, 8 . . ."

She grabbed Seamus's hand and gave it a squeeze.

"7, 6, 5 . . ."

He smiled but pulled free, obviously worried about getting caught.

"4, 3 . . ."

She laughed. He was going to shit a brick when she kissed him.

"2, 1 . . . Happy—"

BOOM!

In Times Square, the big ball exploded in flames and glass.

The auditorium filled with screams, a chorus of terror blasting from the telecast and from the cadets themselves.

The ball wrenched free of its flagpole and shot into the air as if yanked by an invisible cable. For a full second, it hovered ten stories above the ground, and then it rushed back down, not simply falling but hurtling at a sharp angle, and pounded into a packed section of screaming spectators like a half-ton hammer smashing slugs.

The ball rose and struck again and then again and again, each time smashing down on another section.

The tightly packed crowd lurched crazily like a single organism going to pieces as waves of panicked spectators lost their minds and stampeded in all directions, trampling the fallen.

Scarlett stared in a paralysis of terror, understanding, as every cadet around her understood, that they were witnessing *posthuman* terrorism.

The ball came to rest in the middle of Seventh Avenue, burst into flames, and whipped away, rolling along the ground. A tumbling fireball six feet in diameter, it zigzagged back and forth, mowing a gruesome path through the crowd.

THIRTY-FOUR

THE TIMES SQUARE TRAGEDY, AS THE NEW YEAR'S catastrophe came quickly to be known, rattled the nation. The Atlanta event had been shocking, but the Times Square Tragedy was terror on a completely different level: hundreds dead, thousands injured, and millions traumatized.

Rhoads debriefed the cadets in an assembly, regurgitating the same facts that were playing 24/7 on every news station in the world and adding cryptically that The Point would play a role in bringing the terrorists to justice. He allowed no questions.

Rumors flourished, blaming everyone from aliens to high-tech radicals to feral posthumans. Scarlett even overheard false flag whispers claiming that the government had orchestrated the whole thing to justify what was happening here at The Point.

Ridiculous—yet understandable, to a degree.

People all over the world were terrified. Despite the NYPD's amazing security and surveillance, they clearly had no idea what exactly had happened, let alone who was to blame. The terrorists were still at large, almost certainly would strike again, and apparently could attack anyone, anywhere, anytime. The nation gnashed its collective teeth, demanding blood and answers in that order.

Yet life went on, as it does in the wake of tremendous loss.

In the days that followed, the snow melted, fell again, melted partway, fell again, and then Christmas leave was over. The West Point cadets returned, looking forlorn and resigned, no doubt missing their friends and families. January at West Point is known as the Gloom Period. Everything is gray: the sky, the buildings, the river, even the cadets' uniforms and attitudes. Motivation is at low tide. West Point responds by kicking them in the teeth: the second semester starts at a sprint and accelerates along months fraught with high-pressure milestones.

Rhoads had changed since the Times Square Tragedy. His characteristic politician's smile was nowhere to be seen. He pushed Scarlett harder than ever during energy training.

Dalia had changed since the attack, too, dropping her usual apathy to become a yoga Nazi. "Try harder," she'd say. "Focus. Position is everything. Keep your back straight, Scarlett. You call that straight?"

Gung-Ho Dalia, Scarlett soon decided, was even more annoying than Self-Aggrandizing-Slacker Dalia.

Scarlett's new classes were brutal, too, but Seamus was in her mythology class, which gave them an excuse to study together, and they continued to sneak out of The Point most nights.

That was why, despite the miserable weather, Rhoads pressuring her, Dalia harassing her during yoga, and classwork kicking her butt, Scarlett was *happy*.

Unfortunately, Rhoads noticed her lightheartedness.

One afternoon, when Scarlett released the energy even more quickly than usual, Rhoads said, "Perhaps you're distracted." He crushed his coffee cup and tossed it into the wastebasket. "Perhaps your mind is on other things. Maybe I should help you focus."

"No, sir," Scarlett said, sitting up straighter. "I'll break through soon."

"Good," Rhoads said. "Otherwise, I'll have to separate you from your distraction."

She couldn't let Rhoads interfere. Without Seamus, she'd go insane here. She hadn't realized how disconnected and miserable she'd been until after they'd started hanging out. The prospect of returning to that former state, in which she was alone save for her increasingly annoying sessions with Dalia and increasingly infrequent chess games with Lucy, was unfathomable. And what of Seamus? He had been even more alone than she had and for much longer. How would he feel if Rhoads interfered?

She had to avoid that no matter what. If only she could do what Rhoads was asking of her, but it was hard, and it hurt, and she wasn't even sure if it was possible regardless of what Rhoads said. Wanting something to be possible didn't make it possible.

That night, Lucy cursed in German, pushed her books aside, and pulled out the chess board. Scarlett chuckled and helped her set up the board. She really didn't have time for a game—she had fallen behind in *The Odyssey*—but Lucy had even less time. This was a sacrifice on Lucy's part, a sacrifice for friendship. Scarlett wouldn't reject that.

Midway through the game, Lucy began singing "White Rabbit" in her horrible German accent. She pushed a pawn, locking the center. Suddenly, Scarlett was all jammed in with no dynamic moves. It was a simple move she hadn't seen coming.

Lucy said, "Either I'm getting better or you're off your game."

Scarlett snarled, searching for a new plan. She waved her fingertips over the pieces like a woman trying to read Braille for the first time.

Lucy gave her the happy grin that always lit the eyes behind the spectacles with a glimmer less than sane. "I know what's wrong with you, Bro-phelia," she said, and leaned back against the wall, folding her arms over her chest. "You're falling for Seamus."

"What?" Scarlett said, looking up from the pieces. "I . . ." Her face suddenly felt hot, and she realized with some annoyance that she was blushing like some dizzy sixth-grader on a sleepover.

Lucy nodded. "Is that your move?"

Scarlett took her hand off the knight and shrugged. "Yeah. Go ahead."

"Is weak," Lucy said, switching from the horrible German accent to an even lousier Russian accent. Another pawn lifted into the air and advanced, forcing Scarlett's knight to retreat. "I can see it in your eyes, sis, and hear it in your voice."

"Nah," Scarlett said. "I mean, I like him. Don't get me wrong. I like him a lot."

Lucy nodded. "And when you're not with him, how do you feel?"

"I want to be with him."

"You're falling . . . hard," Lucy said, bringing out her queen. "Check."

Scarlett reacted automatically, blocking the threat with a pawn move that simultaneously threatened the queen. "It's just a crush. He's cute and fun and helps me keep my mind off how much this place sucks."

Lucy shook her head. "Nope. It's the real deal. You're falling for him, and he's falling just as hard for you, sister." She moved her knight, leaving her queen in danger. "Check."

Scarlett looked down at the board. Her impulsive pawn move had opened a crucial square for Lucy's knight, which now forked the king and queen. "Grand."

"You must address das check," Lucy said, returning to the abysmal German. Then she laughed, watching Scarlett figure it out. She had to move her king. Lucy would capture Scarlett's queen, blocking flight squares and unveiling a discovered check by the bishop all the way at the other end of the board. This would leave Scarlett's king with one square, and . . .

"Mate in three," Lucy said.

"Anybody ever tell you that you're a pain in the ass?" Scarlett said, grimacing at the board. "A grade-A, rub-a-dog-the-wrong-way pain in the ass."

Lucy grinned with amusement. "Your anger," she said, returning to her deplorable Russian accent. "It is . . . how do you say? Cute."

"Piss up a rope," Scarlett said, and tipped her king.

"You two are a great match," Lucy said, resetting the board, "and I wish you well. Just don't let it destroy you both, all right?"

"We're careful," Scarlett said. She felt funny. Off balance, with this conversation making her excited and nervous at the same time. "We might sneak a kiss or two while you're around, but we know the rules."

"I'm not talking about honor code violations," Lucy said. She finished straightening the pieces and spun the board, offering Scarlett the white pieces and the first move. "Love is a purer form of energy than any of that stuff Rhoads pumps into you. I'm not certain that either one of you is ready to channel that much power."

THE FIRST TIME, they didn't even get all the way out of their clothes.

After hours, they'd slipped out of The Point and come together to the dusty drafting room. On the walk, they'd talked about classes—tough, but at least they had mythology together—and Seamus's upcoming TK testing and Scarlett's continued struggles with energy training, both of them going through the motions of conversation as new energy crackled between them.

Alone in the drafting room, they dropped all pretenses. She popped onto her tiptoes, raised her face to his, and then they were kissing: a long, drawn-out kiss that started slowly and built speed. She smoothed her hands over the rippling muscles of his upper back, and he hooked his fingers into her belt loops and pulled her hips against his. They fell into the kiss, pressing into each other. The kiss slowed again, growing sweeter.

She stepped back and said his name, and Seamus touched her hair and said her name, and they looked at each other for a long second, Scarlett feeling something she'd never felt before, a kind of seriousness, her desire and affection melding to make this more than the simple fun she'd known with guys in high school.

Then they were kissing again, and she pushed him back against the wall and went for his belt. Five minutes later, it was over. They lay together, half dressed, sweating and laughing, both of them shocked.

"Wow," Seamus said. He had a lean body, sinuous in the moonlight, gorgeous.

"Now that we have that out of the way," she said, straddling him, "let's slow down and really enjoy it."

THE NEXT DAY, Scarlett buzzed with happiness. Nothing could destroy her good mood. Not chemistry class, not Hopkins messing with her during lunch, not even training with Rhoads.

Then, two minutes into yoga, Dalia started barking about focus. Day after day, week after week, month after month, Scarlett had been putting up with her, so it should have been easy to put up with her for one more session, but when Dalia screeched, "What are you, stupid?" something inside Scarlett shifted.

"What's up with you, Dalia?" she said. "You blow off yoga for months, can't be bothered to teach me, and now you're G.I. Jane all of a sudden?"

Dalia looked momentarily shocked, then laughed humorlessly, eyes flashing dangerously. "You know what your problem is, Scarlett? You're lazy and selfish."

Scarlett gave her an equally fake smile. She was sick of Dalia. She'd made such a big deal of taking Scarlett under her wing, but what had she done for her, really? Nothing, that was what. And now she was acting like Scarlett owed her everything. "Lazy and selfish; that's two problems. So which one is it?"

"In you, lazy and selfish are all twisted together like a braid. You never work hard, because you don't care about anybody but yourself."

"How would you even know? All you do is talk about how great you are. You don't know anything about me."

Dalia's eyes drilled into Scarlett. "I know more you think. More than you could *dream*."

THIRTY-FIVE

SCARLETT AND HER CLASSMATES SAT IN A LARGE circle, reviewing *The Odyssey*. At the far end, near the door, Dalia doodled, not even pretending to pay attention. Beside her—and apparently back in her good graces, at least for the moment—Clayton lounged, massive and slack-jawed, doing his hayseed routine for anyone who would buy it. Directly across the circle from Scarlett, Seamus sat up straight and achingly handsome, his attention locked with laser focus on their instructor, Major Petrie.

He looked nothing like the wild and playful Seamus who sneaked away to the drafting room with her most nights. One night, she'd joked about his "split personalities"—rebel, lover, hyperfocused student, and chess player—and he'd explained his classroom demeanor. After years of fretting that he'd never be able to afford college, he was determined to make the most of this opportunity. Learning to use his powers was one thing; learning to use his brain—and earning a degree that would mean real job opportunities after he parted ways with the Army—was something completely different.

Scarlett envied Seamus and Lucy for their ability to see the future as a real place, a destination over which they had some degree of control, and the toughness they showed, working toward those futures day after day. Their approach to life made a lot of sense. She just couldn't do it. Literally couldn't. Occasionally she'd make a pact with herself to work toward something, but sooner or later she got derailed. Sometimes she wouldn't even realize that she'd gotten derailed until weeks or months had passed and she no longer even felt like the person who'd put so much value on the thing in the first place.

"In the Underworld," Major Petrie said, "everything was codified and ritualized."

Someone nudged Scarlett's foot.

She glanced from side to side. The chair to her left was empty. To her right, Bentley leaned over his desk, frantic as always, scribbling notes, unaware that she existed.

Another nudge. This time, the pressure lingered, traveling back and forth like someone playing footsie.

She leaned and looked under her seat. Nothing.

When she looked up again, Major Petrie was scowling at her. Petrie was pretty cool compared with the other instructors, but he'd obviously caught Scarlett scanning the floor. "Cadet Winter, how did Odysseus's mother die?"

Scarlett straightened in her chair, face suddenly hot. She'd blown off last night's reading to escape once more to the drafting room with Seamus. Still, she wasn't *that* far behind. Her mind raced over limited possibilities. "The suitors murdered her, sir."

"Very Hollywood, Cadet Winter, but incorrect. I recommend that you read more closely. Your last exam score was less than heroic."

The class chuckled.

Major Petrie said, "Someone help Cadet Winter. How did Odysseus's mother die?"

Seamus's hand shot up.

Petrie called on him.

With his chin held high, Seamus said, "Sir, his mother died of grief."

"Correct, Cadet Kyeong," Petrie said. "Now, if Cadet Winter

is prepared, we will commence with the prophecies and get poor Odysseus out of the Underworld."

When Petrie turned his back and walked toward the white board, Seamus grinned at Scarlett and stuck out his tongue.

She rolled her eyes and mouthed *brownnoser*.

Seamus resumed his focus as Petrie pivoted and paced back in that direction.

"Homer gives us more sacrifice," Petrie said. "In order to enable his deceased mother to speak, Odysseus must give her blood to drink."

Cadets groaned, making faces.

Scarlett was one of them—Stephen King had nothing on old Homer—but the distracting pressure returned, pressed against her ankle, and moved slowly up her calf. She shifted in her seat but kept her face trained on Petrie, who eyeballed her as he glossed over the prophecies.

The pressure moved higher and paused at the knee, tickling her. She resisted the urge to squirm. Looking down, she *saw* the pressure. It pressed her pant leg flat, then smoothed up her inner thigh, an invisible hand feeling her up.

She brushed at it to no avail. Force had manifested out of thin air . . .

She glanced up sharply, but Seamus remained as focused as before, his attention locked on Major Petrie, who said, "For as shocked as Odysseus was to meet his mother in the Underworld, the presence of Achilles must have been even more disconcerting."

Scarlett stared at Seamus for a second, certain that he was messing with her, but he showed absolutely no sign whatsoever. But if not him, who?

She glanced down the row of chairs as Dalia glanced up. Dalia smiled and wiggled one finger in her direction.

Scarlett wiggled her fingertips in a return wave, then swatted as stealthily as she could at the pressure, which had reached the top of her thigh. *What the . . . ?*

She jumped when the pressure moved between her legs. "Hey."

Major Petrie executed a snappy about-face. "Cadet Winter?"

"Sir, this cadet regrets interrupting you, but I'm wondering if you could explain—" She scrambled, trying to hear in her mind the instruction she'd missed. "—why what Achilles said was so shocking."

"Achilles had no business in the Underworld," Petrie explained. "He had died bravely and should have been enjoying a singularly glorious immortality."

Scarlett composed her face, nodding appropriately as the force cupping her began to rub gently back and forth. She tried not to squirm.

Who was doing this?

Petrie said, "Achilles's message—*dead is dead*—must have rattled a hero like Odysseus to the core."

"Thank you, sir," Scarlett said, and shifted in her seat.

"Imagine surrendering your entire life to the heroic ideal, sacrificing everything," Petrie told the class, "only to learn that it was all a lie, that you could have stayed at home with your friends and family and enjoyed a simple yet rewarding life."

Scarlett glanced once more around the classroom, feeling desperate.

Seamus regarded her with a slight smile and mocking eyes, the wild, playful Seamus peeking out from within the focused student.

It *was* him. She shook her head and mouthed *stop*.

Seamus turned away, smirking.

The pressure faded, and Scarlett exhaled with relief.

Then the invisible hand returned, pressing softly against her.

She gestured sharply at Seamus. Several students were looking at her now. Seamus, allowing a satisfied grin, pretended not to notice.

The cruel pressure moved softly back and forth.

She pretended to pay attention to Petrie, who was saying something about Sirens and the importance of music in mythology. She crossed her legs, but that only intensified the pressure, which had begun rubbing her in slow circles.

There was no way to follow what Petrie was saying, and at that point Scarlett didn't care. She had a situation here. Because now, despite her shock and embarrassment, the sensation was starting to feel good . . . no, *great*. She glanced across the aisle at Seamus, pleading with her eyes.

Seamus pretended not to notice.

Then she felt a different kind of pressure down there. A pressure in her, building.

Seamus had to stop, had to cut her a break. She made desperate chopping motions.

Seamus gave her a cocky grin. The invisible force circled faster but stuck to a mercilessly simple rhythm, and—*no, no, no*—she gripped the desk, fighting the urgency rising within her.

Kliener and Bowles, TKs whose grins suggested that they understood exactly what was happening, settled in with the rapt attention of fireworks fans awaiting a grand finale.

Her face burned. *No, no, no!* In mere seconds, she was going to . . .

Someone knocked on the classroom door.

The invisible hand vanished.

Petrie went to the door.

Thankful for the interruption, she glanced across the room and chilled with apprehension. Dalia glared at her, the whites of her eyes showing beneath the irises. Dalia crumpled the paper on her desk and squeezed it in her fist.

Lopez entered the classroom and mumbled a few words privately to Major Petrie, looking even sterner than usual. No, Scarlett realized, not sterner—he looked *somber*—and then the hulking drill sergeant turned in her direction. "Winter," Lopez said, and beckoned.

Great, she thought. *More trouble.*

She rose, embarrassed, and gathered her things, aware of everyone watching her. Seamus grinned as if he'd announced checkmate. She drilled him with death eyes and followed Lopez into the hall.

It wouldn't occur to her until much later that she should have wondered about Lopez's somber face, his uncharacteristically soft voice, and the strange way he'd motioned to her. Normally, the man's every move was as forceful as a throat punch, but he'd beckoned her into the hall with a subtle sweep of the arm, not so much a command as an invitation, a gesture that would, in retrospect, seem almost tender to Scarlett.

Out in the hall, Lopez laid a hand on her shoulder and regarded her with an expression she wouldn't have thought the scarred face capable of making:

Pity.

"I'm sorry, Winter," Lopez said, and patted her shoulder gently. "Your brother is dead."

THIRTY-SIX

BY THE TIME SCARLETT PULLED HERSELF TOGETHER, The Point had assembled in the auditorium.

When she entered, Rhoads, standing at the podium, paused in midsentence.

The cadets stared.

"Scarlett," Rhoads said, "please join us."

She felt the cadets' eyes on her as she slid into a seat at the edge of the row, far from the rest of them. Her eyes burned, but there would be no more crying. Anger had settled over her like a killing frost, freezing her tears and chilling her intentions until they were as hard and cold and pointed as an icicle.

Dan was dead.

She would never see him again. She would never hug him again, never bury the hatchet, never congratulate him on his engagement.

Somewhere, Mom was sobbing uncontrollably, with only the cold comfort of her father to hold her up. But they were safe. Lopez guaranteed that. Safe and on their way to Virginia with a security detail. After the assembly, she was supposed to pack her bags and join them on emergency leave, accompanied by her own set of bodyguards.

Scarlett pushed those thoughts from her mind. No more sorrow, no more tears.

This was *her* fault.

She had caused Dan's death.

"I might as well tell you now," Lopez had said in the hallway as Scarlett reeled. "The terrorists—we know them. They're posthumans, too, and somehow they know about you. That's why they killed Dan. They said as much in the statement they sent to the White House."

Scarlett listened, feeling numb. The news had hollowed out her skull and filled it with cement. Her body trembled and twitched as Lopez spoke. She stared at the drill sergeant, her dumbstruck brain chiming *no, no, no* in a measured cadence of denial. As Lopez explained that the terrorists had followed Dan from his fiancée's house and ambushed him on a lonely stretch of road, the cadence grew louder and faster. By the time Lopez told her about TKs flipping the Jeep and a pyrokinetic torching it, a blaring Klaxon filled her skull. *No! No!! NO!!!*

Finally, her legs had gone weak beneath her, and she'd grabbed Lopez's shoulder to keep from spilling to the floor.

Now her mind and body had reunited in cold purpose. She sat rigidly as Rhoads said, "The president wants a rapid-response strike force. He told me that if he's dealing with posthuman terrorists, he needs a posthuman counterterror unit . . . *yesterday*."

Rhoads panned the cadets. "Alumni of The Point will form the core of the strike force, but the president has authorized me to include a small number of talented upperclassmen."

Excited muttering rippled across the ranks.

Scarlett leaned forward.

"Upperclassmen," Rhoads said, "before I ask for volunteers, I need you to understand that this will be an exceedingly dangerous assignment and one that offers considerable risk even if you never engage the enemy. Training for the strike force will require all of your time for the foreseeable future. You run the very real risk of being recycled and having to repeat a full semester next fall. Firsties, that might mean not graduating this summer."

He cleared his throat, letting the gravity of that sacrifice resonate.

Recycled? Scarlett thought. *Repeat a semester?* No one would volunteer for that.

Rhoads said, "Do I have any volunteers?"

Scarlett watched the hands rise.

One after another, upperclassmen raised their hands—Lucy, Clayton, Dalia—until the room bristled with hands. Even Hopkins raised his arm as straight as a flagpole.

Scarlett felt a lump form in her throat. Whatever these people had done in the past, even Hopkins, all was forgiven now.

As she looked around, gratitude flooded her. Every upperclassman in The Point was—

But no.

One upperclassman sat with his arms folded over his chest, looking sullen.

Seamus. Of all people . . .

"Hooah," Rhoads said. "Those who make the team, Sergeant Lopez will be your leader."

Sergeant Lopez, Scarlett thought. *Not* drill *sergeant. Out of the cadre and into the fire.*

Lopez, standing behind the colonel, gave a short nod.

Rhoads said, "Sergeant Lopez will direct your training and command you in the field. He knows the enemy better than anyone." Rhoads stepped away from the podium. "Sergeant."

Lopez pushed the microphone aside and gripped the podium in his big hands. "The sons of bitches who did this," he said, his inhumanly deep voice filling the auditorium, "are the same ones responsible for all the crazy attacks that you've heard about. Vegas, Atlanta . . . and that Charlie-Foxtrot-tastrophe on New Year's Eve. They call themselves the High Rollers, and the only thing they hate more than normal society is you."

High Rollers echoed through Scarlett's numb mind.

"They're ex-army posthumans trained by Colonel Rhoads before The Point existed."

Rhoads stood at parade rest several feet behind Lopez. If the man felt any guilt at all, it didn't show on his politician's face.

Lopez said, "They were special ops, a banana republic's worst nightmare. Things got hairier than an ape, and the High Rollers went rogue. We're talking major atrocities. Women and children, the whole nine. The details would make you puke. The Army rounded them up and put them in The Farm . . . only they escaped, and now they're pissed."

"We're pissed, too!" Clayton hollered. The meatheads roared agreement. Scarlett loved them for it.

Lopez's animal snort sliced through the bravado. "None of you are ready. The High Rollers spent ten years in the field, honing their powers. They're fanatically loyal to their leader, Jagger. To him, the human race is nothing but a buzzing fly, and all he wants to do is pluck its wings and watch it suffer."

Jagger, Scarlett thought, *and the High Rollers*, and suddenly she understood everything with the burning clarity of a blowtorch flame.

"Jagger is hell in combat boots," Lopez said, "and he's marching this way. I'm the only one who can prepare you." His eyes found Scarlett. "See, I used to be a High Roller."

AFTER THE ASSEMBLY, Scarlett walked to the front and waited for the auditorium to empty.

Passing cadets gave her pitying looks. Several mumbled condolences and reached out to touch her arm. Others avoided eye contact, as if tragedy might prove contagious.

Lucy wrapped her in a hug, promising revenge.

Seamus stepped up, face twisting with emotion.

Scarlett didn't try to hide her dismay. "Seamus, why—"

"I'm sorry," he said, and hurried away.

She watched him go, feeling confused and angry.

Then she was alone with Rhoads, who regarded her grimly.

Scarlett snapped to attention. "Sir, Cadet Winter requesting permission to speak."

"At ease, Scarlett," Rhoads said softly. "Why aren't you packing your bags?"

She didn't want to relax. She was done taking the easy way out. "I want to stay, sir. I want to join the strike force."

Concern wrinkled Rhoads's face. "I appreciate your spirit, Scarlett, and I'm sorry about your brother, but your request is denied. Only upperclassmen may apply. You're a plebe."

"I'm more than a plebe, sir. I'm a Level III."

"A Level III who still hasn't broken through with her training."

"I'll break through," she said. "I'll train harder than anyone."

Rhoads's eyes twinkled briefly—the notion of Scarlett unleashing her full power no doubt sparking his imagination—but he sighed and shook his head. "It's too dangerous."

She felt a surge of desperation. Dan's death was her fault.

She had never lived up to her potential, not as a student, an athlete, a friend, a girlfriend, a daughter, or a sister. Nor had she applied herself here. As soon as she'd tested Level III, she'd coasted. When Dalia had flapped her lips instead of teaching yoga, Scarlett had gone with the flow. When Rhoads had asked her to hold on to energy, she'd claimed it was too painful. She palmed meds, did the bare minimum in class, and blew off much-needed rack time to stroll campus and hook up. She was a lifelong slacker who'd squandered every gift ever given to her.

She wouldn't let Dan down now. "Let me fight, sir. They killed Dan *because of me*."

Rhoads blinked at her. "They did. I won't deny it. But—"

"Give me two weeks, sir. If I haven't broken through, you can kick me off."

"You've had months to harness your power," Rhoads said. "You're telling me that you can break through in two weeks?"

"Yes, sir," Scarlett said. "I've never been so motivated."

Rhoads stared at her.

Scarlett waited, letting the man think. In the distance, Lopez barked orders.

Rhoads pulled TUMS from an inside pocket and crunched a handful. "The strike force will train hard, seven days a week. You would miss classes for weeks, maybe months, and wouldn't have time for homework. That would probably mean—"

"Recycled," she said, nodding gravely. "I understand."

"Your class would move on without you," he said. "You'd have to repeat plebe year."

"With all due respect, sir," Scarlett said, "I don't give a shit."

"Pack your bags, Scarlett. You leave for North Carolina in thirty minutes. You need to say good-bye to your brother." Rhoads started away.

"But sir . . . I—"

Rhoads paused in the doorway without turning back around. "After the funeral, come straight back to The Point, and I'll give you two weeks to prove that you belong on the strike force."

THIRTY-SEVEN

EVERYTHING HURT.

Once more, Scarlett sat in Room 17, receiving a steady flow of current. From the crown of her head to the soles of her feet, pain filled her like boiling oil. Every cell in her body screamed for her to release the torturous energy into the oversized gloves, but she gritted her teeth and stared at Rhoads through blurry eyes stinging with perspiration.

She had never held on this long, had never harbored this much energy.

Rhoads checked the meter. His expression passed from excitement to concern. "All right, Scarlett," he said. "That's enough for today."

"No," she growled. She gripped the chair more tightly, trying to keep her involuntarily flailing body from dropping to the floor.

She couldn't let go, not now, with only one week left to prove that she belonged on the strike force. She had defensive capabilities but could only counterattack. Since the strike force was training primarily for ambush and infiltration, she had no clear role on the team.

To earn a spot, she needed to absorb more power and hold on to that force the way a magazine held ammo.

She would do it or die trying.

The funeral had gutted her. Her parents had been hollowed-out shells of themselves, her mother drugged and sobbing and inconsolable, her father pale and empty-eyed and lost. Dan's fiancée, Daisy, had been sad and sweet. Though Daisy was only in her twenties, her hair was shot through with gray. She'd held Scarlett's hand throughout the nightmarish ceremony, which took place in a dusty conference room at the back of the nondescript building within the industrial-looking complex where government agents were keeping her parents safe.

Dan's coffin was closed, of course. The fire had burned so hotly that the Jeep wasn't even recognizable. Atop the glossy casket sat a framed picture of Dan in uniform and a vase of plastic flowers dominated by yellows, oranges, and reds.

Scarlett, her parents, and Daisy were the only attendees. A Marine chaplain spoke briefly about Dan and sacrifice, but she didn't really listen. She stared at her brother's coffin, thinking, *All my fault, all my fault . . .*

Two Marines entered and played taps, executed the flag-folding ritual, and handed the flag to her mother with whispered condolences. Even Scarlett broke down then, barely aware of Daisy rubbing her back and crying softly beside her.

Then the chaplain said something, and it was over.

Just like that. Time to leave.

Good-bye, Dan. Good-bye, brother. No chance to apologize, no chance to bury the hatchet, no chance for Scarlett to make something of herself, no chance to make Dan proud.

Nothing, nothing, nothing.

Scarlett asked for a moment alone with Dan's coffin. Her parents drifted away like ghosts. Daisy followed, brushing her fingertips softly over the glossy wood as she passed.

Scarlett blew her nose, wiped her eyes, and straightened her uniform before approaching her brother for the last time. From down the hall, she could hear murmured conversation and faint music. Up close, she noticed that someone had left the sticker on the vase of flowers.

AUTUMN BOUQUET, the sticker read, IMITATION. $8.97.

She stared into the framed face. The eyes of her dead brother stared back at her. They were soldier's eyes, hard and fearless.

"Dan," she said, and wrestled against her quavering voice. She had planned to apologize but realized that she couldn't. If she tried, she'd completely melt down. "I'm going to get them." Her eyes burned, but she fought back the tears. "I *promise*."

Now, suffering again in Room 17, she glared at Rhoads. "Turn . . . up . . . the . . . flow."

He hesitated briefly, then increased the current. Fresh pain infused Scarlett's agony.

Since returning to The Point a week earlier, she had driven forward like a machine. *Like a yellow Jeep*, she thought, *with rusted floorboards, blasting classic rock.*

Every second of every day, she focused on making the strike force, which included Lucy, Dunne, and Hopkins, who still sneered but treated Scarlett fairly.

Fine by me. I don't want to be buddies. Just do your job and stay out of my way.

Dalia was a strike force member, too, though she rarely trained alongside them and never joined them for meals. The strike force ate together wherever they were training and shunned the mess hall above ground. They saved a lot of time, not having to change uniforms, form up, or travel to the mess hall, and they maximized that extra time, dispensing with mess hall etiquette to talk tactics through the meals. Scarlett sensed that there was more to their isolation than that, something bordering on pride. The team was coalescing as an elite strike force. The order she'd known since coming to The Point had flipped. Her teammates were no longer freakish cave dwellers, living beneath the *real* cadets. They were preparing to employ incredible skills against enemies who could destroy the surface dwellers literally in the blink of an eye.

The strike force focused on door-buster tactics. Scarlett pushed hard, started taking all her meds, and followed every order. Rhoads was pleased, yet the question hung in the air between them: Would Scarlett prove herself in time?

Scarlett worked hard at yoga and meditation with Dalia. Things between them were much friendlier, and meditation and yoga actually were helping. They did nothing to dull the pain but had enhanced Scarlett's awareness of the energy flowing through her.

She could feel her body handling different energies with different systems. She'd always sensed this, but now she could feel the separate pathways as definitely as she could feel her various muscle groups. Electricity burned along her nervous system, lighting her up like a Christmas tree. Kinetic energy bounced around inside her like shock waves before radiating into the muscles. Sound waves also bounced around, though not so painfully, and built within her bones, which vibrated like tuning forks if she waited too long to release. Sound waves were by far the easiest to hold, though this didn't impress Rhoads, who reasoned that it was highly unlikely that a High Roller would attack with a sonic boom.

Because she had to miss academic classes, instructors provided her with detailed notes, but she barely studied. By the end of every day, she was completely destroyed. She gave up chess with Lucy, stopped taking nighttime walks, and blew off Seamus, all to get more sleep, which she needed in order to break through.

Her sleep was carpeted wall to wall in dreams so shockingly vivid that her nights became a second life, separate from her waking existence yet no less real. She dreamed only of Dan.

Her brother, alive and well, would walk with her along a stretch of deserted beach that she almost recognized but couldn't quite place.

You have to avenge me, Dan would say. *Now, tell me about these magical powers again.*

And they would walk on, strolling the empty beach, Scarlett telling Dan all about her abilities, training, challenges, and goals.

Sometimes Dan would ask questions, his breath redolent of smoke and kerosene and a ghastly scorched smell that made her scars tickle. Other times he would stare into the distance, his eyes narrowing the way they did when he puzzled over an engine block. Mostly, however, he just listened and then told Scarlett again, *Avenge me*.

And in that dreaming world, Scarlett nightly renewed her blood promise.

THIRTY-EIGHT

"ALL RIGHT," LUCY SAID, GATHERING THINGS FROM her desk, "I'm hitting the library. I know you'll miss me terribly, but carry on bravely, soldier."

Scarlett laughed. It wouldn't occur to her until later that Lucy had set her up.

Scarlett sat at her desk, staring through notes and thinking about what Lopez had told them after door-busting drills. *Tomorrow Colonel Rhoads will brief you on the High Rollers*, Lopez had said, his voice growling like tires on gravel. *Tune in and take notes. There'll be a test—whether or not you survive when you finally meet the bastards face-to-face.*

Her stomach did a slow roll. She wished she could bust down Jagger's door right now and blast him between the eyes with 10 million volts, but this intermediate step, learning about her brother's killers, seeing their pictures, hearing their names, made her feel—

"Hey."

She turned.

Seamus stood in the doorway, looking uncharacteristically wary. "May I come in?"

Her heart gave a little hitch, and she smiled reflexively but then came to her senses and straightened the smile. "Sure."

Seamus took a few steps inside and leaned against the bunks, hands shoved into the pockets of his PT shorts. He eyed her cagily. "So, where are we?"

"I guess we're on hold."

"On hold?" he said. "You don't talk to me. You don't smile back when I pass you in the halls. You look away, Scarlett."

"I have a lot on my mind."

He took a step toward her. "Look, I'm no good at this, okay? I don't know how to say this type of stuff, all right? But we have something."

She felt like a chew rope caught between pit bulls, anger and affection.

Whatever. I don't have time for this now. "Yeah," she said, "we had something."

"*Had*, huh?" Color came into his cheeks, and he laughed bitterly. "But not anymore?"

She stood, feeling her face grow hot. Her body ached from training, ached like she'd run a marathon, boxed a heavyweight champ, and thrown herself down a dozen flights of stairs for good measure. She had to study. If she couldn't study, she needed to sleep so that she could be at her best the next day. "Why didn't you join the strike force?"

"I couldn't."

"Bull," she said. "You're the most powerful TK at The Point. Rhoads would kill to have you on the team."

"Screw Rhoads," he said. "I'm not joining his team."

She spread her arms. "The High Rollers killed my brother."

"And Rhoads killed my whole family."

"What? You said that your dad—"

"Rhoads turned my dad into a murderer."

She took a step toward him. "You never—" An invisible hand stopped her.

"Rhoads got our dads gassed in Iraq," he said. "He was in charge. He made the call, despite warnings. That gas—and the so-called treatment that saved them—changed our dads. You said your dad got mean. Well, my dad went psycho."

"I'm sorry about your family," she said. Everything felt weird. Sad and horrible and not quite real. Part of her wished she could hop on a Yamaha and peel out of there. She couldn't, though. Wouldn't. This time she was all in. "You can't blame Rhoads. He couldn't have known what—"

"What if it wasn't a mistake? What if Rhoads knew all about the chemical weapons, knew what was going to happen, and marched our dads straight in there?"

"That's ridiculous."

"Is it? After the gas attack, Rhoads shipped his troops to Germany, where doctors had genetic treatments ready to go even though they'd supposedly never heard of this chemical agent before. Doesn't that strike you as strange? And then Rhoads just happens to find out when kids like you and me start showing off our crazy party tricks? Open your eyes, Scarlett. We've been on a watch list our whole lives. And who happens to be in charge of our training? Rhoads, that's who, the guy who ruined our dads and messed up our DNA. That doesn't strike you as weird?"

She pinched the bridge of her nose. Her skull, which had been filled with booming, flashing fireworks since Room 17, accelerated toward a grand finale.

"Why isn't Rhoads messed up from the gas?" Seamus said, taking a step closer. "Because he took some kind of antidote, that's why."

"Enough." She had a mission—avenge Dan—and wouldn't let Seamus fog her path. "The past is the past."

He shook his head. "You don't believe that."

"All I care about is killing the people who killed my brother."

"Then you're playing right into Rhoads's plans," he said, and stepped even closer. "You'll be his weapon then, and that's exactly what he wants from us. That's the point of The Point: building a posthuman arsenal. We wipe out the High Rollers, Rhoads becomes a hero. The program gets whatever he wants. They'll probably start gassing regular troops. Set them to breeding, build a whole army of superhumans."

"Stop," she said, or meant to say. It came out as a shout.

Seamus stood his ground. "You want vengeance. I get it. When Dad killed Mom and my little brothers and our cocker spaniel, I would've done anything to punish him. *Anything*."

"You understand, then. So help me."

He shook his head. "I'm sorry, Scarlett. I won't let Rhoads turn me into his weapon."

Seamus's eyes glistened with tears that he was too tough to shed. Scarlett realized that they had moved unconsciously closer as they'd argued, as if their very bodies yearned to touch. It would be such a simple thing to lift her hand, caress his face, and end the fight—and end her insane attempt to make the strike force, which so far had been like smashing her face into a brick wall day after day. One touch . . .

His glistening eyes sang to her heart like Sirens along a rocky shore.

But what about Mom's tears? What about Daisy's? What about her own?

She crossed her arms. "Go, then, if you won't help. Get out and leave me alone."

"Fine," he said, and stalked away. He stopped at the door and rounded on her. "But you can't just turn it off, Scarlett. If you let Rhoads turn you into a weapon, you won't be able to change that. Not *ever*."

And he was gone.

SCARLETT RECOGNIZED THE beach now.

It was the stretch of deserted sand that she and Dan had discovered as kids, when they stayed at the north end of Corolla in South Carolina's Outer Banks.

Now, in the dream, they were no longer children. They were both in uniform, Dan in his dress blues, looking like he had marched off a recruiting poster for the Marine Corps, and Scarlett in her PT uniform, the one she wore during energy training.

"You have to break through," Dan said.

"I'm trying," she said. "I only have a few days. Rhoads says that if I don't—"

"You'll do it."

"I'm trying," she repeated, and explained how hard she'd pushed herself that morning, holding on for longer than ever before.

Dan chuckled. "Beating your head against the wall, huh? You always were tough. But you can't just gut this out, kiddo. I've been thinking about the mechanics."

She grinned, partly because it was such a Dan thing, analyzing supernatural power in mechanical terms, and partly in anticipation, because her brother was one of those rare people who could fix anything. "Rhoads says I need to find my capacitor."

Dan shook his head. "That's your problem: trying to hold the energy. The force builds up, reaches critical mass, and explodes. Stop trying to be a battery, Scarlett. Be a power plant."

"A power plant . . ."

He showed her the shining grin that meant his brain was firing on all cylinders. "Power plants aren't just big batteries that we drain and replace. They get energy from windmills, hydraulic turbines, nuclear reactors, coal furnaces, but they don't pump wind or water or heat out to the world. They convert energy into electricity and pump *that* out to us."

"All right," she said, following him but still uncertain where exactly he was headed.

"You want to hold that energy longer, convert it. Keep it moving."

"How?"

"You said that each type of force feels different inside you, right? And you have different channels for each variety. Don't just let the force build in your chest. Reroute it to another channel—or multiple channels. Use more of your body. Change the energy's form, keep it moving and buy time. Then, when you're ready to release, convert it. Rhoads hits you with ten thousand decibels, fry his equipment with a lightning bolt. You won't just make the team. You'll make captain."

THIRTY-NINE

KYLE STEEDE, SCARLETT WROTE. *STRONGEST POST-human ever. Merciless.*

Around her, the dozen strike force cadets, including Lucy, Dunne, and Hopkins, scribbled their own notes. Dalia sat with crossed arms, listening to Rhoads but writing nothing.

When Scarlett woke that morning, she had been excited to test Dan's theory. Maybe it was crazy to follow dream advice, but she was out of options. Yes, she'd improved through toughness, but Rhoads was demanding more, and Scarlett already had pushed herself to the max, so conversion it was. As she pulled on her PT uniform, however, Lucy corrected her. Morning training had been canceled to clear the schedule for the High Rollers briefing.

"Next slide, please," Rhoads said, and the image of the burly post-human with crazy eyes disappeared, replaced by a pale little girl wearing a sparkling silver dress, a pink feather boa, and a toy tiara that twinkled atop her white-blond hair. She looked vaguely familiar . . . and completely ridiculous.

"This is Penny," Rhoads said, "the second most dangerous person in the world."

Laughter rippled across the classroom. The girl was scrawny, eleven or twelve years old. Probably eleven. With her glittering eyes and grin full of braces, she looked like someone had just given her a pony.

Rhoads didn't laugh. "That red-and-white sign behind her is the Fox Theatre in Atlanta. Can anyone tell me what happened in Atlanta last spring?"

He didn't wait for an answer. The Atlanta tragedy had shocked the world.

"Note the time," Rhoads said, and Scarlett jotted "1:38" next to "Penny." "Seven minutes after this photo was taken, Penny killed 117 people. She incinerated them with her mind."

Scarlett struggled to square the little girl's beaming smile with the carnage in Atlanta.

Then a chill went through her.

She's the one. She killed Dan. Burned him to death.

"We don't know who she is exactly," Rhoads said, "only that they call her Penny and that she is the only pyrokinetic free in the world. We suspect that she was also responsible for Times Square."

"You see this little bitch," Lopez said, "kill her on sight."

People shifted, obviously uncomfortable with the command to kill a small child.

Picturing her brother's coffin, Scarlett called out, "Yes, Sergeant," and wrote "Kill her on sight" next to Penny's name.

"Next slide," Rhoads said. "Behold Antonio Jagger, the most dangerous person alive."

Dark-haired and thirtyish, Jagger wore Wayfarer sunglasses and a winning smile. He had sideburns, full lips, and a large nose and managed the rare magic trick of being really attractive without actually being handsome. He didn't look particularly dangerous. He looked like a guy who could tell a good joke.

"I trained Jagger at Bragg, before The Point even existed," Rhoads said. "He was one of the original High Rollers. In fact, he suggested the unit name. When we recruited him, Jagger was a gambler. He drifted casino to casino, hitting it big at blackjack. Based on his winning streak, we assumed that he had a perfect mathematical mind, an eidetic memory, or a remote viewing ability."

Scarlett brushed reflexively at the back of her neck, where it felt like someone was tickling her with a feather. She turned and raised a brow. No one was messing with her, but her classmates were all smiling. Not at Scarlett and not at Rhoads—at the screen.

"Here at The Point, however," Rhoads said, "Jagger tested unremarkably on math, ESP, everything. We began to suspect that he wasn't posthuman at all, that his lucky streak had been just that, a lucky streak. But he was likable and seemed to have leadership skills, so we just sort of kept him on. Eventually, somebody misplaced his discharge papers, and we thought, What the heck? Why not keep the guy, see how he works out?"

The tickling on her neck intensified and crawled up her skull. Was a TK trying to get her attention? She glanced out the classroom door, half expecting to see Seamus, but the little glass square was empty. The disappointment that she felt surprised her.

"The posthuman program was new," Rhoads said. "Things at Bragg were pretty sketchy. We were figuring things out as we went along. The idea was to create a unit of posthuman supersoldiers. But what we did there, it wasn't a leadership program like The Point."

Lopez's snort cut through the air, making Scarlett jump. "You can say that again, sir."

"These recruits hadn't volunteered. They were conscripted. Many weren't cut out to be soldiers. Out of desperation, we used experimental tactics to maintain control. Some were . . . *harsh*."

Lopez nodded, absentmindedly fingering a long scar on his muscular forearm.

"Frankly, we didn't know what we were doing," Rhoads said. "The recruits were frightened and angry. They hated us and fought among themselves. The program was crumbling. Then we made Jagger platoon leader, and—" Rhoads snapped his fingers. "—our troubles were over. He was a natural leader. Suddenly, we didn't care whether or not he had powers. The platoon needed him. *We* needed him."

Lopez said, "Every night, Jagger held a meeting in the back bay. We told him our problems. He listened. Really listened. We could tell that he understood us and cared. He reported our complaints, and things changed. Jagger had our backs. So we wanted to make him happy and wanted to show *Major* Rhoads that we'd work harder for Jagger than we would for him and his goons."

Scarlett noticed her classmates nodding and smiling. Why did they look so enthusiastic? Her skull tingled, and a touch of heat lit in her chest.

What's going on?

A minuscule amount of energy was building inside her. Was she picking up some kind of radiation? Was Rhoads secretly testing her, targeting her with microwaves or something?

Rhoads said, "Much later, after the High Rollers' mass escape, the guards testified that Jagger just *sweet-talked* his way out of The Farm. He simply suggested that the guards should release the inmates, and the guards opened the cells and gates and gave the departing inmates handshakes and high fives, along with cash and car keys and firearms. We took a much closer look at Antonio Jagger then. We went back through his files, all the way to security cam footage of him raking in the chips at Vegas and A.C. and Tishomingo. Analyzing the footage, we realized that Jagger had been playing us from day one.

"When we originally watched the footage, we'd seen what we were looking for—a slim, dark-haired man in sunglasses and flashy clothes, generally in the company of an attractive girl or two, scoring big wins at the blackjack table—but after the escape, revisiting the footage, we were struck right between the eyes by a lightning bolt of understanding.

"Zooming in on Jagger's cards, we saw losing hand after losing hand. Jagger just *acted* like he'd won, and the dealers and players responded as if he'd plopped down a winning hand.

"Jagger is empathy without sympathy. He 'gets' people better than Oprah or Dr. Phil, but he'd draw you a warm bath to soothe your sore muscles, then talk you into slitting your wrists, just for the fun of watching the water turn pink."

Scarlett's classmates once more shifted uncomfortably in their seats.

"I've been watching you smile at his picture," Rhoads said. "Raise your hand if, just seeing his image, you thought he seemed pretty cool."

Hands rose sheepishly. A few at first, then others, and finally everyone but Dalia and Scarlett.

Rhoads nodded. "Like a master illusionist, Jagger projects likability. Add motion, body language, and the sound of his voice, and he can charm people like some kind of vampire."

Lopez came forward. "Jagger would tell me to crush a skull or rip off an arm or spear my fingers into somebody's guts and pull out their spine. I was his pet gorilla, and I did whatever he wanted. I was brainwashed. We all were. I'd still be with him if I hadn't been in surgery when the High Rollers broke out. Once he was gone, my head cleared. When I understood what he'd made me do, I dedicated my life to killing the son of a bitch."

"Tell them about the final mission," Rhoads said.

"We were on operations in South America," Lopez said. "We had business with a certain army officer who also happened to be a major drug trafficker. So we camped out with some villagers on his route. Primitive people, one foot back in the Stone Age. They worked his drug fields, and El Jefe gave them T-shirts and medicine, whiskey, stuff like that. Well, Jagger, he won these people over in a heartbeat, and they put us up. They were simple people. Hunter-gatherer types. Kids and dogs all over. They didn't understand the first thing about the world outside. They just knew that they liked whiskey and candy. El Jefe, he was like a god to them. If they made him happy, they got junk food and firewater. If they pissed him off—and they were lazy and forgetful by nature, truly preindustrial folks—he'd kill one or two of them.

"I felt bad for them. They were small people with innocent eyes and big smiles. I liked them. We all did, even Jagger. But days passed, and then a week, and no sign of El Jefe. Whenever Jagger got bored, he got moody. After a couple of weeks, he got sick of the villagers. Started telling us how worthless they were. We knew that he felt that way about normal humans in general, but these people, they were so primitive, he said it offended him. Good for nothing but slaves, that's what Jagger said. He started playing with them. He'd picked up their language—it's crazy how fast he can learn a language—so he started telling them to do things. It was funny at first. 'Act like a dog,' he'd tell the village elder, and the guy would start barking and shaking his butt like he was wagging a tail, stuff like that. But the longer we waited there, the darker Jagger's jokes got." Lopez paused and looked at Rhoads.

"This is actual video from the village," Rhoads said.

Grainy footage came to life on the screen. One of the villagers, a small man in a ratty Coca-Cola shirt, stood before a dark-haired soldier in camouflage fatigues and sunglasses.

Jagger.

Scarlett rubbed her chest as if she had heartburn. The energy there continued to build.

Jagger rattled something in a strange language that Scarlett had never heard. Subtitles scrolled across the bottom of the screen: "*Your mother died today*."

The smiling villager's face convulsed with shock, and he broke down crying.

Jagger faced the camera. "The dumb son of a bitch," he said in English, his voice deep and full. "His mother's been dead for years!"

Scarlett jumped, startled when her classmates burst into laughter.

Rhoads killed the clip.

The cadets' laughter sputtered and died. They looked at the floor, blushing.

Scarlett glared at them. Why had they laughed at that twisted clip?

Because Jagger's the man, some part of her brain whispered. *Funnier than hell, and smart-smart-smart, and screw that stupid little villager, anyway. Primitive piece of . . .*

Scarlett shook her head. Where had those thoughts come from?

"That was just a small dose," Rhoads said. "Spend time with Jagger, you're his."

"Jagger made the villagers fight for our entertainment," Lopez said. "Men at first. Then he got bored and spiced things up with weird matches: eight kids and an old woman versus a strong man, stuff like that. The High Rollers stood by and watched. We *cheered*." She could hear the shame and humiliation in his voice. "He made us cheer. I could puke just thinking about it."

Lopez didn't puke, though. He just kept talking, his voice cold and leaden, marching dutifully forward with his heavy pack of remorse hiked high on his shoulders. "One night Jagger pulled his Jeep into the center of the village and honked his horn, and everyone came out. The Jeep had a PA loudspeaker in the grill, and Jagger used it like a bullhorn. He got the villagers laughing and told them what he wanted them to do, and they all thought it was a great idea, and he told them all right, have at it. They went completely psychotic. No hesitation. They used machetes and rocks, knives and farming tools, hands and feet and teeth. It was a bloodbath. The last one standing was a boy about seventeen. He was laughing and crying and bleeding, and Jagger told him to slit his own throat, and the kid didn't even hesitate."

The strike force looked sick, shocked, and frightened.

"Making matters worse," Rhoads said, "Jagger appears to be expanding his powers." He advanced to the next slide, which showed Jagger on a rickety stage in what looked like an old country church. A congregation of wide-eyed worshippers crushed against the stage, reaching up toward Jagger with their right hands.

They look crazy, she thought, and felt the tingling again. She hadn't even noticed that it had stopped in the first place, but it was back.

"Notice anything strange?" Rhoads asked.

"They're all using a hand sign," Uba said, and mirrored it. "An outstretched palm with the thumb tucked."

"True," Rhoads said, "but look again. Something's even stranger."

Scarlett saw it. "Jagger is levitating, sir."

"Exactly," Rhoads said, and pointed to Jagger's boots, which were partially obscured by the reaching hands but were hovering six inches above the stage. "We have reports of him using other powers, too. Superstrength, speed, even healing. But using these powers seems to weaken him. We have accounts of him fading out like a narcoleptic, and he disappears for weeks after each terrorist event. We hope to catch him at low tide. Question, DeCraig?"

Lucy sat very straight, her eyes large behind her spectacles. It occurred to Scarlett then that her friend, who relied so heavily on self-control, must be feeling uniquely violated by Jagger's strange influence. "Sir, how can we fight him if he has this type of persuasive power?"

"We're trying to locate Jagger," Rhoads said, and glanced toward Dalia. "We'll use drone strikes to eliminate the threat."

"But we're drilling ambush and infil, sir."

Rhoads nodded. "There's a chance that we won't be able to use drones."

"In that case, sir—"

"In that case," Lopez said, jumping in, "shoot first and ask questions later. Everyone strike at the same time, max power."

Lucy rolled her shoulders, looking like she'd been given a kamikaze mission.

As Scarlett wrote "Shoot first, ask questions later," Rhoads said, "If we zoom in, you'll notice the woman on stage behind him. She's Jagger's closest confidante, Sadie Holt, twenty-five."

Dalia gave a muffled gasp. Scarlett looked up from her notebook and watched Dalia close her mouth and narrow her bulging eyes.

Rhoads said, "Sadie wasn't an original High Roller. She washed out of The Point and was convalescing at The Farm when Jagger escaped and took her with him. Sadie was the first somnopath we'd ever seen."

The class shifted toward Dalia, who now sat with no expression on her face, pen in hand, feigning sudden interest in note taking.

"Jagger keeps her close," Rhoads said. "If you see Sadie, Jagger is nearby."

Scarlett finally looked at the screen and didn't bother to muffle her gasp. She lurched to her feet and pointed at the girl with gray-streaked hair. "That's Daisy," she said, "my brother's fiancée."

FORTY

WHEN SCARLETT CRAWLED THROUGH THE ROPES and into the boxing ring, she was seething with rage and self-loathing. Although logically she knew that she couldn't have known the truth about "Daisy," as Rhoads had pointed out in his office after the briefing, she couldn't help but feel that she should have known, should have sensed the threat in her gut or bones or blood.

But she hadn't. She'd sat beside her and accepted her comfort and hugged her good-bye.

Her first concern then had been her parents, but Rhoads placed the call and learned that her parents were still safe in North Carolina.

"Daisy" had checked out immediately after the funeral. Scarlett listened while Rhoads made several calls, setting agencies into motion. Within an hour, they learned that her apartment was abandoned and the person she'd claimed to be, Daisy Belfort, a psychology student at NC State, just up the road from Camp Lejeune, had never existed. All a lie, all a ruse to . . .

"But why?" Scarlett demanded. "Why bother to seduce Dan?"

"Maybe to get close to you," Rhoads said. "Or to learn more about you. If I know Jagger, though, the main reason was to hurt and disturb you. It wasn't enough to kill your brother. He had to make you feel violated, had to make you—and all of us here at The Point—feel vulnerable."

Rhoads remained in his office, trying to hunt her down, but sent Scarlett to spar with her teammates, saying, "It'll help you to blow off steam."

Coal-burning power plants generate steam, Scarlett had thought, *which spins turbines, creating electrical energy*.

If Clayton felt bad about Scarlett's revelation in the briefing, he didn't show it. Goaded on by Lopez, he rushed at her like a tsunami of muscle.

Just how Scarlett wanted it.

She lay on the ropes and let the gigantic meathead hammer away.

Lopez shouted for her to fire back, but she ignored him.

A few seconds later, when Clayton stopped punching to catch his breath, she mumbled insults through the mouthpiece and beckoned her massive opponent to hit her some more.

Clayton pummeled her with thudding shots, walloping her with wide hooks and looping overhands that filled Scarlett with bouncing force that pumped her muscles full of hissing lava.

Outside the ring, cadets shouted encouragement, though Scarlett couldn't say whether they were shouting to Clayton or to her. She was too focused on channeling energy.

Using the mindfulness Dalia had taught her, she focused on the task, blurring out the world and the voices. Clayton's punches became a kind of cadence, a rhythmic *boom-boom-boom* that was the heartbeat of her concentration as she redirected the pulsing energy from her muscles to her bones, as if it were the result not of concussion but of sound, the force she'd always been able to handle best.

Her bones sucked the force from her muscles, and the urgent burning fire that had been building within her became a manageable vibration throughout her skeleton.

Yes!

Clayton stepped back, huffing like an exhausted draft horse, and stared at her with his mouth wide open.

Scarlett opened her own mouth and released a blast of sound that knocked the meathead off his feet and shattered the glass of the equipment room's door.

After that, no one stood a chance.

One after another, strike force members climbed through the ropes, tried her, and failed.

Soon, she realized that just as she could convert and redirect received force, storing it as sound energy, she also could switch channels upon opening her bones.

With Hopkins, she absorbed a round's worth of telekinetic haymakers, stored them as sound in her bones, and then transmuted them into gravitational force that slammed the TK to the ground and pinned him to the canvas like a bug smashed against a windshield. Truth be told, Scarlett could have smashed him just as flat, but she held back and released extra energy between rounds, battering nearby heavy bags with powerful barrages of telekinetic strikes.

Lopez looked on with a grudging smile.

She'd done it. She'd broken through at last.

Thank you, Dan.

She went easy on her final opponent, Lucy, who, with her great height and skinny physique, looked ridiculous bobbing and weaving in puffy gloves and headgear, like a sunflower in a windstorm. Lucy pattered away with invisible jabs that glanced and grazed lightly off Scarlett's headgear. After the bell rang, Scarlett gave her roomie a hug, turned to Lopez, and said, "That's it. That's everyone. Can we call it a day?"

Lopez chuckled, a sound like a meat grinder gobbling a whole haunch, bone and all. "Anybody want another shot at Winter?" He laughed again. "Going once, going twice—"

"I'll spar with her," a familiar voice said.

Seamus slipped through the ropes.

"No," Scarlett said. "You're not part of the strike force."

Seamus rolled his shoulders as if they were going to have a fist-fight. "You want to be their weapon? Fight the best, then."

"Seamus, this is stupid," she said.

The cadets stomped the bleachers in a thunderous roll and started cheering, "Kyeong! Kyeong the Cannon!"

Scarlett's heart leaped in her chest. "I don't know what you're trying to prove, but I'm not going to fight you."

"Ten seconds," Lopez shouted from ringside.

She stepped toward him. "Seamus, please."

He circled away, looking angry—and sad, too. "No, Scarlett. This is the reality. It's easy to fight someone you hate, like Hopkins, or someone big, like Dunne, who you know can take it, but if you're going to be their weapon, that means that they point you. They pull the trigger."

"Seamus, stop. This is—"

The bell rang.

Seamus's face twisted, and an arc of force smashed her across the back. In all the sparring and hazing and training she'd endured, she'd never felt such incredible force. The abruptness and ferocity of his attack surprised her so much that she didn't have time to channel the force, which boomeranged out of her. A wall locker crunched inward and toppled, spilling gloves and headgear and sending dozens of rolled hand wraps rolling across the mat.

"What the hell, Seamus?" she said.

"They tell you to kill, you kill," he said. "Period." And he launched another attack.

She circled the edges of the ring like a rangy boxer against a heavy-handed puncher, ducking and dodging, but Seamus was relentless, and his invisible blows came from all directions.

"You're giving them everything," he said, pressing forward. "You're ruining your future."

She absorbed a tremendous slashing attack, channeled it into her bones, and opened her mouth to dispute his claim. At that second, he blasted her in the lower back, another surprise attack that ricocheted out of her. A ring post turnbuckle exploded in a spray of vinyl and foam. The remaining force splintered outward, clipping Lopez and bowling him over. "Watch your fucking aim, Winter!" the hulking sergeant bellowed.

"Hear that?" Seamus said. "*Watch your aim*. Good weapons shoot where they're pointed."

"Please stop," she said, panting with effort. "This is crazy. You have to understand."

Lopez shouted for her to fire back, but she refused. Seamus wanted her to blast him. He was so stubborn that he'd get himself killed just to prove a point.

He chased her, blasting away with blistering attacks and a scathing monologue.

She was selling her soul to Rhoads, he said. Ditching herself and their relationship to become Rhoads's magical bazooka.

There was some truth in what he said, of course, but she couldn't let Dan down, couldn't let his murder go unavenged.

No way.

The bell rang, and it was over.

"Time!" Lopez bellowed.

Scarlett spit out her mouthpiece, scowled at Seamus, and released a bolt of lightning that leaped from her with a blinding flash and a deafening crack. Across the gym, a heavy bag vaporized in an explosion of light and heat and crackling electricity. The lights dimmed, went out, and recovered. Behind where the bag had hung, the cinder blocks were scorched and steaming. Cadets staggered, wide-eyed, rubbing their ears and sniffing ozone and casting wary glances at Scarlett. The hair on her arms stood at attention.

She went to the ropes. Lucy climbed onto the ring apron. Her eyes filled her spectacles. Scarlett pushed her gloves through the ropes. "Get these off of me, Lucy."

"You all right, sis?" Lucy said.

"I don't know," Scarlett said. "I just don't know anymore."

Seamus was behind her then, tugging at her arm, apologizing, his voice thick with emotion. "I'm so sorry, Scarlett," he said. "I'm trying to save you."

She refused to turn toward him. Lucy unlaced her gloves and yanked them free. Scarlett unbuckled her headgear and peeled it away. Sweat poured from the chin guard. She chucked the padded helmet out of the ring, and it bounced away across the mat.

Seamus squeezed her arm. "If you go down that path, there's no turning back. I don't want you to suffer like I've suffered."

Lucy held the ropes, and Scarlett slipped from the ring.

"Winter's out," Lopez called. "Who's next?"

"I am." The strange voice, calm and quiet, cut through the commotion.

Scarlett turned.

Dalia entered the ring.

Lopez hesitated for a second and glanced out the main door, perhaps hoping Rhoads would appear. "Well . . ."

"I'm next," Dalia said.

"Knock it off, Dalia," Scarlett said.

Dalia didn't seem to hear or see her. She stared sleepily at Seamus.

"Fifteen seconds," Lopez said.

"No," Scarlett said, grabbing the top rope. "I'll go back in."

Lopez gave his animal snort. "You had your chance."

She jumped down from the ring apron and grabbed Lopez's shoulder. It was like gripping a granite wall. "Sergeant Lopez, I—"

"Lock it up, Winter," Lopez said, "and take your hand off me unless you want to lose your spot on the team."

Scarlett let her hand fall away.

Dalia leaned over the ropes and called to her. The dark circles beneath Dalia's eyes made her look like she'd already gone ten rounds. "Seamus is making you weak," Dalia told her. "He's trying to ruin everything—but I will save you."

"Dalia, don't."

The bell rang.

"Back off, Amer," Seamus said. "Rhoads isn't here to protect you now." And then he was talking over herself, a disembodied version of Seamus's voice calling, "Mom? Dad? Sorry I'm late, but—"

Screaming filled the air.

Both Seamuses were screaming . . .

One Seamus, made of flesh and blood, screamed in the ring, backpedaling in horror.

The other Seamus screamed within the dream, which Scarlett and the other cadets watched in a paralysis of terror.

Scarlett saw Seamus's home from his point of view, staring through his eyes as he entered the living room—such an inaptly named space in this nightmare moment, filled as it was with so many dead. Seamus's mother and twin brothers sat on the couch together, each of their heads a red mess, the work of the pistol sitting atop the fluffy corpse of a cocker spaniel in his father's lap. The gun rose now, pointing at Seamus and, through his perspective, at Scarlett and everyone else. His father said, "I'm sorry, son, but it's better this way. I didn't want to do this. I love Mom and your brothers so much, but . . ." His mouth continued to move, but a string of beeps blocked out his words, as if a TV crew in some parallel universe was editing the dream stream. Even with the beeping, Scarlett could make out one word: *Rhoads*.

"Dad, no," Seamus yelled again in unison, both in the dream and living it again here in public. "Dad, you didn't. Not Mom and—"

"I'm so sorry, son," his dad said, and you could see that he meant it, crazy as that was, could see the tears and the trembling in his hand as he raised the revolver, aiming it at Seamus. "It's my fault that you're the way you are. I can't let them have you. I can't let BEEP turn you into his attack dog. That's all we are to him . . . weapons."

"Dad, no!"

The pistol fired. The gunshot echoed through the gymnasium. Cadets shrieked.

But the pistol had jerked at the last second. Inches from Seamus's head, a family photo shattered, showering glass.

"You killed them, Dad," Seamus's voice in the dream said. "I won't let you kill me. You have to pay for what you did." In the ring, he simply wept, shaking his head from side to side.

Seamus's father grunted with confusion. His left hand flew to his right wrist, struggling in vain as the pistol executed a choppy arc, coming around to point at his face. He shouted at Seamus, but the muzzle jammed into his mouth, muffling the words.

"I'm sorry, Dad," dream Seamus said, and his father's garbled roar ended in the sharp crack of the pistol. His head jerked, spraying red, and his body spilled limply from the chair.

Then the dream was over.

Scarlett's breath shuddered free as she regained full awareness. All around her, strike force members mumbled and cursed. They'd all suffered through the dream.

At the center of the ring, Seamus sobbed. Terrible, tormented, pitiful, alone . . .

"Oh, Seamus," Scarlett muttered, and stepped toward him.

Dalia hunched in a corner, arms spread wide, fingers curled like talons. She panted with intensity, a terrible grin triumphant beneath her dark, glittering eyes.

"Seamus," Scarlett called, "are you—"

"Bitch!" Seamus screamed, and then Dalia flew across the ring as if she'd been struck by a car. She hit the ropes hard enough to stretch them outward, then bounced forward like a professional wrestler, where she smashed into a slashing blow of invisible force. Scarlett heard a terrible whip snap and a crunch. Dalia's head jerked, her face from hairline to chin split open in a line of bright red blood, and her body flopped to the canvas without so much as a twitch.

FORTY-ONE

AFTER CLAYTON LEFT, SCARLETT SAT BESIDE DALIA'S bed in the infirmary. Dalia had no other visitors, though the small room was still cramped with nurses coming and going, a physician who kept popping in and out, and Cramer, who leaned over Dalia, mending her with energy manipulation.

Dalia remained unconscious. She drew long, snorting breaths spaced too far apart, like the snoring of someone with late-stage sleep apnea. One side of her face had ballooned, closing that eye; the other eye stared blankly, the black hole of its pupil dilated to eclipse the iris. Worst of all, however, was the cut that ran between the eyes, dividing her face in halves from top to bottom. Seamus's final attack had split her forehead to the bone, broken and flayed her nose, shattered her front teeth, and sliced through her lips and chin.

Miraculously, Cramer already had closed those wounds and was attending, Scarlett believed, to internal damage. Cramer moved her hands slowly back and forth, a few inches above Dalia's right temple, in the manner of a fortune-teller consulting a crystal ball. Wavering green and purple light shifted in the space between her palms and Dalia's skull, reminding Scarlett of the night so long ago when she'd sat in the backseat of Cramer's car and watched the healer mend Seamus's lacerated eyebrow. The memory didn't seem real. Had things ever actually been that good, that simple, that sweet?

"She'll live," Cramer said, "but she's going to have a horrible scar, and her head's going to hurt like somebody packed it with broken glass."

Scarlett exhaled heavily and patted Dalia's hand. There had been a terrifying moment in the ring, as the guards dragged Seamus away, when Dalia's survival hadn't been certain.

Seamus hadn't resisted the guards. He'd sobbed, apologizing not to Dalia but to Scarlett, who could only stare in wordless terror as the men in camouflage dragged him away.

But Dalia would live. Thank God, she would live.

What she had done, torturing Seamus with that nightmarish memory, had been unbelievably cruel, but Seamus's response had been nothing short of monstrous.

Yet now she understood why Seamus hated Rhoads so much. Rhoads had exposed his father to the chemical that had caused him to kill Seamus's mother and brothers—and had triggered telekinetic power in Seamus. As his father had turned the gun on Seamus, he'd apologized, explaining that he'd done everything to save him from Rhoads. Whether that was true didn't matter. Scarlett could understand to some small degree the guilt that Seamus felt at his powers causing the death of loved ones. Ultimately, Rhoads had both empowered and forced Seamus to turn the gun on his father, who hadn't committed suicide at all. Sure, he'd jammed the gun into his own mouth, and technically, his finger had pulled the trigger, but Scarlett remembered all too vividly how the man had fought the turning of the pistol.

She felt horrible for Seamus, but what he had done to Dalia . . .

Nothing was simple anymore. Nothing was clear.

Well, almost nothing.

She knew one thing to be true.

She would avenge her brother.

Lopez appeared in the doorway. "Come with me, Winter."

She gave Dalia's hand a squeeze, thanked Cramer, and followed the massive sergeant. What did he want this time? He couldn't kick her off the strike force. Now that she'd broken through, Rhoads would do anything to keep her on the team.

Lopez didn't pause to talk. He swaggered down the hallway and disappeared around the corner. Scarlett followed. He made another turn and stopped halfway down that hall, where he unlocked the armory door and beckoned her inside.

She followed warily, remembering the blowtorch.

The room smelled of gun oil. Racks of M14s lined the back wall. Other racks held nightsticks and body armor. Rows of helmets stared like ranked soldiers.

"Close the door," Lopez said.

She closed it.

Lopez put a boot onto one of the wooden benches, rested a forearm across a meaty thigh, and regarded Scarlett with his skull face. Lopez just stared for several seconds, a cigar stub gripped in his teeth. His eyes shone brightly against the dark mask of crosshatched scars. "All right, Winter," he finally said, "I'm gonna level with you, but this is off the record, you read me?"

"Lima Charlie, Sergeant."

Lopez gave a sharp snort. "Your boyfriend is in deep trouble."

"I noticed, Sergeant."

"Lock it up, Winter. We have to make this fast. This is life or death."

Scarlett blinked. *Life or death?*

"Kyeong's been on thin ice since coming here. This time, attacking Amer, he screwed the pooch. And not just any pooch. Rhoads's prize poodle."

"But Sergeant," Scarlett said, "the dream . . . you saw what Dalia did."

Lopez grunted. "Which is why you're here. Amer pushed Kyeong too far. Rhoads won't hear it, but she did. I heard Kyeong talking to you in the ring, and we both saw what happened to his father." He frowned. "That poor kid's been through so much."

For half a second, Scarlett waited for the other shoe to drop—some sarcastic joke about Seamus—but nothing came. Lopez was actually expressing sympathy. "Is he in the Chamber, Sergeant?"

Lopez shook his head. "It's too late for the Chamber. Rhoads doesn't understand Kyeong like we do. He only sees the most powerful TK to ever attend The Point refusing to join his strike force." He shook his head again, harder, like a prizefighter trying to clear blood from his eyes. "Even when Rhoads delivered the ultimatum—join the strike force or ship out—Kyeong refused to join."

"Seamus has no place to go. His family is dead."

"The Farm," Lopez said, and his haunted eyes stared into hers. "Rhoads made him choose between the strike force and The Farm, and Kyeong chose The Farm."

"But that's—"

Lopez grabbed her arm. His eyes burned with something approaching desperation. "Transport will be here soon. I'm buying you five minutes with him. Talk him into joining the team."

"I'll try," Scarlett said.

Lopez squeezed her arm. "If you care even a little bit about that boy, you'd better do more than try." The emotion in Lopez's voice told Scarlett that no matter what the sergeant said, he cared about more than just filling the team roster. "The Farm is hell, pure and simple. He'd be better off dead."

FORTY-TWO

TWO MPS, ONE MALE AND ONE FEMALE, STOOD OUTside the holding cell. Seeing their black uniforms and silo patches, Scarlett understood. Transport already had arrived. They were going to take Seamus to The Farm unless she could persuade him to join the strike force.

Lopez spoke to the MPs, who grudgingly agreed to give Scarlett five minutes. They opened the door and let her inside, then closed the door behind her.

Seamus sat on his cot. He looked up, offered a weak smile, and said, "Part of me wanted to say good-bye. Part of me hoped I'd never see you again."

She crossed the room and crouched in front of him.

He wouldn't meet her eyes.

After what he'd done to Dalia, she'd been shocked and angry. Now, seeing him broken, her heart ached. Her feelings were confused, but she still cared for him. Deeply.

"Hey," she said, and lifted his chin. "We only have five minutes. MPs are here to take you to The Farm."

Seamus nodded, utterly defeated. His mouth wriggled, and tears filled his puffy eyes. "I'm sorry, Scarlett. I'm sorry for everything."

She slid her hands over his jaw and used her thumbs to wipe away his tears. "Just tell Rhoads what he wants to hear and we can talk later."

His head moved back and forth in her hands, and his eyes stared into hers, unflinching. "I won't join. I can't. I'm through with Rhoads. I won't be his weapon."

"You won't fight the people who killed my brother?"

"You saw what I did," he said.

"It was self-defense. Your father killed your family. He was going to kill you."

"That's not what I mean," he said. "You saw what I did to Dalia."

"But she—"

"Stop," he said, his voice suddenly strong again. "I'm beyond help. What I did to Dalia? That's not me, not the real me. I was *nice*. But then . . . what happened, what I did . . . Killing changes you, Scarlett. You can't go back."

"But you could—"

"You don't understand," he said, "and I hope you never do. The person I was before I killed my father, he never would have hurt Dalia like I did. Didn't you ever wonder why Hopkins hates me so much? My first semester here, one of his buddies, Harrison, messed with me. I fought back—and nearly killed him. He'll live, but he'll never be right again. Healers can't fix brain damage."

"That's horrible, but—"

"I'm just a weapon now. That's what Rhoads and my father and this place and the things I've done have turned me into."

"Seamus, listen to me." She had to make him understand. Time was running out.

"I told Rhoads that I wanted chemical stasis."

Scarlett's heart flip-flopped. "Death?"

"Rhoads refused, the coward." He shrugged. "So it's The Farm. Let them strap me down and pump me full of drugs. Just forget everything, and hopefully someday the world will forget that I even existed."

A crazy thought flashed through her head. Go with him to The Farm. Unplug from everything. She'd spent most of her life high, after all. Why not go all in? Be done with the pain and the struggle and letting people down? Just coast into a pharmaceutical haze and fade away . . .

Half an instant later, she shuddered. Psych ward drugs were the ultimate downers. Plunging into them would be like spending the rest of your life in a K-hole. Trapped inside yourself, unable to scream, and with no one to help even if you could. After a while, you'd forget why you were struggling, forget who you were, forget everything, the way a drowning man drifting into the dark depths at some point forgets the surface.

"Seamus," she said, wild with desperation. She pulled him into her arms and hugged him. "You don't have to kill anybody. You just have to tell Rhoads that you'll go back to training, and then, in a couple of years, you'll be out of this place. Seamus, I really care about you."

She felt his head moving back and forth again. "I care for you, too, Scarlett, and I'm sorry to leave you, but I can't stay here. I'd rather go crazy behind bars, where I can't hurt anyone, than stay here and end up killing innocent people . . . maybe friends, maybe even you." He pulled back and looked her in the eyes again, and Scarlett realized that she wasn't the only one desperate to make the other understand. "It's not too late for you. I understand why you joined the strike force, and I know what you think you're doing, but Rhoads is just using you. Once you're his weapon, you'll be his weapon forever. You won't be able to turn that off. Do you really think they'll let you go back to the civilian world?"

She'd never considered it and didn't have time now. "We don't have time for this."

"Even if they let you back out into the world, you wouldn't be *you* anymore."

Tap-tap-tap . . . a light knocking at the door.

Scarlett panicked. "You can't go. What about *us*?"

The door rattled, and she heard the lock turn.

He touched her face. "I'm sorry, Scarlett."

The door opened.

Scarlett stood.

"Time's up," the female MP said, entering the cell. "Cadet Kyeong, my name is Sergeant Khalifa, and this is Sergeant Higdon. We're here to transport you to another facility and do hope that you will be cooperative."

Seamus kissed Scarlett's cheek. "You're better than these people, this place," he said. "Don't let them destroy you."

"Cadet Kyeong," Higdon said, "we're going to need to restrain you prior to transport. Please extend your wrists."

Scarlett waved impatiently. "Just give us a few minutes."

"I'm going to have to ask you to leave now," Khalifa said. Her hand touched Scarlett's shoulder, gently nudging.

Higdon moved past her, cuffs extended. "Nice and easy."

Seamus held out his wrists. "I'm ready."

"No," Scarlett said, and pushed the man's hands aside before he could snap on the cuffs.

Everything happened quickly then.

Khalifa shouted and shoved into her, trying to twist her arm behind her back. Higdon dropped the cuffs and drew a stun gun.

Scarlett yanked her arm free of Khalifa's grip and kneed her hard in the tailbone. Khalifa staggered across the cell. Her nightstick clattered to the floor.

Before Scarlett even fully understood what was happening, Higdon blasted her with the stun gun. Tens of thousands of volts plunged into her chest. Scarlett extended a palm and blasted the force back out. Higdon went stiff as a mannequin and dropped to the floor.

"Run, Seamus!" she shouted.

Seamus looked at her in shock, looked at the guards—and bolted out the door.

Good, she thought, but Khalifa bent for her club, shouting after Seamus.

"No," Scarlett said, grabbed the back of the woman's collar, and yanked.

Then they were in a tangle, wrestling.

"Don't hit her," Higdon said, grabbing Scarlett's shoulders. "She'll use the force."

Khalifa fumbled with Scarlett's hands, trying to apply some kind of finger lock.

Higdon's muscular forearm wrapped around Scarlett's throat and started squeezing like a python.

Scarlett's power provided no protection against finger locks or slow, steady pressure cutting off her circulation.

So she went old school, channeling her girlhood fights with Dan. She twisted her hand free of Khalifa's fumbling, grabbed Higdon's arm, arched her back, and squatted, yanking forward. Grunting with dismay, Higdon followed as she flipped him over her shoulders. His back slammed onto the floor with a jolt. She heard the air go out of him. The choking pressure disappeared from her throat. Higdon writhed, holding his lower back.

Khalifa fumbled with her radio.

Scarlett lashed out with a kick, knocking the thing from her hand. The radio smashed into the wall as one piece and hit the ground as many. "Get out of my way," she told Khalifa, moving toward the door. "I don't want to hurt you."

A wasp stung her neck. Reflexively, she slapped a hand to the spot, felt something sticking from the flesh just beneath her jaw, and plucked it free.

The world tilted, going blurry.

She stumbled, caught herself on the cot, and stared down numbly at the little dart in her hand.

It felt like she was melting into the floor. She couldn't lift herself, couldn't stand. Moving in slow motion, she turned her head to see Rhoads enter the room, brandishing a tranquillizer gun.

"No," she said or, rather, *tried* to say. Even that short word came out slurred. She let the dart slip from her fingers, tried to pull herself onto the cot, and slid to the floor.

"Take her to the Chamber," Rhoads told the guards coming in behind him now.

A wall of blurry camouflage loomed over her. Hands seized her, lifting.

As Scarlett faded, she heard Rhoads key a radio. When the colonel spoke, his words echoed from the guards' belts and the hallway intercom. "All cadets and personnel. Stop what you're doing. Cadet Seamus Kyeong has escaped custody and is trying to flee The Point. He is desperate and dangerous. Stop him . . . *by any means necessary*."

FORTY-THREE

SCARLETT AWOKE SLOWLY, THE ROOM COMING RE-luctantly into focus. She lay on her back, strapped to a table. Metal arms rose on either side, arching over her as if she were trapped within a steel rib cage. The silver disk that she'd watched beam pain and fear and desperation into Seamus's brain hovered over her face like an alien spacecraft.

The Chamber . . .

"I'm terribly disappointed in you, Scarlett," Rhoads said, leaning over her with a sad smile. "You were doing so well. And now—well, we all have our weaknesses, I suppose. Soon your personal weakness will be back in custody and on his way to The Farm."

"No," Scarlett said. Her voice was even weaker than her body, which felt stiff and heavy and unresponsive. "You can't."

"On the contrary," Rhoads said, "I must. He corrupted you, nearly killed Dalia, and refused to join the strike force."

No, she thought, *you have it wrong*. She had so much to say, so much to explain, but her mental steering wheel had gone loose, and her brain was slaloming down a steep and twisting road obscured by fog, with bottomless darkness yawning to either side of the slick and sloping pavement. It would be so easy to surrender the wheel, slide off the soft shoulder, and tumble once more into the void . . .

"I rescued you from the hardships of plebe life," Rhoads said, "and looked the other way when you broke the rules. Even when you assaulted Hopkins and interrupted Kyeong's punishment, I was lenient, but as they say, a spoiled child never loves its mother. Nor its father, it seems."

The tranquillizer's fog thinned, giving Scarlett more control over her racing mind. Rhoads had said that Seamus would "soon be" in custody, so they hadn't caught him yet. He still had a chance.

Come on, Seamus. You can do it.

"You really are like a daughter to me," Rhoads said. "You cadets are the children I never had. I felt the same way about the original recruits, back at Bragg. You see, I created you. All of you. I didn't intend to, but I did. One decision on my part, all the way back in Desert Storm, created everything, the good, the bad, all of it."

"The chemical weapons," she said.

Rhoads gave a slight nod. "Intel said it was a motor pool harboring IEDs. Bush-league bomb builders. I led the assault, and we took the facility with little resistance. Zero casualties. The Iraqis dropped their weapons and fled. We breached the facility unopposed, and that's when the mist rolled out. My first thought was that we'd cracked a refrigerated unit. That's what it looked like by flashlight: steam rolling from a refrigerator into a hot room. Then my soldiers started to drop. Someone behind me was shouting 'Gas, gas, gas!'—but I froze, and the mist rolled over us. All around me, men dropped and started convulsing and vomiting and shouting guttural nonsense like Holy Rollers thrashing on a church floor.

"We were dead. I knew it. I dropped, too. Lost all control of my body. Just lay there, dying, thinking about what I'd done. I'll never forget the pain. Not of the gas but of failure, of knowing that I'd gotten my men killed. That's when someone spiked my thigh with atropine and pulled on my gas mask and cleared the filter and moved on to save someone else. That man, the soldier who'd spotted the gas and gave the warning, the man who saved us all, was your father."

Despite her frustration and desperation and her overwhelming concern for Seamus, Scarlett was rocked by Rhoads's words. "My father?"

"Charlie saved me, saved us all."

Scarlett reeled. *Dad never said anything about that.*

Rhoads said, "We couldn't recognize his action with a medal, of course, because officially speaking, none of this ever happened. The brass locked it down. So you know what we gave him?"

And suddenly she did. What they'd given him for saving all those lives was sitting, all but forgotten, back in her footlocker. *For luck, Dad.*

"A watch," Rhoads said, and shook his head, laughing humorlessly. "That's it. Your father deserved the Medal of Honor, but all we could give him was a watch, a pat on the back, and a one-way ticket to Gulf Syndrome on steroids. Command medevaced Lightning Battalion to Germany, where we underwent weeks of treatment. The docs couldn't ID the chemical agent, so they came at it from all sides, including genetic therapy. Well, the combination ended up having quite an effect on my men. Fatigue, respiratory issues, memory problems. Depression, anxiety, anger management issues. Many struggled with suicidal feelings. Some battled homicidal ideations."

"Seamus's dad," she said, wanting to remind Rhoads of his role in Seamus's tragic life.

Rhoads nodded. "Yes, like Jay Kyeong." He shook his head, looking troubled. Then he shrugged. "It wasn't until much later—sixteen *years* later—that we started hearing about the other side effect. Something—the chemical agent, the treatment, or the combination—had genetically altered my soldiers, activating junk DNA that expressed itself in their offspring."

"Our powers," she said, thinking, *Keep him talking. Keep things civil. He's remembering his men, remembering Seamus's dad. When the time is right, plead Seamus's case again.*

"Yes," Rhoads said, "your powers, which look very similar to supernatural powers reported in countless cultures down through history. Superhuman strength, magical healing, telekinesis. Now we suspect that these stories stemmed from truth, individuals with genetic mutations that had flipped the switch on abilities like those we see here at The Point, although we suspect that most of them operated with a dimmer switch on low. With you cadets, the junk DNA is fully activated, giving you real-life superpowers. All from that night in Iraq when I led my men into the trap that created you."

Rhoads pushed a hand through the ribs of the metal cage and squeezed Scarlett's shoulder. "So yes, I do feel like a father to you, and every father must discipline his child. You aided a prisoner, facilitated his escape, and used your powers to assault military police. I have to punish you."

"I understand, sir," Scarlett said, "but Seamus doesn't deserve The Farm." She didn't care about herself. Her life was a string of punishments. She needed to save Seamus. "Dalia pushed him into this."

Rhoads shook his head. "Scarlett, Scarlett, Scarlett . . ."

"Seamus needs help. Counseling. He's messed up over what happened to his family."

"He is a traitor, and he is too dangerous for normal society," Rhoads said. "What do you do with someone who has no place to go? Seamus wanted death. I am giving him life."

"Give him another chance. But he needs counseling first. He would be amazing."

Rhoads gave her another sad smile. Scarlett wished she could reach through the bars and slap it off his face. "Let him go, Scarlett. He was only using you, destroying your potential."

"Bull," she said. "Keep him here and get him help or I'm quitting the strike force."

Rhoads shook his head. "Quit? You poor child. I've already cut you from the team."

She gaped at him. "Cut? But I promised Dan . . ."

Rhoads stood. "The Chamber offers incredibly effective correctional conditioning." He flicked a switch, and the disk above her face spun with a soft whirring and glowed blue. Underneath her, a flow of electricity tickled. The arched metal arms began to hum, filling her with urgent vibration.

Let it build, let it flow into me and build, and then, when I'm alone, I'll blast this machine to pieces and go help Seamus.

"Unfortunately," Rhoads said, flicking the switch again and killing the machine, "this device works through electricity, light, sound, and a laser that targets specific brain centers. In other words, nothing that will work on you. So I must employ a different method." He stood and opened the door and called into the hall. "We're ready for you. I'm sorry to leave you two alone, but an old friend has come to visit."

Rhoads shut the door, offered one final sad smile through the window, and departed.

"Sir, wait," she called after him. "You have to . . ."

Once more, a face filled the small window. Not Rhoads, though.

Dalia's eyes, less than sane and divided by the ugly purple scar that split her face top to bottom, drilled into Scarlett.

"Dalia," she said, "you're awake."

A smile as hard as barbed wire twisted across Dalia's pale features. "Yes, I am awake," she said, "but you're not."

Scarlett's nose twitched, smelling smoke, and ghostly fingers tickled over her scars.

FORTY-FOUR

OH, NO, SEAMUS THOUGHT. *WHAT IN THE WORLD have I done?*

He left them sprawled there, cluttering the corridor like broken toys—*Please, God, don't let them be dead*—and ran on. He'd considered using his mind to push the unresponsive guards out of the main hallway, but that would have meant taking a closer look at the men he'd clobbered, and what if it turned out that one or two or all three of them weren't breathing? What if it just so happened that he sort of, kind of, you know . . . killed all fucking three of them?

He sprinted toward his only hope: the secret passage he and Scarlett had used night after night to escape from this terrible place. If only they'd kept going, split the academy altogether. They would be free now. Hunted, sure, but free. They could have gotten fake IDs and started over in the teeming underworld of cash and anonymity offered by most large cities.

All a fairy dream now. Because of him, because of what he had done to Dalia—and, if he was honest, because of what he'd done to his father, the memory of which Dalia had used to break him.

And then Scarlett, stupid and brave and impulsive, had attacked the guards, and now—*Oh, Scarlett*—there was no turning back, no way to help her. Now there was only flight. What were his chances of escaping? Slim to frigging none, that was what his chances were, but he took them anyway, slamming through the door marked Do Not Enter and running down the stairwell, his footfalls echoing after him like the clamor of a dozen hunters hot on his trail.

At the bottom of the stairwell, he shouldered through the door and entered the subway, lips peeled back like those of a snarling dog.

Relief rushed through him. The corridor, the train, the tracks: they were all empty. He hopped off the platform and down onto the tracks and started around the train, feeling his first surge of hope when his eyes found the nondescript door waiting for him in the shadowy recesses beyond the tracks.

Maybe he really could escape, blow the whistle on Rhoads, help Scarlett—

But as he hoisted himself onto the other platform, the squeal of metal on metal sliced through his fledgling optimism like a rusty guillotine.

For a fraction of a second, he assumed that the screeching sound was the train, coming to life, but then he noticed that the door he'd been planning to use, the door to Scarlett's secret passage to the surface, was swinging open from the other side.

He dropped back down to the tracks, scrambled under the train, and watched people coming through the secret door: one man, two, a woman . . . others following.

The silver-haired man in the suit had visited The Point before. A politician, one of Rhoads's cronies. He spoke into a phone, saying, "I'm here, by the train, Oscar. Where are you?"

The man beside him, however, stole the show. Short, dark, and strikingly handsome, he walked with the confident fluidity of an unchallenged predator. He wore camouflage BDUs and sunglasses.

Only two types of people wear sunglasses indoors, Seamus's father used to say before he'd gone insane and burned the world: *blind people and assholes*.

But this guy didn't carry a white cane, and he certainly didn't look like an asshole. He looked *famous*, like a celebrity—a cool one if you got to know him, completely down to earth, the type who would conquer the world but crouch down to listen to your cares and concerns.

A haggard-looking woman walked beside him, arm in arm. At first glance, she looked pretty old, like thirty-five or forty, but Seamus looked again and realized that she was in her middle to late twenties, tops, just frazzled and prematurely gray, not old.

His fear had faded, replaced by curiosity.

Others were coming into the subway behind them—Seamus was vaguely aware of someone very large squeezing through the opening now—but his eyes returned to the man in sunglasses. Part of him wanted to crawl out from beneath the train, to welcome the man . . .

A loud bang startled Seamus. The stairwell door behind him—the one through which he himself had come—popped open, and he heard a familiar voice coming into the corridor. "Wes? Where are you? What's with the surprise visit and all this backdoor drama?"

Seamus shuffled around on his belly and inched his way forward and saw who had come through the doors. His fists clenched.

Rhoads.

"Here," the silver-haired politician called.

Spotting the politician across the tracks, Rhoads half smiled, obviously confused. "Who's that with you?"

"I'm sorry, Oscar," the politician said. "I had to see my daughter again. I had to see my baby Penny."

Seamus heard a high-pitched giggle. Goose bumps rose along his forearms. A little blond-haired girl wearing a tiara and a pink feather boa stepped forward and took the politician's hand.

"Penny?" Rhoads said, looking dumbfounded. "Your daughter, Penelope?"

"The same," the politician said. "She's changed. Grown up, dyed her hair, and gained *incredible* talent."

"Oh, Wes . . . I'm so sorry," Rhoads said, and reached for the walkie-talkie that hung from his belt like a six-shooter.

"Colonel Rhoads," a deep voice drawled, its tone warmly mocking. "What a pleasure it is to see you again, sir."

"You," Rhoads said. His face twisted with alarm, and he started to unclip his walkie-talkie, but then his hand fell away from his belt line, any all-call distress signal apparently forgotten.

The man in shades smiled and executed a lazy salute. "Staff Sergeant Antonio Jagger reporting for duty." His laughter was loud and rich. The others—Rhoads included—joined in.

Stranger still, Seamus had to slap a hand over his own mouth to keep from joining in. Instinctively, he glanced away from Jagger and felt a measure of sanity creep back in. Something was wrong here. Very wrong.

"You wrote me off as a regular guy," Jagger said, his voice still ripe with humor, "just some likable dime-a-dozen drifter, lucky at cards."

"You're a charismatic," Rhoads said, his voice throaty with awe.

"Is that what you're calling me?" Jagger said, and Seamus forced himself to look away again, not liking the way the corners of his mouth lifted at the sound of Jagger's amusement. "Well, that's accurate enough, I suppose, as long as you're speaking biblically. Divinely conferred charisma, full of grace. And yes, I have my church. Of course, the church is the *people*, not the place." He spread his palms and swiveled, gesturing toward those who surrounded him. "I've traveled many a mile, baptizing lost souls in hobo jungles, bus stops, homeless shelters, county jails. You see, the human race was in a bad way. They had lost faith. But when they witness a miracle . . ."

He lifted into the air, coasted across the wide gap of the tracks, and landed on the platform five feet in front of Rhoads, who stood there, dumbstruck.

"So the reports were true," Rhoads said. "You can—"

"Levitate," Jagger said. "Yes. And other things. Many, many things, as you will see soon enough." His smile returned, so bright this time that Seamus almost felt like he needed a pair of shades, too. He felt warmth, too, goodwill toward Jagger, who deserved to be happy. If only Rhoads wasn't here, Seamus could crawl out and introduce himself, offer any help that Jagger might need. As it was, he felt like Odysseus lashed to the mast, driven mad by the sweet singing of the Sirens.

"I'm just a people person," Jagger said. "I *really* understand people. So much so that I've learned to duplicate their magic tricks."

Rhoads's walkie-talkie lifted from his belt and hovered in the air between them.

"Even telekinesis," Jagger said. The radio whipped sideways and smashed into the tracks inches from Seamus's face. He shut his eyes and felt walkie-talkie shrapnel scratch his face, and suddenly dread flooded over him, cold as a bucket of ice water, bringing him back to reality. He was lying on the hard ground beneath a train, face stinging, and . . .

Somehow Jagger had enchanted him even though the man didn't even know Seamus was here.

Seamus closed his eyes tightly. That helped clear his head.

How had Jagger done that? And how had he mesmerized Rhoads so easily, so completely?

"Trouble is, using multiple powers takes a lot of energy. It drains me like a sink." Seamus could *feel* Jagger's smile. "Luckily, you just happen to have the solution that I need: *Scarlett Winter*."

FORTY-FIVE

SCARLETT WEPT.

Somewhere nearby, the woman burned, howling with pain. Scarlett could hear her and smell her but not see her. Oh, no, not that. She wouldn't look, couldn't look . . .

"You're too late," her father's voice said. "Always too little, too late. Because you were too busy having a good time, too busy looking out for number one."

Scarlett held the crying baby in her arms. She'd done her best to peel away the burning fabric, but some of the material had melted into the baby's flesh and into hers. That was how she had gotten her scars, the ones that were itching like crazy now . . . itching yet not hurting. There was no pain. No physical pain, anyway. Reliving this moment, the moment of her great failure, was incredibly painful, especially with her father here, saying all these terrible things that Scarlett knew deep down were true.

"You're pitiful," her father said. "You disgust me."

"I don't want to die," the woman in the car screamed.

Did she really shout that the night of the crash?

"Please don't let me die!"

Now Scarlett turned and could see the woman's face pressed against the window, staring out at her, blood draining from the split in her hairline, tears streaming from her face. "Why won't you save me?"

Scarlett could hear the woman plainly, as if she, too, were in the car, could hear her and hear the crackling flames and feel the tremendous heat.

I have to help her!

She handed the baby to Sav—only it wasn't Sav; it was Scarlett's father—and rushed back in to save the woman . . . or rather, she *tried* to rush forward again. Her legs barely moved, they were so heavy with fatigue.

The corners of her mouth betrayed her, lifting into a mocking smile. *You're not tired. You're high and drunk, and this is it, this is the life, right here . . .*

She felt a wave of intense pleasure and saw Seamus's head between her legs.

"Please save me!" the woman cried.

You really should help her, she thought, but a warm breeze soothed over her and carried that thought away.

Why bother? The woman didn't say those things. This isn't real. In reality, Scarlett had saved the baby, but there hadn't been time to save the woman.

Besides, she felt awesome now. Why in the world would she interrupt Seamus?

"You don't care about me," her mother's voice said.

She turned her head and saw not her mother but the woman behind the wheel, speaking to her in her mother's voice. "Is this what you want? Are you trying to kill me?" The flames rose all around her, leaping from her burning clothes to ignite her hair in a halo of flame, and Scarlett smelled her burning.

Do something, she told herself. *Get her out of there!*

But she couldn't move, could only lie there, high as a kite, the smell of her mother's burning flesh filling her nostrils as Seamus pleasured her.

Scarlett gagged.

"Don't you dare puke," her father said. "You're so weak."

All pleasure disappeared. She wasn't high or drunk. Seamus had vanished. She was just a little girl, and her father was back from the war, and the house was cold, and she was shaking like crazy, shivering from fear, and she just wanted to make it stop, wanted to escape, wanted to run away or fall asleep . . . anything to make it stop.

"You only care about yourself," her father said, and Scarlett ached, knowing it was true, hating that it was true. Always had been, always would be.

I'm nothing but a self-centered piece of shit.

"You had so much potential," her father said. "Good brain, good looks, good family. School, sports, boys . . . everything was easy for you. And what do you do with all those advantages? Nothing, that's what. You don't care enough to try. You just coast along until you get into trouble, and then you sweet-talk your way out of it."

The truth burned into her, seared into her mind and heart and soul like battery acid.

"You don't deserve to attend The Point," her father said. "You just lucked out and woke up one day with superpowers. And still you coasted. Why? Because you're lazy and weak and don't care about anyone or anything."

She wanted to shout back at her father, wanted to tell him that it wasn't true, that her whole life she really had cared, that she really had tried, it was just that something always ended up happening . . . but those thoughts died beneath the roar of her own self-loathing.

Soft and weak and lazy like a little baby.

The woman screamed, burning.

"You didn't even try to save her," her father said.

"I tried to save her."

"You didn't try to save him. You weren't even there."

Him?

The screaming changed, deepening . . . and called her name. "Scarlett! Help me!"

No, Scarlett thought, filling with terror. *Not this. Anything but this.*

Hands turned her head, forcing her to look at that which she did not wish to see.

Flames engulfed Dan's overturned Jeep. He hung upside down in the driver's seat, trapped, burning . . . staring out at Scarlett, pleading to her, "Please help me, Scarlett!"

"Your own brother," her father's voice said, "and you just let him die."

No, Scarlett thought, *I never would have . . . I didn't know . . .*

Her excuses scrambled for purchase within her, found none—*everything is my fault*—and tumbled into the pit of fire burning at her center, the white-hot hell she'd been tending with pride and greed and sloth, the hell in which she'd burned those foolish enough to trust or love her, the hell to which she herself would one day go, and not a moment too soon . . . for it was she who deserved to burn, she who deserved damnation in the lake of fire that she'd made of her life.

"Your own brother," her father said again. "Your own mother."

And everything changed.

No more fire, no more screaming, no more pressing heat.

Now everything was still and cold and quiet . . . quiet as death. The field was gone. The burning woman was gone. Dan was gone, taking his screams with him. All that remained was the terrible knowledge that Scarlett was selfish and worthless and everything was her fault.

Her father's voice spoke as the cold room came into focus. "Your own mother."

Scarlett gasped and let out a strangled cry, "Mom?"

"All your fault," her father said. He stood behind her, one hand on her shoulder, both of them staring down at the bed where her mother lay dead beneath a blanket of empty prescription bottles, spilled wine, and vomit.

This isn't real, Scarlett told herself as an icy corkscrew of terror drilled into her heart. *Mom is alive. This is just a dream, a nightmare. I'm almost certain that Mom's still alive.*

Her father's voice said, "How could she possibly carry on with only you for a child?"

"I didn't mean to—"

"Spare me, Scarlett," he said. "You never deserved The Point. Dan did. But you fixed that, didn't you? Dan's dead, and your mother's dead . . . all because of you."

Scarlett stared into her mother's cloudy, lifeless eyes. "I'm so sorry, Mom. I never—"

"It's okay," a voice said. "It's all right now, Scarlett." The voice was deep and smooth and familiar. A hand stroked her scalp gently. The image of her mother faded. "You are forgiven. You are delivered."

Scarlett was awake. She lay trembling and soaked in sweat within the machine, tears leaking from her burning eyes. Was it true? Was she really forgiven? The room came slowly into focus, and joy leaped in her heart when she saw who sat beside her, stroking her head. "Dan?"

But that wasn't possible. Dan was dead—*all your fault, all your fault!*—and this was reality. She had escaped the dream, so . . .

She shook her head.

It wasn't Dan beside her. Not at all. Dan never wore Wayfarers.

FORTY-SIX

"YOU'RE JAGGER," SCARLETT SAID.

"Correct," Jagger said with a nod, "and you are the answer to all my problems." Behind him, people crowded into the Chamber: Rhoads, smiling excitedly; an enormous man, even larger than Lopez, whom Scarlett recognized as the High Roller Kyle Steede; and silver-haired Senator Ditko, staring down at Scarlett as if she were something nasty squashed into the sole of his shoe.

Scarlett shook her head, confused. She was badly rattled from the dream torture. Was this real? Was this really happening? Why would Sav's dad be here?

Then, seeing Dalia leering at her from behind Jagger, Scarlett cringed, and an involuntary huff escaped her lungs.

Jagger smiled down. "Don't be afraid, Scarlett."

"Yes," Rhoads said, stepping forward with a goofy grin. "Everything is as it should be."

What was going on here?

But she knew. Even rattled and hurting and fogged over from Dalia's torment, she knew.

Jagger laid a hand on Rhoads's arm. "Call your cadets and cadre to the auditorium. I want everyone in attendance. Tell them they're about to have a special visitor but don't spoil the surprise. My people will help you set up. Oh, and I'll be needing the big projector screen, okay? Great. Now you go ahead. I'll be down momentarily to give them a nice pep talk."

"Yes, sir," Rhoads said. He saluted crisply.

"Colonel Rhoads!" she shouted, but Rhoads exited the Chamber without looking back.

"It's Jagger," she called after him. "He charmed you."

"Shh," Jagger said.

"Go to hell," she said, wishing she could get her hands around Jagger's throat.

Dalia stepped forward, anger flashing in her crazy eyes. "If you speak to him that way again, Scarlett, I'll *hurt* you."

Oh, no, Scarlett thought, so terrified of Dalia that she almost didn't notice the tickling at the back of her neck. *No, no, no . . .*

"That won't be necessary, Dalia dear," Jagger said. He regarded Scarlett with a small smile. "Interesting." He stepped closer to the machine. "Scarlett, my friend, relax, okay? Will you do that for me?"

"I'll kill you for what you did to my brother," she said. The tickling on her neck strengthened, vibrating up the back of her skull, and she felt heat building in her chest.

Jagger laughed. "Very interesting, indeed. Kyle, would you please cover Scarlett's mouth?"

Steede moved forward.

"Leave me alone," she said. Restrained as she was, she couldn't even turn away.

A huge hand closed over her mouth, muffling her complaints.

She squirmed to no avail. She could barely breathe. She had to get out of here, but she couldn't move, couldn't even speak.

"Don't suffocate her, Kyle," Jagger said. "She's still quite valuable. Priceless, in fact." Then he spoke over a shoulder, asking, "How long until lunch?"

"Fifteen minutes," a woman's voice said.

"Are the cameras up and running?"

"Affirmative."

"And we're recording?"

"Roger that."

"Excellent," Jagger said. "Head down to the auditorium with Senator Ditko. Bring the laptops online and double-check the sat phones. Senator, are you ready to do your duty?"

"Yes, sir," Sav's dad said, obviously mesmerized like Rhoads. Taking a closer look, Scarlett started thrashing again at her restraints. Holding Ditko's hand was Penny, the little pyrokinetic who'd burned Dan to death, the absurd plastic tiara still sitting atop her hair, which was pale blond, just like . . .

It's Sav's missing sister, Penelope . . .

Jagger reached through the metal ribs of the machine and patted Scarlett's shoulder. "I understand that you must be upset, Scarlett, and I do apologize about your brother. We felt horrible about that, didn't we, Sadie?"

"I feel positively monstrous," Daisy said, stepping into view and speaking in a Southern accent exaggerated with cloying sweetness. "Really I do. Daniel was such a fine young gentleman."

"Yes," Jagger said. "It was a shame, but I needed to get close to Dan, needed to learn about him so that when I had a chance to visit your dreams, I could do a good impersonation. And Sadie—I'm sorry, I guess you'd prefer that I call her Daisy—needed to meet you. She's not quite so powerful as dear Dalia, so she needs to meet someone in order to walk within his or her dreams."

Jagger turned to smile at Dalia. "Unless, of course, that person happens to be a dream walker herself. It was simple for Sadie to find and interact with Dalia after we peeked into the mind of a friend of ours who's unjustly quarantined at The Farm, and wow—what was this? If Sadie's a ham radio, Dalia is every radio station on earth, broadcasting at a billion decibels. So yeah, it was easy for Sadie to connect. We watched Dalia's dream walks for a while before Sadie introduced us. By that time, I understood that you were the answer to my problems, and your brother was the key to connecting you with Sadie and allowing her to tap into your mind so that I could dream walk with you, as him. After all, there's no more surefire way to summon someone than to arrange the funeral of her only brother."

He killed Dan just to get close to me?

Scarlett screamed into the meaty palm covering her mouth, fueled by rage and guilt and desperation. She was tempted to lash out telekinetically with the force in her bones, but it would probably do no more than bloody Jagger's lip, and if she was going to strike, she needed to take his head off.

Jagger squeezed her shoulder and spoke in a stern voice: "Stop struggling, Scarlett."

She felt energy at the back of her neck and head again, this time in a blast, as if someone had hosed her down with a flamethrower, and a buzzing heat sizzled within her skull, just as it had during Rhoads's briefing. She shoved this force into her bones like a woman thumbing ammo into a magazine.

Jagger tilted his head. "This is more than interesting. It's amazing. Honestly, I'm used to having my way. I tell people to jump, they don't bother to ask 'How high?' They just jump as high as they can, trying to make me happy. But you . . ." He laughed. "Unfortunately, I don't have time to crack this egg right now. The big show is about to begin, and I need you . . . or, more precisely, I need your power. I mentioned dream walking. As Rhoads might have told you, I have this nifty little trick where I learn other posthumans' abilities. It's pretty cool, but it's also very taxing. I'm like a computer. Each program takes up space, and after a while, my system lags. Not enough RAM, right? Like I'm running on eight gigs and need sixteen. Well, that power of yours, now that you've learned to store and convert it, like I showed you, it's not just sixteen gigs . . . it's limitless RAM. Once I learn your ability, I'll be able to absorb explosions, shatter eardrums with a shout, crisp troops with a blast of flame, lift a tank, walk into someone's dream ten thousand miles away, and sweet-talk a rabid dog into licking my hand . . . all at full power, all at the same time."

Jagger clapped his hands. "All right, folks. Nonessential personnel, please report to the auditorium. But don't let the cadets see you until after my speech, okay? Clear out. That means you, Sadie, and you, Dalia."

"But you promised," Dalia said, touching Jagger's shoulder. "You said—"

"I know what I said," Jagger told her, brushing her hand away with barely concealed annoyance. "Now be a good girl and step outside. I don't want to risk your getting hurt, all right? Once we're finished, you can play some more."

Dalia's smile wriggled, and she blinked away tears. "Thank you," she said, her voice thick with emotion, and she followed Sadie out of the Chamber.

No, Scarlett thought, *not that; anything but Dalia . . .*

She considered lashing out with the energy vibrating within her bones and striking Dalia with a telekinetic blast, but she wasn't sure that she'd stored enough to really hurt her. Besides, as much as she feared Dalia, she wasn't the main problem. Scarlett needed to absorb more, let it build, wait for Jagger to get close—after all, she wasn't a telekinetic, so her aim was poor at best—and blast him right between the eyes.

At that moment, Jagger leaned closer and placed his fingertips on Scarlett's forehead.

She couldn't miss from this range, but she needed more force.

"Show me how this works," Jagger said. "Kyle, please punch Scarlett in the stomach."

Yeah, hit me, she thought, but she had the sense to feign fear.

The meathead kept one hand pressed over Scarlett's mouth. With the other, he bent a few of the machine's metal ribs aside. Then he drove a big fist into her gut. An explosion of kinetic energy rushed into Scarlett, flooding her muscles with burning energy, which she rerouted to her bones, where it joined the strange energy that Jagger had beamed into her skull.

Had she absorbed enough? Perhaps, but she had to be certain. She would get only one shot. She needed to crush Jagger's skull, pulp his brain.

Jagger removed his fingertips from Scarlett's forehead, a huge smile lighting up his face. "So that's how you do it. Amazing. You pull the force into your bones, like sound." He chuckled. "Okay, Kyle, hit her one more time so I can fine-tune things."

Yes, she thought. *One more time* . . . and Steede hit her—hard. The force punched into her, carpet bombing her muscles with napalm, which exploded back out of her, bound to the force she'd been holding back, in a telekinetic shotgun blast.

Steede flew backward as if he'd been hit by a Louisville Slugger. The light overhead shattered, and debris rained down from the damaged ceiling, rattling off the metal ribs and pattering along her uniform.

Yes!

Her real target, however, just grinned down at her. "Fantastic," Jagger said. "I feel so strong!"

Scarlett stared in disbelief and dawning terror. Jagger had absorbed the blast, just as she would have.

Steede rose, cursing, and glowered at her with a bloody face.

Jagger patted Steede's huge shoulder. "Let's go, Kyle. My audience awaits. It's show time."

Scarlett sputtered, helpless and hurting. She'd tried her hardest, put everything into her last-ditch effort, her final shot . . . and had failed. Nothing could stop Jagger now, and nothing could save her.

Of course, she didn't understand then, suffering in the depths of her failure and misery, just how much worse things could get.

Then she heard Jagger speaking in the hall just outside the door. "Dalia dear," he said, his voice oozing sweet syrup, "your toy awaits."

FORTY-SEVEN

GLORIOUS, JAGGER THOUGHT, PACING THE STAGE before his mesmerized audience. *Absolutely glorious.*

"Again," he said, and spread his arms.

Steede interlaced his fingers, reared back, and lifted his doubled fist overhead like a man with an invisible sledgehammer trying to ring the carnival bell. And then, with a savage roar, the strongest man in the world swung the invisible hammer.

The hammer blow exploded into Jagger's chest. The sound echoed through the auditorium, reminding Jagger of the heavy, hollow *whump* of an M203 grenade launcher.

He laughed.

Steede stared, still bewildered. The man was strong enough to punch a fist into a person's chest and rip out the spine and had, in fact, done just that, several times, to people all over the world, at Jagger's suggestion. Yet . . .

"It doesn't even hurt," Jagger said. He said it to himself, but he stood close enough to the mic that the High Rollers and *future* High Rollers—all the wide-eyed cadets and cadre in attendance—nodded and smiled.

His claim wasn't entirely true, of course. The strike didn't hurt on the surface, but deeper within him a beautiful agony now burned like a sun. Like a dozen suns. A thousand . . .

So much energy. So much *power*.

Scarlett Winter's energy-channeling ability had proved the final piece in the puzzle, the key not only to using his various abilities simultaneously but to supercharging whatever power he used. How easy it had been to charm those in attendance. Rhoads assembled them, and Jagger said a few words in the mic before stepping into view. Now they were his.

And there was no fatigue, no fading, no sign of the blackouts he normally suffered after employing borrowed powers. At long last, he was fully awake and ready to set things right.

"Cadets," he said, and nodded to Rhoads, who bent dutifully over the multimedia station. A second later, the towering projector screen at the back of the stage came to life, streaming a live feed of the West Point mess hall far above them, thousands of cadets and cadre just sitting down to their meals.

By this point in the spring semester, the West Point cadets were completely institutionalized. It was actually impressive to see how effectively West Point had managed to coerce a diverse population of superstars to surrender their individuality and dedicate their every waking second to operating as cogs in an incredibly complex, amazingly efficient machine, the highest purpose of which currently appeared to be the training of young men and women to cut desserts in the most challenging convolutions. Such of waste of time, talent, and energy.

Especially energy.

Energy was everything.

That was clear to him now. Everything was clear, throbbing as he was in this supercharged state. This was incredible. His whole body thrummed with power. On a whim, he considered blasting Steede with a lightning bolt, reducing him to ash just for the fun of it. But that would be a mistake. Steede was still of value to him.

He had to remember that this euphoria was not the end. It was the *means* to an end. This was the Day of Reckoning, to be followed by the Days of Woe, aka the Era of Jagger Doing Whatever He Wants . . . and *that* was the end.

He smiled at his audience of slaves, savoring the sight of that self-righteous son of a bitch Rhoads, who had underestimated Jagger again and again, first at Bragg, patting Jagger on the head and writing him off as a nice guy with a few leadership skills, never suspecting that Jagger was, even at that early point in the development of his abilities, manipulating the colonel's thoughts. Hilarious. Again in the field, again at The Farm, again and again and again since Jagger had decided to break free. And the underestimation continued, Rhoads thinking that he could defeat Jagger by training a bunch of kids here, as if wearing a West Point ring granted some kind of power all by itself, as if sitting up straight and taking Ivy League physics would mean diddly out in the field . . . against the High Rollers, for crying out loud.

A five-star fool, Rhoads. But not without his usefulness. Even he would play a role in this, Jagger's moment of fruition. His vengeance, his reordering.

"Today is the dawn of a new age," he told the rapt audience beaming up at him, "the dawn of *our* age."

The auditorium thundered with applause and cheers and stomping boots.

"Look at them," he said, gesturing toward the live feed of the mess hall streaming on the giant projection screen. "All those shiny West Pointers. Aren't you sick of their stares and smirks when you enter the mess hall? Of course you are. Because you know the truth. They're elitists, born into privilege, with parents who reinforced all that duty, honor, and country nonsense. Duty's for slaves, countries aren't real, and honor . . . ? They wouldn't know honor if it marched up and pinned a medal on them.

"Honor comes from here," he said, and thumped his chest, stirring the bright flames within, "and here." He rapped on his skull. "West

Pointers don't use their hearts or their minds. They follow orders, that's it, just like they did in high school, doing what Mommy and Daddy told them, becoming class presidents and team captains and earning admission to their personal wet dream—West Point—their golden ticket to a life spent bossing people born without the same advantages."

He shook his head with mock disgust. "Look at them. Look at their spiffy uniforms and perfect posture. They're robots, not people. Is that what you want?"

The audience stared, waiting to be told what it wanted.

"No," Jagger said. "You're too real for that. And unlike these crisp young fascists, you don't think you're better than everyone else, which is actually kind of funny if you think about it." He grinned at the cadets, who'd been grumbling after he'd explained that they were angry.

Now they grinned back.

"Because you are the special ones," he said. "But these cadidiots laugh every time you walk in the mess hall. They act like they're A number one, God's gift to the universe, the high and mighty West Point supertroopers."

Lopez's snort cut through the air.

Jagger had forgotten that snort, the way it startled people. Very amusing. He'd missed it, missed having Lopez around.

But no one here so much as flinched at the sound. They were locked on to Jagger. A bomb could go off, and not one of them would bat an eye.

"The only reason they're sitting in that dining hall up there," he said, "is luck. They were born with tremendous advantages. Internal and external. Nature and nurture. Sure, they worked hard, but what of it? They were wired to work hard *and* raised to work hard. At birth, they were dealt a royal flush. The way our world is set up, they could do anything. And with all that potential, all those choices, what do they decide to do? Cure cancer? No. Embrace a passion, become great painters or musicians or poets? No. Dedicate their lives to public service, rescuing the oppressed? Again, no. They come to

West Point, because this is where they can get the two things that they want more than anything else in the world: bragging rights and the ability to spend the rest of their petty lives rubbing other people's noses in their supertrooper status."

His audience snarled like so many vicious dogs.

"So yeah," he said, "they can sense that you're different. They smell it on you. And they're right. You are not like them. But they misinterpret the difference. They think you're misfits, some ragtag outfit of third-rate losers who came here on the short bus. Well, fuck them."

"Yeah!" someone shouted.

"Fuck them!" someone else hollered.

Jagger grinned, savoring the hateful clamor. Their anger vibrated and sizzled, pulsing off them like actual energy, and in truth, it was force that he could—and would—use. "You are so much better than them. Difference is, you were dealt mixed hands. You didn't have perfect little families giving you pep talks every day. Your fathers were enlisted men, just like mine. Our fathers drank and had mood swings, and maybe sometimes they went upside your head or beat your mom and siblings in front of you."

He paused, watching them nod. When he spoke again, his voice was lower, full of emotion. "I am sorry. I am so damned sorry. I wish that I could have been there for each and every one of you. I wish I could have stopped all that trauma and given your fathers the help they needed and deserved. I wish that I could have been there to tell you the truth. That you are far more amazing than those shiny assholes upstairs. You can do things that they could never dream of. You can kick through brick walls or stack the rubble with your minds. You can light fires with your eyes or heal third-degree burns with your hands. You can run fast as cheetahs or leap straight into someone's dreams. But do we ever look at them the way they look at us? Of course not. Because we're not a bunch of stuck-up, self-important elitists who love bossing people around. Am I right?"

The audience roared approval.

Jagger chuckled. "Wow . . . I guess we're speaking the same language. Well, today is going to change everything. Today we're going to send the golden children a message, and they in turn will *become* our message. Watch. You're going to love this."

The cadets nodded, eager.

"And when the president of the United States sees this footage . . ." He swiveled his gaze toward Rhoads. "We *are* recording, aren't we, Colonel?"

"We sure are, sir," Rhoads chimed.

"And we've contacted the major news networks?"

"Yes, sir."

"Excellent," Jagger said. "You could tell the mainstream media exactly what we're about to do, and rather than try to stop us, they'd start running teasers. Well, we'll give them the story they want, and they'll show the whole world. The White House will demand answers, and thanks to our very own Senator Ditko—" He paused, gesturing to the far left of the stage, where Ditko took a little bow. "—we'll be able to provide them. When the president interrupts programming to give an emergency State of the Union address, he'll patch me in, and I'll have a little chat with millions of viewers across the nation, thousands of whom have been waiting for this moment, the Day of Reckoning, for a long, long time. I'll give them *our* message, and they'll do what I say."

The cadets roared.

Jagger cracked his knuckles near the mic, and the speakers gave what sounded like a twenty-one-gun salute.

"But first we have a little fun with the lunch bunch upstairs," he said. "Watch this, kids." He clapped his hands, and a pillar of fire ten feet high roared to life on stage.

The cadets leaned back in their seats, *oohing* and *ahhing*.

Jagger spread his arms, and the columnar inferno curved and stretched, lifting slowly into the air like an uncoiling serpent knit of hellfire. Then, with a loud whoosh, the flames whipped over the audience in an airborne river of fire. Cadets cried out in surprise and fear and elation, then cried out again when the flames curved back over them and plunged straight into Jagger's chest.

Yes!

He stiffened with the rush.

The flames rushed out of his back, arched over his head, and flowed again into his chest . . . and out his back again.

Out, over, back in . . . out, over, back in . . .

The flames cycled faster and faster, burning more brightly with each revolution, until Jagger spread his arms, impaled by an unbroken loop of blinding flame.

He straightened an arm, spread his fingers, and tucked his thumb, pointing the Crown of Glory at the ceiling, where a large overhead light wrenched away with a terrible screech, raining sparks. The unit crashed to the stage, making cadets jump and laugh nervously. Overhead, severed wires lowered, spraying sparks. They twisted and hissed like snakes, moving lower and lower until they struck, plunging their sparking ends into Jagger's loop of flame, which swelled and quickened and shone brighter than ever, huffing flame.

Yes, this was power! This was glory!

Using telekinesis, he tore away additional light fixtures and guided their sizzling wires to his power loop, which grew and grew and grew, illuminating the auditorium in a hissing, flickering light that played in a flickering chiaroscuro across the wide-flung eyes of his captivated audience.

He bared his teeth in a grin and willed the top of the loop to lower slowly, then punched it straight into his forehead.

The cadets gasped.

Jagger stumbled backward, steadied himself, and cackled static laughter.

His audience writhed with awe.

When he spoke, his voice, inhumanly deep now, boomed from the speakers high above in the mess hall.

"Attention!"

The West Point cadets upstairs shot to their feet and stared up with wide eyes toward the ceiling, as if God himself had spoken.

Which was appropriate, Jagger thought.

"This is your supreme commander," he said. "On the count of three, I will give you an order, and you will all comply immediately. One, two, three . . ."

FORTY-EIGHT

SCARLETT TRIED TO SCREAM BUT HAD NO VOICE.

"I never cared about you," Seamus said, and threw back his head with a gale of cruel laughter. His features were exaggerated somehow, sharper and more beautiful and completely merciless, not entirely human.

She moaned in this private hell, unable to speak, unable to apologize, unable to agree.

"You're so stupid," Seamus said. "Look at yourself. You really thought I could fall for a loser like you? I just used you. Now I'm free, and you're paying the price."

Another wave of cruel laughter crushed down on her.

And then the dream vanished, and Scarlett returned once again to the Chamber. She fought to catch her breath. Her eyes burned from crying, her muscles throbbed from struggling against the restraints, and her throat itched, raw from screaming.

Please, she prayed. *Please, make it stop.*

She wanted to end this, needed to end it, even if that meant dying, and now, thinking of herself, how stupid and selfish, how reckless and cruel she'd been, she understood that she deserved to die . . . and yes, she longed for death.

Her death wouldn't fix the damage she'd done—she could never atone for her mistakes—but at least she would end her suffering, erase her shameful squandered life, and save others from the pain she would no doubt otherwise inflict.

Yes, death . . .

But for now she was trapped, facing the facts, facing Dalia, whose face filled the square window of the Chamber door: Dalia standing outside, looking in at her, poor Dalia, whom she had so wronged . . .

She had no idea how long the dream torture had been going on, only that she couldn't bear another second. "Mercy," she pleaded. "Death . . ."

"Death?" Dalia said, and smirked. "I'm afraid not, sweetie. Jagger wants you alive. He wants to know how you managed to resist him. But of course, I can answer that. I know all about how stupid and stubborn you are, how you can disregard those who try to help you. Death? I don't think so. We're just getting started."

Scarlett squeezed her eyes shut and trembled. She was wrung out. She didn't have the energy to argue or tears to shed.

"I've been watching your dreams since you came here," Dalia said, "and a lot of people want to chime in. Consider this an intervention. All the people you've hurt, coming together to help you understand what a self-centered bitch you've been."

"I can't take it anymore," Scarlett said. She was broken. Dalia had shown her everything: the people she'd hurt, people suffering in private, things she'd never even considered, guys she'd jilted, friends she'd ditched, elderly drivers she'd scared, blasting past on the Yamaha. She saw her brother, decomposing in the grave, asking again and again why Scarlett had done this to him; her mother, dead from an overdose, whispering that it was all her fault; her father, alone, weeping like a child, the man a hero both for the lives he'd saved and for the degree to which he'd suffered, protecting his family from the rage that burned inside him, all while Scarlett treated him like dirt. She watched tragedies yet to come, things she would have done, people she would have let down, without this intervention. She wanted death, deserved death, *needed* death. "Please kill me."

"Not a chance," Dalia said. "We could have been such good friends, Scarlett. I welcomed you here, saved you from your tormentors, and made Rhoads give you every privilege. And what did you do with these privileges? Used them to sneak around with Kyeong. I tried to warn you, but would you listen? Of course not, because you're stupid and selfish and cruel. Well, now we'll—"

Her words cut off abruptly, and things *shifted*.

Scarlett was still in the Chamber, still hurting, still wanting death, deserving it, *needing* it, yet Dalia's dream thrall was lifting away like a poisonous gas. Dalia was out of her head, and the somnopath's face was gone from the window.

But then—*no!*

Dalia's face filled the window again, and Scarlett cried out—not for mercy; she knew now that Dalia was utterly merciless—but out of sheer terror.

"Scarlett!"

That voice . . .

She looked again.

It wasn't Dalia at the window.

"Scarlett," Seamus said, his face pressed to the glass. "Are you okay?"

Not Dalia at all . . . *Seamus . . .*

"I took care of her," Seamus said. "I saw her at the window and heard what she was saying, and—I took care of her."

Took care of her? She didn't know what he meant, and her mind shied from the possibilities. Seamus's cruel laughter echoed from wherever her mind stored its nightmares. "Leave me alone."

"I heard what she was saying," Seamus said. He put his hand to the glass. "It was all lies. She was just playing on your fears, trying to break you."

When Scarlett spoke, her voice was a tortured rasp. "You said it was all my fault."

And it is. It is all my fault.

"Snap out of it," Seamus said. "Dalia messed you up. That's it. None of that was real. I came back for you, didn't I?"

"Yeah, but—"

"Stop," Seamus said. "We don't have time for this. Sort your shit."

Sort your shit, she thought, and heard another echo, not from her nightmares but from the past: Ginny laughing as Scarlett panicked, Ginny saying, *Sort your shit. It's just a trip. It's all in here,* and tapping Scarlett's skull.

That was what they'd always said during moments like that, when one of them had taken the Paranoia Express to Terrorville.

She took a deep breath. *Sort your shit*, she told herself. It was code, and it took her back to her partying days, anchoring her. A curious place to find strength, perhaps, but a drowning woman doesn't complain if someone throws her a garden hose instead of a rope. "All right," she said. "Okay. Yeah."

Seamus was describing things he'd seen on his way there, things he'd heard. "Something's going on, something big, like an invasion."

"Jagger," she said, remembering. Her panic spiked again, recalling Jagger's excitement as he had probed her mind and ability.

"We have to get you out of there," Seamus said, "but it's locked, and I don't have a key. Hold on for a second. I have to check Dalia's pockets."

"Don't leave me," Scarlett pleaded. Without Seamus, she was afraid that she would slide back into the black pit of self-loathing.

Seamus disappeared from the window, filling her with panic. Whose face would next fill the glass square? Dalia's? Jagger's? The charred face of the woman she'd failed to save?

Scarlett lay there hurting and helpless, reminded of her first night here at The Point, when Hopkins and his telekinetic goons had pummeled her from behind a similar door. All the work she'd been through, all the Level III torture, and she was still trapped behind a door, helpless as a baby in a crib.

Seamus's face returned, twisted with concern. "No keys. I don't know what to do."

Scarlett, returning to her senses, said, "Can't you break it down?"

He shook his head. "The door and lock are too strong. They were designed to contain TKs."

It was hopeless. Again she was reminded of her first night, the helplessness she'd felt, lying there with no way to fight back as Hopkins and his thugs pounded her through the door, all of this before she'd learned how to—

"I have to look for a guard," Seamus said. "Try to overpower him, take his keys."

"Wait," she said. "Don't leave. I've got it."

For a fraction of a second, she feared that he hadn't heard her, but his face appeared again in the glass square. "What?"

"Hit me," she said.

"Huh?"

"Blast me with your mind . . . hard."

FORTY-NINE

"HOOAH!" A BOOKISH-LOOKING PLEBE SHOUTED AS he plunged a fork into the stomach of the upperclassman beside him. The upperclassman convulsed, yelped with laughter, and buried his fingers in the plebe's eyes.

The West Point mess hall was a collage of terrors soaked in blood and set to insane music: screams of pain and rage, maniacal laughter, orders bellowed on top of orders, most of them absolutely nonsensical in the current context.

In one corner, a silver-haired officer shouted "About-face!" again and again to the cadet whose face he pounded rhythmically into the tiled floor.

Nearby, a quartet of cadets overturned their table atop a trio of lunatics and then turned on one another.

Beneath the giant mural, a pair of female cadets twirled, locked in a gruesome embrace, plunging knives into each other's abdomen, their mutual screaming and laughter entwined in an uncanny braid.

All of this played out on the large screen at the back of the stage behind Jagger, whose leering grin was mirrored by the cadets and cadre staring up from the auditorium seats, an absolutely rapt audience riveted to the bloody spectacle.

Beautiful, Jagger thought. *Absolutely glorious,* much like the sizzling ring of electricity filling him with unimaginable power now. He'd discharged only a fraction of it when he'd commanded the West Pointers to fight to the death, and since then it had continued to build.

"Colonel Rhoads," he said. "Patch in the media. No exclusives. Footage for everyone."

"On it," Rhoads said, tapping away at the laptop.

Soon every network in the world would be broadcasting the footage, and the web would follow. Fear would go viral, unsettling millions of people, which would only make them more malleable. In mere seconds, tens of thousands whom he had prepared, all the bums and runaways, college kids and congregations, would understand that the Day of Reckoning had at last arrived. All across the nation, they would swing into action, spreading mayhem. The terrified masses would run for cover, lock their doors, turn on their television sets, and look to their government for help.

"Senator," Jagger said, turning to Ditko. "Now it's your turn. Contact the president. By the time you get through, his people will be showing him the breaking footage. Give him the basics, then tell him that you're handing the phone to the man with all the answers. I need to speak to him before he addresses the nation."

Before I *address the nation*, he thought. But Ditko didn't need to know that. The man's usefulness was nearly at an end. After that, who knew?

Maybe I'll have Penny burn him alive.

Ditko saluted and turned away, pulling out his phone.

Using his mind, Jagger peeled a section of electrical conduit from the wall, snapped the pipeline, severed the wires inside, and sucked sparking electricity into the glowing globe of power now engulfing him. The power ring burned more brightly than ever, impaling and empowering him. Other rings formed, circling him, and between those rings arced tendrils of electricity, creating a pulsing latticework sphere of white static shot through with bolts of yellow and veined in propane blue.

This was omnipotence. This was euphoria.

By then the news was spreading, and in thousands of towns across the land, his sleeper cells were leaping into action. Horror stories from all over would flood the news, making even the gentlest souls pick up weapons.

"Yes," Ditko said into the phone, "I need to speak with him directly. As in now. Yes, we have a situation here." Then, after the pause that Jagger had made him practice, he said, "A *posthuman* situation."

FIFTY

WITH EVERY STRIKE FROM SEAMUS, SCARLETT GREW stronger.

After the third blast, she snapped the restraints and shoved aside the metal ribs of the machine's cage. Stepping free, she spread her arms and thrust her chest forward. "Again—as hard as you can!"

Seamus blasted her once, twice, three times, each strike harder than the last.

She shouted for him to step away from the door. Her first kick bent the door and snapped a hinge. The second strike ripped the door free and tossed it across the corridor, where it clanged loudly off the block wall and fell to the ground. She stepped free of the Chamber, bones still thrumming with pent-up force.

They embraced.

On the floor, Dalia murmured softly, still unconscious but starting to come around.

"She's Jagger's puppet now," Scarlett said. "So are Rhoads and Ditko." She quickly explained Jagger and his power.

Seamus frowned. "Rhoads gave an all-call to the auditorium."

"And Jagger's the guest speaker," she said. "They're his by now, all of them."

"We have to get out of here before they come for us."

Dalia stirred, mumbling.

"What about Dalia?" she said. "We can't protect ourselves from her."

Seamus smiled grimly. "I know how to make her leave us alone."

A short time later, as they hurried away down the hall, Scarlett wished that she hadn't kicked the Chamber door completely off its hinges. It would have been good to block Dalia's screams as the machine shone its merciless spotlight on whatever nightmares she had stored in that dark mind of hers. By the bloodcurdling sound of her screams, she must have been harboring some terrible dreams indeed.

They reached the intersection. To the left was the auditorium and Jagger. To the right was a clear path to the subway stairwell, safety, and freedom.

Scarlett turned left.

Seamus grabbed her arm. "What are you doing?"

"We have to stop Jagger, Seamus."

He tugged in the opposite direction. "He's too powerful."

"If I don't try to stop him, I'll spend the rest of my life hating myself," Scarlett said. She remembered the pain Dalia had put her through and shivered, knowing that most of it was true. She'd hurt a lot of people. Whenever the going had gotten tough, she'd quit or begged off or stuck her head in a sand made of weed and booze and boy toys: anything to ignore the problem. The sum total of her life had led her to this crossroads. If she turned right, she would set all the things Dalia had shown her in stone, but if she turned left . . . "I have to try."

"Even if you could stop Jagger, it wouldn't bring Dan back."

"It's not just about Dan," she said. "It's about everyone. And this place, and West Point, and duty. I know that sounds stupid, but we're part of something here, and we swore an oath. That's bigger than me or you or Dan or what we think of Rhoads."

He looked at her with thoughtful eyes, the corners of his mouth drawing downward.

"Think about Lucy DeCraig," she said. "How are you going to feel if—"

"Shut up," he said, and closed his eyes. "Just shut up, all right?" He reached into his pocket, pulled out a pack of gum, and handed her two pieces.

She raised one eyebrow. "Gum?"

Unwrapping a piece, Seamus said, "Hubris kills."

"Huh?"

He plucked the chewed gum from his mouth and stuffed it into his ear. "Let's not fool around like Odysseus."

FIFTY-ONE

SCARLETT CROUCHED IN THE SHADOWS JUST OFF-stage and stared in terror at Jagger, who levitated several inches above the stage, impaled on a ring of sparking power that swelled and swelled.

I hope Seamus lost his nerve, she thought, and, glancing across the stage, saw no sign of him. They had split up, agreeing to attack from opposite sides. *I hope he lost his nerve and ran.*

Now, standing here, seeing Jagger and feeling his unbelievable power, she understood how foolish she and Seamus had been, coming here, thinking they could intervene.

Jagger gestured toward the ceiling, and a large light tore away, dangling by a twist of metal over the heads of the mesmerized cadets, who took no notice whatsoever. They were utterly transfixed on the dining hall horror show playing out on the screen behind Jagger. Wiring tore away from the damaged light and descended, weaving through the air and spraying sparks, and joined Jagger's glowing ring of electricity.

Jagger was using the ability he'd stolen from her to build an incredible power loop—but for what?

Jagger spoke, and his voice was crackling static. "Senator Ditko, what is our status?"

With one hand, Senator Ditko held a phone to his ear. With the other, he still clutched the tiny hand of Sav's murderous little sister, Penny.

You see this little bitch, Lopez's voice echoed in her mind, *kill her on sight.*

But Scarlett knew that she couldn't do that. She couldn't kill Penny for things she'd done under Jagger's spell.

Ditko gave Jagger a thumbs-up and said into the phone, "Yes, Mr. President, that's correct: a *posthuman* situation. I have someone here who can answer all of your questions."

Jagger extended an arm, and the phone whipped from Ditko's hand to his.

For a fraction of a second, Scarlett thrilled, hoping the phone would pop against Jagger's pulsing aura like an insect hitting an electrical bug zapper, but no—Jagger had mastered force in a way Scarlett wouldn't have thought possible. He raised the phone to his ear, clearly planning to charm the president of the United States. For what purpose? Jagger might find it hilarious to launch nukes around the world.

She edged closer. She needed to do something now—but what could she possibly do?

She'd absorbed strikes from Seamus, storing their force in her bones, but Jagger would gobble any energy Scarlett threw at him. If she charged Jagger instead, the High Rollers would mob her and pull her limb from limb with the help of the cadets and cadre, who gaped up at Jagger like an audience of ventriloquist's dummies.

Jagger's electrical loop pulsed with terrible power, suffusing the very air with a crackling undercurrent that made the hair on Scarlett's arms stand at attention.

How had Jagger generated so much power? How could he hold it? Throughout training, Rhoads had warned Scarlett about overloading. *Take on too much power*, Rhoads had told her, quoting the battery of scientists at his disposal, *and you'll explode like an overloaded fuse box.*

"Hello, Mr. President," Jagger said, his voice ripe with charm that Scarlett not only heard but *felt* at the back of her neck. She had plucked the gum from her ears as soon as she'd parted ways with Seamus. It was a good idea for Seamus to protect himself, but she was betting everything on an assumption now, and if her success or failure came down to chewing gum, she was dead. Better to hear what the enemy was saying. "I'm going to tell you just what to do."

This is it, Scarlett thought. *You have to stop him now.*

But how? Blasting Jagger now would be like trying to use a barbecue lighter to extinguish an erupting volcano.

The curtains parted slowly across the stage, and Seamus emerged from the darkness. If she didn't strike now, *he* would, and—

"Call an emergency State of the Union address," Jagger said, "and allow me to speak with the American people directly."

To hell with Rhoads and his half stepping, Scarlett's true self blurted. Her old mojo, which she'd been suppressing since day one at The Point—and which had more to do with popping wheelies than with following orders—flooded back in. *If I overload, I overload.*

She crouched, released the pent-up force from her bones, flooded her muscles with energy, and leaped straight at Jagger. She spread her arms wide and stuck out her chest as she had done countless times back home at the quarry, pulling a theatrical swan dive in one more impulsive, death-defying stunt, spitting into the face of the crushing boredom and unbearable depression that wanted so badly to define her life.

And then, barking laughter, Scarlett exploded into the supernova surrounding Jagger.

FIFTY-TWO

JAGGER GRUNTED WITH SURPRISE, SPOTTING THE hurtling shape—*A person? Scarlett Winter?*—just as the girl slammed into his loop of power.

A blinding flash, a loud zap, and Jagger hit the stage with a heavy thump. The phone spun away across the floorboards.

His assailant—yes, it was Scarlett—blasted away from the explosion, pinwheeling through the air like a bird killed by a speeding automobile. She slammed into the side wall and collapsed to the ground in a lump, steaming and sparking.

"Exit stage right," Jagger said, and emitted a burst of static laughter.

But something was wrong.

I'm not on my feet anymore.

He looked around woozily and realized that he was several feet from where he'd been standing when Scarlett had hit the ring—and apparently destroyed it.

His consciousness twisted in and out of focus like a face in a fun house mirror.

She rocked me.

His confused mind tumbled back in time to a night long ago, before he'd mastered his powers, when a pit boss had chased him down in a parking lot outside an Oklahoma casino. The pit boss started shouting about cheating and giving back money. The guy had brought an employee out with him. Not one of the security types you see in Vegas, burly goons with cauliflower ears and cheap suits. No, the pit boss had a skinny dishwasher with him.

Jagger remembered the guy now, in this cloudy moment. The dishwasher was tall and dark and wiry as a whip handle, with a sopping wet apron and huge knuckles gnarled with scar tissue. The guy just stood there, looking bored, while the pit boss yelled and threatened, and Jagger had made a mistake then, trying to charm the pit boss instead of asking himself, *Why bring a dishwasher outside?*

The dishwasher's right cross had shattered Jagger's orbital bone and knocked him out cold. Jagger had awakened on his back, coughing blood, the macadam warm and hard beneath him. The dishwasher stood over him with no real expression on his face. No anger, no excitement, no sorrow, and Jagger . . .

What the hell?

He shook his head.

Jagger, old buddy, you are fucked up. That girl rocked you harder than the dishwasher.

The confused burble building among the cadets roused him. He had to shake off the cobwebs and fix this shit before everything went south at approximately the speed of light.

Ditko leaned over him, looking concerned, and offered a hand.

Jagger pushed the hand aside and sat up on his own power.

His head was clearing now. The air smelled strange. Ozone and singed hair and burned rubber and some other smell, like overheated metal . . .

Get your head straight, he told himself, and struggled to his feet. He felt spent, wobbly. The world tilted and came back into focus.

The cadets stared up at him, looking confused—some were clearly more agitated than others—and he understood that the blast had fractured his hold on them.

Fractured but not destroyed. Good.

Meanwhile, his High Rollers, long conditioned to doing his bidding, remained on point, watching him, ready to act, and over all of this played achingly beautiful music, the discordant symphony of the still-raging dining hall chaos.

A wall of muscle crossed the stage, Steede moving toward where Scarlett had fallen.

The stupid bitch had gotten herself killed, breaking the loop. What a waste. She could have been a convenient backup battery.

"Oh, well," Jagger said. "The show goes on." He gestured toward the phone, and it flew into his grasp. He just needed to calm the president and buy a few minutes to build another loop before addressing the nation.

Across the stage, Steede reached for Scarlett—and spun away with a *thwack* sound. One of Steede's massive arms flopped free, as if hacked from his body by an unseen machete. Steede roared in pain and shock, spraying blood, then flew from his feet, hit by an invisible snowplow doing fifty miles an hour.

A male cadet—lean yet muscular, with black hair—emerged from the wings, glaring fiercely at Jagger.

The missing boy, Jagger thought. *Scarlett's sweetheart, Kyeong.*

And then the invisible snowplow that had blasted the life from Steede slammed into Jagger.

He jerked with the impact. Then he straightened and smiled at Kyeong. "Ooh, you're *strong*," he said, and sent the force boomeranging back at the boy.

Kyeong tried to dodge, but the blast caught him broadside. He cried out sharply, spun away, and lay on the stage, twitching like fresh roadkill.

"Colonel Rhoads, what have you been feeding these cadets," Jagger said, smiling at the crowd, "whiskey and vinegar?"

"Hooah!" Rhoads roared back.

"Hooah!" the audience echoed.

Yet Jagger felt a twinge of concern. Kyeong's blast had actually *hurt*. Yes, he'd handled the force, but not cleanly. How badly had Scarlett damaged him?

Eyes on the prize. Take care of business now and worry about all that later.

He lifted the phone to his ear and almost laughed to hear the president's concerned voice. "No worries, Mr. President," he said. "Everything's squared away, and I'm ready to rock and roll."

But at that second, a bright light shone from the wing, illuminating the auditorium in a strange, wavering light. Scarlett rose to her feet and squared with Jagger like a gunfighter, encircled by a blue-white halo of power.

"You can take a punch," Jagger said. "I'll give you that much." He spread his arms. "But what are you going to do? Anything you throw at me, I'll just throw back at you. We'll do the do-si-do a couple of times, but then my soldiers will eat you alive." He gave the phone a shake. "And then I'll get the real party started."

A crackling whip of force lashed across the stage. The phone exploded in his hand.

"*Schweinehund!*" a tall, skinny cadet with spectacles shouted up at him. Somehow she had shaken off his control and destroyed his phone, his *plan*, with a telekinetic attack.

Jagger stared at the empty hand into which the force of the exploding phone had rushed. He tightened the throbbing hand into a fist, but he knew better than to spend it on the TK sniper, just as he knew better than to waste a telekinetic blast on Scarlett. Oh, no . . . she could handle *that* kind of force.

Instead, he smiled brightly.

"Very impressive, Scarlett," he said, and lowered his voice an octave, infusing it with warmth and goodwill. "You really are amazing." He stretched out a hand. "Come, join me."

Scarlett smiled back at him, and the halo surrounding her shone even more brightly.

Yes, Jagger thought. *It's working.*

"And what then?" Scarlett said. "Rule the world together like a couple of supervillains?"

Jagger laughed. "See, that's where the villains get it wrong. Why bother to manage the herd? That's just another version of the duty-country-honor lie that this place sells. Why rule the world when you can just do whatever you want?" Then he took his voice lower still, tightening it like a flashlight beam, and stared straight into Scarlett's eyes. "Now, be a good girl, get down on all fours, and bark like a dog."

"I have a better idea," Scarlett said, and snapped her fingers. The corona of light around her shimmered, and her voice boomed like a salvo of artillery. "Everyone . . . help me fight!"

FIFTY-THREE

EVERYTHING WENT CRAZY.

Jagger's power to manipulate had been one more form of force, a literal manifestation of personal magnetism. She hadn't understood what was happening when she'd felt energy building during Rhoads's presentation on the High Rollers. It was only after she'd resisted Jagger in the Chamber and felt similar energy building in her neck and skull that she'd begun to wonder.

Scarlett had absorbed the charismatic attack and counterpunched with her own command. She knew that Jagger was weakened, just as she was, and she hoped that everyone would attack him simultaneously with enough power and variety to overload and destroy him.

The cadets and cadre, free of Jagger's hypnotic yoke, came to their senses immediately.

Unfortunately, the High Rollers, apparently under a much stronger spell, resisted her command and attacked the cadets.

The auditorium exploded in a posthuman battle royal. TKs on both sides launched devastating attacks. Meatheads roared forward, smashing skulls and snapping spines. Speedsters jumped and flashed past the enemy ranks, snapping necks. Guards from The Point waded in with Tasers and nightsticks. Rhoads fired his tranquillizer gun.

A massive female High Roller lifted Vernon overhead and pitched him screaming over several rows of seats but then screamed herself when Cramer stepped forward and bathed the meathead's face in a billowing charcoal miasma streaked in crimson. This was the dreaded antihealing mentioned only in whispers at The Point. The big High Roller's face twisted into a grimace and then ballooned, going purple. Fissures opened over the distended flesh, spraying pus. The meathead choked horribly and clawed at her own face, which sloughed away in bloody hunks. She retched and gasped and toppled heavily forward, dead as a stone.

In those opening seconds of the melee, it appeared that the cadets, through initiative and superior numbers, would overwhelm the High Rollers.

Then Penny screamed, and a napalm strike of flames rolled across the auditorium, engulfing cadets, cadre, and those unfortunate High Rollers who had rushed forward to engage the enemy. People dived for cover. Many, however, were too slow. They writhed, burning brightly, completely indistinguishable in the hot flames.

In a single instant, the battle had swung. Combat-hardened as they were, the High Rollers seized the initiative and launched blistering, unrelenting attacks against the survivors hiding behind the burning auditorium seats.

Chantel Uba, the firstie TK who embodied integrity, rose from cover and fired a calculated attack.

Penny spun as if struck by a bullet and collapsed to the stage.

A fraction of a second later, Uba's head jerked and lost its shape as one side caved beneath an invisible hammer blow. She collapsed, dead before she hit the auditorium floor.

Her killer, a TK named Gans, started barking orders then, coordinating the High Rollers' attacks to eradicate the surviving cadets.

FIFTY-FOUR

ONSTAGE, SCARLETT AND JAGGER FIRED SIMULTA-neous blasts of concentrated force. Both of them were hurt, and both were hoping to catch their weakened opponent with a decisive blow. Instead, their attacks collided at center stage, forming a river of sparking energy that ran like a conduit between them. They both staggered, caught themselves, and pushed harder.

Scarlett shouted and strained. Everything hurt.

In the space between them, at the point where her energy met his, she could feel energy condensing, crushing in on itself, growing denser and denser, as if they were creating a singularity.

When she surged, the singularity pushed toward Jagger. When he struggled back, she felt the singularity edge in her direction.

She didn't know what precisely would happen if Jagger managed to push the singularity all the way to her, didn't know whether she would explode or vaporize or be crushed down to nothing, but she knew without a doubt that touching the singularity would mean instant death.

She growled, pushing the mass of condensed energy back toward Jagger.

She wouldn't quit. No matter how much it hurt, no matter how strong he was, she wouldn't surrender.

Jagger was immensely powerful. Alone, he could destroy anyone, any *one*, but Scarlett was not alone.

She fought with the power of love and hatred.

Jagger, meanwhile, fought only with the urge to survive and destroy.

It wasn't enough.

Scarlett was strengthened by the desperate need to avenge her brother, to save her friends, and, yes, to rescue this place, this place that she once had loathed but had come to respect, this place where people sacrificed their lives to safeguard the lives of people who didn't even know that The Point existed, people who would brand them as freaks and burn them at the stake.

As a mother will starve to feed her child, as a father will surrender his life one factory shift at a time to support his family, as a soldier will charge into withering fire to rescue a fallen brother in arms, Scarlett summoned that which is most beautiful in humanity, the power to fight harder, suffer longer, and endure more, all for the good of others. She endured not merely for herself but also for her fallen brother, for Seamus and Lucy, Cramer and Vernon, and even, somehow, the likes of Lopez and Rhoads and Hopkins. She transcended herself, fighting for this place, these people, her family, her world. And filled with that determination, she braced herself and pounded forth more power so that the deadly knot of force edged back in Jagger's direction, closer and closer, and she could see panic widening his eyes, closer and closer . . .

"High Rollers!" Jagger barked. "Forget them! Fire on me!"

His fanatical soldiers turned their attacks away from the beleaguered cadets and blasted Jagger with their various energies.

She felt his power surge, felt the singularity push in her direction, forcing energy back into her. A volcano of churning heat pulsed within her. She stumbled, tripping backward until her back slammed into a wall. Jagger pressed forward, laughing, and she was pinned against the wall by their joined force, with the singularity and certain death edging closer and closer.

She gritted her teeth, summoning every bit of courage and determination. She wouldn't quit. She battled back, straining, but Jagger, fueled by the High Rollers' attacks, was too powerful to withstand.

At that moment, the cadets rose bravely from their defensive positions and blasted the High Rollers, who had been left defenseless by Jagger's command. The High Rollers fell as one, blindsided by a simultaneously barrage of telekinetic force, projectiles, and the bone-crunching tackles of speedsters.

Jagger's gambit, however, had paid off. He had sacrificed the High Rollers, but his power had surged incredibly. He pressed the singularity forward. Its sizzling force was blinding now, eclipsing everything.

Feeling like her insides had turned to boiling oil, Scarlett screamed in pain and rage and desperation. Her body would explode at any second.

"Hit Scarlett with everything you've got," the familiar voice of Lucy DeCraig shouted.

In an instant, the maddening heat and pressure rushed out of Scarlett, riding a thundering river of new power. The cadets and cadre of The Point had turned their energy on her—and not a moment too soon.

She pushed.

Jagger staggered backward, cursing, and slammed into the wall. Pinned there, he shouted frantic, unintelligible commands that melted into wordless screams of pain and terror as the singularity edged to within inches.

"This is for Dan," Scarlett said, and shoved out one last time.

There was a bright flash and a faint scream that was cut short, and Jagger imploded. In a fraction of a second, he crushed down on himself and disappeared with a crackle into the singularity, which released a flash of light, a blast of wind, and a tremendous thunderclap—and was gone.

A geyser of power gushed from Scarlett and blasted a steaming tunnel through the wall into an adjacent corridor.

Then it was over. Alarms sounded, and sprinklers rained down.

Scarlett stood there, alone at center stage, shuddering, her consciousness dimming in and out like a dying lightbulb. With the last strength remaining to her, she stumbled toward a shape lying in the shadows, and called to the healers, "Help Seamus!"

FIFTY-FIVE

WEEKS LATER, WITH A MILD SUN SHINING DOWN from a perfect blue sky, Scarlett marched with her fellow plebes across bright green grass to join the upperclassmen already in formation between the bleachers, where their families cheered, and the stage, where Colonel Rhoads stood, smiling down, flanked by Drill Sergeant Lopez and The Point's official West Point liaison, Captain Fuller. Lopez, once more a drill sergeant, even wore his Smokey the Bear campaign hat for the graduation ceremony, which was being held not at West Point—The Point had struggled too hard to stay out of the news to hold a formal service in broad daylight upon the field—but at a local high school football stadium secured by Senator Ditko, who eschewed the stage to sit in the bleachers alongside his family, including Sav, whose voice Scarlett could hear, and little Penny, who, having completed rehabilitation, would be joining The Point as a Level III recruit on R-Day, making her the youngest plebe in history. She was lucky to be alive. If someone other than Chantel Uba had delivered the blow that had knocked her out of the fight, Penny probably would have died. Uba, however, had taken the time to attack precisely, with restraint, and it had cost her everything.

Following decorum, Scarlett took only a quick glance toward the bottom row of the bleachers, where her parents applauded happily. Consciously or unconsciously, they had left a gap beside them.

Dan.

Despite the beautiful day, cheering families, and triumphant music, a funeral dirge moaned within Scarlett's heart and certainly within the hearts of those in attendance, as well as tens of thousands not in attendance, who had no idea that The Point even existed. The Point had suffered fifty-seven deaths. Nearly two-thirds of those killed were cadets. Virtually every survivor had suffered significant injuries. Above, in West Point proper, the losses were nothing short of staggering. Although the cadets had stopped fighting seconds after Jagger's death, nearly 1,500 of the nation's finest young officers had lost their lives.

The White House had officially blamed the tragedy on terrorists and a chemical agent that had induced temporary psychosis. America was largely mollified by the explanation, and that was no real surprise. With a scapegoat identified, fear and outrage had paradoxically calmed the masses. That being said, in the weeks since the attack, a steady stream of black suits and white jackets had scoured The Point. Government agents had grilled everyone—*and no one more than me*, Scarlett thought bitterly—and government scientists had subjected cadets and cadre to an exhaustive battery of tests. They'd collected blood and urine, run MRIs and stress tests, administered polygraphs, done narco-analytical interrogations, and even conducted bizarre empathy examinations like the ones Scarlett had seen in that old movie *Blade Runner*. Testing was over, thankfully, but a team of government "observers" would remain at The Point indefinitely. They lurked in classrooms, patrolled hallways, eavesdropped within the barracks, and had the authority to question anyone anytime about anything.

Recently, General Christian Paul Baca, the secretary of the army, had visited The Point to voice the president's gratitude and hold a Q&A session for the cadets. When General Baca stated that the president viewed The Point as the nation's answer to all posthuman threats, foreign and domestic, Lucy, who'd been badly rattled by losing control to Jagger but otherwise had come through the event without serious injury, asked, "Sir, are other countries training posthumans?"

General Baca smiled. "We have every confidence that the United States will be well prepared to win the arms race of the Posthuman Cold War . . . should one arise."

Not exactly an encouraging response.

But also not something to think about today, Scarlett reminded herself.

Today she would set aside her grief, suspend her anxieties, and celebrate. Despite the tragedy, the firsties were graduating, and the other classes were moving on, which made her very happy. She now felt proud to be part of The Point, but the notion of repeating plebe year held about as much appeal as gargling battery acid.

She and her classmates maneuvered into formation beside the surviving yearlings, who soon would be declared cows.

Someone goosed her. She managed not to jump, didn't look around, and didn't need to. She knew that the perpetrator wasn't standing behind her. He was standing in the adjacent formation, probably suppressing a grin.

Nothing could erase the awful events of this year, but Seamus at least made things better. If the tragedy had a silver lining, it was his recovery and the second chance he'd not only earned but accepted. Still no fan of Rhoads, Seamus at least had begun counseling and committed to moving forward with his class.

Unlike his fellow yearling, Dalia.

"It's not an ideal solution," Rhoads had said, explaining that Dalia would remain at The Farm, under heavy sedation. "It's the *only* solution."

They couldn't take chances with Dalia, Rhoads explained. She was too damaged and too powerful.

Most of the High Rollers remained at The Farm, undergoing rehabilitation. A few, like Penny, had been out-processed after completing rehab. At Rhoads's insistence, The Farm also was undergoing a transformation. Apparently, falling under Jagger's spell had caused the colonel to reevaluate the facility. Security remained priority one, but The Farm was evolving from a terrifying prison asylum into a legitimate correctional facility. Only the most severe and dangerous cases—including Dalia and Sadie—would remain underground.

Scarlett felt bad for Dalia despite what Dalia had done to her, but she hoped Sadie suffered every second of every day for the rest of her life. Maybe that wasn't very forgiving, but everyone had limitations, and she would never forget Sadie's soft embrace at Dan's funeral.

The music stopped, and Rhoads asked those in attendance to stand for the Pledge and the playing of the national anthem. Then he thanked the parents for attending, outlined the day's significance, and began speaking again of the tragedy. "The dead will never be forgotten," he said, "and their sacrifice will persist in strengthening our resolve."

Rhoads segued into his recognition of the cadets "in whose honor we are today gathered upon this verdant field." He spoke in hallowed tones, and Scarlett couldn't help but think of Jagger, whose voice had been as deadly as an atomic warhead.

But not to me, thank God, not to me.

Otherwise none of this would be happening. How many of these people would even be alive? You wouldn't need a set of bleachers to seat them, that was for sure.

Yet she felt no pride. Her resistance to Jagger's commands had, after all, had nothing to do with resolve or resourcefulness. Her ultimate gamble, which had hinged on not only resisting a superpowered blast of charisma but repurposing that energy to free everyone and defeat Jagger, had been incredibly reckless.

So no, she didn't feel proud. She only felt lucky.

Rhoads called Uba's parents onto the stage. Scarlett had seen Mr. and Mrs. Uba at the Christmas feast. Mr. Uba had struck her as large and powerfully built, with a loud voice that floated on a sea of rich laughter. Mrs. Uba had been athletically compact and absolutely vibrant with her expressive face, animated gestures, and fluid movement. Now, however, they moved slowly and stiffly, as if they'd aged thirty years. They looked small and frail in clothes that hung loose on their stooped frames, like trick-or-treat mock-ups of their former selves.

Rhoads spoke of their daughter's accomplishments and character and the phrase that haunts every service member's parents: *the ultimate sacrifice*.

"It is my great honor," Rhoads said, "to announce the institution of the Chantel Uba Memorial Award, which will be presented at the conclusion of each academic year to a cadet who has displayed exemplary courage, character, and commitment to The Point."

The Ubas smiled and nodded and wiped at tears, obviously moved, and Scarlett felt a lump form in her own throat. Uba had been 100 percent squared away, a totally committed cadet who ate, slept, and dreamed The Point. If anyone deserved the award Rhoads was describing, it was Uba.

"Mr. and Mrs. Uba," Rhoads said, "I would ask you to stay onstage and help me congratulate this year's recipient of the Chantel Uba Memorial Award, a cadet who displayed courage, character, and commitment while *saving* The Point."

Scarlett felt her face go red.

"Cadet Scarlett Winter," Rhoads said, "please come forward to receive your award."

Scarlett's legs followed orders, moving her out of formation and toward the stage, but her face burned, and her thoughts were a string of question marks. The moment didn't feel real. It felt like her head had disconnected from her neck and was bobbing high above her marching body like a red balloon filled with air that was growing hotter and hotter as she registered the smiling faces awaiting her on stage and the loud applause thundering behind her. Invisible fingers goosed her again and again as she marched up the steps and across the stage, Seamus's telekinesis nipping at her butt like a Chihuahua.

Rhoads started talking about the things Scarlett had done, but she didn't hear it, not really. She was too shocked and overwhelmed and far too conscious of the Ubas, who smiled at her with admiration that she didn't deserve. Then Rhoads handed her a plaque and shook her hand, and Mr. Uba shook her hand, and Mrs. Uba hugged her. She was surprised by the firmness of Mr. Uba's handshake and the fierceness of Mrs. Uba's embrace. Despite outward appearances, despite their unfathomable loss, impressive strength still dwelled within this man and woman. Realizing this, Scarlett experienced another surprise: a surge of unfettered optimism.

She belonged here and was proud to be part of The Point. If the nation did face posthuman threats, foreign or domestic, she would draw strength from this moment and annihilate those enemies.

"Thank you," she said, and started back toward the ranks. Glancing toward the bleachers, she saw her mother clapping. The torturous nightmare images that had shown her mother dead from suicide fortunately had turned out to be an illusion that was based on nothing but a manifestation of Scarlett's deep-seated fears and Dalia's cruelty. Despite her mother's bright smile, Scarlett knew that she was still struggling, still hurting, but for today at least, she was happy. Sometimes that was all you had. Sometimes *happy for today* was all you could hope for and all that mattered.

Her father stood ramrod straight beside his wife. And then Master Sergeant Charles Winter, U.S. Army, retired—a man who'd tormented his family but who'd obviously battled demons not to do far worse, a man who'd saved hundreds of lives and never breathed a word of his heroism—broke Scarlett's heart when he raised his hand in a salute.

Scarlett returned the salute, rejoined the ranks, and spent the rest of the ceremony in a kind of happy haze—thankful for her family and friends, her life and this place, her future, the warmth of sunlight on her face and fresh air and the smell of flowers and the sound of birdsong on the spring breeze—until Rhoads announced that the cadets were shifting ahead into the future.

Scarlett and her classmates, now yearlings, cheered loudly.

Finally, to the wild cheers and applause of all in attendance, the new graduates tossed their caps into the air. The hats fluttered against the blue sky like a flock of disoriented birds, and then, with TKs throughout the ranks grinning conspiratorially, the shiny black caps gathered into a wedge formation, whooshed in a wide circle overhead, and settled squarely down onto the heads of The Point's newest senior class.

ACKNOWLEDGMENTS

On the long road from initial concept to published book, I was lucky to march alongside a platoon of incredibly talented and hardworking people:

Keith Clayton, my publisher at Del Rey. You made this book happen, unwittingly convinced me to purchase a standing desk, and introduced me to bacon-dusted tater tots.

Tricia Narwani, the most metal editor in the universe. I love working with you. Thank you so much for your killer ideas, high-octane enthusiasm, and supremely sinister coolness.

Matt Schwartz, a top-notch friend and the smartest guy I know. When I wandered, lost in the wilderness of this book, your bright ideas led me not out but *deeper*. Thanks for everything, bud.

David Moench, Julie Leung, David Stevenson, Eric Lowenkron, Ryan Kearney, Nancy Delia, and everyone at Del Rey. Thank you for your kindness, hard work, and support.

Lieutenant Colonel Bryan Price at the United States Military Academy. Thank you for showing me West Point, sharing hilarious stories, answering countless questions, and buying me lunch. There were no bacon-dusted tater tots, but the view and the company were second to none.

Don Bentley, my friend and first reader. You're not very good at Ping-Pong, but thanks for making this a better book and for encouraging me every step of the way.

Frank Parisi and Craig DiLouie, who helped me get this book off the ground and who were always there when I needed to talk. You guys are aces.

Thanks to my beautiful wife and best friend, Christina, without whom I would achieve nothing. Thank you for your unwavering support, faith, and encouragement. I love you so much.

Our amazing daughter, Ellie, who showed up during the writing of this book to steal my heart and make my life perfect. Daddy loves you!

Allison Skiff, Carole McLean, and Claire DeLise, for keeping Ellie safe and happy while I battled giant centipedes in the writing cave.

Finally, thanks to you, dear reader. Without you, these words would remain in the cold, dark void between the covers of an unread book. Thanks for giving Scarlett's story a chance.

ABOUT THE AUTHOR

JOHN DIXON's first two novels, *Phoenix Island* and *Devil's Pocket,* won back-to-back Bram Stoker Awards and inspired the CBS TV series *Intelligence.* A former boxer, teacher, and stonemason, John lives in West Chester, Pennsylvania, with his wife, daughter, and freeloading dog.

johndixonbooks.com
Facebook.com/johndixonbooks
Twitter: @johndixonbooks

ABOUT THE TYPE

This book was set in Bembo, a typeface based on an old-style Roman face that was used for Cardinal Pietro Bembo's tract *De Aetna* in 1495. Bembo was cut by Francesco Griffo (1450–1518) in the early sixteenth century for Italian Renaissance printer and publisher Aldus Manutius (1449–1515). The Lanston Monotype Company of Philadelphia brought the well-proportioned letterforms of Bembo to the United States in the 1930s.